By Treason We Perish

A.J. Mackenzie is the pseudonym of Marilyn Livingstone and Morgen Witzel, an Anglo-Canadian husband-and-wife team of writers and historians. They write non-fiction history and management books under their own names, but 'become' A.J. MacKenzie when writing fiction. Morgen has an MA in renaissance diplomacy from the University of Victoria, but since the late 1990s has concentrated on writing books on leadership and management. Several of his books have been international best-sellers. Marilyn has a PhD in medieval economic history from the Queen's University, Belfast. She is a musician who writes music and also plays in a silver band and sings in an a capella trio. They have written two books of medieval history together, and also several novels, including the Hardcastle & Chaytor mysteries set on Romney Marsh during the French Revolution.

Also by A.J. MacKenzie

The War of 1812 Epics

The Ballad of John MacLea
The Hunt for the North Star
Invasion

The Hundred Years' War

A Flight of Arrows
A Clash of Lions
The Fallen Sword

The Simon Merrivale Mysteries

By Treason We Perish

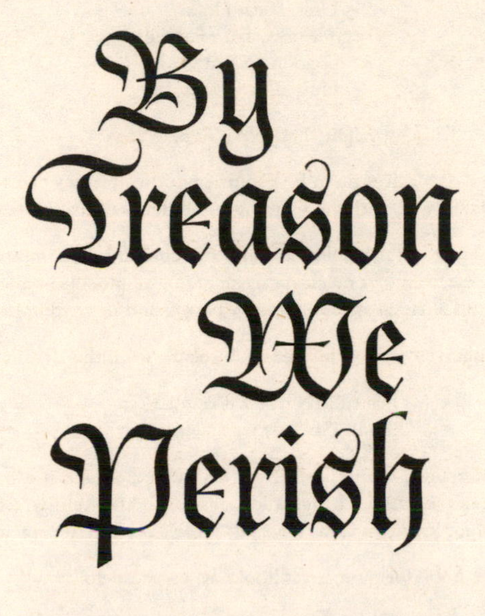

A.J. MACKENZIE

CANELO

First published in the United Kingdom in 2023 by

Canelo
Unit 9, 5th Floor
Cargo Works, 1-2 Hatfields
London SE1 9PG
United Kingdom

A CIP catalogue record for this book is available from the British Library.

Print ISBN 978 1 80436 426 0
Ebook ISBN 978 1 80436 427 7

Printed and bound in Great Britain by Clays Ltd, Elcograf S.p.A.

1

This book is dedicated to all NHS staff, especially to those working with cancer patients.

A king ought not to go out of his kingdom to make war
Unless the commons of his land will consent
By treason we often see very many perish
No one can tell in whom to trust with certainty
Let not the king go out of his kingdom without counsel

—English protest song,
mid-fourteenth century

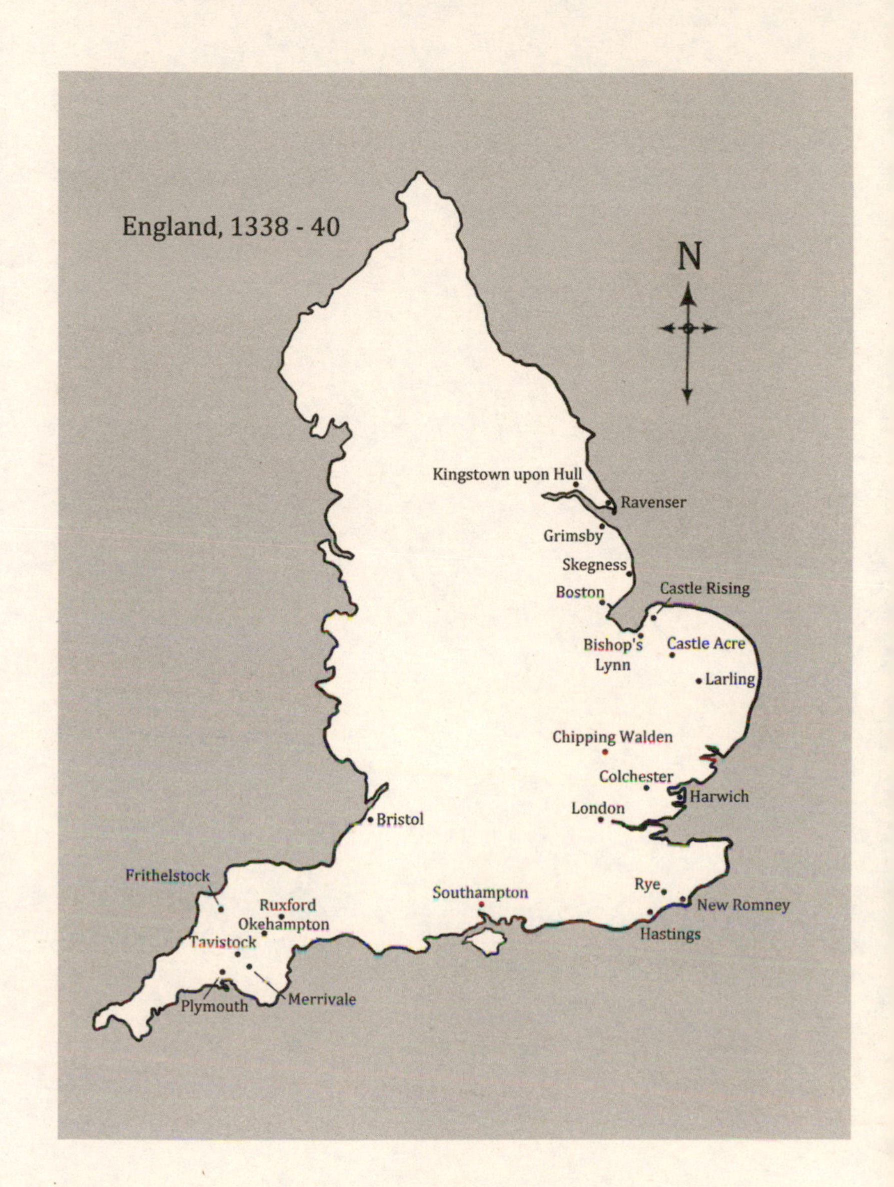
England, 1338 - 40
N
Kingstown upon Hull
Ravenser
Grimsby
Skegness
Boston
Castle Rising
Bishop's
Lynn
Castle Acre
Larling
Chipping Walden
Colchester
Harwich
London
Bristol
Frithelstock
Ruxford
Okehampton
Tavistock
Plymouth
Merrivale
Southampton
Rye
New Romney
Hastings

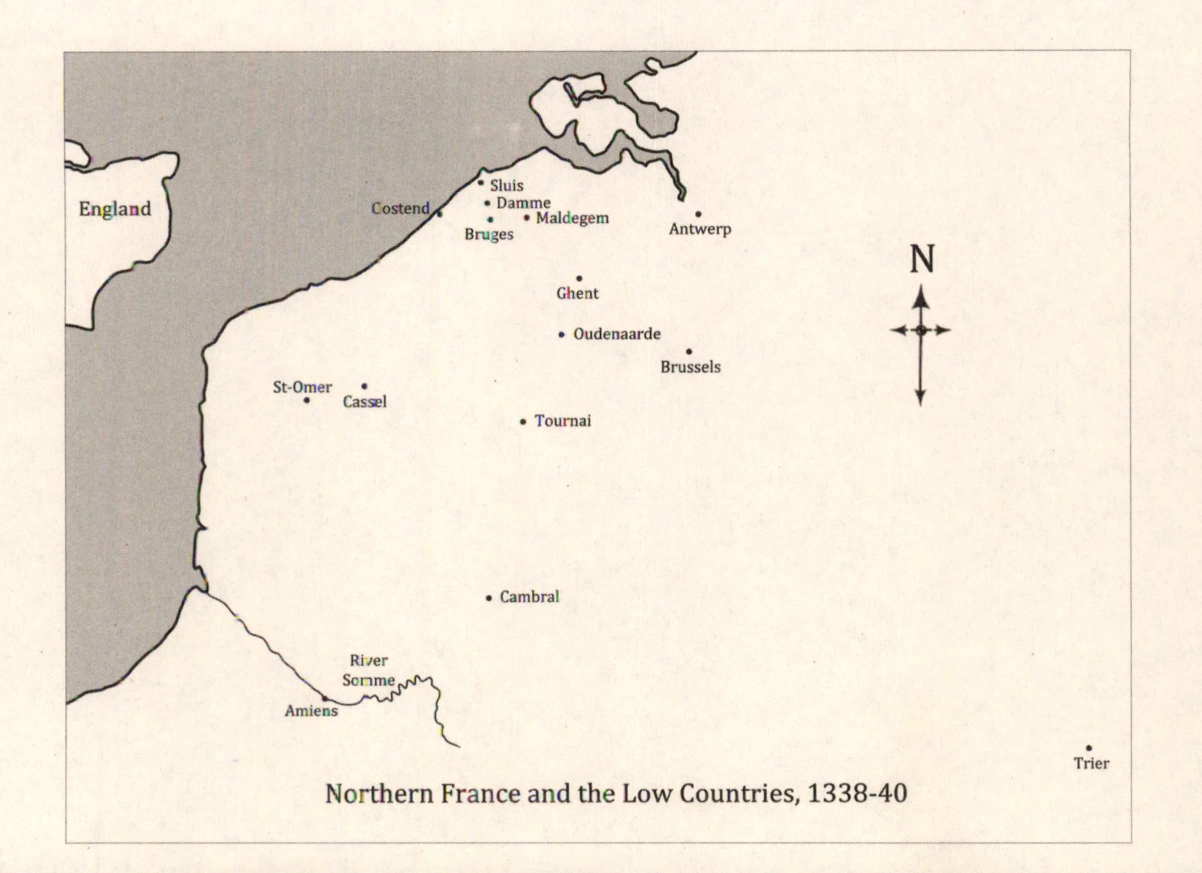

Northern France and the Low Countries, 1338-40

Dramatis personae

In the household of King Edward III

Edward III, king of England
Philippa of Hainault, his wife and queen of England
Simon Merrivale, King's Messenger
Edmund Gonville, king's clerk
Sir John Moleyns, lord of Stoke Poges and treasurer of the king's chamber
Sir Geoffrey Scrope, lawyer, man-at-arms and royal advisor
Henry Burghersh, bishop of Lincoln and royal advisor
Alice Bedingfield, the queen's lady-in-waiting

In the household of the queen mother

Isabella of France, former queen of England and mother of Edward III
John Hull, chaplain
Peter Ellerker, treasurer
John Stanton, sarjeant
Ralph Dunham, clerk
Robert Brigget, marshal
Warin of Hexworthy, groom

Administrators in London

John Stratford, Archbishop of Canterbury
Robert Stratford, his brother, bishop of Chichester and Lord Chancellor

Edmund Grimsby, senior official at the Chancery
William de la Zouche, Lord High Treasurer and later Archbishop of York
William Kildesby, Keeper of the Privy Seal

Physicians and apothecaries

Mercuriade of Salerno, physician
Cassandra Wesenham, apothecary
Jordan of Canterbury, physician to the king of England

Saffron growers and dealers

Nicholas le Flemyng (Nicolaes Engels), croker
Juan Moreno, croker
James Westacre, croker and former shipmaster
William (Guillaume) Gonville, spice merchant

Englishmen involved in the wool trade

William de la Pole, merchant and banker from Hull
Robert Denton, Pole's agent and attorney, controller of customs
John Wesenham, collector of customs in Bishop's Lynn
Roger Wolsthorp, collector of customs in Boston
Reginald Conduit, merchant of London, vintner and banker

Other bankers and financiers

Sir John Pulteney, formerly Lord Mayor of London
Donato di Pacino de' Peruzzi, banker from Florence
Aufrej Solaro, partner in the banking house of Solaro, Antwerp branch
Orland Turc de Castel, head of the Company of the Leopard in Antwerp
Anton Turc, partner in the Company of the Leopard
Sinibald Solaro, partner in the banking house of Solaro, Strassburg branch

Velvl Roth (Vivelin Rus), banker from Strassburg

Other clerics and religious leaders

Raimon Vidal, secretary to Étienne Aubert, Bishop of Noyon
John Courtenay, abbot of Tavistock
Balduin of Luxembourg, Archbishop of Trier
Rabbi Levi ben Gershon, philosopher, mathematician and astronomer

Knights, pirates, dukes, counts and archers

Sir John Sully of Iddesleigh, friend and patron of Merrivale
Enric, man-at-arms from Savoy
Sgond, man-at-arms from Savoy
John Crabbe, Anglo-Flemish shipmaster, engineer and pirate
Jan III Reginar, Duke of Brabant (Cousin Jan)
Willem II Avesnes, Count of Hainault (Brother Willem)
Jacob van Artevelde, captain general of the League of Three
Robin Pinn, archer from Sidmouth in Devon
Jack Giffard, archer from Torrington in Devon

A note on measures, money and names

Two similar terms appear in this book, but they have slightly different meanings. A *woolsack* is a large and durable cloth sack which is filled with raw wool. A *sack of wool* on the other hand is a unit of weight, the amount of wool each sack should contain when filled. According to the *Assize of Weights and Measures*, each sack of wool should have weighed twenty-six stone, that is, 364 pounds or slightly over 165 kilograms. A *wey* was half a sack. A stone was, and still is, fourteen pounds.

Saffron was measured using the apothecaries' system of weights. Without going into detail, an apothecaries' pound weighed three-quarters of a Tower pound (later known as avoirdupois), or around 340 grams.

Money in medieval England was accounted for in two ways. The first and most common for smaller transactions was pounds, shillings and pence, written as £, *s* and *d*. There were 12*d* in a shilling, and 20*s* or 240*d* to the pound. The second was the mark, purely a unit of account worth 13*s* 4*d* or two-thirds of a pound.

The largest coin in common circulation in England was the groat, worth 4*d*. There were also half-groats (2*d*), pennies, half-pennies and farthings, the latter worth a quarter *d*. The most common gold coin was the florin, minted in the city of Florence. The value of gold versus silver fluctuated depending on political and economic issues, the relative scarcity of each metal and the purity of the coinage itself, but data compiled at the London School of Economics and Political Science suggests that in the mid-fourteenth century the value of a florin ranged from three to four shillings, or 36*d* to 48*d*.

Some of the places we mention had names different from those they bear today. The port of Bishop's Lynn changed its name to King's Lynn following the sixteenth-century reformation, and the market town of Chipping Walden eventually became Saffron Walden after the establishment of saffron growing in the area. Otherwise, we have used modern English names such as Antwerp, Ghent, Turin and Florence. The exceptions are where the medieval place was named in a language different from the modern name; for example in Chapter 1 we use several Provençal names including the river Isèra instead of Val d'Isère, and La Chasa Dieu instead of the French La Chaise-Dieu. Strasbourg, the capital of modern Alsace, was known throughout the Middle Ages as Strassburg, part of the distinctly Germanic culture of s'Elsàss; the French influence and name only came several centuries later.

The characters in this book would have spoken the usual mix of languages including several dialects of English, north French, west Flemish, east Flemish, Elsàss (Alsatian), various dialects of Occitan, Piedmontese, Tuscan Italian and Czech. As ever, for the most part we have rendered their speech into modern English for the convenience of the reader.

Flight

1

Valley of the Isèra, October 1338

A man was climbing for his life. His hands were bloody from hauling himself up the cliff, and his breath rasped in his throat. His tunic and hose were both soaking wet, their weight dragging at his arms and legs. All his mind and body concentrated on the fissures in the stone a few inches from his face.

A bitter wind whistled around him. He could hear noise in the abyss beneath him; at least two other men were climbing after him. He shifted his weight, trying to traverse across the cliff face towards a stone chimney to his left. The rock beneath his boot broke, fragments clattering away below. For a moment he dangled by his hands, ignoring the pain in his bleeding fingers while he searched desperately for a foothold.

His right boot brushed against a spur of rock. He planted his foot and tested it; this time it held firm. He reached up and found a stone ledge, dragging himself up and using the ledge to move sideways towards the chimney. The men below him were growing closer.

Having reached the chimney he could climb faster, bracing his feet against the stone walls. Once he looked down. And his heart froze in his chest. A group of dismounted men-at-arms stood at the foot of the cliff looking up at him. Their leader wore a blue cloak with a device of a black eagle with spread wings.

He climbed on. The chimney widened and the cliff became less steep. He scrabbled up the slope on all fours, boots scraping and slipping, more shards of stone tumbling down into the void. Sobbing for breath, he reached the top of the cliff and fell on his face for a moment.

They're coming. Get up, get up.

He staggered to his feet. Flakes of snow curled like ash on the cold wind. Ahead, a bowshot away, lay a thick dark forest stretching up the lower slopes of the nearest mountain, its shoulders rising like the buttresses of some gigantic cathedral. The man ran towards the woods, looking for shelter, just as a horseman rode up the steep hill to his right and turned, cutting him off from the forest.

The man stopped. The horseman, who wore the same black eagle device on his blue surcoat, dismounted and drew his sword. The climber had no weapons; his sword and dagger had been taken before they put him in the river. He waited, crouching a little, watching the man-at-arms's face as the latter came closer.

From behind came the scrape of boots on stone; his pursuers nearly at the top.

The man-at-arms raised his sword. '*Na kolena!*' he snarled. 'On your knees!'

The other man shook his head. 'I prefer to die on my feet.'

The sword blade flashed in the dull light, swinging towards his neck. He ducked under it, hurling himself bodily at the man-at-arms and driving him backwards. The other man stumbled and the first man seized his arm and twisted it, wrenching the sword out of his hand. They grappled, each trying to throw the other off his feet. Rocking his head back, the climber butted the man-at-arms hard in the face, breaking his nose. They parted, the man-at-arms streaming blood as he pulled his dagger from his belt. The first man kicked it out of his hand and charged into him again, tackling him low and driving him around in a half circle, back towards the cliff.

The man-at-arms realised the danger. He hit his assailant hard across the side of the head, again and again. The first man staggered but did not loosen his grip, continuing to push the man-at-arms back. For a moment they stood locked on the brink, the man-at-arms with his back to the void. The other man kicked him, loosening his grip, and a fist like a hammer hit the man-at-arms in his bloody face.

The man-at-arms swayed. His knees folded and he fell backwards, body bumping down the steep slope and hurtling off into space. A moment later came a dull thud, his body hitting the ground far below.

A rush of excitement swept through the first man. Reinvigorated for a moment, he turned towards the horse. Spooked perhaps by the scent of blood, the animal whinnied and bolted back down the hill. Cursing, the man turned and ran towards the woods. He was halfway there when three more men climbed over the top of the cliff and raced after him.

The chasers were tired from their climb, but the fugitive was even more exhausted and weighed down by his sodden clothes. His burst of energy quickly faded, and he heard their rapid footsteps behind him and knew he could not outpace them. Despairing, he reached the forest and ran through the pine trees, feet crunching on the dry cones carpeting the ground, looking for a place to hide.

Something reared up in front of him, an enormous dark shape; black eyes, a shining muzzle, an open mouth with rows of enormous pale teeth looming over him. He halted abruptly, clinging to a pine tree. After a long moment the bear dropped onto all fours again, nostrils twitching, staring at him suspiciously. He froze, barely breathing, hoping the creature would forget about him and go away.

The pursuers hurtled through the trees, sliding to a stop when they saw the bear. '*Ježíš Kristus!*' one of them said sharply, and they turned and fled. The bear paused for a moment, sniffing the wind; deciding it disliked what it smelled, it charged after them, lumbering through the trees with astonishing speed. Screams echoed in the distance, fading slowly away, leaving only the wind roaring in the pines.

Lyon, October 1338

Lights shone from the cathedral of Sant-Jean and the houses in the lower town, but up on the hill above the river Saône, all was dark. Groping through the streets the man found the house he was looking for opposite the church of Sant Irénée, and knocked at the door.

The cold wind whistled in the streets. Around him, the shadows seemed to crawl with motion. The man cursed his imagination and knocked again. Finally, a man's voice responded.

'Who is there?'

'I seek Marcus the Magician.'

The door was unbolted and a servant with a lamp ushered him quickly inside. Securing the door behind him the man led him across a dim courtyard into a small hall. 'Wait here.'

The fugitive waited. The fire was covered, but a little light still leaked out into the hall. Eight days had passed since his escape in the high Alps. Since then he had hidden by day and travelled by night, always watching the horizon, waiting for the sound of hoofbeats or a rustle in the dark that might warn of an ambush. His only sustenance had been a loaf of bread stolen from a village along the way.

The door opened and a woman entered, holding a lamp. Long white hair framed her face. Her dress was white also, simple with loose sleeves and no adornment.

The servant followed her, waiting by the door. She held up the lamp, studying him. 'What is your business with Marcus the Magician?'

The servant waited by the door. The man shook his head. 'Marcus Magus lived a thousand years ago. His name is the password I was given. I was told that if I needed help, I should come to this house.'

Silence fell. The lamp flame burned steadily. 'Who are you?' the woman asked finally.

'I am Simon Merrivale, a messenger in the service of King Edward of England. I am being pursued, and I have no money, no food and no weapons. I am desperate.'

She walked close to him, holding up the lamp. He saw the flame reflected in her eyes, and could almost feel her searching his soul.

'Yes,' she said finally. 'You are telling the truth. The Father of all sees your spirit before his face.'

Relief flooded through him. He folded his hands in prayer at his chest. 'Grace has descended upon you.'

She made the sign of the cross in the air. 'I have come to behold all things, those which belong to myself and those which belong to others. Be seated.' She turned to the servant. 'Bring food, and a cup of wine.'

Merrivale sank down onto a bench. His hands were shaking a little. 'May I ask who you are? If you prefer not to tell me, I understand.'

'My name is Mercuriade of Salerno, and I am a physician. Formerly I practised in Florence, but now I minister to the needs of the Italian bankers in Lyon.'

A thought stirred in Merrivale's weary mind. 'Bankers like the Peruzzi?'

'They have an office here, yes. Why do you ask?'

'I had some dealings with them recently. It did not end well.'

The servant arrived with cold chicken, a loaf of coarse bread and a cup of well-watered wine. Merrivale began to eat, slowly. Bitter experience had taught him that eating too quickly after being half-starved could be just as dangerous as not eating at all. The woman sat down opposite him. 'Who is pursuing you?' she asked.

'King Jean of Bohemia's men.' He took a sip of wine. 'There may be others.'

She watched him for a long time. 'There is much that you are not telling me,' she said finally. 'Some of it I can guess, and the rest matters not. You need to rest and recover your strength.'

'I hoped Lyon might offer me a place to hide until I can shake off Bohemia's hunters. Out in the open country I am exposed.'

'And where will you go once you have shaken them off?'

'I must return to England and my king. *Ma dòna*, if you can aid me I will be grateful, but I don't wish to put you in danger.'

'My soul is prepared for God. I am not so sure about yours, however.'

Merrivale said nothing. 'The best place to hide is usually in plain sight,' she said. 'Tomorrow, go to the inn next to the church and ask the landlord for work. Tell him I sent you. He is one of us, and will ask no questions.'

A wave of relief and fatigue washed over him. 'Thank you.'

'There is no need to thank me.' Mercuriade studied him again. Her white hair shone in the lamplight. 'You spoke the words of our faith,' she said. 'Are you also a Marcosian?'

Merrivale shook his head. 'I respect your faith, as I respect all those who are sincere.'

'The Pope would not agree. He regards us as heretics.'

Merrivale swallowed a mouthful of bread and cut another piece. 'I find some of your doctrines attractive. You believe that women have powers of prophecy.'

'Marcus Magus believed that. I am not so sure.'

'I am sorry to hear it. I was hoping you could tell my future.'

'How old are you?' Mercuriade asked.

'Twenty-six.'

'Really? You look older.'

Merrivale smiled a little. 'It is not time that ages us, it is the roads we travel.'

'Then I think you already know your future. Your soul is battered and broken, Simon Merrivale. I can heal wounds of the body. Only you can cure the suffering of your spirit.'

'How do I do that?'

'Through knowledge. The Marcosians speak of many kinds of *gnosis*: who we were, what we have become, where we were, whither we have sunk, whither we hasten, whence we are redeemed. Find the answers to those questions. They will help you to heal.'

It was only twenty-five years since France had seized Lyon from its imperial fief-holder. In the streets people spoke a dialect of Provençal rather than French and did their best to ignore their Parisian masters. No one paid any attention to the new groom in the stables at Lo Lion d'Aur, a quiet man who performed his duties well and seldom went out.

It took Merrivale several days to fully recover physically from his ordeal in the mountains. The mental scars, as Mercuriade had said, would take longer to heal. The conspiracy in Savoy, which he and Brother Geoffrey of Maldon had spent months putting together, had collapsed in utter ruin; English hopes of converting Savoy into a powerful ally against France were gone. Many of their friends had been killed. It was entirely possibly that Yolande was dead too; King Jean of Bohemia was quite capable of ordering his own daughter's execution.

Brother Geoffrey had disappeared, and the presumption must be that he too was dead.

Do not think about them. That way madness lies.

He knew he could not stay here forever. Sooner or later he would have to return to the English court and face whatever awaited him there. The king would be bitterly angry, of course, but he had to return and make his report. Death was the only thing that prevented a King's Messenger from carrying out his duty.

Lo Lion d'Aur was busy. Lyon lay on the main route from Paris to the papal court at Avignon and over the mountains to Italy, and the city played host to a steady stream of travellers coming overland from the north and upriver from the south. On the fifth day the head groom came into the stable.

'Get this place cleaned up and be quick about it. An outrider just came in. There's a big party from Italy arriving this afternoon. They'll need stabling for at least thirty horses.'

One of the grooms grunted, scratching himself. 'Another cardinal on his way to Paris. Better make sure we lock the women away. And the boys.'

'This one's a banker, not a priest,' the head groom said. 'Same thing applies, though. Go on, get to work.'

The party arrived that afternoon, the banker, his secretaries, his servants and a strong party of men-at-arms bristling with weapons. Standing by the stable door, Merrivale watched them ride into the courtyard and dismount. The leader wore a cloak trimmed with fur and a dark blue coif embroidered with gold, surrounding a long face with a beaked nose.

Merrivale's breath hissed with sudden shock. He ducked into the stable quickly, before the other man could see him. The Florentine banker was Donato di Pacino de' Peruzzi, the man who had promised to bankroll the failed conspiracy in Savoy, right up until the last minute, when he broke his pledge and supported Jean of Bohemia instead.

He had no idea what Peruzzi was doing in Lyon, nor did it matter. It was unlikely that Peruzzi had seen him, but he could not afford to take a chance. He needed to get away from here, as soon as possible.

He looked up at the sky. Dusk fell early at this time of year. As soon as it was fully dark he would slip out of the inn and leave by the nearest gate. He had money now, not much, but at least enough to buy him a little food along the way.

The autumn day drew to its end. The other grooms were going drinking. One turned to Merrivale. 'Coming with us, Simó?'

Merrivale shook his head. 'I need to finish mucking out. Go ahead, I'll join you later.'

The grooms departed. The bell of Sant Irénée rang vespers. As its echoes died away Merrivale stepped cautiously out into the street. A dog barked. Another joined in, its high-pitched yelp a counterpoint to the deeper growl of the first. Merrivale listened for a moment, and walked towards the Sant-Etiève gate.

Boots scraped on the cobbles ahead.

He knew beyond doubt what the noise meant; King's Messengers were used to being hunted. He turned back towards Lo Lion d'Aur. Dark figures spilled into the street, some with swords in their hands, cutting him off from the inn. The tower of Sant Irénée loomed overhead. Flinging open the west door of the church he hurried inside, slammed and barred the door behind him, and looked around for somewhere to hide. Dim light showed the door to the sacristy, unlocked. Pulling it open he found a postern leading to the outside, unbolted this and threw it open. Beyond was a narrow lane full of foul smells and shadows.

He halted. His pursuers were hammering on the west door; it would not take them long to break it down. The sacristy was the first place they would look. Leaving the postern open, he ran back through the church into the tower. Already the west door was shuddering with strain; the enemy must be using a ram. More dogs, roused further by the noise, barked hysterically.

In the darkness of the tower a bell rope brushed against his face. He found the wooden stair to the belfry and ran up it with reckless haste, stumbling on the steep steps. At the top he crouched low behind the stone parapet, listening. The silent bell hung from its headstock beside him, rope dangling into the darkness.

The church door broke with a crash of splintering wood. '*Hledejte všude!*' a man's voice barked. '*Najděte ho!*'

High in the belfry, Merrivale listened to the sound of men below searching the aisles and chapels. Another voice called out. '*Maršik! Utekil přes sakristii!* He has escaped through the sacristy!'

'Go after him, you fools!'

Gradually their footsteps faded away. Merrivale let the silence last for a long time before he stood up, easing the cramp in his legs. If he could get safely out of the church he might still win through to the gates…

Soft footsteps moved slowly up the stairs towards him.

His scalp began to tingle, his head aching suddenly with the promise of violence. He searched quickly but there was nothing he could use as a weapon. His pursuer took the final few steps in a rush, jumping up into the belfry with a gleaming sword in one hand and a dagger in the other. Merrivale backed away, hands empty at his sides.

'Simon Merrivale,' the other man said. 'Peruzzi was right. You *are* alive.'

So, Peruzzi had spotted him after all. The banker had eyes that could see through walls. 'Who are you?' Merrivale demanded.

'I am Maršik Jankovtsi of Vlašimi. Say your last prayers, you filth, because I am going to kill you.'

'Why? What harm have I ever done you?'

Jankovtsi growled at him. 'You violated my king's daughter, and for that you are condemned to death. And the man you killed in the mountains, the one who fell to his death, that was Jaroš, my brother.'

'Sorry,' Merrivale said.

'Bastard! For my brother, I shall kill you twice over.'

'You do realise that isn't actually possible.'

Jankovtsi snarled again. 'By the time I am finished—'

'Oh, for Christ's sake! Are all Bohemians so long-winded? Get it over with, before we both die of old age.'

Merrivale dodged the thrusting sword, lunged at Jankovtsi's sword arm and twisted his wrist. He could not evade the dagger that ripped down his side and glanced off his ribs. Another blow cut through the soft flesh of his shoulder. Gritting his teeth, Merrivale straightened and kicked the Bohemian hard on the knee. The other man staggered back, and before he could recover Merrivale jumped onto the headstock. Pain clouded his brain and he wavered for a moment, stretching out his arms for balance. There was nothing to hold onto; the stone floor of the belfry lay sixty feet below.

'There is no escape,' Jankovtsi said.

Escape was the last thing on Merrivale's mind. He knelt carefully on the headstock and reached down. Finding the bronze canons on top of the bells, he hooked his fingers through them and slid down onto the bell itself. Summoning his fading strength, he reached for the bell rope.

Whither we have sunk, whither we hasten.

Too late, Jankovtsi realised what he was doing. '*Sakra!*' he shouted, and threw the dagger. Its blade clanged off the bell and went spinning down to the belfry floor. Holding onto the rope, Merrivale jumped off the bell into space. The rope seared his hands as he slid down; a second later the bell boomed, deafening in the confined space of the tower, and the rope jerked sharply upwards, so hard he nearly lost his grip. Another deep boom and the rope descended again; this time Merrivale slid all the way down, releasing his grip and falling headlong on the stone floor.

The bell was still booming, and through the echoes he could hear Jankovtsi pounding down the wooden stairs. Groping in the dark, Merrivale found the dagger and stumbled into cover under the stairs. Jankovtsi, descending into darkness, was effectively blind. As he reached the bottom of the stairs, Merrivale stepped out and drove the dagger hard into his back.

A mist of pain clouded his eyes. When it cleared, he saw Jankovtsi stretched on the belfry floor, hand clawing at the dagger embedded in his body. The Bohemian's strength was fading fast; after a moment his hand went limp and his body relaxed into death.

Merrivale felt suddenly sick. Clutching his bloody shoulder, he staggered out of the church. He got as far as Mercuriade's door before he lost consciousness.

'You should not travel,' Mercuriade said. 'You have lost too much blood.'

'I cannot stay. I killed Jankovtsi, but he was not alone. His men will enlist the help of the city watch, and they will search every house in Lyon. I must get away tonight.'

She examined him for a moment, lips pursed. 'Why did you kill this man?'

'He attacked me. It was him or me.'

Mercuriade shook her head. 'Tell me the truth.'

A long silence followed. 'I was angry,' Merrivale said finally.

'At him.'

'No. At myself.'

'For what happened in Savoy, I think. There was a woman involved, wasn't there? I see it in your eyes.'

He winced a little. 'Are you certain you are not a prophet?'

'I read men's pasts, not their futures. Who was she?'

'She was the fire and the flame,' Merrivale said softly. 'She was the lily, and the rose.'

'So, you have the capacity for love,' she said after a moment. 'I hoped that was the case, and not that you were just another fool who lived for killing. But all the same, your soul is full of darkness. You must overcome that. Find your love, and set your anger aside.'

Merrivale gazed at the candle flame for a moment. 'I lost my love in Savoy,' he said. 'And I don't know if I can forget my anger.'

'Time will tell,' she said cryptically. 'Assuming you live that long, of course. The cut on your ribs is clean and will heal well. I am less certain about the shoulder. I have cleaned the wound as best I can and sewn it up, but if you over-exert yourself it might become infected. You could lose your arm, even your life.'

'I must take that chance.'

'You are an extraordinarily stubborn man.' She studied him again. 'Perhaps that is what will save you.'

'Perhaps.'

'Where will you go?'

'North, perhaps. If I can reach Strassburg I will be in Imperial territory, safe from the Bohemians and French.'

'If you need help in Strassburg, call upon a friend of mine, a man named Velvl Roth. For my sake he will aid you. Now, my servants will find clean clothes for you. How much money do you have?'

'...A little.'

'I will give you more. No, do not thank me. May the Grace who is before all things, and who transcends all knowledge and speech, fill your soul and multiply her own knowledge in you.'

'Thank you for your blessing,' he said quietly. 'You have been my salvation.'

'Your salvation lies within you, Simon Merrivale. Follow the path of light, if you can, and let it bring you safely home.'

La Chasa Dieu, November 1338

At the last moment, Merrivale changed his mind. He had no doubt that Jankovtsi's men were still looking for him, and they would know too that the shortest route to safety was north towards Strassburg. They would lay traps and ambushes along the way, and he was no longer strong enough to fight them off.

There was another way, longer and harder, over the mountains to the west towards English-held Gascony. There, despite the lateness of the season, he should be able find a ship bound for England. He remembered suddenly the words of his old friend and patron, Sir John Sully: 'Never do what they expect you to do, boy. Always keep them guessing.' Ignoring the pain in his shoulder, he turned his face towards the western hills.

Two long days on foot brought him to the town Sant-Etiève, but he knew he could walk no more. Mercuriade's fears had come to pass; the wound in his shoulder was red and hot to the touch, the skin straining against the careful sutures she had sewn. The village blacksmith sold him a tough little Auvergnat cob. The horse cost most of his remaining money, but it was his only chance of reaching Gascony.

Riding helped to conserve his strength, a little, but by the end of the fifth day he was weak with fever and vomiting when he tried to eat. He could go no further. In the light of a cold sunset he saw ahead the dark silhouette of a fortified monastery on a hilltop. Hunched in the saddle, he urged the horse towards it.

At the gate he leaned down and rang the bell. The sound of the monks singing vespers in the chapel drifted on the wind. A grille in the door opened and a black-robed man looked out. 'Who are you, stranger?'

'I am Aimeric de Gensac.' The Auvergne had been a French royal fief for centuries; if the monks discovered his real identity they would hand him over to the civil authorities, who might well inform the Bohemians. 'I am wounded and need help.'

Strong hands helped him down from his horse, and he heard a quiet voice send for the infirmarer. 'Where am I?' he asked.

'This is La Chasa Dieu.'

The world spun around him. They took him into a chamber that smelled of soap and lavender, and gently drew off his tunic and shirt. The infirmarer, a tonsured Benedictine monk with drooping jowls like a bloodhound, examined the sewn-up wound. 'The wound is infected. Already the flesh is becoming corrupted. We must act quickly. Bring me the leeches, and prepare a poultice and a cordial of saffron. This man needs his strength to fight the corruption.'

After that, everything became a dream of fever, chaotic visions of violence and flame. Once he found himself back in his own village during the famine, fighting another child for a piece of bread. The child suddenly turned into a raging giant with a horned head who seized him by the neck. Then he was in the belfry of Sant Irénée wrestling with Jankovtsi, only this time the Bohemian pushed him out of the belfry and he fell endlessly through the air, watching the cobbled street rise towards him. Once Yolande's face swam into view, coming closer, her lips brushing his, and then he realised it was her disembodied head amidst leaping fire. He woke up screaming.

'Hush,' said a voice. 'Here, drink a little of this.' A spoon was held to his lips and a little liquor dribbled into his mouth, tasting of brandy and saffron. He swallowed it and fell asleep again. Gradually the flames and visions faded, replaced by a peaceful darkness.

He woke again to find cold daylight coming through the windows of the infirmary. The skin of his shoulder was cool to the touch. He sat up, feeling dizzy, and reached for his clothes. The dizziness passed and he found he could walk, albeit a little unsteadily, and he went out into the cloister where late autumn sunlight shone through the pointed stone arches. All was quiet; the air was chill and the monks had wisely found work indoors.

A man sat on a stone bench reading a small wooden-bound codex. Unlike the black-robed monks of the abbey, this man wore the plain brown habit of a Franciscan friar. He smiled pleasantly at Merrivale. 'Lazarus arises from the dead,' he said.

'Raimon Vidal,' Merrivale said slowly. 'What are you doing here?'

'Looking for you. Do not worry, I haven't come to cut your throat. I could have done that while you slept. I must say, you have made a remarkable recovery. Leeches and saffron brandy are clearly a sovereign cure.'

'How did you find me?'

'I know how your mind works. I found the blacksmith who sold you the horse, and followed your trail from there. Aimeric de Gensac is an excellent alias, by the way. I may use it myself one day.'

'Where are the Bohemians?'

'Looking for you, but in all the wrong places.'

Merrivale paused, gathering his clouded thoughts. 'Why are you here?'

'Admirable. No prevarication, just a direct question straight to the heart of the matter. My master Étienne Aubert, the Bishop of Noyon, has formed a certain respect for you. He invites you to join his household.'

Young by church standards, highly intelligent and almost insanely ambitious, Aubert was a rising star of the papal court at Avignon; wagers were being taken on when he would receive a cardinal's hat. Merrivale shook his head. 'My fever appears to be returning. I thought I heard you say that Bishop Aubert wishes to employ me. Even though we were on opposite sides in Savoy.'

'At times I found it difficult to tell who was on which side in Savoy. His Grace respects talent.'

'No matter where it comes from?'

Vidal smiled and held up the book. 'Marsilius of Padua, the *Defensor Pacis*. Have you read it? Laws should only be made by the people, he says, and enforced by their sovereign prince. Popes should have no authority over the populace, and their interference in temporal matters is the greatest cause of strife in the world. Utter heresy, of course, but entertaining to read. His prose style is excellent.'

'What in God's name are you talking about?'

'Marsilius has been condemned by the Pope. But Bishop Aubert has corresponded with him in the past, and even offered him protection if Marsilius was willing to write tracts favourable to His Grace. Do you see what I mean?'

'Your master is amoral and ambitious, and will use any means to further his own ends.'

'I could not have summed him up better myself. He will pay you very well, far more than your debt-ridden king can afford. And of course, under the bishop's protection you will have nothing to fear from the Bohemians.'

Merrivale paused, looking at the Franciscan. Somehow this conversation had made him feel stronger. 'I do not fear the Bohemians, and Bishop Aubert is a rectum in human form. I would sooner serve the devil.'

'I will not make the obvious comparison.' Vidal rose to his feet, tucking the book into a pocket of his robe. 'His Grace will be annoyed, but there it is. Is there anything that might make you change your mind?'

'No. I know where my duty lies.'

'I shall remind you of the words of the prophet Isaiah. "The godly perish, but no one cares." You need to look to your own interests, Simon. No one else will do it for you.' Vidal paused. 'I have some good news for you. Your friend, Brother Geoffrey of Maldon, escaped from Savoy.'

After a moment Merrivale said, 'Where is he now?'

'I don't know. We searched the city, but found no sign of him. Do you want to know about the girl? Princess Yolande?'

Weak and tired though he was, Merrivale felt a surge of anger. 'God damn you to hell. Why did you do it? Why did you betray us to Peruzzi and her father?'

Vidal shook his head. 'I said nothing to King Jean. He is unpredictable at the best of times and I did not feel he would receive the news particularly well, so I let Peruzzi take the risk and tell him instead. As to why, I was following orders. As you were, perhaps, when you first seduced the beautiful princess.'

'You are an utter shit, Raimon.'

Vidal's eyebrows rose. 'Ah. So it was true love after all. How interesting.'

'How did you find out about us?'

'I didn't. I invented a rumour in an attempt to discredit you, hoping to cause dissent within your camp. I was as surprised as anyone when it turned out to be true.'

'I don't believe you.'

'Don't you?' Vidal's normally pleasant voice had turned hard. 'Time to make a choice, Simon. What do you want to believe? How do you want to remember Yolande? Because memories are all you have now.'

Merrivale said nothing. 'I shall take my leave,' Vidal said. 'Stay here and rest for as long as you wish. Do not fear, I shall not inform anyone that you are here.'

'That would be most unlike you.'

'There are times when even I can be trusted. Farewell, Simon. I feel certain we shall meet again.'

2

Merrivale, December 1338

Winter on Dartmoor, cold wind and rain; the rolling fields and rugged granite tors were shrouded in gloom. Simon Merrivale stood on a hilltop, holding the reins of his horse and looking down at a stone village on the banks of a little river. His shoulder still ached a little and he was tired and weak from illness and travelling. It had been a long journey across the mountains of the Auvergne and down the valley of the Dordogne to Libourne, where he had taken passage on the *Maudelyn*, a roundship out of New Romney carrying the last of the season's cargo of wine back to England.

Somewhere off the north coast of Brittany they encountered a fishing boat, whose crew warned that French warships were still active in the Narrow Sea. The master of the *Maudelyn* decided to take no chances, and instead of making for New Romney he turned the ship's head north towards the safety of Plymouth. Merrivale had hired a horse and, acting on an impulse that he could not entirely explain, ridden up over the moor to the little village he had once called home.

Behind him stretched a long double row of standing stones, erected by unknown hands in a far earlier age, disappearing into the mist. As a child, Merrivale had played among those stones. Foolish people maintained that they were the devil's work, or that they were haunted by witches, but they had never held any terrors for Merrivale or the other children of the village. They had been his friends, back then; he was a gentleman's son, his father the lord of the manor, and his playmates were the sons and daughters of blacksmiths and tin miners and shepherds, but rank and station mean nothing when you are five years old. Watching the silver rain drift across the moor like banners floating on the wind, Merrivale thought about happy times, a kind father, a gentle and loving mother, two playful older sisters who sometimes teased their little brother and pulled his hair, but never failed to love him.

Then came the rain, day after day without cease. The moorland became saturated; water poured off the granite crags of the tors and foamed in the valleys. The Walkham, the gentle stream that flowed across the moor through the village, turned into a raging torrent that washed away several cottages and the mill. Seven bodies had eventually been recovered from the river; others were never found. That was just the first disaster.

Without sun, the crops rotted in the sodden fields. They got through the first year by eating the seed corn they had saved for the following year, but come spring they had nothing to plant; not that any seed would have sprouted in the waterlogged ground. Grass would not grow and the sheep and cattle grew weak with hunger. A murrain struck and the animals began to die too. Merrivale remembered the rotting carcasses piling up between the ancient lines of stone. When the last of the sheep and cattle were gone the people ate draught ponies and dogs, and when those too were gone, they began to starve.

No help came from the outside world, from Plymouth or Tavistock in the lowlands, for they too were afflicted; so, according to rumour, was the entire country and the lands beyond. Up in the little village on the moor, Merrivale learned to fight his former playmates for scraps of food, and to ignore the grip of hunger in his gut and carry whatever he could win back to the manor house to share with his family and the two remaining servants, the ones who had not already fled.

It was not enough; it was never enough. The servants were the first to die, followed by Matilda his youngest sister. He remembered her cries of pain growing weaker and weaker, and the silence that followed. His older sister, Eleanor, followed her days later. A month later their mother turned her face to the wall and died too, out of heartbreak and sorrow as much as hunger. Only he and his father survived. Wiping the rain from his face, Merrivale realised that although he remembered the beginning of the famine clearly, he could not recall its end; only that slowly, gradually, there was bread once more and the pain in his gut began to ease. He was young and strong, and in time he recovered. His father did not.

Wind lashed across the moor and Merrivale pulled his cloak more tightly around him. At the far end of the village was a little granite church where they had buried his sisters and his mother. He thought about going down to the church, walking inside and kneeling by their graves, praying for their souls. *What would that achieve?* he asked himself. *I could not save them while I was alive. What use am I to them in death?*

Mercuriade of Salerno had suggested redemption might be possible. *The Marcosians speak of many kinds of gnosis: who we were, what we have become, where we were, whither we have sunk.* Well, there were answers here, if he could bear to face them. He had been born here in this village, and it had made him. He had gone on to become a King's Messenger, but at heart he was still a boy who had survived the Great Famine and could not understand why he had been spared while those he loved had died.

He wiped the rain from his eyes. *I tried to save Yolande*, he thought, *just as I tried to save my family. I failed.*

Why am I still alive, when so many others have died? He knew it was a futile question, but he could not stop asking it. Of course, no answer came. His mind was a mass of black sorrow and bleak, bitter anger. He recognised the truth in what Mercuriade had said, but he could not break free.

Smoke came from the chimney of the manor house and from some of the cottages. The new owner of the manor had clearly tried to make good the damage caused by the famine; there were sheep in the fields again, and a new mill wheel turned in the stream. Turning his horse, Merrivale rode away down the hill.

Tavistock, December 1338

He knew there would be trouble when the abbot's servant returned saying the abbot was too busy to see him.

Merrivale paused for a moment, looking around. Tavistock Abbey, rich and powerful, lay on the banks of another river, surrounded by green hills streaked with low-hanging clouds. Rain gurgled in the lead drainpipes and sluiced through the gutters.

'Tell Abbot John I shall not detain him for long,' he said. 'I simply want to see my father.'

'I'm sorry, sir. Father Abbot was quite clear.'

Merrivale paused again. He had visited Tavistock many times and been impressed by its serenity and order, but today something was different. Black-robed monks hurried through the cloisters, some clutching rolls of parchment or wooden tablets. Some looked close to panic. Voices called out in the chapter house, sharp with urgency.

'What is happening?' Merrivale asked.

The servant looked uncertain. 'What do you mean, sir?'

'An abbot, no matter how powerful, refuses to see a King's Messenger at his peril. What is going on?'

'It's the bishop,' the servant said. 'He has threatened us with a visit of inspection. All of the office holders of the abbey have been asked to produce their accounts for examination.'

'Ah.' John Courtenay, Abbot of Tavistock, was the brother of Hugh Courtenay, Earl of Devon, and the earl and his family had been at feud with the Bishop of Exeter for the past fifteen years. This was clearly the bishop's latest move.

'Tell Abbot John he has a simple choice,' Merrivale said. 'I can speak to the king on his behalf, and suggest His Grace instructs the bishop to back down. Or, if he refuses to see me, I can recommend to Bishop Grandisson that his clerks go through the abbey's finances with a fine-toothed comb. The results would not be in your best interests.'

'Why not?' The servant was clearly not the sharpest knife in the block.

'Because someone, the cellarer or the feretrar or the sacristan, is hiding something in his accounts. They always are.'

'Five minutes,' John Courtenay snapped a few moments later. He pointed to a sandglass on a side table. 'That is all I can give you.'

The abbot's hall was a handsome building with painted walls and bronze lamps. A fire roared in the hearth, keeping winter at bay. 'I wish to see my father,' Merrivale said.

'He's not here. The money ran out.'

Merrivale stared at him. 'What do you mean, the money ran out? I left ample funds for his upkeep.'

'Apparently you didn't, or so the infirmarer says. Look, Merrivale, don't blame us. Bishop Grandisson is like a leech, sucking money out of the diocese to build his precious cathedral in Exeter. Our costs have gone up and there's nothing we can do about it.'

'You disapprove of cathedrals?'

'I disapprove of anything that man does. My family have been lords of Devon for two centuries, and Grandisson is just some upstart from Savoy. What right does he have to come in and start reordering things?'

Aware that he sounded petulant, the abbot glanced at the sandglass. 'And then there's the war. Ever since it began, the king's purveyors have been stripping the country like carrion crows. They bought the wool from our sheep on compulsory purchase, but only paid two-thirds of its market price. How are we to make ends meet?'

'You haven't explained what happened to the money I left to pay for my father's upkeep.'

'I have, but you haven't been listening. Look, we didn't just throw him out. The canons at Frithelstock offered to care for him so I sent him there. I'm sure they are looking after him very well, in their own… eccentric way.'

'My father is a broken man,' Merrivale said. 'He needs care and kindness, not to be passed around like an unwanted parcel. What happened to Christian charity, Father Abbot?'

'Christian charity? Ask the royal purveyors about Christian charity. Ask the Exchequer. Ask Scrope and Burghersh and Gonville and all those other vultures around the king, demanding more and more money to fight their precious war. I have to feed my flock, Merrivale, my monks and my tenants. I have to keep them warm through the winter, and ensure they have bread in their mouths, and put tiles on the roofs when the storms come.' The abbot nodded towards the sandglass. 'Your five minutes are up.'

Merrivale picked up the sandglass and hurled it to the floor. Shards of wood and glass spun across the tiles. 'Pray that my father has come to no harm,' he said. 'If he has, then whatever has befallen him will be visited back on your own head.'

Frithelstock, December 1338

He had allowed his emotions to get the better of him, again, which was a mistake. A sensible man would simply have walked away.

Merrivale rode north, passing Hugh Courtenay's impressive new hunting lodge at Okehampton on his way; clearly, neither the exactions of the purveyors nor the demands of Bishop Grandisson had affected the wealth of the Earls of Devon. From there the road led north through deep valleys to the sleepy town of Torrington. The roads were nearly empty, the fields bare and bleak. Wolves howled from the high ground to the east, and riding into town Merrivale saw wolf traps hanging over some of the doors.

Beyond the town, the road crossed the river Torridge on a long bridge. Otters played in the current around the stone piers. Frithelstock Priory lay on the high ground above the river, a collection of simple stone buildings surrounded by green fields. Merrivale dismounted at the gate and rang the bell. After a very long time the gate opened to reveal a black-robed man holding a half-eaten chicken leg in one hand. 'Welcome, stranger. Oh, dear, the weather do be dreadful. Come on inside now, and get yourself warm.'

The priory was small, but the Augustinian canons who welcomed him were friendly and smiling. 'Aye, your father is here. What a fine old gentleman he is! He'll be so happy to see his son. He speaks of you all the time, bless him. Now, he's usually asleep around this time, so you have a cup of wine to warm yourself while we wake him.'

The rooms were plain white plaster without paint or hangings, but there were warm fires everywhere. An atmosphere of cheerful anarchy prevailed. There was no infirmarer to care for the sick and elderly ('We just muck in and do everything ourselves, you see.') and no sign of the prior, though Merrivale heard female laughter coming from the prior's quarters. The sour mood that had gripped him ever since Tavistock began to fade a little. *Perhaps this is all for the best*, he thought.

'Come now,' one of the canons said. 'He's ready to see you.'

Reginald Merrivale sat in a chair in his own little cell, wrapped in a warm robe with a cap over his white hair, warming his hands over a charcoal brazier. He stood up as Merrivale entered, his eyes cloudy with emotion. 'My boy,' he said softly. 'My boy.'

They embraced tightly. 'I am sorry it has been so long,' Merrivale said.

'No, you must never apologise. You've been doing your duty. I'm proud of you, you know. Have I ever told you that?'

'Every time you see me,' Merrivale said smiling. 'I am glad I can make you happy.'

'You've restored the family honour. There were times when I never thought that would happen.'

Impoverished by the famine, Reginald Merrivale had been unable to pay the rents and tithes he owed to the church and his overlords. Several years after the death of his wife and daughters he had been deprived of his lands, and he and his son had been forced to live off the charity of friends. This final indignity, piled on top of the other tragedies, had broken his already frail spirit. He was only in his mid-fifties, but there was a palsy in his hands and at times his speech was slurred, worse than Merrivale remembered.

'So, where have you been, my boy?'

'Savoy,' Merrivale said.

'Savoy? That's a long way to travel. What took you there?'

Merrivale talked a little about Savoy, but he realised his father was not really listening. After a minute or so he changed the subject. 'How are you, father? Are they looking after you here?'

'Oh yes, very well, very well. Much better than Tavistock.'

'That is good to hear.'

'Much better,' his father repeated. 'I never really liked Tavistock, you know. All those puffed-up Benedictines, thinking they're better than everyone else. Especially that man Courtenay. Pompous prick.'

'I'm sorry I put you there.'

In a moment his father was contrite. 'Oh, don't mind me, my boy. It was all right, really, I just prefer it here. But you must do whatever is necessary. I don't want to be a burden to you.'

'Who has been paying for your care here?'

'Sir John Sully. He's always been so generous, John. I'm so grateful to him.'

'I'll make the arrangements from now on.'

His father's eyes filled with tears. 'You shouldn't have to. You shouldn't need to look after me. I'm just a burden to you,' he repeated. 'I'm a burden to everyone.'

Merrivale took his father's wrinkled hand in his own. 'Stop,' he said softly. 'Don't vex yourself. I'm glad I am able to help.' He paused. 'At least I can help someone.'

His father watched him for a while. 'You're young,' he said. 'You still think it's possible to change the world. When you grow older, you'll realise you can't.'

If that is so, I hope I never grow old, Merrivale nearly said, but he bit the words back. 'So we just accept what the world gives us?'

'That's what the monks said. We carry on and do our duty.' His father looked at his hands. 'Well, I don't, not any more. I just wait until God calls me.'

Merrivale forced a smile. 'That will be many years from now.'

'Will it? I don't know. I get tired, so easily, and I can feel the clouds gathering on the edges of my mind. I forget little things. I can remember the past as clearly as the ring of a bell, but when I go out to walk around the fields, I get lost. One of the canons has to come with me, or sometimes one of the girls. Pretty girls. The canons aren't supposed to have them in the house, but no one seems to mind.'

Merrivale watched him, feeling a soft pain in his chest. 'Perhaps this is where you belong,' he said. 'The canons are dedicated to caring for the needy and the sick. You are their vocation.'

'Really? I never looked at it that way.' His father looked up at him, eyes suddenly brighter. 'Something is troubling your soul, my boy.'

'I went back to our old home a few days ago. That may have been a mistake.'

'Aye,' his father said slowly. 'I understand what you mean. I've never been back, you know, not since... I've never been able to bring myself to go back.'

'They've rebuilt the mill,' Merrivale said. He could feel his throat closing. 'There are sheep again.'

'Good. Good. I'm glad.' His father looked up and suddenly his eyes were bright with understanding. 'What happened in Savoy, Simon? You were telling me, but I fear my mind was wandering.'

He wanted to tell his father everything, about Yolande, and Bishop Aubert's machinations, and Peruzzi's betrayal, but he could not bring himself to do so. How could he share his own suffering with a man who had already endured so much? Telling his father about Yolande would only upset him further still. He swallowed his pain.

'Savoy did not go well,' he said, trying to keep his voice light. 'Don't worry. I'll soon pick up the pieces again.'

'I'm sure you will. You were always a single-minded young beggar.'

'I come by that naturally.'

'Aye, from your mother. She was the strongest woman I've ever met, until the famine came... I think of them every day, you know.'

'Yes. Me too.'

'I'm so tired,' his father said, and he stared at the brazier again. Merrivale leaned over and took both his father's hands between his own palms, trying to still the shaking. It subsided after a time but he could still feel the underlying tremor, soft as a heartbeat.

They sat together in silence for a long time. 'You should go,' his father said finally. 'You mustn't worry about me. They look after me very well here, you know. Much better than Tavistock.'

'I'm glad of that.'

'Go back to the king, my boy. Do your duty. Make me proud.'

Merrivale sat for a moment longer, unable to speak. Slowly he rose to his feet, and bent and planted a soft kiss on his father's forehead before turning and leaving the room. Outside in the little cloister he paused for a moment, looking up at the wind-whipped clouds. In the prior's lodge the women were laughing again.

3

Ruxford, December 1338

'Simon Merrivale! Hail and welcome! By God, boy, you're thin as a rake. Where have you been?'

'Here and there,' Merrivale said. 'You, John, have not changed a bit.'

Sir John Sully was fifty-six years old, the same age as Merrivale's father, but unlike the old man at Frithelstock, he was full of boundless energy. His hair was white and his face weather-beaten from countless campaign trails, but his blue eyes were young and all-seeing. 'Untrue, untrue,' he said, clapping Merrivale on the back. 'I've been at home too long, I've grown idle and fat. Come in, come in. Isabelle will be glad to see you.'

Sully's principal manor was at Iddesleigh on the high ground north of Dartmoor, but in winter he preferred his wife's property at Ruxford, down in the mild valley of the river Creedy. Merrivale knew the place well. His father had once been one of Sully's retainers, and after Reginald Merrivale had been dispossessed of his lands, Sully had brought the frail, shattered man and his pale, nearly mute son to live with himself and his family. Under the spell of Ruxford's warmth and peace the horrors of the famine had begun gradually to fade. Even today, the place still felt like home.

The hall was redolent of woodsmoke and dogs; Merrivale could not recall ever seeing Sully without at least one dog in attendance, even on campaign. Lady Isabelle, a merry brown-haired woman somewhat younger than her husband, greeted him cheerfully. 'How long will you remain with us, Simon? At least until Twelfth Night, I hope.'

Merrivale shook his head. 'I am sorry, I cannot stay for long. I must return to London and report to the king.'

Sully and his wife glanced at each other. 'The king is in Antwerp,' the former said. 'He and the queen and court are spending the winter there, as guests of Cousin Jan and Brother Willem. What a happy family party they will make,' he added ironically.

Cousin Jan was the king's cousin, the Duke of Brabant and lord of Antwerp; Brother Willem was his brother-in-law, the Count of Hainault. Despite their family relationships, none of the three was very fond of the others. 'Then to Antwerp I must go,' Merrivale said. 'I really only came to say thank you for looking after my father. You must let me know how much money I owe you.'

'We will speak of it later. Come, sit by the fire. Have a glass of wine, you look in need of it. Have you seen your father?'

A fire blazed in a hearth that could have been used to roast whole oxen, and probably had. Merrivale pulled up a bench while Sully dropped into a high-backed chair and Lady Isabelle poured wine. 'I went to Frithelstock,' Merrivale said. 'He seems happier there than at Tavistock. Getting away from that prick of an abbot has probably helped.'

'Aye, don't blame Abbot Courtenay. He has deeper problems on his hands. Like every landlord in the country, myself included, he's being squeezed by the king's purveyors. Those bastards are bleeding the country dry to support the king's war.'

'Yes,' Merrivale said reluctantly. He disliked John Courtenay, and did not want to stop disliking him. 'The abbot blamed several people in particular. Sir Geoffrey Scrope and Burghersh, the Bishop of Lincoln. And someone named Gonville.'

Sully shook his head. 'We both know Geoffrey Scrope, Simon. He's a good and honourable man. And Burghersh is full of choler, too much so for a churchman, but he's still a loyal servant to the king.'

'I reckon Burghersh could start a war with his own reflection, but I take your point. Who is Gonville?'

Lady Isabelle made a moue. 'The king's new secretary. Some puffed-up little clerk. He comes from East Anglia,' she said, in a voice implying that nothing good ever came out of East Anglia.

'He's harmless,' Sully said. 'He's a collector of benefices, true, but there's plenty of those around. It's the purveyors and treasurers and moneymen who are doing the real mischief to the country.'

'Spoken like a true gentleman,' his wife pronounced. 'Knights are always contemptuous of money, until they want some.' She looked at Merrivale. 'All the same, this war with France is causing real discontent in the country.'

'Why? We've had wars before.'

'Yes, with Scotland,' Sully said, 'but the Scottish wars have always been popular. Close neighbours make good enemies, and apart from Bannockburn and a few others we'll not mention, we always win. The conflict with France is different. The people don't understand why we're fighting.'

'Never mind the people,' said Lady Isabelle. '*I* don't understand it. On top of which, the war is not going well. New taxes are being levied to pay for armies, but there are no victories to boast about. The French and their corsair allies roam the seas at will. They burned Portsmouth last spring, and then there was that horror in Southampton in October.'

'What happened in Southampton?'

'Of course, you were away. The French burned the entire town and killed half the people, and carried the rest away to sell as slaves.' She sighed. 'It is hard to tell which suffered the worst fate. Understandably, that did not help the public mood.'

Sully nodded. 'I correspond with Geoffrey Scrope from time to time, just to stay informed about affairs at court. According to his last letter, the king is growing worried. He knows how quickly unrest and mutterings in dark corners can turn into plots and treason. His own father was removed from the throne and murdered. He won't want to go the same way.'

The fire popped, sparks shooting up the chimney. 'All the more reason why I need to go to Antwerp,' Merrivale said. 'My place is with the king.'

Husband and wife glanced at each other again. 'I'd bide here a while, if I were you,' Sully said gently.

'Why? What has happened, John?'

'Tell him,' Lady Isabelle said, and her voice too was gentle.

'Geoffrey Scrope's last letter also mentioned you,' Sully said. 'He's in Antwerp too, of course, sitting at the king's right hand. The king blames you for what went wrong in Savoy. Geoffrey tried to persuade him to give you a second chance, but His Grace wouldn't listen. I am sorry, Simon, but the king has dismissed you from your post. You are no longer a King's Messenger.'

It took some time to sink in. He knew Sully was distressed on his behalf; it was Sully who had used his influence to get Merrivale appointed to the post six years ago at the start of the Scottish wars. He had served all through that conflict, and in France too and beyond, and he had thought he had won the king's trust and respect.

Now, he had lost the woman he loved and he had lost his vocation, the work that gave purpose to his life. He felt like a drowning man, with the water closing over his head.

'What in God's name am I going to do?' he asked aloud. 'That post was my whole life. Where do I go now?' Another thought struck him. 'Holy Mary, John, what about my father? How do I pay for his upkeep? The canons will put him out, he'll be abandoned and alone.'

'The canons will do no such thing,' Sully said. 'If there is any question of fees for his maintenance, I will cover the cost.'

Desperation, grief, anger all woke within him. 'I cannot let him live off your charity, John. Not again. For God's sake, can there be no forgiveness? Was what I did in Savoy so terrible?'

'Tell us what happened,' Lady Isabelle said.

He wanted to tell them, and yet he did not. Slowly he resolved the struggle in his mind and found his voice. 'Geoffrey of Maldon and I were sent to Savoy,' he said finally. 'Geoffrey was the king's agent, and I was there to support him. Our purpose was to bribe the Count of Savoy to come over to our side and declare war on France. Unfortunately, the count proved to be a peaceful man who didn't want to go to war at all, so we hatched a new plan. We knew King

Jean of Bohemia was in Italy trying to carve out a domain for himself, and we offered to help him overthrow the count and seize Savoy. We bribed others to join too, Carlo Grimaldi the lord of Monaco, and Ottone Doria the Genoese mercenary captain. Donato de' Peruzzi was prepared to finance the venture.'

'What went wrong?' Sully asked.

'The French had agents in Savoy, too. One of them was Étienne Aubert, the Bishop of Noyon. His spy, a man called Vidal, discovered… something he should not have discovered. He informed Peruzzi, who decided it was too risky to support us and changed sides. He then bribed Grimaldi and Doria to follow him back to their French allegiance.'

Sully frowned. 'There is a rumour at court that Bishop Aubert had offered to take you into his service. Is that true?'

'The offer was made, yes, but I doubt very much if it was genuine. I suspect this was part of a plot to slander me and encourage the king to dismiss me. If so, it worked.'

'What secret did this man Vidal discover?' asked Lady Isabelle.

'That I was the lover of Princess Yolande of Sicily,' Merrivale said after a moment. 'King Jean's bastard daughter.'

Both of his hosts stared at him. 'Oh, my dear boy,' Lady Isabelle said softly. 'You certainly reached for the stars.'

'And the stars came down to me, and I held them in my hands,' Merrivale said. 'Right from the beginning we knew this was no passing fancy, this was something that would last for a lifetime. We dared to dream. We planned to live together forever.' He paused for a moment. 'Or so I thought.'

Sully shook his white head. 'Love makes a man careless.'

'That's the hell of it, John. We *weren't* careless. We knew how vindictive her father could be, and we covered our tracks with great care. How Vidal discovered us, the devil only knows… Strangely, I don't really blame Vidal for betraying us. The person I blame is myself.'

'For what?' asked Isabelle.

'For forgetting my duty. For falling in love.'

She smiled a little. 'I sometimes forget how young you are. Do you really think you had a choice? You must know the *Roman de la*

Rose. Love is a dream from which we wake, only to find ourselves still dreaming.'

'I dream of her every night,' Merrivale said. 'And I wake to emptiness.'

Her face was full of sympathy. 'What happened?'

'I realised everything was falling apart and I rode to Turin to find her, but her father's men had already taken her and set a trap for me. I escaped and rode up into the mountains, but they followed and this time they caught me. On King Jean's orders, I was tied inside a sack and thrown into a river.'

'Dear God,' Sully said.

'I escaped, God knows how, and made my way back to England, mostly because I didn't know what else to do. I don't even know if she is still alive. Even if she is, her father will have walled her up in a nunnery or married her off to one of his retainers. I will never see her again.'

Sully stirred. 'Nothing is impossible. Don't give up hope, boy.'

'I must,' Merrivale said bleakly. 'Hope causes pain, more than I can bear. I can live with despair. I learned how to do so, during the famine.'

'Do not speak like that,' Lady Isabelle exclaimed. 'Simon, my dear, you cannot spend the rest of your life mourning her.'

'Why not? I have spent most of my life in mourning. My mother, my sisters, the children I played with as a boy, and now Yolande. I thought I could return home and find solace in my duties. Now, that too is gone.'

They persuaded him to stay the night, and he agreed because he had nowhere else to go. They were kind, and somehow that made things worse.

In the morning, Sully came to his chamber. 'Isabelle and I have been discussing you.'

'I thought you might,' Merrivale said.

'You need an occupation. Something to keep you busy and stop you dwelling too much on the past.'

Merrivale forced a smile. 'I am open to suggestions.'

'Well, I might have something for you. It could get you back in the king's good books, or it could get you even deeper into trouble. I reckon the chances are about even.'

'What is it?'

'Would you be willing to serve the king's mother?'

Merrivale was startled. 'Would the king approve? To say he is protective of his family is an understatement.'

'The queen is unlikely to disclose this matter to anyone outside her own household, least of all to her son. Her chaplain is an old friend of mine, a man named John Hull. He tells me Her Grace is experiencing financial difficulties.'

'Nothing new there. She spends money like most people pass water.'

'Aye, but this is different. She reckons someone is defrauding her. One of her clerks was ordered to investigate, but he has disappeared.'

'What happened to him?'

'That's what Her Grace wants to find out. She needs a reliable man to conduct a discreet inquisition.' Sully hesitated. 'I should warn you, Queen Isabella can be... difficult.'

'And the king can't?'

'You know where you are with the king. He wears his heart on his sleeve. No one is quite sure where his mother keeps hers.'

The clerk had probably been knifed in a tavern fight, or gone missing in the stews. Tracking him down would likely be dull, sordid and unrewarding, but it was better than doing nothing. 'Very well,' Merrivale said. 'I'll take the commission, if it's still available.'

Sully smiled. 'Good. I'll write to Master Hull now.'

In the quiet, dog-friendly comfort of Ruxford, Merrivale waited for Hull to reply. Rain drifted down the valleys and snow settled on the high moors. Twelfth Night came and went.

Two days later a messenger arrived bearing a letter for Sir John Sully. He broke the seal and read it, then handed it to Merrivale.

To my esteemed friend John Sully, miles, *greeting. From your description, it would seem your friend is amply qualified. He should not be concerned about the king, for even if he should come to hear of this appointment, Her Grace will deflect his wrath away. She has always derived a certain amount of pleasure from annoying her son. If Master Merrivale still wishes to accept the commission he should go to London and call at Surnes Tower on Bucklersbury, where he should ask to speak to Master Stanton. I wish him good fortune. I remain your friend and servant, John Hull,* capellanus.

Merrivale handed the letter back. 'Thank you.'

'There's no need to thank me, boy. Make a success of this, and you will have a friend for life in the queen mother.'

'Yes,' Merrivale said wryly. 'For better or for worse.'

4

London, February 1339

'Master Merrivale? I'm John Stanton, one of Queen Isabella's sarjeants. Thank you for offering your services.'

'Thank you,' Merrivale said. He looked at the other man; stocky in build, middling height with a pleasant face. 'You look familiar. Have we met?'

'I believe we did, in Perth during the last Scottish campaign. I was in the king's service then. I was seconded to the queen mother's household shortly thereafter.'

They were standing in the great hall of Surnes Tower. Its walls were painted white with red masonry patterns and rosettes, and the ceiling beams were patterned with red and blue traceries, the beam ends supported by gilded angels. Candlelight gleamed off a painted statue of Saint Michael impaling a dragon on his lance. 'I see Her Grace's tastes have not changed,' Merrivale said.

'Ah, this has nothing to do with the queen mother. A London merchant built this place about thirty years ago. He was a collector of customs, so he had enough money to splash the paint around. After he died, an Italian banker took possession, and he gave the house over to the queen.'

'In exchange for what?'

'Best not to ask. Things were a bit chaotic back then.'

'Back then' referred to the reign of the king's father, Edward II, a time of famine, rebellion and civil war that finally ended when the king was overthrown by his wife, Queen Isabella. She was appointed regent of England, ruling on behalf of her son, but much of her power was exercised by her lover Roger Mortimer, who ordered the murder of the king and, later, the arrest and execution of the king's brother. At this point, the young Edward III, guessing that his name was next on Mortimer's list, decided to get his retaliation in first. The royal lover ended up dangling from a gallows at Tyburn, and the king's mother was sent into retirement.

A servant brought a jug of spiced wine and two finely polished silver cups. Stanton watched while the wine was poured and picked up one of the cups, inhaling the fumes. He winced. 'I do wish Her Grace would keep a decent cellar. But the treasurer keeps telling me there isn't enough money.'

Merrivale nodded, picking up the other cup. 'I understand you wish me to find a clerk who has gone missing. What can you tell me about him?'

Stanton looked slightly taken aback. Perhaps he was not used to people coming to the point so quickly. 'His name is Ralph Dunham. He has been in the queen mother's household for about a year.'

'Before that?'

'He was educated at Castle Acre Priory and took minor orders. The prior recommended him to Edmund Gonville, one of the king's secretaries. Gonville paid for him to go to Cambridge and he spent three years in the studium there.'

A collector of benefices, Sir John Sully had called Gonville. 'What does Dunham look like?'

'Middle height, slender, black hair. Rather fine-featured, I would say. He wears a silver signet ring on his right hand.'

'Any vices? Drink, gambling, women? Men?'

'Not that I know of.'

'Anything else I need to know?'

Stanton shook his head. 'I didn't know him well. He was with Her Grace at Castle Rising and I spend much of my time in London. But I know the queen liked him and trusted him.'

'This bothers me,' Merrivale said. 'Royal clerks don't disappear without attracting attention. When they do, the crown moves heaven and earth to find them. Sheriffs are summoned, the posse comitatus is called out, commissions of oyer and terminer are appointed to oversee the search. Why has that not been done?'

Stanton paused. 'It is a bit hard to explain,' he said finally. 'Let us say Her Grace is doing something she would prefer other people not know about.'

'You mean, something she would prefer the king does not know about.'

'Yes. Look, I'll explain what is happening, but this must be kept confidential.'

'You have my word.'

The serjeant drew a deep breath. 'When the king assumed direct rule eight years ago he gave his mother a generous pension, derived partly from lands and rents and partly from exports of wool. Most of the time, at least, this was enough to keep Her Grace in the manner she believes she is entitled to. However, money from both sources has dried up.'

'Why?'

'Well, many of her lands were in Southampton, and those were laid waste by the French and are paying no rents. As for the wool money, the king placed the entire export of wool in the hands of a company of merchants led by William de la Pole, one of the king's bankers. Pole was instructed to pay the queen what she is owed, but he claims the syndicate hasn't managed to sell the wool and cannot meet its obligations until it does.'

'Why the delay?'

'We don't know. Pole can't say, or won't say, what the problem is. My own job at the moment is to investigate the wool trade and find out what is holding up the queen's payments.' Stanton took a sip of his wine. 'Now we come to the heart of the matter. The queen wishes to become more financially independent. Some time ago, on the advice of her treasurer, she decided to engage in a venture of her own and bought six acres of land near Chipping Walden in Essex.'

'Only six acres? What crop is she planting?'

'Red gold,' Stanton said. 'Her Grace is growing saffron.'

'Ah,' Merrivale said slowly. 'Is it possible to grow saffron in our climate?'

'It's a matter of finding the right kind of soil, I am told. If the initial venture is successful, Her Grace intends to purchase more land.'

'And she would no longer need to rely on her pension from the king?'

'No. An acre of good land will produce anything up to thirty pounds of saffron, and a London apothecary will pay between fifteen and twenty shillings a pound, even more if the quality is good. Ship the crop over to Antwerp or Ghent and you can double your money. Now, imagine that six acres is expanded to sixty, or six hundred. Her Grace would recoup everything she lost in Southampton, and more besides.'

Indeed, Merrivale thought. *It might be enough money to redeem some of the queen mother's tenants who had been sold into slavery, or compensate the families of those who had died.*

'Was this experiment successful?'

'At first it seemed so. Reports suggested there would be a good crop last year, but around October everything went quiet. We stopped receiving reports from the crokers, the farmers growing the saffron. That's when Dunham was first sent to Chipping Walden to investigate.'

'Why keep this secret from the king?'

For the first time Stanton looked uncomfortable. 'The queen borrowed money to finance this venture. If the crop is lost she will be unable to pay back the loan, and will be forced to call on the king for help. The king is short of money himself and, well...'

Merrivale nodded. 'This could cause a rupture between them. She wants this matter sorted out quickly and quietly before it reaches the king's ears. Which does she really want me to do? Find her missing clerk, or ensure the saffron crop is safe?'

Stanton had recovered his composure. He grinned. 'I think she is hoping for both,' he said.

'When did Dunham go to Chipping Walden?'

'Early November.'

'Did he send any word after he departed?'

'No. At first we thought he might have met with an accident on the road, of course.'

'What effort has been made to find him?'

'Robert Brigget, the queen's marshal, rode down to Walden in December but found no sign of Dunham. He also reported that the crokers had vanished, taking the crop with them. We sent a message to Dunham's family, but they have heard nothing from him.'

'Tell me about the crokers.'

'There are three of them, Juan Moreno, Nicholas le Flemyng and James Westacre. Moreno is from Castile and has experience of saffron growing. Flemyng comes from Colchester and Westacre from Norfolk. All three came highly recommended.'

'By whom?'

'Peter Ellerker, the queen's treasurer, recruited them. Where he found them, I do not know.'

Merrivale nodded. 'Very well. I shall go to Chipping Walden and see what I can discover.'

'Thank you,' Stanton said. 'I'm afraid you will be on your own. The investigation into the queen's wool subsidy is taking up all my time, and we cannot spare anyone else. We're having difficulty keeping servants at the moment. They have heard the rumours and think they won't be paid.'

Thinking of his father, Merrivale gazed up at the gilded angels for a moment. 'Will *I* be paid?'

'You have my word of honour,' Stanton said.

Merrivale stepped out into the street as the bells of Saint Stephen's church on Wallbrook began to ring sexts. Other bells joined in. The clouds had blown away and watery sunlight filled the streets. Stocks Market was busy with people selling brassicas and dried herbs. Beyond it, Poultry was crowded with draymen and porters, archers in the white-and-red livery of the city, blue-robed Sack Friars from their house on Lothbury, demure Franciscan nuns in grey habits, cordwainers in leather aprons and mercers in dark robes, German merchants from the Steelyard, vendors selling smoking hot chestnuts, sweet wafers, pigs' feet, eel pies, hot ale.

Walking up Grocers Lane, Merrivale passed the shops of pepperers and spicers and apothecaries, smelling the tang of pepper and cloves in the air. Stone jars of ginger and galangal stood behind mounds of ground turmeric and cinnamon and pots of mustard and aromatic gums. There were little wooden boxes of saffron too, the costliest of all spices, kept conspicuously away from customers' reach. *Red gold*, Stanton had called it, and he was not wrong; at times the price of saffron and the price of gold were not far distant from each other. The prices he had quoted were conservative. Merrivale had seen far higher in his travels.

Partly this was due to scarcity. There were a few saffron meadows in France, but most were in Spain or even further afield. But saffron also had its own mystique. It was one of those luxury goods that only the very wealthy could afford, and that helped to keep the price high. If Queen Isabella could establish saffron fields in England, she would indeed have created a gold mine.

And gold mines, of course, opened the doors to temptation. Men and women had committed fraud, or worse, for far smaller sums of money.

He reached Lombard Street and turned east towards his lodgings, passing the gates of the big house belonging to William de la Pole, the powerful wool merchant and banker from Hull. A man sat in front of the gates playing a symphonia, one hand turning the crank and the other pressing the keys. Beside him stood another man, holding out his hands like a supplicant and singing.

A king ought not to go out of his kingdom to make war
Unless the commons of his land will consent
By treason we often see very many perish
No one can tell in whom to trust with certainty
Let not the king go out of his kingdom without counsel

A group of people had gathered to listen. Some were nodding in agreement. Several city watch archers were among them, listening too and making no move to stop the performance. London always danced to its own tune, not to whatever music the king called.

Since the king is determined to take so much
He will find enough to satisfy himself among the rich
And it seems to me he would get more, and do better
To take from the great ones, and leave the little people alone
He sins who takes money from the needy without cause

Merrivale glanced at the archers again. One said something, and the others laughed.

We should not blame such wickedness on the king
But on his bad and rapacious councillors
The king is a young man, not yet of an age
To encompass any malice. But listen, for I speak the truth
His counsellors are doing great harm.

Merrivale walked on. Sully was right, the people were not blaming the king, yet, but they *were* patronising him. 'He is only young, he doesn't yet know what he is doing, he is being deceived by his corrupt councillors.' It was hard to know which sentiment would make Edward III more angry.

Distracted by the song, Merrivale did not notice the man with the wooden cudgel until the latter had moved up beside him. He ducked under the first blow aimed at his head, but a second blow from behind cracked across his back and knocked him to the ground. He struggled to rise as the cudgel hammered into his ribs; his heavy cloak absorbed some of the force, but the blows still drove the air out of his lungs. Unable to shout for help, he curled into a ball, protecting his head and belly. His attackers stood over him, cudgels raised. '*Copé!*' one said. 'Finish him.'

Another voice spoke, sharp with anger. 'Stand away!'

'Don't interfere, *monsù*,' one of the attackers said. 'There are three of us and only one of you.'

'I don't care how many you are,' the other man said. 'You walk away, boy. Else you don't, I'm going to carve your guts out and twist them into garters.'

'You threaten us, bastard?'

'Enric, we don't have time for this!' a new voice hissed. 'If the watch spot us, we're finished. *Mòrt!*'

'*Già*,' the first man said reluctantly. '*Andè, andè*.'

Merrivale heard their footsteps hurrying away. He sat up slowly, looking at his rescuer. The other man was about his own age, short and squarely built with thick red hair. 'Dartmoor,' Merrivale said. 'I'd know that accent anywhere.'

No one else seemed to have noticed the attack; everyone was still listening to the musicians. The red-haired man slid his knife back into its sheath and helped Merrivale to his feet. He could feel bruises beginning to swell, but no worse damage seemed to have been done. 'Thank you,' he said. 'May I ask your name?'

'Warin of Hexworthy. And who might you be?'

'My name is Simon Merrivale. I'm a King's Messenger.' He checked for a moment; the words had come out automatically. 'That is, I used to be.'

Warin's attitude changed at once. 'I didn't realise, sir. I beg your pardon for speaking so familiar.'

'No pardon is needed. You arrived in the nick of time.'

'King's Messenger, you said. Is that why those men attacked you?'

'No,' Merrivale said. 'They were robbers, I expect. Sadly, the city is full of them. What brings you to London, Master Warin?'

'I thought I'd come and see the world.' That seemed unlikely, Merrivale thought. 'I'm a free man, by the way, just in case you get ideas.'

'Don't worry, I didn't think you were a runaway serf. I hail from Devon myself, I know Hexworthy is a tin mining village and the miners are free tenants. Now that you've seen the world, what do you think of it?'

'Some good, some bad. The ale's good here, when you can afford it. Which hasn't been too often of recent.'

Merrivale looked at him. 'Are you short of money?'

'No, sir. I'm just travelling around at the moment. Living off my fat,' Warin added, unconvincingly.

'And in danger of being arrested. London has laws against vagrancy.' Merrivale pointed. 'Go to Surnes Tower on Bucklersbury and ask to speak to Master Stanton. Tell him I sent you. They'll find work for you.'

Warin looked stubborn, unwilling to accept help, but common sense told him that refusal would be both ungracious and foolish. He bobbed his head. 'Thank you, sir. I'm in your debt.'

'Consider the slate wiped clean.' Merrivale stood for a moment, watching the red-haired man walk away up the street. The drone of the symphonia still hung in the air.

He had not told Warin that he knew exactly where his attackers came from. They had spoken in Piedmontese dialect. He knew it well; he had heard little else for the past year, in the streets and markets and taverns of Savoy.

5

Chipping Walden, February 1339

The ride from London to Chipping Walden should have taken two days but Merrivale took twice as long, staying off the high roads and doubling back to check for any signs of pursuit. The London attack had made him cautious. The attackers were Savoyards, not Bohemians, so they were unlikely to be King Jean's men, but something did not make sense. They could easily have killed him; the city watch had been oblivious to their presence, and for all his defiance it was unlikely that Warin of Hexworthy could have stopped them. So why had they not finished their work?

He reached Chipping Walden late on the fourth afternoon, the winter sun shining low over the fields. The air was bitterly cold and the ditch surrounding the town was covered with a thick layer of ice. Next to the marketplace were an inn, a forge and some fine houses; most of the rest of the town was a huddle of thatched cottages and yards full of frozen mud, dominated by the tall lantern tower of the church. Sheep bleated in the fields and a cow complained in her byre. Across the meadows to the west was a stream fringed by a line of trees with long shadows; beyond these, the rooftops and tower of an abbey could be seen. To the north were the ruins of a small castle, slighted in some earlier civil war.

Merrivale dismounted outside the inn, handing over his horse to a groom. Inside the common room a woman was lighting lamps. A man sat in a corner, nursing a pot of ale. Both watched him in silence.

He laid a coin on the counter and the woman drew another pot of ale and pushed it over to him, pocketing the coin. Still no one said a word. He waited to see what would happen.

The woman finally broke the silence. 'We've not seen you here before, sir.'

'I've not been here before,' Merrivale said. 'Is it always this quiet?'

'Lambing has started,' said the man. He was fair-skinned with short hair and a thin, pointed nose. 'Most folk are out in the fields.'

Silence fell again. Merrivale sipped his ale, which was surprisingly good. 'What might your business be?' the woman inquired after a moment.

'I'm looking for a clerk named Ralph Dunham. I'm told he came here last autumn.'

The man stared into his ale pot. 'I don't recall anyone of that name, sir,' the woman said. Her reaction seemed genuine.

'He had business with some people here. James Westacre and Nicholas le Flemyng, and a Spaniard named Moreno. Do you know them?'

'They're gone,' the man said. 'Long gone.'

'When did they go?'

'Couple of days after All Hallows.'

'I don't suppose anyone knows where they went?'

The landlady pursed her lips. The man's shoulder lifted in a shrug.

Merrivale rose to his feet. 'Thank you,' he said. 'I have enjoyed our conversation. Perhaps you could tell me where I might buy some saffron?'

The woman looked vague, but the man's head came up sharply. 'Ask the wise woman,' he said. 'You'll find her on Church Street. She might know.'

'You are a fountain of information,' Merrivale told him.

Church Street was full of small shops, a bakery, a malting, a cutler's booth and a house with a familiar badge over the door, a snake coiled around a winged staff. Merrivale opened its door and stepped into the lamplit interior. Rows of painted pottery and stone jars stood on shelves around the room. A confusion of smells filled the air; rosemary and mint, mustard and spikenard and some bitter scents he did not recognise.

A woman came into the room. She wore a plain gown with a dark apron; a white wimple covered most of her fair hair. There were lines on her forehead and at the corners of her eyes but the rest of her face seemed ageless. He guessed she was about forty, but there might have been ten years either way.

'How may I help you?' There was an edge of challenge in her voice. Perhaps she did not like strangers either.

'I am looking for the wise woman,' Merrivale said.

'My name is Cassandra Wesenham,' she said. 'I am an apothecary by trade, and a fully qualified physician trained at the Schola Medica Salernitana. I am also versed in law, geometry and logic, and no one *ever* calls me a "wise woman".'

Merrivale bowed. 'I apologise unreservedly. You were at Salerno? Did you perchance study with Mercuriade?'

Her eyes widened a little. 'She was one of my professors, yes. How do you know of her?'

'I met her last year. If you were her student, then you have my full respect.' He paused for a moment. 'Are you also a Marcosian?'

'A heretic? Not that it is any of your business, but the answer is no. Mercuriade sees faith and reason as two halves of the same coin, but I prefer to keep them separate. I try to follow the path of logic and truth.'

This conversation was not going where he expected. 'You believe that logic and truth are related?'

'Of course. Logic, if used correctly, leads us to the truth. Without logic, no science can ever be fully known.'

'You're quoting William of Ockham, which means you probably *are* a heretic,' Merrivale said. 'Or so the Pope has decreed. On the other hand, most popes have very little interest in logic and are only distantly acquainted with the truth. Allow me to introduce myself. My name is Simon Merrivale and I am looking for a man named Ralph Dunham.'

He watched her reaction. Her face gave nothing away. 'Has something happened to him?'

'I don't know. That is what I hope to discover.'

She glanced towards the door, as if she expected an armed posse to be waiting outside. 'Are you alone?'

'It is pointless to use more to achieve what can be done with less.'

Her lips twitched a little. 'Don't tell me you've met Ockham as well.'

'In Munich, two years ago. Travel is one of the privileges of my work. Did you meet Dunham?'

'Yes,' she said. 'He came into my shop and asked me questions about saffron.'

'What sort of questions?'

'Why should I answer you?' she countered.

He considered this. 'You don't have to, of course, but it would be helpful. The queen mother would like to know what has happened to her servant. I owe Mercuriade a great deal,' he added. 'I would never do anything to harm a friend of hers.'

She relaxed a little. 'He asked about prices and markets, mostly. Where to sell it, how many shillings per pound's weight a croker could expect to receive. I wasn't much help to him, because I know very little about the market. I never buy saffron myself.'

'You do not stock it?'

'Of course I do,' she said calmly. 'I grow my own.'

The back room of the shop contained a long wooden bench with mortars and pestles of various sizes, pottery bowls and glass jars and a variety of tools scattered across the surface. More jars stood on shelves, and there was a locked chest, which he guessed was where she kept the more toxic ingredients of her trade. A drying kiln stood to one side of the room. A large silver-grey cat with tufted ears sat on the flagstones next to the kiln, calmly grooming itself. Cassandra removed the stopper from a jar of wine and poured two glass beakers full, handing one to Merrivale.

'Had I stayed in Italy, I could have become like Mercuriade,' she said. 'A respected physician with a practice of my own, perhaps even a professor. Here in the north, ignorance and superstition mean women are not allowed to practise medicine or trade as apothecaries. Even in my home town, Bishop's Lynn, I was shunned. So, I had to go out into the country and become a hedge healer. A *wise woman*.'

'Why choose Walden?'

'Because I could grow saffron here. I made a study of its medical properties while I was at Salerno. Because saffron is so expensive, most of it goes to feed the vanity of the rich. Their cooks buy it to flavour a dish of eggs, or glaze a capon so it looks to be made of gold.'

'Isn't it the same with physicians? The more expensive the medicine, the more efficacious the cure?'

She was impatient. 'You mean nonsense like drinking powdered sandalwood, or dissolving pearls in vinegar. Saffron is different. The ancients all knew its properties, Galen, Pliny, Dioscorides. Galen tells us that certain foods like saffron help to regulate the body and keep us healthy. It aids digestion and acts as a diuretic, draining fluid from the lungs and provoking a healthy flow of urine. Dissolved in a potion, it can also be used as a narcotic to aid sleep. This is not belief or superstition, Master Merrivale. This is science.'

'What made you decide to grow saffron yourself?'

'Anger at the absurd prices charged in Grocers Lane, mostly. But I had also found a place where the growing conditions are right. Unlike much of East Anglia, the soils at Walden are light and well-drained. I obtained some crocus corms from a medical colleague in Spain and planted my own saffron meadow. It is not large, only a few perches, but it meets my needs.'

'Very enterprising,' Merrivale said. He pondered for a moment. 'Presumably you know about the crokers who began planting saffron here a few years ago.'

'Two years ago, to be precise. Yes, I am aware of them.'

'Did you ever have dealings with them?'

'I had met one of them before, James Westacre. He was formerly a shipmaster, and my brother had owned a share in his ship. I recognised him as soon as he arrived in Walden.'

'What about the other two? Moreno and Flemyng?'

'Moreno was a little older than the others, quite professional. I think he comes from a family of saffron growers in Spain. I disliked

Flemyng. He came into my shop a couple of times, asking all sorts of questions about which drugs I kept in stock and whether any of them were toxic. I did not think his interest was particularly healthy.'

'Did anyone else work with them?'

'Only at harvest time, otherwise they did most of the work themselves. For the harvest they brought in people from Colchester and Mildenhall for a few weeks.'

'Not local people?'

'No. At harvest time the locals are busy bringing in their own crops. It is not uncommon to hire labourers from the towns.'

'How many workers did they employ for the harvest?'

'Several dozen at least.'

Merrivale raised his eyebrows. 'For six acres? That seems a great many.'

She shook her head. 'Picking saffron is hard, concentrated work. When the crocus flowers are fully open they must be harvested immediately, before they go over. Then the chives, the stamens, must be removed from the petals and sorted for quality. It takes about two hundred thousand chives to make a pound of wet saffron, and a good harvest brings in about thirty pounds per acre. As you can see, it is no small task.'

The cat rose to its feet, swishing its long tail, and stalked out of the room. 'What happens once it is harvested?' Merrivale asked.

'The wet chives are wrapped in paper and pressed before being dried in kilns. Once they are dried the harvest is ready to sell.'

Merrivale thought for a moment. 'Where are the crokers now?'

'I believe they took their harvest to London to sell it, and went off to enjoy their money. In winter the plants are dormant, and there is nothing to do until the corms begin to sprout again in spring.'

'Is there anything else you can tell me about them?'

'You ask a great many questions, Simon Merrivale. May I ask one of my own? What has all this to do with your missing clerk?'

Merrivale watched her face as he spoke. 'Ralph Dunham was employed by Queen Isabella, as were the four crokers. Any profit from the saffron meadows is due to her, but the crokers took the harvest and disappeared. Dunham's task was to find them and recover the saffron. For someone versed in logic, lady, you seem strangely unaware of what is going on. Or are you?'

Cassandra rose and fetched the wine jar, refilling their beakers. 'I was unaware of Her Grace's involvement,' she said calmly. 'My assumption about their actions was logical, but I was not in possession of all the facts.'

'Thereby demonstrating the limits of logic,' Merrivale said. 'Tell me more about Westacre.'

'There is not a great deal to tell. He comes from Westacre, a manor near Castle Acre. As I said, he was a shipmaster. He voyaged often to Spain, and he told me that he learned about saffron cultivation there. He acquired some crocus corms and returned home with the intention of retiring from the sea and becoming a farmer.'

'And all over the country there are farm boys who dream of going to sea. Let us return to Dunham. When did you first meet him?'

'A week ago.'

Merrivale was startled. The clerk had not been heard of since November. 'Only a week?'

'Last Thursday, to be precise. He called on me in the afternoon and we had a short conversation as I said. He departed, and I have not seen him since.'

'Dunham also comes from Castle Acre. Had you not met him before?'

'No, but I know of his family. His father builds wagons and hires them out to merchants needing transport. My brother uses his services.'

'You said Dunham asked about prices and markets. Anything else?'

She thought. 'He asked about a man named Brigget, but I don't know who he is. He also asked whether saffron could be adulterated.'

'Can it?'

'Yes, of course. You can mix it with stamens from other similar flowers, or dampen it with oil to make it heavier.'

'Did he ask about the crokers? Where they had gone, for example?'

'No.' She paused. 'Which is strange, given what you have said. If he was looking for them, why did he not ask me?'

Merrivale frowned, trying to pull together the loose thoughts nagging at the edge of his mind. 'Is there anything else, anything at all that might help me find him?'

'There is one thing,' she said finally. 'Dunham was impatient, like a man in a hurry. He was angry too, I could hear it in his voice. And all the time we spoke, he kept glancing over his shoulder towards the door.'

'Was someone following him?'

'Quite possibly. I cannot be certain because I do not have possession of all the facts. But he behaved like a man who thought he might be in danger.'

The saffron meadows lay to the west of town, next to the abbey's lands. Merrivale walked across the fields towards them, seeing the abbey buildings dark against the sunset. Sheep bleated in the distance, and he heard the faint baa-ing of a lamb seeking its mother. His breath steamed and the grass under his feet crunched with frost. It was bitter weather for lambing.

The saffron meadows were surrounded by a fence of strong wooden hurdles. The drawstring had been removed from the gate latch, but Merrivale used the point of his dagger to pry up the latch and open the gate. Inside were open fields full of spiky plants flattened by frost. The drying kilns stood empty, their doors open; the ovens were full of ash and cobwebs. An open-fronted shed next to the kilns was full of tools; a plough and a harrow, rakes, dibbers, wooden baskets hanging on the wall. The broken shards of a pottery cup lay on a wooden bench, surrounded by a dark stain where something – wine, perhaps – had soaked into the wood.

There was another stain on the wall below the baskets, a black smear on the wood. Merrivale scratched one corner of it with his fingernail, and the stain crumbled to powder. His boot bumped against something on the ground, a wooden spade, carelessly discarded. Picking it up, he saw more dried blood on the back of the blade.

Something gleamed on the grass beside his foot. He had not seen the object at first, as it had been covered by the spade. He picked it up, lifting it to catch the dying light. It was a silver signet ring.

Swiftly he searched the rest of the meadow, looking for any sign of disturbance in the earth. He found none. Nor was there any trace of the saffron crop itself. Cassandra Wesenham was right; they must have taken it with them. There was little doubt now that the crokers had absconded with the crop.

Closing the gate behind him he saw the distant stream fringed with trees, their branches black spiderweb silhouettes against the orange glow of the sky. He walked towards them.

Standing at the top of the bank above the frozen stream he saw a dense bank of young willows, narrow wand-like stems rising from the ice. There was just enough light to see a dark bundle lying behind them. He scrambled down the steep bank and drew his sword, cutting back some of the willows until he could drag the body free. The cloak wrapped around the corpse crackled with ice and the body itself was frozen stiff and heavy as lead.

He heard a movement on the bank above him, and reached again for his sword. Someone stood at the top of the bank, looking down. Even in the dim light it was just possible to recognise the man from the inn.

The man turned and fled. 'Stop!' Merrivale shouted. He started up the bank but slipped and fell, swearing. By the time he reached the top the man was far away across the fields, running into the shadows.

6

Chipping Walden, February 1339

Tracking the fugitive was impossible; darkness was falling rapidly and the fields were frozen hard. The other man's boots left no trace on the earth. Giving up, Merrivale called at Walden Abbey to ask for help in retrieving the body. The abbot, who had been about to retire for the night, grumbled for a while but finally agreed to send a couple of servants with torches and a handcart. Half an hour later they carried the body into the infirmary and laid it out on a table.

'Not much left of the poor fellow,' the infirmarer commented. 'How long do you reckon he was lying out there?'

It was too cold for maggots, but the small rodents who lived along the stream had been at work, chewing through the cloak and into the flesh beneath it. Some of the soft tissue had gone, the feet, most of one arm, part of the face. The rest was curiously shrunken, like it had been pressed under a heavy weight.

'I was hoping you could tell me,' Merrivale said.

The monk pulled up the sleeves of his black cassock and peered at the body. 'Can't say I have much experience with this sort of thing. Most of the cadavers I see died of illness, or an accident in the fields. They're fresh, if you see what I mean.'

Merrivale waited. The infirmarer rubbed his chin. 'Hmm. Probably a young fellow, judging by his teeth. No sign of deformities. Hmm-hmm. Slender build, so far as one can tell. Black hair.'

'I can see all that. What might have killed him? Are there signs of a blow to the head, for example?'

Rather gingerly, the infirmarer ran his hands over the head of the corpse. 'No lesions or marks on the skin. Hmm-hmm. No sign of a skull fracture. I mean, so far as one can tell.'

Merrivale glanced at the intact hand. Pale lines ran in parallel across the fingernails. 'What about poison?'

'Poison?' The infirmarer peered at him, and Merrivale realised the man was short-sighted. 'That seems rather unlikely, don't you think? People poison each other in romances, not in real life.'

'So what *do* you think happened?'

'Hmm.' The monk studied the body again for a moment. 'Most likely the poor fellow slipped and fell down the bank. The fall knocked him unconscious and he ended up in the water and drowned.'

'The stream is frozen.'

'Yes, so it is. He could have fallen through the ice, of course.'

'And after he drowned, he crawled out of the water again, wrapped himself in his cloak and secreted himself in the middle of a bank of willows?'

'Well, no, of course not. Hmm-hmm. But this is surely a case of accidental death. So far as one can tell.'

Merrivale tried not to grind his teeth. 'As you say, brother, you lack experience. Send a message to the town, if you please, and ask the apothecary to join us.'

'What apothecary? Oh, you mean the wise woman. We can't do that.'

'Why not?'

'This is a monastery. We cannot have women in here, it's against the rules.'

'She is a Salerno-trained physician, not a prostitute. Bring her here.'

The monk turned away from the body, rolling his sleeves down. 'Out of the question.'

'Brother, I am in the service of Queen Isabella. Would you care to explain to the queen mother why you have thwarted my wishes and obstructed my inquisition? Or to the king?'

'It's against the rules,' the monk repeated. 'I'll have to inform Father Abbot.'

'Then do so.'

'He has gone to bed. He'll be asleep by now.'

'*Then wake him!*'

Cassandra Wesenham arrived an hour later, wearing a dark cloak with a hood and carrying a basket. At the sight of her, the infirmarer crossed himself and withdrew. 'I'm sorry,' Merrivale said. 'This will be unpleasant.'

Her voice was calm. 'Only a heartbeat separates the living from the dead.'

Merrivale drew back the shroud covering the body. She studied it for a moment, her face calm. 'This is Ralph Dunham,' she said.

'You are certain?'

'The face is badly deteriorated, but there is enough left to recognise him. Where was he found?'

Merrivale told her. 'I believe he was killed at the saffron meadow, and the body taken to the stream.'

'Why not simply bury him?'

'Perhaps they were short of time. Also, I suspect they were hoping for rain, so the stream would rise and cover the body. They wanted him to disappear and not be found.'

She lifted the intact hand, studying the fingernails. 'Dunham was poisoned with arsenic,' she said.

'Yes, I thought I recognised the lines on his nails. I found a broken wine cup at the meadow. There were bloodstains too, suggesting someone had been struck a very hard blow with a spade, probably on the head, and staggered back against the wall.'

Her hands felt around the corpse's head, her fingers firm and probing. 'There is no sign of a head injury. Men do die of bleeding on the brain without the skull being fractured, but I would still expect to find some evidence of contusion, even after immersion in water. There is nothing here.'

She looked up. 'Of course, it may have been this man who struck the blow. Arsenic requires some time to take effect. He may have realised he had been poisoned, and attacked his poisoner.'

'How long ago?'

She studied the corpse, frowning a little. 'The rodent damage suggests he has been dead for at least several days. In my opinion, about a week. Which means he was killed not long after he came to my shop.'

'Have you sold arsenic to anyone recently?'

She looked up and met his eyes. 'I would never sell pure arsenic. I use very small amounts in some of my medicines, that is all. The arsenic itself is kept in a locked chest in my workroom, and I have the only key. I account for my stock regularly, and nothing is missing.'

She had anticipated all his questions. Logical thinking, or something else? Merrivale nodded again. 'There is nothing more we can do here,' he said. 'I shall find the infirmarer and give him money for a mass. Then I will escort you home.'

They walked back to Walden, crossing fields white with frost in the light of a gibbous moon. Fires twinkled in the distance, around the pens where the shepherds had gathered the ewes for lambing.

'What will you do now?' she asked.

'Discover who killed him, and bring them to justice.'

'Justice is important to you?'

Merrivale thought of his father, far away in Frithelstock. There had been no justice in the famine that killed his family, or in the actions of the greedy bailiffs who deprived a broken man of his lands and home. 'Where there is justice, there is hope,' he said. 'Without it we might as well be dead.'

She glanced at him, as if not sure whether to believe him. 'I'm probably one of the last people who saw Dunham alive, and as you pointed out, I possess arsenic. It might have been me.'

'Did you have reason to kill him?'

'No.'

'Then I shall start with the people who did. I want to talk to the crokers.' He paused. 'Also, I must speak to Dunham's family in Castle Acre. I shall depart tomorrow.'

'I am coming with you.'

Merrivale considered this. 'Are two people required? Ockham would say there should be no plurality without necessity.'

'This is not a subject for levity,' she said coldly.

'I'm not joking. Why do you want to come with me?'

'I am travelling back to Lynn in any case, and require an escort on the road. More importantly, if an officer of the queen mother's household marches into Castle Acre and starts demanding information, people will close up tighter than an oyster. Dunham's father does business with my brother, and I know Westacre. They will talk to me.'

'What about your practice here in Walden?'

'I have an apprentice who will keep the townspeople supplied with mustard poultices and love potions. Let me help you, Master Merrivale.'

They walked on in silence, Merrivale listening to the darkness and thinking about the man from the inn. Why had he followed Merrivale across the fields that evening? Had he too been searching for the body? Or did he already know it was there?

Castle Acre, February 1339

Castle Acre was dominated by the pale stone walls and towers of its eponymous castle. More walls enclosing a deer park could be seen in the distance. 'Who owns this place?' Merrivale asked.

'The Earl of Surrey,' said Cassandra. 'He is rarely in residence. He brings his mistresses to hunt here a few times a year, that's all.'

'He hunts his mistresses?'

'You know what I mean,' she said severely. 'The steward's representative calls once a month to collect the rents. Otherwise, the place is usually empty.'

'Why doesn't the steward come himself?'

'I assume his other duties don't allow it. He holds several benefices and is also a clerk to the king. He is away in Antwerp at the moment.'

Merrivale glanced at her. 'This steward. Is his na…
chance?'

'Yes, Edmund Gonville. He has care of all of Surrey's lands in …
county.'

Dunham's wagon yard lay next to the Norwich road, almost in the shadow of the castle. Merrivale dismounted next to a row of wooden wagons with canvas covers, standing opposite a big open-sided workshop. A dozen men were hard at work, assembling wagon boxes, turning axles on a lathe, fitting iron rims to wheels. A forge roared, sending welcome blasts of heat out into the yard. A stone house and stables stood beyond the shed.

A man came down the steps of the house, bearded, greying, wearing a heavy cloak to keep out the wind. He walked across the yard with a confident step. 'Greetings, sir and lady. Are you looking to hire a wagon? I can provide a team of horses, even a driver if required.'

'You must be Master Dunham,' Merrivale said. 'My name is Merrivale, and I am in the queen mother's service. This is Mistress Wesenham.'

Cassandra smiled. 'You know my brother, the alderman in Lynn.'

'Of course! Welcome, welcome to you both. Come inside out of the weather.'

The hall was small but handsomely painted, and there were Dinant bronze candlesticks on the table. Dunham called for a servant to bring hot wine. 'Now then, how may I help you?'

Quietly, Merrivale told him what had happened. He watched the other man's face crumple with shock, and felt the bile rising in his own throat. *Delivering such news never gets easier*, he thought.

The hot wine arrived, unwanted now. 'He is gone,' Dunham said quietly. 'My boy, my heir. My pride and joy. He's gone.'

'When did you last hear from him?' Merrivale asked.

Dunham was swaying on his feet. Cassandra hurried forward, helping him down onto a bench. 'Hush,' she said softly, shooting a withering glance at Merrivale. 'Be still now. Grief is like poison. Don't keep it trapped inside you, let it out.'

After a moment Dunham covered his face with his hands and began to weep, whimpering softly in his throat. Cassandra rested her hand on his back, her eyes full of sympathy. 'Have you other family?' she asked softly.

'My wife went to her grave four years ago. I have two daughters, both married. Ralph was my only son.' Slowly, as if they were being squeezed from his body, the words came out. 'I was so proud of Ralph. He had a fine patron in Master Gonville. When he joined Queen Isabella's household I thought… he'd soon move on to the king's service. He was a good lad. Everything you could ask for in a son. I was so proud of him,' he repeated.

Merrivale's father had used almost exactly the same words. He felt an ache in his chest, like the returning pain of an old wound. After a long time, the other man raised his head, eyes red and cheeks streaked with tears. 'Who did this to Ralph?' he asked.

'We don't yet know,' Merrivale said. 'But we will find them.'

'You asked when I last heard from Ralph. He came to see me about two weeks ago. He couldn't stay long, he said, he was on Queen Isabella's business, and it couldn't wait. He wouldn't say what that business was, of course, he never did. He was always very discreet.'

'You were right to be proud of him,' Merrivale said. 'He was a good servant to the queen.'

Dunham had begun to weep again. Cassandra reached into her reticule and drew out a small bottle. Taking out the stopper, she poured a few drops into one of the wine cups and placed it before Dunham. 'This will make you sleep,' she said. 'That is what you need now, sleep and rest. Time will heal you.'

Outside Merrivale took a deep breath, inhaling air raw with sea damp. 'Will time really bring mercy?' he asked. 'That has not been my experience.'

'Some people recover from grief and grow stronger, others are broken by it.' Cassandra looked at him. 'Do you really intend to find the killer?'

'That is what I said. Do you not believe me?'

'My apologies if I have misjudged you,' she said levelly.

He turned to face her, fighting down his anger. 'Did you not hear what I said in Walden? I have seen men die of arsenic poisoning. It is a painful and degrading death. Do you really think I can walk away from that?'

'Perhaps not. But the crokers have disappeared along with their crop. Dunham might have been working with them, and this could have been a falling out among thieves.'

'Does that make his death any less cruel?' Merrivale asked. 'Or his father's grief any less painful?'

'So, I *have* misjudged you. You are going to right the wrongs of the world.'

'Not all of them,' Merrivale said, giving her a hand up into the saddle. 'For the moment, just this one.'

The hamlet of Westacre lay a mile or so west of Castle Acre town, a small manor house with a range of outbuildings and a few thatched cottages huddled along the banks of a frozen river. People were chopping holes in the ice to draw water. A grey-bearded man looked up, raising his hand in salute. 'Mistress Wesenham. It has been a long time.'

Cassandra smiled. 'I am glad to see you again, master. How are you and your family faring in this cold?'

The man stood with his axe resting over his shoulder, his eyes watchful. 'We are well.'

'The wind is bitter. May we alight for a while and warm ourselves?'

'All right,' the man said after a moment. 'Come along inside.'

The hall was old, with a smoky central hearth rather than a fireplace. The man with the axe was James Westacre's father; a grey-haired woman with a deeply lined face was introduced as his mother. Two younger women and a boy in his early teens sat to one side, both looking worried.

'I met your son recently in Walden,' Cassandra said. 'He said he had bought land nearby, and was giving up the seafaring life.'

'That's right,' Westacre's father said.

'I was surprised. He always seemed to enjoy adventure, and was full of tales of the faraway places he had visited. But I suppose we all feel the urge to settle down as we grow older.'

Silence. 'I haven't seen him since the autumn and wondered where he might be,' Cassandra said. 'Don't tell me he has grown bored already and gone back to sea.'

The grey-haired woman's voice crackled with hostility. 'Why do you want to know?'

Cassandra looked surprised. 'I was curious, mistress. My brother always spoke well of your son, and I had taken an interest in him.'

'He is dead,' the woman said.

Silence. Westacre's father looked down at his hands. The boy fidgeted. The two younger women stared at Cassandra and Merrivale, their eyes full of fright. 'May God grant him mercy,' Cassandra said. 'I am so sorry to hear this news, mistress. How did it happen?'

'Robbers killed him and stole his money,' the grey-haired woman snapped. 'The roads are full of thieves these days, ever since the king went over the sea. All these wicked new taxes, there's no money to be had, everything is going to ruin. All poor Jamie wanted was to live in peace and work his land.'

'Please accept my condolences,' Cassandra said, her voice quiet. 'When I return home, I shall ask the priest to say a mass for his soul.'

One of the women gave a convulsive start. The other one looked frozen. 'I think you should go,' the older woman said.

Not until they were riding away from Westacre did Cassandra speak again. 'So much for them opening up to me,' she said dryly. 'Are they still watching us?'

'Yes.'

'What do you think?'

'First, they are the worst liars since Judas Iscariot. Second, James Westacre is alive and well.'

'I agree, they're hiding him. But from whom? Us?'

Merrivale remembered the man from the inn, and the mysterious assailants in London. 'No,' he said. 'We're not the only ones hunting him.'

The house of John Wesenham, merchant and alderman in the port of Bishop's Lynn, was on the Saturday marketplace near the guildhall. He welcomed his sister warmly, and thanked Merrivale for escorting her on the road. 'You are welcome to stay the night. The day is half gone, and it is bitter cold to be travelling.'

'Thank you, but I must be on my way.'

'Let me provide you with an escort, at least. French ships have been spotted off the coast. You might run into a landing party.'

Riding into the town, Merrivale had seen archers manning the walls and workmen digging out the ditch around the southern suburb. After the destruction of Southampton, every coastal town was looking to its defences. 'If the French do come, you will need your men to defend the town.'

'At least have some food and wine before you go.'

Merrivale smiled. 'I shall not refuse. Master Wesenham, might I ask you a question? Your sister tells me you owned a share of a James Westacre's ship.'

'Yes, until last year. Westacre decided to buy out the shares of the other partners. He wanted to be sole owner as well as shipmaster.'

Merrivale paused. Westacre's family had said he intended to retire from the sea; he himself had said much the same to Cassandra. Something did not add up.

Cassandra came to sit with him while he ate. 'Are you certain you won't stay the night?'

'I cannot.' Merrivale glanced around the hall. 'Your brother is clearly a man of substance.'

'He was recently appointed a collector of customs, and has hopes of further preferment. He is a rising man, it seems.'

'You said you also have property here.'

'Indeed, I am comfortably provided for. My father left me four houses and two messuages in Lynn, along with two houses and a warehouse in Boston. I inherited another house in Ghent from an aunt.'

Merrivale was surprised. 'Forgive me, but why practise medicine? Surely your rents would allow you to live a life of leisure.'

'Medicine is my vocation.' She smiled. 'Helpfully, it also renders me less desirable to potential suitors. What sensible man would want to marry a wise woman?'

'I admire your double meaning,' he said. 'You are happy to live in solitude?'

'Blissfully so.' Her smile faded a little. 'I hope you don't mind, but I asked my brother where you might find the other crokers. He didn't know about Moreno, but he says Nicholas le Flemyng is a wool merchant in Colchester. It's not much, I know.'

'It is a start.' He wiped his lips with his napkin and rose to his feet. 'Mistress Wesenham, I know that at times I have sounded ungracious. Please believe that I appreciate all the help you have given me.'

'I have done very little.' Her brown eyes were serious now. 'Be careful, Master Merrivale. There has been one death already. I fear there may be more to come.'

Thoughtfully, Merrivale rode through the south gate and down the long causeway over the fens. The Marcosians, he remembered, believed women had the gift of prophecy. He hoped they were wrong.

7

Colchester, March 1339

Lent had arrived, the Christian world's annual exercise in self-denial and austerity. *Why do we still do this to ourselves?* Merrivale wondered. *Surely living through the famine was penance enough?*

At Colchester there were guards on all the gates, and the gaps in the crumbling Roman walls had been filled with new stone. A sentinel at the north bridge held out a spear to bar Merrivale's way. 'Who are you, stranger?'

'My name is Merrivale, and I am with Queen Isabella's household. The sheriff will confirm my identity.'

He had already spotted the device of Sir John Coggeshall, the sheriff of Essex, on the castle walls. 'Are you expecting trouble?'

The watchman lowered his spear. 'Doria's galleys have been raiding around Shoebury, sir. Word is they're moving north.'

In theory, Lent was covered by the Truce of God when war was suspended and all fighting ceased. It seemed someone had forgotten to tell Ottone Doria. 'Sir John and his men will hold them off,' Merrivale said.

'Yes, sir.' The watchman did not look convinced. He too had heard news of Southampton.

'I am looking for the house of Nicholas le Flemyng, the wool merchant.'

'Wool merchant? Well, I suppose he is, after a manner of speaking.'

'What do you mean?' Merrivale asked.

'He trades in wool, all right. He buys wool from the purveyors and sell it overseas. But you'll not find a cocket seal on any of his woolsacks, nor does he pay a penny in customs.'

'He is a smuggler.'

'Among other things. You'll find his house on the Cornhill, sir, by Saint Runwald's church. Keep an eye on your purse while you talk to him.'

The weather was a little warmer and the wind felt soft on his cheek as he rode through the little town, but Merrivale's mood was bleak. He knew Doria, the Genoese admiral; he and his partner, the corsair leader Carlo Grimaldi from Monaco, commanded fleets of heavily armed war galleys. King Philip of France had hired them both at the start of the war. One of the aims of the Savoy project had been to detach them from their French alliance and bring them and their ships over to the English side. Initially, they had agreed.

And then I ruined the entire plan, and now Doria's galleys are raiding our coasts. And where Doria is, Grimaldi will not be far away. A hard and bloody season is upon us, and it is my fault.

Oh, God, Yolande. What have we done?

The Flemyng house was large and well-built, the servants discreet and helpful. 'Yes, the master is at home. If you care to wait, sir, we'll let him know you are here.'

A few minutes later he was conducted up to the solar, where a man sat behind a table reading a set of accounts on a small parchment roll. He was young, fair-haired with a strong nose and a broad pleasant face; in keeping with the season, he wore a plain dark tunic and hose. A pewter scallop shell was pinned to one shoulder, the badge of a pilgrim who had been to Compostela.

'I am Nicholas le Flemyng,' the man said. 'I understand you wished to see me.'

Merrivale introduced himself. 'I am inquiring into the murder of Queen Isabella's clerk, Ralph Dunham.'

It was a deliberate tactic, intended to shock, and it worked. Flemyng stared, open-mouthed. 'His murder? My God, what happened?'

Merrivale disregarded the question. 'When did you last see Dunham?'

Still stunned, Flemyng shook his head. 'Last autumn, after the harvest. He arrived in Walden just after All Hallows.'

'What did he want?'

'He had come to collect the saffron crop. He had instructions from the queen mother's treasurer, Master Ellerker.' Flemyng hesitated. 'We weren't very happy about it, if I am honest.'

'Why not?'

'Well, you see, our original contracts instructed us to take the crop to London and sell it to the Guild of Pepperers. A fixed rate per pound would go to the queen, and we could keep the rest. We'd have made more money that way.'

'Did Dunham pay you?'

'Yes, but a flat rate per pound, and not a very good one. Westacre and I were seething, but there wasn't much we could do about it.'

'What about Moreno?' Merrivale asked. 'Did he object?'

'No, he didn't seem to mind. We handed over the crop, and Dunham paid us our shares and took the saffron away in a wagon. That's the last I saw of him.' Flemyng shook his head. 'I still don't understand why anyone would want to kill him.'

Apart from the fact that he had a wagon load of saffron in his possession. 'Was he armed? Did he bring an escort?'

Flemyng looked puzzled, as if he had only just thought of this. 'No. Not to the handover, anyway. They might have been waiting elsewhere, I suppose.'

That was improvised, Merrivale thought, and not very well, either. He paused for a moment, letting the silence drag on until Flemyng became uncomfortable. 'I understand you paid several visits to the apothecary in Chipping Walden,' Merrivale said finally.

'Who? Oh, you must mean the wise woman. Yes, I was looking for some poison. We had a problem with rats, you see.'

'Do rats eat saffron?'

'No, but they'll dig up the corms out of the ground and eat them, and the corms are even more valuable than the chives. I saw what rats could do to a saffron meadow, in Spain.'

'When were you in Spain?'

'Four years ago. I went on pilgrimage to Compostela. That was where I learned about saffron growing, you see.'

The shrine of Santiago de Compostela was in the far northwest of Spain, hundreds of miles from the great saffron meadows of La Mancha in the sun-baked south. 'How did you get involved in Queen Isabella's project?' Merrivale asked.

'Westacre recruited me. He knew of my interest in the subject.'

'And who recruited Westacre?'

'A royal clerk, a man named Edmund Gonville. He was advising on the project, I'm not sure why.'

Merrivale thought for a moment. 'One more question. Where might I find the other two crokers?'

'Moreno said he was going to London. I'm not sure about Westacre. He didn't mention any plans to me. I know this sounds vague, but you see, we didn't really talk about much of anything except saffron.'

For men who had spent nearly two years working together, that seemed unlikely. 'Where were you two weeks ago, Master le Flemyng?'

'Here in Colchester. I've been here for the past month. The servants will confirm it.'

'Very well. If I need to ask further questions, where will I find you?'

Flemyng gestured around the room. 'Here, of course. None of us are going anywhere, not with Doria's pirates roaming the seas. You still haven't told me how Dunham died.'

'No,' Merrivale said. 'I haven't.'

London, March 1339

The clerk of the Guild of Pepperers knew all about Juan Moreno. 'We've known the *señor* for many years. He was one of our most reliable partners in Castile, and supplied spices to several of our members.'

'Is he also a member of the guild?'

The clerk shook his head. 'As an outland merchant, he is not entitled to membership.'

'He lives in England now,' Merrivale pointed out.

Another shake of the head. 'Not long enough to be resident. You're right, some foreign merchants do eventually become members, like Master Gonville, but only if they take up permanent residence here.'

'Are you speaking of Edmund Gonville?'

'No, his father, William Gonville. Formerly Guillaume Gonville, though I doubt if he has used *that* name since the war started.'

'He is French?'

'Aye, he's French. You can change the name, but you can't change the man. If you want to speak to Señor Moreno, he is currently lodging near Saint Bride's church beyond Ludgate. Shall I ask someone to show you the way?'

'I can find it. Has anyone approached the guild recently and offered to sell a large quantity of saffron?'

The clerk wagged a finger. 'The commercial affairs of the guild and its members are strictly confidential, Master Merrivale. You need a writ from the Chancery to get that sort of information.'

Merrivale smiled a little. 'Never mind,' he said. 'Forget I asked.'

He had thought for some time that he was being followed, and as he passed Saint Paul's he became certain of it. Turning his head and glancing from the corner of his eye he saw two men, both in dark cloaks with hoods, coming purposefully after him.

He hesitated for a moment. It would be an easy matter to lure them into one of the many narrow lanes and alleys that ran off to the side, and kill them. He had done it before, and for a moment he found himself excited by the thought. His hand reached inside his cloak and closed on the hilt of his sword.

Then, suddenly, a wave of revulsion washed over him. For a moment he was back in Lyon, listening to Mercuriade. *Many kinds of* gnosis. *What we have become, whither we have sunk.*

My God, he thought quietly, *is this what I have become? Am I prepared to take the lives of two men just because they are following me through the streets? What if there is actually a perfectly good explanation for their behaviour?*

He doubted this, but he released his grip on his sword and walked down the hill to Ludgate. Archers of the city watch stood guard at the gates, looking bored. Merrivale beckoned to them. 'See those two men, the ones cloaked as pilgrims? If they attempt to pass through the gate, seize them and interrogate them. Find out who they are and where they come from.'

The archer looked him up and down. 'On whose authority?'

'The queen mother's. Do as I say.'

Arriving at Juan Moreno's house he found the Spaniard watching his servants pack his possessions into painted wooden trunks. 'I leave tomorrow for Castile,' he said. He was brown-skinned with black hair and a short, carefully trimmed beard; he spoke good French with an accent that was somewhere between Castilian and Occitan, and a tinge of something else besides. 'You caught me just in time.'

'May I speak with you alone?'

Moreno nodded to the servants, who left the room. 'What is it?'

'Ralph Dunham is dead. His body was found near Walden about two weeks ago. Where were you at that time?'

Moreno's face gave nothing away. 'I was here in London. I can provide witnesses to attest to this.'

'When did you last see him?'

'Early in November, when we handed over our saffron crop. I assume you know about that.'

'I do. Were you disappointed by the amount you were paid?'

'No,' Moreno said after a moment. 'To be honest, I was glad to get away. I knew things were going to go very badly wrong.'

'You will have to explain that.'

'Señor Dunham was in great haste. He did not inspect the saffron for quality before handing over the money, he did not open even one of the packets. Had he done so, he would have quickly seen that both Señor Westacre and Señor le Flemyng had defrauded him. Both had adulterated the crops they sold, mixing stamens from marigolds and other flowers with the saffron chives before drying. The crop they gave Dunham was not more than twenty per cent pure.'

'What did they do with the rest?'

'I do not know. I assume they kept it to sell privately.'

'Did you say anything to Dunham?'

'I did not,' Moreno said emphatically. 'I am a foreigner in a country at war, Señor Merrivale. I do not meddle in other men's affairs. Besides, there was something more.'

'What was it?'

'I said Señor Dunham was in great haste. All the time we were loading the saffron into the wagon he was looking around, as if he was afraid someone might see us. Once the loading was complete he drove the wagon away at great speed. Señor Merrivale, I do not believe he was acting on the queen's instructions. I think he was attempting to steal the saffron for himself.'

'How did you know the others had adulterated the crops?' Merrivale asked.

'To me it was obvious. I have many years' experience dealing in saffron.'

'Were you not tempted to follow their example?'

Moreno stared at him. 'My family are *azafrános*, Señor Merrivale. We have been cultivators of saffron for generations. Our reputation is our pride. We would never betray it.'

'I apologise, I did not mean to offend you. In your opinion, how much would the entire crop have been worth? Without the adulteration, I mean?'

'The quality was good. Had we taken the crop to London to sell as intended, I expect the total value would have been in excess of six hundred marks.'

Or about four hundred pounds, Merrivale thought. More than enough to tempt a man to steal. Or to kill.

'How did Dunham pay you?' he asked. 'In silver?'

'No, by a note of credit drawn on the Peruzzi bank in London. I have redeemed the note and now I am leaving the country before trouble starts.'

A cold finger ran its way down Merrivale's spine. 'Why the Peruzzi bank?'

'I do not know. Does it matter? All banks are the same.'

'No,' Merrivale said emphatically. 'They are not. Who recruited you into the queen mother's service?'

'A man named William Gonville, a merchant and trader in pepper and spices. He is a member of the Guild of Pepperers in London, which is how I know him. If you wish to speak to him you will find him at his manor at Larling, near Norfolk.'

'How well did you know the other two crokers? Westacre and Flemyng?'

'Not at all. Westacre was very secretive and did not talk much about himself. Flemyng was fair-seeming, but I would not trust him. He stole something from me before we departed, something I treasured very deeply, a pilgrim's badge commemorating my visit to the shrine at Compostela.'

'A silver scallop shell?'

'Yes.'

Merrivale thought for a moment. 'One last question, Señor Moreno. Did you have a problem with rats at Walden?'

'Rats?' Moreno looked surprised. 'No, not at all. I know how much damage they can do to a saffron meadow and I kept watch for signs of them, but I saw nothing.'

Merrivale nodded. 'Your journey back to Spain could be perilous. Doria and Grimaldi are at sea.'

'I should be safe enough. My ship sails from Bristol, and their corsairs have not yet ventured so far west.'

'Then I wish you a fair journey,' Merrivale said.

Back at Ludgate he summoned the archers of the watch. 'Well?'

'They're foreigners, sir. Gave their names as Enric and Sgond, from the city of Ast. We've never heard of it.'

'I have.' Ast was the Piedmontese version of Asti, the centre of the Lombard banking community. 'Where are they now?'

'We had no authority to hold them, sir. They said they are employed by the Peruzzi bank, and threatened to inform their masters.' The archer looked embarrassed. 'We didn't want trouble, sir. We know the Peruzzis have powerful friends.'

Merrivale pushed a groat into the man's hand. 'You did well. Thank you.'

John Stanton was working in the painted hall at Surnes Tower, the high table stacked with rolls of parchment. 'Customs records,' the yeoman explained. 'The King's Remembrancer sent them over this morning. I'm still trying to find out what happened to the queen's subsidy from the wool money, but it's a bit like cleaning the Augean stables. Have you found anything?'

'Yes, and it stinks worse than any stable.' Briefly, Merrivale related the tale of the adulterated saffron and Dunham's disappearance and death. 'I think Moreno was telling the truth, or most of it. Whoever killed Dunham probably has the portion of unadulterated saffron Moreno handed over. Flemyng and Westacre kept their portions back. I shall ask the sheriff of Norfolk to institute a search for Westacre, and I am returning to Colchester to confront Flemyng.'

'Flemyng and Westacre defrauded Dunham, and one or both killed him to cover their tracks?'

'It is certainly possible, and Flemyng has an interest in poisons. He also lied to me, repeatedly.'

Stanton threw down his pen. 'We need wine,' he said, clapping his hands for a servant. A maid came, bearing a silver jug and two pottery cups. Stanton poured wine into the cup and held one up to his nose, inhaling deeply. 'Rheingau wine,' he said. 'Made from muscat grapes, harvested late when there is dew on the vines. There is an aroma of… violets, I think. According to the learned scholar Jofroi of Waterford, wines from Rheingau are "wet", meaning they impact on the red and blue humours, blood and phlegm. Consumed in moderation, they cool the blood and clear the mind, if you believe such things. For myself, I call it sweet as music and smooth as silk on the palate.'

'You are fond of wine?'

Stanton smiled. 'Wine is one of life's consolations. A reminder that not everything or everyone on this earth is bad. Whoever made this wine, for example, could keep company with the angels.'

He sipped his wine again. 'Back to the problems of the present. Whoever has the saffron will eventually try to sell it. That means they'll have to come out of hiding. As soon as they break cover, we can arrest them.'

'In theory, yes. I asked the Guild of Pepperers, but they refused to cooperate. But Flemyng and Westacre could also sell the saffron to a third party, who might sell it on or even send it out of the country. A bank, for example.'

Stanton nodded. 'You mean the Peruzzis.'

'Are they lending money to the king at the moment?'

'I believe so, yes.'

'And the queen mother?'

There was a short pause. 'Yes. She borrowed money from the Peruzzis to finance her saffron meadows.'

Merrivale felt the surge of anger again. 'Why? Of all the banks she could have chosen, why them?'

'I don't know,' Stanton said.

'Then I shall damned well find out.' Merrivale rose to his feet. 'Thank you for the wine, John. I shall report again as soon as I have news.'

'I've been summoned to Castle Rising next week,' Stanton said. 'Send word to me there.' He paused for a moment. 'Thank you, Simon. This is turning out to be a wretched business. I'm glad you are here.'

Colchester, April 1339

The Flemyng house was closed, its windows shuttered and the gates locked. Merrivale knocked several times, loudly, but no one answered. Once again, Merrivale felt the clouds of anger boiling up in his mind, and once again, he fought to suppress them.

You find killing easy, don't you? Yolande had once said. *It is not one of the things I admire about you.*

I would kill for you, he had replied. She had gazed at him with those beautiful eyes, pools in which his soul could drown, and said, *I have never asked you to do so, and I never will.* But he knew these fits of murderous anger came more easily now, and in his lucid moments he wondered how much of this anger was directed at himself.

He rode to the castle, seeing the sun shining dull orange in a sky stained with smoke. At the sheriff's office, faces were grim. 'Doria attacked Harwich a few days ago. It was Southampton all over again, every ship taken, the port and half the town burned, God knows how many dead. He missed the wool ships, which we reckon were his target, but everything else is gone. Now his galleys are burning their way along the coast towards Yarmouth.'

Harwich was only twenty miles away. 'Christ,' Merrivale said quietly. 'Where is Grimaldi?'

'Prowling in the Narrow Sea. His men haven't yet landed, but it's only a matter of time.'

'I'm sorry to add to your burdens, but I need to find Nicholas le Flemyng. Does anyone know where he went?'

'Flemyng? His ship sailed at the end of last month, and that's the last we saw of him. Doria's war galleys were all over the sea, and they're not taking prisoners. He'll be dead by now, and his ship at the bottom of the German Ocean.'

'I didn't know he had a ship.'

'He acquired one recently from somewhere, a roundship called the *Witschip*. Not that it matters now. His creditors will mourn him, but I doubt if anyone else will.'

'To whom did he owe money?'

'Half the tradesmen in the town, if you believe the reports, but he was also heavily in debt to one of the Italian banks.'

'Peruzzi,' Merrivale said grimly. 'By God, now this is starting to make sense.'

Larling, April 1339

William Gonville, formerly known as Guillaume, received Merrivale at his manor near Norwich with the grave, dignified air of a doctor of philosophy admitting a new student to his studium. His black robe and long grey beard added to the impression, as did the shelves of books behind him. 'Be welcome, Master Merrivale. Tell me how I may assist you.'

At twenty-seven, Merrivale was old enough to dislike being patronised. 'You may start by telling me what you know about a plot to defraud Queen Isabella of her saffron crop.'

'Ah, yes. The saffron.' Gonville stroked his beard with one finger. 'I feared Her Grace might come out of this badly. The risk was always there.'

'What is your role in this business, if I may ask?'

'The queen's treasurer, Master Ellerker, asked my son for help, and he came to me. I used my connections to find the crokers and procure the land. When harvest came, I arranged the sale to a willing buyer.'

'The Guild of Pepperers in London.'

'No. I am a member of the guild, of course, but I felt I should do my best for the queen mother. I used my connections again to secure a buyer in Ghent. He was willing to pay a very good price, nearly double what the saffron would have fetched on the London market. Ghent is a cloth town, and saffron is in great demand for dyeing.'

'What happened next?'

'Master Dunham took delivery of the harvest, and I began to make arrangements to ship it to Ghent. However, I then learned that Dunham had stolen the saffron and was intending to sell it for his own profit. After that, of course, I washed my hands of the entire affair.'

'Who told you about Dunham?'

'The queen's marshal. Brigget was his name, I believe.'

'Do you know where the crop is now?'

'I assume Dunham still has it in his possession. Are you searching for him?'

'We have found him. He is dead, and there is no sign of the saffron.'

Gonville's face did not change. 'Then you would appear to have a problem.'

'Whoever has the saffron is probably trying to sell it. Have you heard any rumours?'

Gonville gestured to the books around him. 'My interests are now largely confined to scholarship. I only agreed to help Ellerker as a favour to Her Grace. Others handle my quotidian business affairs.'

'Do these others include your son Edmund?'

Gonville managed to look both surprised and superior. 'Edmund? Of course not. He is far too busy with his duties.'

'Ah yes, his duties. How many rectories has he collected now? Still just the three? And he's steward of Surrey's lands, I hear, and a commissioner of the fens too. He's a busy fellow, your son.'

'I mean, of course, his duties with the king,' Gonville said sharply. 'He is in attendance on His Grace in Antwerp as we speak. He has nothing to do with the saffron.'

'I never said he did.'

'I have behaved honourably, Master Merrivale. Do not attempt to cast aspersions on my good name or that of my family. My servants will show you out.'

8

Castle Rising, April 1339

A couple of miles from Larling, Merrivale glanced over his shoulder and saw two horsemen on the road behind him. When he next looked back they were still there, trailing him by about three furlongs. For the moment, they seemed content to keep their distance.

Evening fell. Bars of cloud streaked a brilliant sunset. Hundreds of dark silhouettes crossed the glowing sky, flocks of wild geese coming down to rest on the marshes along the Wash. Merrivale urged his tired horse up to the gates of Castle Rising and dismounted. 'I am here to see Master Stanton. My name is Merrivale.'

'We have been told to expect you, sir.' He led his horse into the courtyard, listening as the gates closed behind him. The two horsemen had dropped back as soon as the castle came in sight, but he knew they were still out there; and where there were two there might be others. A groom, a stocky man with red hair, came out of the stables and touched his forehead in salute. 'I'll take your horse, master.'

'Thank you, Warin. It's good to see you again. How long have you been up here?'

'About a month now. They transferred me up here from Surnes Tower. Thank you for recommending me, sir. I've been grateful for the work.'

A servant in the queen mother's blue-and-gold livery conducted him into the massive square keep and up to a first floor chamber. More servants brought him hot water for washing, a jug of wine and a dish of cod with ale sauce and a pottage of cabbage and onions flavoured with pepper and garlic. Lent meant fish.

Another servant knocked at the door. 'Her Grace is waiting, sir. If you are ready, I will take you to her.'

Merrivale puffed out his cheeks. He had been hoping for a quiet talk with Stanton, alone. 'I will come directly.'

The queen mother's private chambers were vivid with colour. Candles gleamed off painted walls where leopards stalked peacocks through forests of brilliant flowers. Carved and gilded stools and benches were cushioned with crimson cloth. Cats, the queen's favourite Syrian tabbies, stalked around the room or sat grooming themselves, ignoring the four men standing behind the queen's chair. One was Stanton. Next to him was a tall thin man whose white cassock seemed to droop from bony shoulders; the third man was small with narrow-set eyes and a pinched, nervous look to his face. The fourth had short hair and a long pointed nose. Merrivale had last seen him staring down into the stream near Chipping Walden, looking at Dunham's body. Their eyes met for a moment, but the other man's face gave nothing away.

Merrivale bowed to the queen. In her mid-forties, Isabella of France had inherited the bright hair and piercing blue eyes of her father, Philip the Fair. Her green gown was embellished with lines of tiny pearls, and the white wimple framing her face was shot with gold thread. Her fingers, clasped in her lap, were crusted with rings.

'Thank you for joining us, Master Merrivale,' she said. Her voice was firm, her tones those of a woman used to giving orders. 'Master Stanton you already know.' The cleric was Sir John Sully's friend the chaplain, John Hull; the nervous man was the treasurer, Peter Ellerker, and the fourth man was introduced as Robert Brigget, the queen's marshal.

'Make your report,' Isabella said.

'Ralph Dunham was killed after he tried to steal your saffron crop. The principal suspects at this stage are Westacre and Flemyng. Westacre is in hiding; men are looking for him but so far without success. Flemyng recently took passage for Flanders. The sheriff's men are convinced he was caught and killed by Doria's men, but I do not believe it. I think he is safe in Flanders.'

'Why?'

'Because both Flemyng and Ottone Doria have a connection with Donato de' Peruzzi,' Merrivale said. He looked straight at the queen. 'As indeed, Your Grace, do you.'

There was a moment of silence. When Isabella spoke there was an edge to her voice. 'What are you implying, Merrivale?'

'That Peruzzi is manipulating you. All of you. It only remains to understand why.'

Ellerker looked suddenly like he wanted to vomit. 'Do we know where the saffron is?' asked Hull, the chaplain.

'We may assume that Flemyng took his portion with him. Westacre has hidden his, and we are unlikely to find it unless we find Westacre. That leaves the crop that Moreno handed over to Dunham. I believe Dunham hid it somewhere near Walden, intending to retrieve it once he found a buyer.'

Merrivale looked hard at the marshal. 'Don't you agree, Master Brigget? You were in Walden waiting for Dunham to return. Or did you already know he was dead?'

'No, I did not,' Brigget said. He rubbed the back of his head. 'I travelled to Walden in December on Her Grace's orders to find Dunham, but I could discover no trace of him. In February I learned that Dunham might still be alive and working in secret to sell the saffron. I returned to Walden to investigate further.'

'And you did not inform me?' demanded the queen.

Brigget bowed. 'My apologies, Your Grace, but I had very little to go on, only the word of one rather unreliable source. I wanted to be certain of my facts before I came to you.'

'Who told you Dunham had the saffron?' asked Merrivale.

'A merchant named William Gonville.'

Merrivale's eyebrows rose. 'According to Gonville, it was you who told him that Dunham had stolen the saffron.'

'He is lying,' Brigget said. 'As I said, he is unreliable.'

'When you discovered me with Dunham's body, why did you run away?'

'I had no idea who you were. You might have killed Dunham yourself, and intended to kill me next to get rid of a witness.'

Silence fell. One of the tabby cats stalked past the queen's chair and she leaned down, snapping her long ringed fingers. 'Here, Gyb!' she said. 'Gybbe-Gybbe-Gybbe! Come to mistress.'

The cat jumped into her lap and rubbed its chin against her hand, beginning to purr. 'Good cat,' Isabella said, stroking it. 'You, at least, are faithful and loyal to me. Unlike my clerk, who robbed me, or my marshal, who ran away from danger, or my treasurer, who advised me to embark on this foolish and ruinous venture, or my sarjeant, who still cannot tell me when my silver from the wool subsidy will arrive. One way or another we have lost a great deal of money, haven't we, Gybbe? How shall I afford milk for you now? You will have to go out and catch mice for yourself, like the barn cats.'

Now all of her retainers looked sick. The queen gazed at Merrivale, her eyes hard as sapphires. 'And you,' she said. 'My son's faithful servant, his messenger who turned triumph into disaster and destroyed our hopes in Savoy. What have you brought me? No money, no saffron, only a sorry tale of treachery and the corpse of a dead thief. I suppose you will want to be paid for your services.'

'Whether Your Grace pays me is a matter for your own conscience,' Merrivale said. 'What I want is to find Dunham's killer.'

'Why?' she challenged him. 'Why does Dunham matter?'

'We all matter,' Merrivale said. 'Had things gone differently in 1330, I would have done the same for Your Grace.'

Silence fell. The cat yawned, jumped down from the queen's lap and wandered away, waving its tail.

The queen motioned to the men behind her. 'Leave us.'

They filed out of the room. Ellerker and Brigget did not meet Merrivale's eye; Hull the chaplain seemed amused. Stanton glanced once at Merrivale before closing the door behind him.

'You play dangerous games, Master Merrivale,' Isabella said.

Merrivale shook his head. 'In my profession, playing games gets you killed. Your Grace might profit from this lesson.'

'I have ordered men whipped for saying less.'

'You embarked on a venture to grow the most costly spice in the world without adequate support or security. You exposed the crokers and the officers of your own household to dangerous temptation. Men have killed each other for the price of a pound of saffron; what did you imagine they would do when three hundredweight was at stake? And now, you have left yourself vulnerable.'

'Explain.'

'You borrowed the money for this venture from the Peruzzi bank. The Peruzzis then encouraged the crokers to adulterate the saffron and steal the crop, which the bank would then buy. When Moreno proved to be an honest man, they suborned Dunham to steal his portion as well, and when they learned that Dunham had got greedy and tried to recover the other two portions, they paid someone to poison him. All of this was done to ensure that you would fail, and be in debt to the Peruzzis.'

'Why?' the queen demanded. She was angry still, but she was thinking hard.

'Because they want to control you. They want more of the king's banking business and they want you to help them get it. If you refuse, they will take this story to the king and use it to drive a wedge between him and you. He will be furious when he hears the story, won't he? At this critical moment, when the war is going badly and people are singing seditious songs in the street, the last thing he needs to hear is that his impecunious mother has run up another debt.'

'I do not require a lecture from you on my relations with my son,' she snapped.

'Then make good on your threat. Have me whipped.'

Silence fell. One of the cats, perhaps sensing its mistress's mood, hissed at Merrivale. He ignored it.

'Are you always this insubordinate?' Isabella demanded.

'No, Your Grace. Only when the occasion demands it.'

'I want my saffron, Merrivale. As much of it as you can find. Even part of the crop will enable me to repay my debt to the Peruzzis.'

'First I shall bring Dunham's killer to justice,' Merrivale said. 'Then, I will bring the saffron to you.'

He was offered a lodging for the night, which he thought showed remarkable forbearance. In the morning he found Stanton in the hall. 'I want a word with Brigget.'

The serjeant looked at him, his face wary. *He is surprised I'm not chained up in the oubliette*, Merrivale thought. *Frankly, so am I.*

'He rode out, very early,' Stanton said. 'He hasn't returned.'

'Did he say where he was going?'

'Not to me.'

Merrivale nodded. 'I need a favour from you. Two men followed me here, and I want to make sure they don't track me to where I'm going next. Can you assign some of the queen's archers to watch my back when I leave? If they see anyone following me, drive them off.'

Stanton looked worried. 'I'll send an escort with you as well.'

'No. Remember, she wants this handled discreetly.'

Warin was waiting in the courtyard with the horse. 'I've changed my mind,' Merrivale said. 'I'll take a groom with me, if I may. This one, for preference.'

The fields and marshes of the Fens were shrouded in mist. Merrivale looked back to check whether anyone was following, but saw only drifting sheets of vapour. 'I hope you don't mind my co-opting you,' he said to Warin. 'But Stanton is right, I could use an extra pair of hands. Do you have your knife?'

'I'm never without it, sir. And I'm happy to be of service. Life in the stables gets a bit dull after a while.'

'I know,' Merrivale said. 'I was a groom myself once. Longest week of my life.'

Warin blinked in surprise. Merrivale changed the subject. 'What can you tell me about Robert Brigget, the marshal?'

'Not a great deal, to be honest. I don't see much of him, he's always coming and going.'

'When he leaves the castle, does anyone go with him?'

'No, sir. He rides out alone, and comes back alone too.'

'Did you see him leave this morning?'

'Yes, sir. I saddled his horse.'

'Did he speak to you or anyone else before he left?'

'He spoke to Master Ellerker for a few minutes.' Warin paused. 'Neither of them looked happy.'

'Were they quarrelling?'

'I'd say so, sir. Then Master Ellerker went back inside, and Master Brigget mounted up and rode away like the devil was chasing him. He never said where he was going.'

'I know where,' Merrivale said.

The streets of Bishop's Lynn were quiet and full of fog. Dismounting outside Wesenham's house, Merrivale called for the porter. 'Is Mistress Cassandra at home? I must speak to her, urgently.'

She came out to see him at once, her face full of concern. 'Master Merrivale? What is it?'

'I know where the saffron is, and you must be with me when I find it. How soon can you depart?'

'Give me half an hour.'

Chipping Walden, April 1339

Spring was on its way now; the lambs born in late winter were bounding in the pastures and the air was full of birdsong. Green shoots of corn were already rising from the soil.

The apothecary's house in Church Street was exactly as Cassandra had left it. Her apprentice greeted them, bowed and withdrew. 'What makes you think the saffron is here?' Cassandra asked as they walked through the shop.

'Dunham and his confederates intended that you should take the blame,' Merrivale said. 'After his death the narrative changed, but only a little. You will be named as the person who stole the crop from Dunham, murdered him and hid the saffron. You have knowledge about saffron, you have arsenic in your possession and you are a "wise woman". People will readily believe that you are also a poisoner. Do you see where I am leading you?'

'We need to find the saffron before the killer does.' Her voice was calm. 'Otherwise he will denounce me as a murdering witch, hand over a portion of the crop to prove his good faith and abscond with the rest. How much saffron did Dunham have?'

'At least ninety pounds. More, if he managed to recover any of the saffron Westacre and Flemyng stole from him.'

'That quantity would not be easy to hide, and this house is not large.'

'We must search anyway. Dunham didn't come to see you to talk about markets. He was spying out a place to conceal the saffron.'

Walking through the house and shop, she threw open every cupboard and chest and aumbry. Nothing was amiss. The only saffron to be found was a small amount of her own stock in a sealed glass jar. Merrivale stared at it for a moment, thinking. 'Did you tell Dunham about your saffron meadow?'

'Yes.'

'Take me there.'

Cassandra's saffron meadow lay to the south of the village. It was much smaller than the others, a sliver of land between two larger fields and fenced off with high hurdles. A small wattle and daub hut stood in one corner.

'What are we looking for, sir?' asked Warin.

'Anything out of the ordinary,' said Merrivale, dismounting and handing over the reins.

Cassandra surveyed the meadow. The muddy soil was bare save for a few weeds; the dead leaves of last year's crocuses had largely rotted away. 'Nothing has been disturbed.'

'What about the hut?'

Cassandra opened the door of the hut and stopped. Much of the interior was filled with a large heavy sack made of coarse cloth, which Merrivale recognised at once as a woolsack. A broken portion of its cocket seal was still attached. Drawing his knife, he cut the seal away and slit the sack open. Inside were dozens of smaller parcels, each wrapped in cloth and bound with ribbon.

Cassandra opened one of the parcels. The hut was full of a musky aroma, sweet and dry, intense and elusive at the same time. 'Is this genuine?' Merrivale asked.

'Yes,' she said quietly.

'Sir,' Warin said, low-voiced and urgent. 'There's someone coming.'

'Get inside, quickly.' Warin hurried in and Merrivale motioned for silence. They heard the gate open and close and footsteps coming nearer. 'Remember our deal, Brigget,' a man's voice said. 'Half for you, and half for me.'

'Are you certain it is here?' Robert Brigget asked.

'I helped Dunham shift it myself. I want your word, Brigget. Each takes half. I'm not moving another step until you agree.'

'All right, all right. But by God, Westacre, if it's not here, I'll do for you like I did for Dunham.'

'It's here, I'm telling you… Christ, I don't feel right.'

'What is it?'

'Something in my guts. I knew there was something wrong with that beer.'

'For God's sake, Westacre, stop complaining… Wait. Those are fresh footprints. Someone's here.'

'Jesus! We need to get away!'

'Don't be an idiot, we've come too far to turn back now.' There came a faint metallic noise, the sound of a sword being drawn. 'Follow me,' Brigget said.

In the hut, Merrivale looked at Warin. The latter nodded. Merrivale opened the door of the hut and stepped swiftly out, Warin following him. Brigget and Westacre stopped, staring at them.

'Merrivale,' the marshal said. 'What are you doing here?'

'You know perfectly well what I'm doing here. Lay down your sword and surrender yourself to the king's justice.'

'Me?' Brigget walked forward again, his sword a moving ribbon of light in the dull afternoon. 'I don't think so. You're the one who is going to pay, Merrivale, you and the witch. You won't be able to cover up her crimes now.'

Cassandra brushed past Merrivale and marched forward, hands clenched at her sides. '*My* crimes! You've already admitted your own. "I'll do for you like I did for Dunham." You murdered that man!'

Brigget advanced towards her, raising his sword. Merrivale reached for his own weapon, but before he could draw it something hissed in the air and Brigget stopped like he had run into a wall, looking down at the hilt of Warin's knife protruding from his chest. He took another step, but his strength was already failing. His sword fell to the ground and he collapsed beside it.

Westacre stood a few yards behind him, bent over and gasping for breath. Hurrying to him, Merrivale saw he was shivering and sweating, saliva hanging in long strings from his mouth. He sank to his knees, clutching at his chest. 'Air,' he gasped. 'I need air.'

Cassandra knelt beside him, still perfectly calm. 'He has been poisoned,' she said quietly. 'I think it must be hemlock.'

'Is there an antidote?'

'No.'

Merrivale knelt too, raising Westacre's head and looking into his dazed eyes. 'Tell me the truth,' Merrivale said. 'It cannot save your life, but it might save your soul.'

The truth came out, gasping and choking as paralysis set in and Westacre's windpipe began to close. Fearful of retaliation, he had hidden his portion of the stolen crop at his home and instructed his family to pretend he was dead while he tried to work out a way to sell it. The Guild of Pepperers had refused to deal with him, and he was at his wit's end when a message from Dunham arrived, asking for help.

'Why would he trust you? Did he not blame you for passing off the adulterated crop?'

The words were slow and slurred now. Death was not far away. 'He thought that was down to Flemyng. Not me. He wanted to hide the rest of the saffron from Brigget. I said, use the wise woman. Anyone finds it, they'll blame her. When we go, leave a little behind. Tell sheriff she stole it, he arrests her, we get away.'

'Did you see Dunham again?'

'No. Brigget found me, don't know how. Said Dunham is dead. He'd kill me if I don't help. Had no choice. Tried to bargain...'

The convulsions began then, Westacre rolling over and clawing at the ground while his body quivered with spasms. Merrivale stood up, looking at Cassandra. 'How long?'

'Minutes at most.'

Merrivale turned and walked back to where Brigget lay sprawled on the ground. Kneeling again, he ran his fingers around the dead man's head. Finding what he was looking for, he nodded.

'Go to the hut,' he said to Warin, 'and find a couple of spades. While we bury the bodies, Mistress Wesenham, go into town and hire a horse and cart. I want to get the saffron away as quickly as possible before any more of our enemies come down around our ears.'

'There are more?'

'Someone has been following me for most of the past two months. Quickly, mistress. Already the abbey bells are ringing nones. By vespers we must be well away from here.'

9

Castle Rising, April 1339

Queen Isabella and her officers received him in the same painted chamber. It was Easter morning, and the air inside the castle smelled of incense and hot wax, mingled with the smell of roasting meat and spices. There were fewer cats than before; the others were probably down in the kitchens looking for food to steal.

'Well done,' Queen Isabella said. She wore a gown of blue Lucchese silk and a headdress framed with pearls that made her look like a Byzantian empress. 'Thanks to you, Master Merrivale, my fortunes are partly restored.'

Merrivale bowed. 'I have left the saffron under seal in a warehouse owned by Wesenham, the alderman in Lynn. I thought that was best, rather than bringing it here and exposing any more of Your Grace's officers to temptation.'

Ellerker winced, but Hull the chaplain looked like he was hiding a smile. 'I regret that it was not possible to recover Flemyng's portion of the saffron,' Merrivale said. 'What about Westacre?'

Stanton shook his head. 'He had hidden the saffron in a barn near the family manor. Unfortunately, he hadn't told his family what it was. They had never seen saffron before, and they thought it smelled like the devil's weeds.'

'What did they do with it?'

Stanton sighed. 'They fed it to the pigs,' he said.

There was silence for a moment. 'Well,' Hull said dryly, 'whoever eats those porkers should have clear lungs and a healthy flow of urine.'

After a moment Isabella chuckled. 'Fortune's wheel,' she said. 'I shall not punish the Westacres. Let their stupidity be their curse.'

'Along with the death of their son, of course,' Merrivale said. 'May I recommend a course of action to Your Grace? Let Wesenham handle the transport of the saffron to London and its sale to the Guild of Pepperers as soon as possible. We have only about a third of the original crop, but even that should allow you to repay the loan to the Peruzzi bank.'

Judging by the look on her face, the queen was thinking instead about Badakshan rubies, reputedly her favourite gems. Either that, or more cats. Ellerker cleared his throat. 'We could ask Master William Gonville to handle the transaction,' he offered.

'No,' said Merrivale. 'It was Gonville and his son who recruited Westacre in the first place. Stay away from them.'

Ellerker went red in the face. Hull the chaplain looked thoughtful. 'Dunham, Brigget, Westacre, Flemyng; they all wanted the saffron for themselves.'

'Dunham tried to take it all for himself, but was foiled by Westacre and Flemyng. He then made a pact with Westacre, but Brigget caught up with him and poisoned him. When Dunham realised what had happened, he attacked Brigget with a spade. I found evidence of a wound on Brigget's head before we buried him.'

Hull nodded. 'I recall Brigget being laid up for several days, and wearing a bandage on his head. He said he had been kicked by a horse. Ironic for a marshal. After he recovered, he must have tracked down Westacre and persuaded him to join forces, which Westacre seems to have done without a second thought for his previous partner... It would seem the Apostle Paul was right. The love of money really is the root of all evil.'

'So Brigget killed them both,' John Stanton said. 'I would have put money on it being Flemyng.'

'Oh, Flemyng was involved,' Merrivale said. 'He may have procured the poisons, or at least gave advice on their use. And if he was acting on the orders of the Peruzzis, it may well have been Flemyng who passed on the instructions to kill Dunham and Westacre in the first place. I wonder how much longer Brigget would have survived, had he recovered the saffron.'

'You said Flemyng has left the country,' the queen said.

'The Peruzzis have long arms, Your Grace,' said Merrivale, thinking of the men who had followed him. 'Flemyng was not their only agent in this country. I want to know what connection they have with the Gonvilles.'

Ellerker spoke up. 'William Gonville is a respected merchant, and his son is a trusted servant of the king.'

Merrivale turned to him. 'Neither of which means that they could not have colluded in murder.'

'Edmund Gonville is not a murderer,' Ellerker said sullenly.

'Then let us find out what he is,' said Merrivale.

John Stanton cleared his throat. 'There is something else you need to know, Simon. Edmund Gonville is the royal secretary charged with special responsibility for ensuring the wool subsidy is gathered in. All official correspondence with Pole's syndicate goes through Gonville.'

Merrivale thought for a moment. 'I said I thought the Peruzzis was trying to take a larger share of the king's banking business. But what if this is something different? What if they are trying to take over the wool trade?'

'Gonville would be perfectly placed to help them do so,' Stanton said.

'And perhaps at last we are beginning to understand why my wool subsidy has not been paid,' said the queen.

She rose to her feet, pearls gleaming in the candlelight. The silk of her gown shimmered like a waterfall. 'A few pounds of saffron do not matter,' she said. 'The wool trade is the lifeblood of the kingdom. Without revenues from wool exports we are incapable of raising an army or fleet. We will be defenceless in the face of the enemy.'

'And if Donato de' Peruzzi gains control of the wool trade he will use it against us,' Merrivale said. 'He betrayed us once in Savoy, and he will do so again.'

'Then he must be prevented from doing so,' said the queen. 'By serving me in this matter, you also serve the king, and the country. Very well, gentlemen. Make it so.'

'What exactly does she want us to do?' asked Stanton. '"By serving me in this matter." What does that mean?'

'It means she wants her money from the wool subsidy,' Merrivale said. 'That is her primary objective. If we can protect the wool trade at the same time, that will be an incidental good. How serious is the problem with her finances?'

They stood on the ramparts at the top of the keep, looking out over the fens. The waters of the Wash lay in the distance, gleaming silver under a cloudy sky. 'Very serious,' Stanton said. 'Income from the saffron will enable her to pay off the Peruzzi loan. But unless the wool subsidy comes through, it is only a matter of time before she is forced back to the moneylenders again.'

'She could adopt a less lavish style of living,' Merrivale said. 'Stop buying jewels. Pension off some of the cats.'

Stanton snorted. 'She'd sooner sell her rubies than lose any of her cats.'

'Is Ellerker to be trusted?'

'Depends what you mean. Is he honest? Yes, I think so. I've never had reason to think otherwise. Is he competent? Absolutely not. His records are in a terrible state. It took me a week to understand the household's financial affairs, and I was trained in civil law and accounts at the Temple and the Chancery.'

Royal serjeants were expected to be men of many parts; they fought for their sovereign in the courtroom as well as on the battlefield, and their duties might range from issuing writs against recalcitrant nobles to exercising the royal dogs. 'Tell me again about this wool syndicate,' Merrivale said. 'How does it work? Remember I was out of the country for nearly a year.'

'The king granted the right to collect thirty thousand sacks of wool to a consortium of merchants, led by William de la Pole from Hull and the London vintner, Reginald Conduit, in exchange for an upfront payment of two hundred thousand pounds. The Exchequer also collects customs duties on every sack of wool exported, plus half the sale price of each sack. The merchants were supposed to take most of the risk, putting up the money to buy the wool and hoping they could sell it for profit.'

'That doesn't sound like much of a risk to me. The cloth-making cities in the Low Countries are always hungry for wool.'

'It wasn't as easy as you might think,' Stanton said. 'The consortium was given the power to make compulsory purchases of wool at below the market rate, which angered the landlords. Many resisted handing over their wool, or only sold wool of lower quality. It also took longer than expected to gather thirty thousand sacks and transport them to the east coast ports. Finally, thanks to the king requisitioning so many ships for his own service, there weren't enough bottoms to bring all the wool overseas to market. Some of last year's wool is still sitting in warehouses. Now, Pole and his associates say they have run out of funds. They spent everything they had on the initial payment, and cannot remit any further money to the king until they sell the wool. Or so they say.'

'Rich men are always the first to plead poverty,' Merrivale agreed, 'and Pole is the richest man in the kingdom. When I saw you in London you were neck-deep in parchment rolls. Did they tell you anything?'

'Only what we already know, that the wool exports aren't yielding enough money to pay even the ordinary expenses of government, let alone the conduct of the war. The officials I spoke to at the Chancery and Exchequer were suspicious, but so far they had found no evidence of wrongdoing.'

'What did they think might be happening?'

'The best guess is that some of the wool traders are smuggling wool out of the country and selling it privately rather than through the Staple. That way they evade the export taxes as well.'

'I know a London merchant who may be able to tell us more. We need to look for anything that might connect the smugglers with Edmund Gonville. And anything that might connect Gonville to Peruzzi.'

Stanton hesitated. 'I know something went badly wrong in Savoy. What happened?'

He did not want to think about Savoy, because whenever he did he heard Mercuriade's voice repeating, *where we were, whither we have sunk, whither we hasten*, and then he started thinking about Yolande and wanted to weep. 'We were trying to bring Savoy and Jean of Bohemia over to the English side,' he said finally. 'Donato de' Peruzzi was our backer. Partway through the plot, he decided he could make more money out of supporting the French. He also bribed Ottone Doria and Carlo Grimaldi to join him, and it is thanks to him that they are raiding our coasts at the moment.'

It was almost true. *Peruzzi knew that if King Jean discovered my affair with Yolande, he would break our pact and return to the French allegiance, and the entire scheme would collapse. He didn't want to be on the losing side. He betrayed us, but I cannot blame him alone.*

'How do you know this?' Stanton asked.

'Grimaldi told me. He liked me, I'm not quite certain why, given that he is a vicious old pirate who respects neither God nor man. He warned me that our plot was collapsing and advised me to get away. Instead, I went back to Turin and got caught by the Bohemians.'

'Why did you go back?'

'It is a long story,' Merrivale said finally. 'Some other time, perhaps.'

'You clearly dislike Peruzzi. Are you certain you are not letting that dislike cloud your judgement?'

'Yes to the first question, no to the second,' Merrivale said. 'I know Peruzzi for what he is. He serves his own interests first and foremost, and believes the laws do not apply to him.'

'There are rumours that the Peruzzi bank in Florence is facing difficulties of its own,' Stanton said. 'They made a number of bad loans to kings, who can't or won't pay them back. According to one report, the bank is on the brink of collapse.'

'All the more reason why Donato will stop at nothing to get what he wants. If he has set his sights on the wool trade, then God help us. We need to go to London and talk to these merchants, Pole and Conduit. Did you say Conduit is a vintner?'

'He is head of the Mastery of Vintners. I don't know him.'

'What? An enthusiast like yourself doesn't know the head of the guild of vintners?'

'I drink wine, I don't sell it.' Stanton clapped Merrivale on the back. 'There's the trumpet, summoning us for the feast. We must go.'

The painted walls of the great hall were hung with swags of woven green grass and reeds. Candles blazed from torchères, winking off crystal and silver glasses and jugs and salt cellars. Hundreds of intricately painted Easter eggs, some of them gilded or silvered, were scattered across the tables. Music played softly, viols and rebec and shawm interweaving with the gentle hum of conversation.

Queen Isabella entered the hall and was seated at the head table. Her favourite cat jumped into her lap, resting its front paws on the edge of the table. The rest of the guests bowed and took their seats. Merrivale, sitting between Stanton and Hull the chaplain, saw that they were few in number; the queen's ladies and the rest of her household, her old friend Marie de Saint-Pol who lived not far away, a handful of others. The company was small, partly because the queen could not afford to entertain more lavishly, but partly because people had long memories. It was nine years since she had fallen from power but in the eyes of many, Isabella of France was still a dangerous friend.

Trumpets sounded again, announcing the first course. Servants in blue and gold processed into the hall carrying silver and bronze platters, accompanied by more musicians. The cat flattened its ears at the noise. A sculpted subtlety in the form of a ship drawn by swans was placed on a stand before the high table to polite applause. More dishes followed, steaming and fragrant with spices; beef in red wine and pepper, capons glazed with honey, simnel bread dyed in bright colours, pastries filled with minced lamb, cumin and ginger, rabbits in garlic gravy, chicken cooked in almond milk with saffron and raisins, mutton stewed with plums and currants, pigeons roasted with pepper and herbs, rosewater pudding, custard tarts decorated with flaked almonds. Lent was over; there was not a fish in sight.

The guests were enjoying themselves, Merrivale thought. The queen ate and chatted with Madame de Saint-Pol, feeding the cat bits of capon with her ringed fingers and looking like she had not a care in the world. Stanton and Hull began to argue about wine, Hull making the case for vintages from Sancerre, Stanton complaining that they were too strong and lacked flavour. Merrivale looked at the food on his trencher, but the smells of spices seemed flat in his nostrils and he had no appetite.

A year ago at Easter, he had been at a similar feast at the court of Savoy, and there he had first met Yolande. He remembered little else, save that when she walked into the room it seemed like the day grew brighter and the air warmer. The dam holding back his memories broke down and he sat for a moment, staring down at his plate.

'Gathering wool, Master Merrivale?' asked Hull.

Stanton had turned away and was flirting with one of the queen's ladies. 'Thinking of the past,' Merrivale said.

The chaplain helped himself to a pigeon and a handful of pastries; for a thin man, he had a prodigious appetite. 'Now then,' he said. 'Was a woman involved?'

'... Yes.'

'Aye, I thought so. I know that look in a man's eyes. Don't worry, I won't pry any further. This is a feast, not a confessional.'

Merrivale smiled a little. 'From your name and accent, I'm guessing you're from Kingstown upon Hull.'

'I am, though it's many years since I've been back.'

'It is a fine town.'

Hull considered this. 'A fine town to be from, perhaps. Not a place you would choose to live, unless you enjoy the rule of a dictator.'

Merrivale raised his eyebrows. 'Are you thinking of William de la Pole?'

'In Hull, my lad, you think of no one else. Pole and his lieutenants control everything. Not just there of course, but most of the east coast ports, Skegness, Boston, even Lynn. He runs them all.'

'Where does he come from?'

'The family were from Ravenser, I think, but he grew up in Hull. His father died when he was young, but his guardian gave him money to set up his first business. Thereafter he prospered, very rapidly. No matter what the vagaries of war or weather, Pole always seems to profit.'

'You don't like him.'

The chaplain surveyed the platters in front of them, finally selecting a thick slice of roast beef and a ladle of green sauce flavoured with herbs and verjuice. 'I have a certain respect for his acuity, but I fear it ends there. Saint Thomas Aquinas once wrote that God permits merchants to make a profit, provided they do so lawfully and use that profit to the benefit of others. Pole would have told Saint Thomas to mind his own business. You see, there's one important difference between Pole and God.'

'What is that?'

'God doesn't think he is William de la Pole.' Hull chewed his meat. 'This beef is overdone, again. I have spoken to the cooks before, but apparently to no avail.'

'Perhaps that's how the cats like it.'

'Ah, now, you may be onto something there. You are interested in Pole?'

'Yes.'

'Is this to do with the wool?'

Merrivale nodded.

'Be careful,' Hull warned. 'He is in high favour at the moment. The king relies on him.'

'I'm sure he does. The king needs his home-grown financiers, if he is to stay out of the clutches of the Italian bankers.'

'Ah, yes. From the compound interest of the Florentines, oh Lord, deliver us.'

The musicians continued to play, largely ignored by the assembled company. Satiated, people began to rise from their seats and move around, carrying goblets of wine and talking to friends. Another trumpet call announced a group of mummers, brightly robed and masked, who began to perform in mime accompanied by the viols and shawm. Merrivale stopped beside Ellerker, the queen mother's treasurer, who was watching the play and looking even more unhappy than usual.

'They are depicting the triumph of good over evil,' Ellerker said. 'If only that were so in real life.'

Merrivale smiled a little. 'Easter is supposed to be a day for optimism. Christ is risen, the world is renewed.'

'I find it hard to be optimistic at the moment,' Ellerker said.

Merrivale watched him for a moment. 'Do you mind if I ask a question? What is your connection with Edmund Gonville?'

Ellerker looked wary. 'What do you mean?'

'Gonville's father told me that you asked his son for help with the saffron venture. I wondered how well you knew him.'

'We both studied at Cambridge. He was a little younger than me, but we read law and estate management together.'

'You can study estate management?'

'Of course. There are books about it, Grosseteste's *Praecepta*, Walter of Henley's *Book of Husbandry*, that sort of thing.'

'Was that before or after he started collecting rectories?'

'It's not unusual to hold multiple benefices,' Ellerker said, a little defensively. 'Gonville is very capable, and works hard. He deserves his reward.'

'I'm sure he does, or the king would never have appointed him. Presumably you knew his father was in the spice trade.'

'Yes. When Her Grace decided to invest in saffron I asked him to introduce me to his father.'

'One thing puzzles me. Why saffron? Where did that idea come from?'

'God knows,' the treasurer said, glancing at him. 'Her Grace has all sorts of ideas. It might have come from one of her friends. Madame de Saint-Pol, perhaps.'

'Yes, that might be it.' They stood in silence for a few minutes, watching the mummers. The play came to an end and a lively stamping dance began. People rolled the painted Easter eggs across the floor, shouting with laughter when the dancers accidentally stepped on them. 'There's another thing too,' Merrivale said finally. 'Some of the crokers told me they were instructed to sell the crop in London, but when I spoke to William Gonville he said he had been commissioned to arrange a sale overseas. Why the discrepancy?'

Ellerker looked perplexed. 'Perhaps the plan changed.'

'You don't know?'

'I'm afraid not. Once the scheme was established, I was no longer involved.'

'Who was? Dunham?'

'Yes, Dunham knew all the details.'

Another egg was crushed under a dancer's foot, bits of gilded shell spinning across the floor. *There's a metaphor here*, Merrivale thought. He understood now why John Stanton had been brought into the queen mother's household. He wondered whether Ellerker knew this, and whether he resented it.

He wondered too why he felt so strongly about all of this. Dunham's murder had made him angry, and that anger had not gone away; if anything, it had grown stronger. Brigget was only the instrument of death, he thought. The men responsible for the killings are still out there. I will find them, or by God I will die trying. This is not yet over.

Wool

10

London, May 1339

'Come in, Simon. Be seated. I am pleased to see you again.'

Sir John Pulteney, draper, banker and four times mayor of London, was in his mid-forties. His dark velvet robe and cap spoke of wealth and taste, as did the finely carved pearwood table and chairs in his private rooms. A copy of Aristotle's *Secretum Secretorum* lay open on the table beside him. *This is what William Gonville aspires to*, Merrivale thought.

There was a second man in the room, one Merrivale had not expected to see; John Sully's friend, Sir Geoffrey Scrope. A grave man in his fifties with silver-grey hair and close-trimmed beard, he was a man of many parts; lawyer, judge, diplomat, secretary, soldier, councillor. The king relied on him closely, and had once said that he learned more about the art of kingship from Scrope than he had from his own father. Merrivale knew him well; he had been a steady presence at court for the past decade and more.

Merrivale sat down, looking at Pulteney. 'It is good to see you too, Sir John. I trust the Knights of Saint John have given you no more trouble?'

Pulteney smiled. Several years earlier he had made a large loan to the Knights, a loan which the Grand Prior of England, Philip de Thame, had signified that he did not intend to repay. Merrivale had uncovered some correspondence between the grand prior and the Pope in Avignon, including a series of letters that the grand prior most certainly did not want to become public knowledge. No more was said, and the loan was paid on time.

'None whatsoever,' Pulteney said. He picked up a piece of parchment from the table. 'I am intrigued by your letter, Simon. You indicated that you wanted to talk about the Peruzzi bank. By coincidence, Sir Geoffrey and I have just been discussing them.'

'One of their big dogs, Donato de' Peruzzi, has just arrived in London,' Scrope said. 'Word has it that he wants to re-establish his bank as a power in the land, as it was back in the days of the king's father. He'll find things are a little different now.'

'Donato de' Peruzzi betrayed our interests in Savoy,' Merrivale said sharply. 'He paid Doria and Grimaldi, and for all we know he is still paying their corsairs to attack us. Why has he been allowed back into England?'

Scrope frowned. 'I think you are mistaken, Simon. Doria and Grimaldi are in the service of the French crown, not Peruzzi. As for Peruzzi himself, he has friends at court and they have used their influence with the king. His Grace has also opened negotiations with one of the Lombard banks, the Solaros, through their branch in Antwerp. No source of finance is being left untapped, it seems.'

'Is this because of the problems with the wool trade?' Merrivale asked.

'Partly.' Scrope was watching him closely. 'How much do you know about this, Simon?'

'I know that there are delays in remitting money to the king, and to the queen mother, and the wool syndicate cannot or will not say when the money might arrive.'

'Forgive me for asking, Simon, but for whom are you working now? Does the king know you are asking questions?'

'The king knows nothing about this. I report to Queen Isabella, who wants to know why her own money from the wool subsidy has not been paid. I came to see Sir John in hopes that he might have some information for me.'

Pulteney shook his head. 'I am not directly involved in the wool syndicate, I'm afraid. I was invited to join it, but I turned down the offer. Throughout my career in commerce I have stuck to one basic rule. If something looks too good to be true, it usually *is* too good to be true.'

'That's rather cryptic, Sir John.'

'Pole and Conduit and their friends saw a chance to make a fortune. Buy low, sell high. Purchase wool cheaply under royal licence, sell it for high prices in the cloth towns of Flanders and Hainault and Holland, and split the profits with the king. But it was never going to be that easy. Wool is a bulky commodity, expensive to store and transport, and the prices being offered in the Low Countries are nothing like so high as anticipated. They have also neglected security. According to my information, some of the wool they gathered has simply disappeared.'

Merrivale remembered what Stanton had said. 'By "disappeared", do you mean the wool has been smuggled abroad?'

'Almost certainly. Pole and Conduit are like Icarus, flying too close to the sun. There is a real danger that they will come crashing down again.'

Merrivale handed over the broken seal he had taken from the woolsack in Walden. 'Can you tell me anything about this, Sir John?'

Pulteney looked at the seal lying in his hand. 'It's a cocket seal, the kind that is affixed to a woolsack before shipment abroad. It certifies that the collector of customs or his officers have collected the export duty. This seal is from the port of Bishop's Lynn. Or it would be, if it were genuine.'

Geoffrey Scrope looked up sharply. 'How do you know it is not?' Merrivale asked.

'You need to brush up on your heraldry, my friend. See that creature on the seal, part lion rampant and part fish? That's the badge of Lynn, but it is facing the wrong way. Someone was careless.'

'Is forging seals common?' asked Scrope.

'It wasn't when I was collector of customs.' Pulteney smiled a little. 'Collectors take a portion of the revenue from export taxes. Smuggling hits our income as well as the king's, so smart collectors clamp down on forgeries and fraud. May I ask where you found this, Simon?'

'Affixed to an empty woolsack in a field worker's shed in Essex.'

'Well, that's damned strange,' Pulteney said. 'Woolsacks are expensive, and are reused time and again. People don't leave them lying around, especially not smugglers.'

'It was being used for a different purpose at the time,' said Merrivale. That the woolsack had been full of stolen saffron was not something Pulteney and Scrope needed to know. 'But from what you have said, Sir John, it was clearly supplied by someone with connections to wool smuggling. Sir Geoffrey, I am fortunate to find you here also. I assumed you were in Antwerp with the king.'

'I had some business in London,' Scrope said. 'I am returning to Antwerp as soon as it is concluded.'

'May I ask you about the king's new secretary, Edmund Gonville? Who recommended him for his post?'

'The Earl of Surrey put his name before the king, but he is also a protégé of the Bishop of Lincoln, Henry Burghersh. I believe it was Henry's influence that swayed the king to appoint him.'

'Gonville handles all matters concerning the wool trade on the king's behalf, am I correct?'

'You are.' Scrope's eyes narrowed a little. 'What are you implying, Simon?'

'Gonville must be aware that the wool trade is being undermined by smugglers. What is he doing about it?'

'Ah, yes, I see what you mean.' Scrope gazed out of the window for a moment. 'In theory, as the king's secretary, Gonville wields an enormous amount of power. He can issue orders that have the power of royal command. In practice, there is very little he can do to enforce those orders. The only ones who can stop the smuggling are the collectors and controllers of customs who oversee the ports and shipments of wool. Each port has its own collector, and neither Gonville nor anyone else can keep watch on all of them.'

'Are you saying the problem cannot be solved?'

'It can, but you would first need to find evidence against the smugglers and then persuade the king to take action against them, and neither will be easy. Some of them are likely to be powerful people, men on whom he relies for money.'

'You mean some of the members of the syndicate are also smugglers.'

Scrope looked at Pulteney. 'I think it is very likely,' he said.

'I agree,' said Pulteney.

Scrope glanced out the window again and rose to his feet. 'Gentlemen, forgive me, but I must depart. I have pressing business that will not wait.' He glanced at Merrivale. 'I am sorry about what has happened,' he said quietly. 'I tried to persuade the king to give you a second chance, but he would not listen.'

'Sir John Sully told me. I am grateful for your efforts, Sir Geoffrey.'

'You were a good servant to the king, and I am sure you will render similar good service to the queen mother. I am glad you have found a place again, Simon. Farewell.'

After Scrope departed, Pulteney looked at Merrivale. 'You're not just investigating the queen mother's subsidy.'

'I am acting on her orders, but you are right. I'm not.'

'A word of advice. Be careful what questions you ask about Gonville.'

'Oh? You think there are questions that should be asked?'

'It is not for me to say. Just remember that walls have ears. If you antagonise the king's favourite it could go badly for you.'

'When you stepped down as collector of customs for London, Sir John, who took over the post?'

'Reginald Conduit.'

'Who is also a member of the wool syndicate, even though he is a master vintner. Something does not smell right. Would you not agree?'

Pulteney did not answer directly. 'Be careful,' he said again. 'Conduit is a reckless man, and a dangerous enemy.'

'So am I,' Merrivale said.

Warin was waiting outside Pulteney's house in Candlewick Street. 'Master Stanton sent me, sir. He asks you to call on him at Surnes Tower.'

'Tell him I will be there as soon as possible. There is someone I need to see first.'

'I'll come with you, sir. Master Stanton suggests you might take me into your service permanently.' Warin hesitated. 'If you'll have me, that is.'

'Does Stanton think I need a nursemaid?'

'Well.' There was a glint of mischief in Warin's eyes. 'Those weren't his exact words, sir.'

'Tin miners,' Merrivale said. 'Sarcastic beggars, to a man. Keep your eyes open and tell me if you think anyone is following us.'

The house of the Peruzzi in London was a quiet, undistinguished building in Lombard Street. There was no sign or coat of arms to identify the house, but there were large men in leather jerkins in the street keeping watch. When Merrivale stepped towards the gate, they barred his way. 'Who are you?' one demanded.

'My name is Simon Merrivale. I have business with Donato de' Peruzzi.'

After some discussion among themselves they agreed to send for Peruzzi's secretary. He arrived a few minutes later, a grey-haired Florentine in Peruzzi livery, blue with silver pears stitched into the fabric of his tunic. 'The master is not at home,' he said, hooking his thumbs into his belt.

'He will see me,' Merrivale said.

'No, *signore*, he will not. I must ask you to be on your way.'

The large men crowded around them. Merrivale hoped Warin had enough sense to keep his hand away from his knife. 'Then give him a message,' he said. 'Ask him if he is still paying Doria and Grimaldi. I know they are in French service, but the money must be coming from somewhere.'

'Do not be ridiculous,' the secretary said stiffly. 'Signore Doria and Signore Grimaldi are being financed by the Solaro bank from Asti. They have nothing to do with us.'

A long silence followed. The large men shifted their feet. 'You weren't supposed to tell me that,' Merrivale said. 'Were you?'

'Go at once,' the secretary said, his voice sharp with anger.

Walking down the street, Merrivale could feel the watching eyes boring into his back. And as he and Warin crossed the bridge over

Wallbrook he spotted the men following him again. There were three of them this time.

Stanton was waiting at Surnes Tower. 'I have secured an interview with Reginald Conduit. I'd like you to come with me.'

'Secured an interview? My friend, you are the queen mother's sarjeant and I used to be a King's Messenger. When we want to see someone, they admit us without question. Sometimes we don't even bother to knock first.'

'Mm. Are you familiar with concepts such as tact, and subtlety?'

'Vaguely.' Yolande had once asked a similar question. Swiftly, Merrivale summarised his conversation with Pulteney and his brief visit to the House of Peruzzi. Stanton frowned. 'It sounds as if Pulteney knows more than he is prepared to admit.'

'Scrope too, I am certain of it. They are protecting themselves. Come, let us go and see Conduit. I promise to be on my best behaviour.'

They found Reginald Conduit in his warehouse at Queenhithe, supervising the loading of pipes of wine onto wagons. He was a big man, broad-shouldered with fists like hams, his face red in the spring heat. 'Say what you want quickly and get out. I have business to attend to.'

'So I see,' Stanton said. He looked around the warehouse, which was nearly empty. 'How is the trade faring?'

'Trade? What trade? The sea is swarming with enemy ships and our wine ships can't make port. Last year's vintage is still stuck in Bordeaux and Libourne.'

'Can't our ships get into Plymouth, or Bristol?'

'Not any more. Carlo Grimaldi's corsairs are raiding the coast of Devon and Cornwall. He attacked Plymouth three days ago, and burned or took every ship in the port. Much more of this and the wine trade will be gutted like a herring.'

'What about wool?' asked Stanton. 'In a month's time they'll be shearing again. Can our wool ships get through?'

'Not as things stand. Grimaldi's friend Doria controls the German Ocean.' Conduit stared at them, shoulders hunched a little. 'Are you here to talk about wine or wool?'

'We'd like your professional opinion as a collector of customs. How easy would it be to smuggle wool?'

'Don't be stupid. A full sack of wool weighs twenty-six stone and it takes several men to shift it. You can't exactly hide one under your cloak when the customs officials come calling, can you? Or disguise it as ballast, or a sack of coal.'

'Could smugglers be colluding with customs officials?' Merrivale asked.

'That's an even more stupid question than the last one. Every single woolsack is examined and sealed. The accounts are checked by the collector of customs, and double-checked by the controller who oversees the collector and his staff. There's no chance of anything slipping through.'

Merrivale cleared his throat. 'Unless the collector of customs is also a member of the wool syndicate,' he said. 'Then, I think it would be quite easy to arrange.'

Conduit took a step forward. The men around the wagons stopped working to watch. 'This is none of your concern, boy,' the vintner said.

'Is it not? If merchants in your consortium have resorted to smuggling wool and you know about it, or even worse, if you are colluding with them; that, master vintner, *is* our concern.'

They stared at each other for a long moment. 'Maybe a few sacks are slipping through here and there,' Conduit said. 'So what? There's no harm done. It's not enough to affect the trade, or the king's finances, which I assume is what you are really concerned about. Leave it alone, boy.'

'As collector of customs for London, you are a royal official. If the king finds out you are conniving at law-breaking, it will not go well for you.'

Conduit's hands clenched. 'I'll ride out the storm,' he said, his voice harsh with anger. 'The king needs men like me, more than he needs men like you. Now walk away, boy. And if you try to interfere in my affairs, then by Christ I'll smash you.'

'I know you need to bluster in front of your men to retain their respect,' Merrivale said. 'But three men are dead, I do not surrender to threats and my name is not *boy*. Is that clear?'

Conduit's fist was already in motion, travelling towards Merrivale's face. Merrivale stepped sideways, seized Conduit's arm by the wrist and yanked it out straight, twisting the other man's forearm around into a painful angle. Grimacing, Conduit struggled to pull away but Merrivale held his arm in a vice-like grip. 'Stop,' he said commandingly. 'Or I will break your elbow.'

Conduit stopped. After a moment Merrivale released his arm and stepped back and bowed. 'It was a pleasure to meet you, master vintner,' he said. 'We'll leave you to get on with your work.'

'Was that you on your best behaviour?' Stanton asked as they walked out into the street.

'I didn't actually break his arm. What did you make of all that?'

'The same as you. There is smuggling, and he knows about it. Why did he get so angry?'

'Some people are always angry. Or perhaps he is just a bully who likes to dominate everyone around him. I have met men like him before.'

Stanton shook his head. 'I think that is unlikely. Yes, there is distress in the wine trade, but Conduit is not short of money. He knows something, but how do we prove it?'

Merrivale turned to Warin, who had waited outside watching the three hooded men who had followed them. 'Can you get close to Conduit's household? Not the warehouse workers but some of his clerks. Find out if they know anything.'

Warin touched his forehead. 'I'll need money for ale, sir.'

Merrivale handed over some coins. 'Buy yourself a new tunic, too, so you can blend in.'

Warin walked off down the street. One of the three hooded men followed him. An idea came into Merrivale's mind and he turned to

Stanton. 'Are you going back to Surnes Tower? I'll join you there presently. There is something I must attend to first.'

'Will you be safe?' Stanton asked. He had seen the hooded men too.

'I can look after myself. Go on, my friend. I will join you soon.'

Stanton went up the hill away from the river. Another of the hooded men followed him. Ignoring the third man, Merrivale turned and walked down Skinners Lane towards the Steelyard. Just before he reached the church of Saint James at Garlickhythe he halted for a moment, hand to his forehead as if thinking of something, giving the other man plenty of time to catch up. Then, very deliberately, Merrivale turned and walked into a narrow lane between two houses. His pursuer followed him into the lane and stopped suddenly, raising his hands as the point of Merrivale's dagger touched his throat.

'I know Enric and Sgond,' Merrivale said in Piedmontese. 'You, I do not recognise.'

The man leaned back, trying to avoid the knife point. His voice came out in a strangled croak. 'Aufrej Solaro.'

'Solaro?' Merrivale said in sudden surprise. 'Are you one of the bankers?'

'I am a partner in our Antwerp branch.'

'Why did you try to kill me back in February?'

'We didn't. Our orders were to threaten you, give you a good beating and frighten you off.'

The dagger grazed Solaro's Adam's apple, drawing a thin red line of blood. 'Orders from Donato de' Peruzzi,' Merrivale said. 'Why is he hiring Lombard thieves to do his dirty work? Does Florence not have enough cutpurses of her own?'

'I am no thief,' Solaro said angrily. 'As well as the bank, my family are rulers of the city of Asti. I am as much of a gentleman as you.'

'Bankers clearly have many more skills than I appreciated. Moneylending and assault make an interesting combination. What venture are you engaged in now? Funding Ottone Doria and Carlo Grimaldi, perhaps, so their galleys can raid our shores and burn our ports? Don't try to deny it, Peruzzi's secretary has already admitted it.'

'I have nothing to do with Doria and Grimaldi,' Solaro said. He was starting to sound less frightened. 'They are paid through another branch of the bank. We keep our business separate from each other.'

'I don't believe you,' Merrivale said.

Thud-thud-thud on the cobbles in the lane outside, the sound of running footsteps; before either of them had a chance to move, four more men rushed into the alley. They wore rough workmen's jerkins and were armed with knives and heavy staves. The leader raised his staff and hit Merrivale on the shoulder before he could duck. His padded coat absorbed part of the force and he stabbed his assailant in the shoulder, and the man dropped his staff and reeled back, streaming blood. Retrieving the staff, Merrivale rammed the butt end into another man's stomach, spun it in his hands and hit the third a crashing blow over the head. The fourth man was fighting with Solaro, who slammed the other man's knife hand against the wall, tore the knife from his nerveless fingers and stabbed him in the leg. The man screamed and hobbled back into the street, leg streaming blood. The others stumbled after him.

The smell of blood was thick in the warm air of the alley. Breathing deeply, Merrivale and Solaro faced each other, the latter still holding his bloody knife. 'Who were they?' Solaro asked.

'Angry wine merchants. You are working for Peruzzi, aren't you? Is he the real paymaster for Doria and Grimaldi?'

Solaro shook his head. 'Enough, now. Abandon your inquisition. Otherwise, next time we meet, my orders may be different.'

'More threats,' Merrivale said. 'More empty noise.' He stared at Solaro. 'Why are you doing this? Why prostitute your bank and your reputation for Peruzzi? For God's sake, it's only money.'

'Only money,' Solaro repeated. 'Only money.' He shook his head in disbelief, and started to laugh. 'Very funny. Oh, very funny indeed. You are wasted in your present profession, Merrivale. You should have been a jester, with parti-coloured hose and bells on your head.'

'This is not finished,' Merrivale said.

'But soon it will be, finished and done with the dead buried. Be careful, Merrivale, that you are not on the losing side.'

'You let him go?' Stanton asked.

'Yes. Kill him and Peruzzi would just send another. I would sooner have my enemies in plain sight. This concerns me deeply, John.'

'Here.' Stanton poured a goblet full of dark red wine and pushed it across the table. 'Spanish, full of fire and blood from the high plains of La Mancha, down where they grow the saffron. I fancy you can taste a little saffron in it.'

'Please don't ever mention saffron to me again.'

Stanton smiled. 'Are you certain those were Conduit's men? It was bold of them to attack you, even more so in daylight.'

'I recognised one of them from the warehouse. Conduit is a powerful man, and he knows I am in disgrace and have no protector other than the queen mother, whose influence is limited.'

'All the same, we could ask the sheriff's men to investigate.'

Merrivale shook his head. 'Let us wait and see what Warin learns.'

Warin of Hexworthy returned to Surnes Tower three days later, wearing the deeply thoughtful expression of a man nursing a colossal hangover. 'Those clerks certainly can drink,' he said. 'I reckon some of them must be tin miners.'

'Did they tell you anything?'

'It took a while to gain their confidence, but we got there in the end. They wouldn't say anything about wool smuggling in London, no matter how drunk they were. But they say it's common practice in the Cinque Ports and the east coast harbours.'

'Common practice? Conduit claimed it is only a few sacks here and there.'

'It's much more than that, sir. Thousands of sacks of wool are being smuggled past customs. One of the clerks said that if the king gets his revenue from even half the wool collected, it will be a miracle.'

Merrivale and Stanton looked at each other. 'I know the Cinque Ports well,' the latter said.

'Then I'll take the east coast. Warin, go put your head in a bucket of water and wash away your hangover. We ride in an hour.'

11

Bishop's Lynn, June 1339

'Thank you for your hospitality, Master Wesenham,' Merrivale said. 'I feel like I have been journeying endlessly. It is good to stop and rest for a while.'

'My door is always open,' John Wesenham said smiling. They were sitting once more in the painted hall of his house next to the Saturday marketplace in Lynn. It was early summer now, the weather bright and calm; through the open windows came the sound of wagons in the street, the creaking of timber from ships moored in the river, and the shrill calls of waterfowl in the marshes along the Wash.

'I trust you were able to dispose of the saffron?' Merrivale asked.

'Nothing easier. The Guild of Pepperers were most receptive, and their graders pronounced the crop to be of very high quality. I was able to secure a good price for Her Grace.'

'I trust Her Grace expressed her gratitude.'

Wesenham smiled. 'You said in your letter that you had some questions for me. I am happy to help if I can.'

'Thank you. I am looking for evidence of wool smuggling.'

Wesenham looked startled. 'Who is employing you, if I may ask?'

'I'm still with Queen Isabella's household. She wants her share of the wool subsidy, and is concerned that the smugglers are defrauding her of her money.'

He and Stanton had agreed to stick to this story for the moment; it gave them a good excuse for making inquiries without betraying their real purpose. 'Is it true that smuggling is on the increase?'

'Yes,' Wesenham said bluntly. 'This year's revenues from export duties are the lowest I have seen, and that's not just because of the war.'

'What has happened? Why are people tempted into smuggling?'

'It's the same old story,' Wesenham said. 'The more you tax any form of merchandise, the more attractive you make it to smugglers. Before the war, according to the ancient custom, the export duty on wool was fixed at 6*s* 8*d* per sack. High-quality wools are valued at upwards of £8 per sack, making the rate of tax about four per cent. Because the duty was so low, very few merchants were tempted to engage in smuggling.'

'What changed? The war?'

Wesenham nodded. 'Shipping became more costly, and prices on the continent have fallen. But the main issue was the king's demand for an extra tax of 40*s* per sack to finance the war, which puts the duty up to about thirty per cent. That makes it much more profitable to smuggle.'

Merrivale nodded. 'You are the collector of customs for Bishop's Lynn. What are you doing to prevent the smuggling?'

'Whatever I can, but it is not enough. My officers inspect warehouses and ships and check all the cargoes, but they cannot be everywhere.'

'Who is the controller of customs? The man who checks and verifies your accounts?'

'His name is Robert Denton, from Kingstown upon Hull. Each of the east coast ports has its own collector, but Denton has been appointed controller for all of them. He is a reliable man, but he is responsible for a large area with many ships. He too cannot be everywhere at once.'

'Who appoints the controllers and collectors?'

'The Lord High Treasurer, William de la Zouche, makes formal recommendations to the king, who approves them.'

'Zouche? Yes, I know him. I wondered if it might be Edmund Gonville.'

Wesenham paused, and Merrivale could see him choosing his words carefully. 'Gonville is influential, yes.'

'Did he use his influence on your behalf?'

'No. I know Gonville, of course, but I do not flatter myself that he holds me in high esteem. I hope I hold my position thanks to my own diligence. One never knows for certain, of course.'

Merrivale wondered how much influence Wesenham really had, and whether money had changed hands to help him secure his post. It didn't matter; this was not part of his remit, and Wesenham had answered all his questions.

Although, in fact, the information he had divulged amounted to very little.

On the heels of the thought, Wesenham spoke again. 'You did my sister a good turn. She has not told me all the details, but I gather you foiled a rather unpleasant plot against her. For that, I thank you.'

'I was pleased to be of service.'

'In exchange, may I offer a piece of advice? If you intend to inquire further, proceed with care. In response to my attempts to prevent smuggling, my servants have been assaulted and my wife and children threatened. The men you seek are dangerous.'

Merrivale smiled. 'As it happens I have already been warned off, several times.'

Wesenham watched him for a moment. 'You are a resolute man.'

'Stubborn is the word favoured by most people. Ox-brained has been employed as well.' Yolande had called him both of these things.

'The men you are up against are resolute as well. Take care, my friend. For my sister's sake, I should not like to see you come to any harm.'

Dinner was enlivened by the late arrival of John Hull, the queen's chaplain. Thin and bony as ever in his loose black cassock, he smiled at Merrivale. 'I see you managed to rid yourself of young Stanton.'

'He had some business to take care of in Rye,' Merrivale said.

'Probably involving wine. Not since my Oxford days have I heard a man talk so eloquently about a subject he does not understand.'

There were five of them at the table, Wesenham and his wife, Merrivale, Cassandra and Hull. Wesenham's wife did not speak a word through the entire meal and never once looked at Cassandra. Hull filled the silence amicably, reminiscing about his time at Oxford, his fellow students, the lectures by eminent professors, the town–gown riots he had witnessed. 'You should have gone to Cambridge,' Merrivale said. 'I gather things are much quieter there.'

Hull, helping himself to roast lamb, looked faintly surprised. 'There is a university at Cambridge? Well, well. How refreshing it is to learn new things.'

Cambridge had been founded a century ago by scholars fleeing the violence at Oxford, something which both universities seemed unable, or unwilling, to forget. 'Perhaps we could hear about Mistress Wesenham's time in Salerno,' Merrivale offered.

Cassandra glanced at her sister-in-law. 'Everything I might say has already been heard,' she said dryly. The other woman shuddered but remained silent.

After dinner Merrivale went into the solar to watch the evening sky and try not to think about Yolande. Cassandra found him there an hour later. 'Am I disturbing you?'

'Yes, and I am grateful for it. What is on your mind?'

'My brother told me about the wool smuggling. Is this connected to the saffron?'

'Very probably, but I am trying to work out how.'

Her brown eyes were serious. 'John says he warned you, but you did not take him seriously. Heed me instead. Be careful.'

'Everyone keeps telling me to be careful. I am always careful for myself. It is not my fault if I have no control over what other men do.'

'I am not sure I believe either of those statements.'

Merrivale smiled a little. 'When do you return to Chipping Walden?'

'Next week, but only to collect my more valuable stock and hand over the rest to my apprentice. I am moving on.'

He raised his eyebrows. 'You have grown tired of being a wise woman?'

'I have. Nor do I have any great wish to grow saffron in a meadow where corpses lie buried. And yes, before you say it, I know that isn't logical.'

'What will you do now? Stay here in Lynn?'

She sighed. 'No. Lynn is just a larger, muddier version of Walden, with the same short-sighted, old-fashioned views. And you may have noticed that I don't get on with my sister-in-law, who regards me as some sort of colliquation of Hecate and Fata Morgana.'

'Where will you go?'

'I have my house in Ghent. As soon as it is safe to cross the sea, I shall go there and endeavour to practise the medicine I learned in Salerno.'

'I wish you good fortune,' Merrivale said. 'Journey safely, mistress.'

In the morning, Hull offered to accompany Merrivale and Warin on their journey up the east coast. 'These are wild and perilous parts for Devon men. You could use some local knowledge.'

'What about your duties with Queen Isabella?'

'She has other priests. She would encourage me to help you, I think.'

Long natural causeways crossed the grey water and reedbeds of the fens. 'What are we looking for?' Hull asked as they rode down one of these.

The church towers of Spalding began to emerge from the mist ahead. 'Evidence of wool smuggling,' said Merrivale. 'At the moment we have only a forged cocket seal and rumours from some clerks in London. We need firm evidence, and we need names.'

'Was Wesenham helpful?'

'He knows more than he is willing to say, but I understand his reasons for holding back. He has more to lose than I do.'

Hull glanced at him. 'What do you have to lose, lad?'

'Honour. Self-respect. Pride.'

'You value these things?' the chaplain asked after a moment.

'Without them, what else is there in life?'

'You are thinking of this world, but there is also the life eternal. You cannot take pride or honour beyond the grave.'

Merrivale thought of his father in Frithelstock, a man who had given up on life. He was sitting in death's antechamber now, waiting for his name to be called. He wondered if he would see his father again.

'I'm not thinking that far ahead,' he said.

Boston, June 1339

Boston bustled with energy, its streets full of wagons. The docks along the Haven were crowded with ships from a dozen ports loading bushels of salt, bales of linen, pigs of lead shipped downriver from mines further inland and of course, sacks of wool. Scandinavian and German dialects could be heard all along the waterfront.

'The collector of customs in Boston is Roger Wolsthorp,' Hull said. 'He owes his post to the patronage of Edmund Gonville.'

Merrivale looked at him sharply. 'How do you know this?'

'From the horse's mouth. Wolsthorp often boasts about how much Gonville esteems him. What he doesn't say is that he pays Gonville £100 a year to help him secure the post.'

'I asked Wesenham about Gonville too. He says he is too lowly to merit Gonville's interest.'

'I suspect he was being self-deprecating. In fairness, I know of nothing to link him with Gonville, but he has another useful connection. Edmund Grimsby, an official at the Chancery in London.'

'Is Grimsby influential?'

'Oh, yes. He has held a number of high posts, including master of the rolls over in Ireland. He and I were at Oxford together, and he had a talent even then for making friends with people who matter. Also, Wesenham has lent him money in the past.'

'For God's sake,' Merrivale said. 'Is there a merchant or clerk in the country who is *not* connected to all the others through debt?'

Not for the first time, the chaplain looked mildly surprised. 'No, of course not. Did you think there would be?'

'How do we find Wolsthorp?'

'Let us start with the customs house.'

They rode on along the waterfront. No one seemed greatly worried about the possibility of an attack by Doria's ships, Merrivale thought. The only armed men in sight were two watchmen bearing the town's mermaid badge on their tunics, leaning on their spears outside the customs house. Both were overweight and unshaven; neither looked capable of stopping a petty thief, let alone a Genoese war galley.

Merrivale and Hull dismounted, Warin coming up to tether the horses. 'We are servants of Queen Isabella,' Merrivale said to the watchmen. 'Tell Master Wolsthorp we wish to see him.'

One man turned his head and bellowed. 'Queen's man here to see the collector!'

A short pause, followed by the slamming of a door and the sound of running footsteps. 'Christ,' said Merrivale, and he ran around the building just in time to see a man in a dark coat disappear into one of the narrow lanes leading towards the centre of town. Cursing again, Merrivale ran after him.

He was fast and light on his feet, but the other man was on home ground with a head start. Within a few minutes, his quarry had disappeared from sight. Merrivale stopped outside Saint Botolph's church, panting as he gathered his breath. A flicker of motion caught his eye, and he turned to see the man in the dark coat slipping out of the west door of the church.

'Stop, damn you!' Merrivale shouted. The other man looked around, face full of panic, and fled once more.

This time the chase took them back towards the waterfront, down past the piers where the fishing boats lay moored next to racks of drying nets. The fugitive picked up a couple of inflated bladders, floats for the fishing nets, and hurled them at Merrivale's head. He dodged them easily and ran on. Ahead lay a big wooden warehouse. The other man flung open its door and ran inside, slamming the door behind him. Merrivale heard the bar drop inside just as his hand closed on the latch. He kicked the door hard, several times, but it did not yield.

Someone ran up behind him and stopped, breathing hard. He turned to see Hull bent over with his hands resting on his knees. 'I'd say that fellow doesn't want to talk to us,' he gasped.

'Whatever gave you that idea?'

'We can't get in and he can't get out. An impasse, I would say... What was that?'

The sound of splintering wood was followed by a shout and a cry of pain. A moment passed before the warehouse door swung open. Warin stood in the doorway, rubbing his knuckles. 'There's another door on the riverside, sir,' he said. 'I caught him trying to sneak out of that.'

'Where is he?'

'Inside. I gave him a thump to keep him quiet. He'll be awake again in a few minutes.'

Merrivale and Hull followed the groom into the warehouse. 'How did you know we were here?' Merrivale asked.

'I came after you. When I saw he was heading for the river, I circled around to get in front of him.'

The warehouse was full of woolsacks high from floor to ceiling. The musty, faintly greasy smell of raw wool filled the air. The man in the dark coat lay slumped against one of the sacks, a trickle of blood leaking from a split lip.

Hull peered at the woolsacks. 'They all appear to have the town's cocket seal. Except... Hmm. No, these aren't right.'

'What do you mean?'

'The mermaid on these seals is rather more generously endowed than the one on the town's badge. She appears to have two of those fishing floats attached to her torso.' Hull broke off a seal from one of the sacks and handed it over. 'I think the forger let his imagination get the better of him.'

The mermaid figure was crude but it would probably pass casual inspection, especially if the customs officers had been paid not to look too closely. The man at their feet stirred and sat up slowly, holding his head. Warin grabbed him by the front of his coat and lifted him upright, pushing him back against the woolsacks. 'Who are you?' Merrivale demanded.

The man shook his head a little, touching his chin and looking at the blood on his fingertips. 'Roger Wolsthorp.'

'The collector of customs?'

'That's right. Who is this vulgar fellow, and why did he hit me?'

'Why did you run from us?' Merrivale countered.

'They said you would be coming. They warned me to say nothing. I should stay away from you, they said.'

'Who are *they*?'

'For God's sake! I can't tell you their names!'

Merrivale signed to Warin, who shook the collector until his eyes rolled back in his head. 'Edmund Gonville procured this post for you,' Merrivale said.

'So what? Everyone has a patron. Even you, I'll be bound.'

'Did Gonville tell you I was coming to Boston?'

The collector of customs shook his head. 'All Gonville does is send out letters ordering us to remit more revenue. Him and the Treasury and the Exchequer, all demanding, more money, more money, all the time. For Christ's sake, what are we supposed to do?'

'Tell us who the smugglers are. You don't need to fear them, we can protect you.'

Wolsthorp stared at him. 'Mother of God. Do you have any idea who you are dealing with? Some of the smugglers are sea rovers and pirates. They've sailed all the seas from Bothnia to the Pillars of Hercules. They're not going to take much notice of a puffed-up queen's clerk and a hayrake in a cassock.'

Hull stirred a little. 'I am a priest, which means that if I break your nose, I will have to do a heavy penance. But I am willing to bear it if necessary.'

'I'm not telling you anything,' Wolsthorp said. 'My life is worth more than that.'

Merrivale nodded. 'Let him go,' he said to Warin.

Warin released his grip on the collector's tunic and stepped back. Wolsthorp watched them, wary again. 'Why does this matter to you?' he asked. 'What is so important about the wool that you will risk your own lives for it?'

'Someone is also stealing from Queen Isabella,' Hull said. 'We intend to find out who is responsible.'

Wolsthorp started to laugh, then winced with the pain of his split lip. 'Is that what this is about? The queen mother's subsidy?'

'What do you know about that?' demanded Hull.

'Enough to know you're barking up the wrong tree. It isn't smugglers who are defrauding the queen. It's her own household who are robbing her blind.'

Skegness, June 1339

Wind and waves had been at work in Skegness, tearing away the sea defences of the little port. Many of the buildings around the harbour were derelict, and a spring tide boiled around their skeletal timbers. The collector of customs did not try to run; he locked himself in his own house and refused to come out.

Warin watched the tide washing around nearby buildings with a sceptical eye. Born on the high moors, he did not trust the sea. 'We're being followed again, sir.'

'Where?' asked Merrivale.

'See that house with the fishing nets hanging outside? Two of them just beyond, dressed like fishermen. I reckon there's another as well.'

'Solaro again? And his friends Enric and Sgond?'

'Could be.'

'See if you can find out.'

Warin slipped quietly away. Merrivale stood looking at the collector's house, hands on his hips. 'Do you think Wolsthorp was telling the truth?'

'About what? Someone in Queen Isabella's household is stealing from her? That might be old news. Perhaps word of Dunham's activities has got out. He was definitely lying about Gonville, though.'

'How do you know?'

'I've heard many confessions in my time. I can tell when a man is admitting to a lesser sin in order to conceal a greater one.' Hull paused for a moment. 'Now then, in a moment you're going to remind me that you are the inquisitor and I am merely the local guide, before telling me to mind my own business.'

'I don't pass judgement until I know the full story. You probably learned that in the confessional too.'

'Man, are you serious? We heard the same stories over and over, so often that we knew what was coming before they'd finished the first sentence. Forgive me, father, for I have lain with another man's wife. Forgive me, father, for I have coveted another man's sheep. On a good day, it was t'other way around. We spent most of our time thinking up amusing forms of penance.' Hull looked up at the house. 'He's not coming out.'

'No. Let's find a tavern and wait for Warin.'

The tavern was on the water's edge, a row of fishing boats drawn up on the sand outside. Merrivale sat hunched over the table, staring into his ale and trying not to think. Hull watched him for a little. 'I told you I had heard many confessions,' he said. 'Enough to know when a man is in pain.'

'Aren't most men in pain? And even more women?'

'Aye, you could be onto something. It must have been hard to lose your post with the king.'

'I will get by. I'm used to looking after myself. I learned that during the famine.'

'Ah, yes. How old were you?'

'I was seven when it began.'

'Too young. I was sixteen and up at Oxford. We fared better than many; we always had something to eat, even if a lot of it was rat. Funnily enough, I'm still partial to a bit of rat.' Hull paused. 'This isn't making you feel any better, is it?'

'I fought my friends for food. I injured some of them, badly. I think I may have killed one of them. I was a child, John. Why was I made to endure this? Why did I survive when my mother and sisters died?'

'As a clergyman, I am bound to say that it was God's will,' Hull said. 'As a man, I have absolutely no idea. Fate is blind and random. Some she kills, the others she leaves behind to wrestle with the guilt. Sometimes it is hard to know which is worse.'

Merrivale looked at him. 'Are we talking about me, or you?'

Hull nodded. 'Like you said, most men. Ah, here is your groom.'

Warin pulled up a bench and sat down opposite Merrivale. 'They're local boys, sir, not the Piedmontese. They've been ordered to watch us and report back to their paymaster, a fellow called Robert Denton in Kingstown upon Hull. That's all he knew.'

'All who knew?' asked Merrivale.

'The one who saw me and came back to get rid of me. I pushed him against a wall and threatened him a bit, and he sang like a lark. But he didn't know very much. They're hired hands, nothing more.'

Hull cleared his throat. 'Robert Denton is controller of customs for the east coast ports. He supervises all the collectors.'

'I know. Shall we go?'

Ravenser, June 1339

From Grimsby, whose little port smelled of mud and herring guts, they took passage across the grey sweep of the Humber. Twilight was falling; the clouds overhead were the colour of slate, streaked with bars of fiery pink in the west. Seals bobbed in the water between the sandbars, and lamps twinkled in the fishing villages along the estuary, reflecting off the water like the faerie lights of Elfland. Or corpse candles, Merrivale thought.

Ravenser was an ancient town huddled behind the long sandspit known as the Spurn. As at Skegness, the sandbars had eroded and the town was being reclaimed by the sea. The ground floors of many buildings had been abandoned. At high tide boats rowed up and down the streets. Near the docks was a row of apothecaries' shops, each with lobster pots hanging from its walls. According to Hull, each shop had its own fleet of lobster boats. 'I'm sure you'll explain why,' Merrivale said.

'Now then, I thought a clever fellow like you would know. The gizzard stone of the lobster has medicinal properties. It is said to be most efficacious for the cure of stomach aches. Especially those brought on by eating too much lobster.'

There were times when Hull's whimsies were amusing, but this was not one of those times. 'Denton is in Kingstown upon Hull and not Ravenser,' Merrivale said. 'What are we doing here?'

'We can find Denton later. I am intrigued by this tale of shipmasters involved in smuggling. Most of the rovers of the northern seas call at Ravenser, and I happen to know one of them. If he is here, we might learn something useful.'

The tavern called the Raven's Tongue was on slightly higher ground, but even so there were water marks halfway up the interior walls. At first Merrivale thought the common room was empty, but as his eyes adjusted to the dim glow of rush lights he saw a lone man sitting on a bench, contemplating a pot of ale in his hands.

'We are in luck,' Hull said quietly. 'That is the man of whom I spoke.'

The man looked up as Hull approached. He had a broad, blunt face with deep-set dark eyes and his shoulder-length hair and beard were streaked with grey. 'Forgive me, father, for I have sinned,' he said.

'You don't surprise me.' Hull sat down on the bench beside him, wrapping his cassock around his knees. 'It has been a long time, John Crabbe.'

'Berwick-upon-Tweed, '33. You weren't a clergyman then.'

'And you weren't an Englishman, or at least you hadn't yet pledged allegiance to England. This is Simon Merrivale.'

'I've heard of you.' Crabbe's accent had overtones of both Scotland and Flanders. 'You were at Berwick too, though our paths never crossed. Have you come to rake up the past?'

'I am only interested in the present.' Merrivale pulled up a wooden stool and sat. 'We're told that some of the shipmasters on the east coast are smuggling wool out of the country. Is this true?'

'Are you asking me to give information about my friends?'

A woman had come out of the taproom and stood watching. Merrivale signalled to her to refill the ale pot. 'I don't want to make trouble for anyone,' he said when she had gone. 'But I need to know who is organising the smuggling.'

Crabbe remained silent. 'Someone is stealing the king's wool,' Hull said gently. 'There is a price on your head in three countries, Master Crabbe. Your continued survival depends on the king's goodwill.'

'You'll not blackmail me into helping you.'

'Perish the thought,' said Hull. 'But given your reputation as one of the most skilful and daring captains ever to sail the German Ocean, I'd say you're already involved, one way or another. I can think of two possibilities. One is that you're up to your neck in smuggling. The other is that King Edward has hired you to put a stop to it.'

'You can help yourself by removing some of the smugglers from play,' Merrivale said. 'You would be carrying out the king's wishes, or alternatively, eliminating some of your competitors. Either way, you win.'

Crabbe studied Merrivale for a long time. 'The shipmasters are not the thieves,' he said. 'They are contracted to carry the wool, and they receive a handsome fee for doing so. They facilitate the trade, no more.'

'Who else is involved?'

'Everyone. Landlords, who sell poor quality wool to the king's purveyors and hold back the best stuff so they can sell it untaxed overseas. Impecunious merchants, who have borrowed heavily to pay for wool and then watched their profits eroded away by the king's new taxes. The king's officials, who take a cut of every transaction.'

'Every transaction?' asked Hull. 'Including smuggling?'

'Master Merrivale asked earlier who is organising the smuggling. The orders are anonymous, but everyone knows they come from royal officials. Some are signed with the privy seal, meaning they have royal authority.'

Hull stared at him. 'Body of Christ. The *government* is behind the smuggling?'

'That should not surprise you, Master Hull.'

'You mentioned orders,' Merrivale said. 'Orders to do what?'

'Which cargos to load at which ports, which customs collectors are to be paid off, which cocket seals are to be forged. All the details necessary to make the trade flow smoothly.'

'You have seen these orders?'

'I have.'

'And Denton the controller is involved too, along with the collectors in Kingstown and Skegness and Boston.'

'You are missing one.'

Merrivale closed his eyes for a moment. 'John Wesenham,' he said.

'Don't blame him, or the others. They're cogs on a wheel. You know what the engine of government is like. Office after office, department after department, the Exchequer, the Chancery, the Treasury, the Chamber, the Wardrobe, the Great Wardrobe, the Privy Wardrobe, the Privy Seal, each with their own keepers and officials all grasping for power and money, each intent on building their own little empire. That's where the rot lies.'

'Is Edmund Gonville one of the rotten ones?'

'I've no idea. I'm not a familiar at court.'

'You must have heard rumours.'

Crabbe shook his head. 'I don't stick my neck out. I used to be a pirate, but these men are far more ruthless than me. If they turn against you, they will nail your balls to a table and hammer them flat like *pannekoeken*.'

'When you have been tied in a sack and thrown into a freezing river, other threats lose their piquancy,' Merrivale said. 'What about the Italian bankers, the Lombard houses and the Peruzzis? Are they involved too?'

'Not directly. But I am sure they are finding a way to make a profit.'

'What can you tell me about Robert Denton?'

'Nothing you haven't already guessed.'

Merrivale rose to his feet. 'Thank you, Master Crabbe. You have been most helpful.'

Warin was waiting on watch outside the tavern. Darkness had fallen. The lamps of the town gleamed off the receding tide. Out in the estuary more lamps winked, fishing boats making their way towards the sea.

'What do we think this is about?' Merrivale asked. 'Power or money?'

'Both,' said Hull. 'You can't separate them. Money buys you power, and power gives you access to money. It was ever thus.'

Merrivale smiled a little. 'What were you before you became a cleric?'

'A lost sheep, looking for a shepherd. How do we stop these men?'

'We expose them. Corruption hates sunlight. I want to speak to Robert Denton.'

Something hit Merrivale hard on the back of the head. His last conscious vision was of the muddy foreshore coming up towards his face.

12

Burstwick, June 1339

Consciousness came back in little waves like the tide lapping at the shore. For a moment his dazed mind thought he was drowning and he struggled to move, but his hands were tied behind his back. A canvas hood had been pulled over his head. The hood stank of fish, which was probably what had made him think of the sea.

'He's awake,' someone said. Merrivale recognised the accent, the swallowed consonants and long vowels peculiar to the riparian settlements along the Humber.

'Get him up,' said another voice. 'Let's see what he has to say for himself.'

Hard hands dragged Merrivale upright. The hood was pulled from his head and for a moment he stood dazzled by the lamplight, his eyes throbbing a little. He was in a castle hall, quite an old one judging by the smoke stains on the timbers overhead; there was a strong smell of damp in the air. Dim light leaked through high windows and he heard seabirds crying outside. They had not taken him far, then.

His sword and dagger were both gone. His captors held him firmly between them, their fingers biting into his arms. He moistened his lips with his tongue. 'Where am I?' he asked.

One of the men cuffed him hard across the side of the head. Pain shot through his skull.

A door creaked open on rusty hinges. Two more men entered the room, both cloaked against the damp. One was tall and broad-shouldered and looked like a fighting man; the other was slender with a pale face and long elegant hands. He has never seen a tiltyard, Merrivale thought, let alone a battlefield.

'Simon Merrivale,' the big man said. 'It's time we met. I am Robert Denton.'

Merrivale stared at him. 'Is this a typical northern welcome?'

That earned him another blow to the head. He stood for a moment, staring at the floor and waiting for the pain to subside. 'That's enough,' Denton said. 'Cut him loose and let him sit down.'

His bonds were cut and a stool placed before him. He sat down, rubbing his chafed wrists. 'For Christ's sake. If you wanted to meet me you should have sent an invitation, not abducted me off the street.' He looked around the hall. 'What is this place?'

'This is the castle of Burstwick,' Denton said. 'The seat of the lordship of Holderness.'

Holderness was a vast fief with at least a dozen manors, spanning the coast from the Spurn north to Flamborough Head. 'This is a royal castle,' Merrivale said.

'Yes,' said the pale-faced man. 'Now do you begin to understand?'

Merrivale said nothing. 'Time to start talking,' Denton commanded. 'What are you doing here?'

'You already know. Wesenham and Wolsthorp will have reported our conversations, and your men have been watching us at least since Skegness, and probably before that.'

'In London you called on the Italian banker, Donato de' Peruzzi. What are your relations with him?'

The question caught Merrivale by surprise. 'Ah,' he said after a moment. 'I am guessing that Reginald Conduit had me followed as well. Conduit is Pole's partner in the wool consortium. You, Master Denton, are controller of customs in Kingstown upon Hull as well as various other places, and nothing happens in Hull without Pole's consent. That means you must be Pole's creature. Am I right?'

Denton took a pace forward. 'Tell us what you discussed with Peruzzi.'

'Nothing,' said Merrivale. 'He refused to see me.'

The pale man snapped his fingers. 'This is false. You are colluding with Peruzzi.'

'Colluding? To do what?'

Silence. After a moment Merrivale answered his own question. 'Of course. Peruzzi is trying to wrest control of the wool trade away from Pole and Conduit. But if you think I am Peruzzi's agent, you are dead wrong.'

From outside came a faint noise, like the creaking of a door. The pale man held up a hand and hurried outside. He returned a minute later. 'Nothing. Probably just dogs. The fog's settling in thick.'

'Good,' said Denton. 'It will give us cover.' He gestured towards Merrivale. 'He might be telling the truth, you know.'

'It hardly matters either way,' said the pale man. 'He has meddled in something that was not his concern. I wonder if he is aware of how much damage he has already caused? Probably not. Men of his sort lack imagination.'

The hurt and pain were gone, and Merrivale was angry again. He rose to his feet. 'Damage? Christ! You're the ones who are smuggling wool, defrauding the king and stealing the queen mother's subsidy!'

The pale man raised one long finger. 'Listen to me, Merrivale. The king is aware of your actions, and to say that he is deeply displeased is an understatement. On His Grace's orders, I have had to interrupt my own important work in Antwerp and return to England to deal with you. I am not in a tolerant mood.'

'You must be Edmund Gonville,' Merrivale said after a moment. 'And you claim to have the king's writ?'

'My warrant bears the privy seal.'

'Oh? Did Kildesby seal it himself, or did you purloin it from his office while he slept off last night's wine?'

William Kildesby was the Keeper of the Privy Seal. Denton took another step forward, but Gonville put a hand on his shoulder to restrain him. 'You have interfered in matters of state, Merrivale,' he said.

'You will need to explain that.'

'An explanation is more than you deserve, but very well. Wool is indeed being taken out of the kingdom, secretly and untaxed, but this is at the orders of His Grace. He is willing to forgo export duties so that the wool can be sold quickly and profits from his share remitted at once to the Treasury. He needs ready money to finance the war with France.'

Light began to dawn. 'The king is conniving at the smuggling of his own wool. So what? Why the secrecy?'

'The king is breaking the law,' Denton said.

'The king is sovereign. He can break whatever laws he likes.'

'No, he can't, not where the wool trade is concerned. The arrangements for export and customs were subject to long and careful negotiations between parliament and the crown.'

Gonville nodded. 'Public confidence in the law would erode, at a time when people are already murmuring against the government.'

They have stopped interrogating me. Now they are telling me a story. Why?

Another thought emerged from the clouds in his aching head. 'You said this is at the orders of His Grace. Is it really? How much does he know about the smuggling?'

Gonville paused. 'It is not necessary for the king to know everything that is done in his name,' he said finally. 'Sometimes, indeed, it is better that he remains ignorant. We can protect him better that way.'

'Let's get back to Peruzzi,' Merrivale said. 'Why are you so worried about him? You are close to the king. It would only take a word from you to poison the wells against Peruzzi.'

Gonville did not blink. 'Donato de' Peruzzi has other friends, more powerful than myself. If he gains control of the wool trade he will manipulate it for his own advantage. We must keep control of the trade.'

'I agree. Among other things, Peruzzi might well use the profits from trading in English wool to pay Doria and Grimaldi to attack England. You did know he is financing our enemies, didn't you?'

Gonville went very still. 'Can you prove this?'

'Not yet,' Merrivale said. 'But I will.'

Gonville paused for a long time in thought, one long finger pressed to his temple. 'You know too much,' he said finally.

'We can dispose of him,' said Denton.

'No,' Gonville said. 'The queen mother would ask questions, and if the truth came out it could provoke a rift with the king. We don't want that, or at least not yet.'

He turned to the two men standing behind Merrivale. 'Lock him away. We'll decide what to do with him later.'

Outside, his captors walked him across the courtyard through pale pre-dawn light towards the gatehouse. The castle itself was lifeless and partly derelict; some of the outbuildings were crumbling and part of the stable roof had fallen in. The dogs slinking around the kitchen door looked half feral.

At the gatehouse they pushed him into the guardroom and locked the door. The only windows were arrow slits and the walls were solid and strong. Merrivale sat on a bench, resting his aching head in his hands. His anger began to recede, replaced by an all too familiar sense of failure. He thought again of his father, far away in Frithelstock. *I have failed him too*, he thought. *I cannot even keep the family name alive. I am the last Merrivale.*

Memories, the same memories that cursed his dreams, stirred and formed in the shadows. Rain, endless rain and dead animals rotting in the fields. Children of the famine, fighting like wild dogs for food, blood on their faces and hands. White-shrouded bundles, his sisters and his mother being lowered into the ground.

Yolande, her face glowing with love, her hand held out to him, and the same face but full of fear, crying out in the distance, *help me, Simon, please, you are the only one who can help.* And Mercuriade's voice, *where we were, whither we have sunk.*

I really must get rid of that voice, he thought.

How did Vidal know? How?

Morning came slowly. Through the arrow slits he saw mist rising in coils from the wet ground. Far in the distance a bell tolled prime. He heard voices in the courtyard, and the whinny of horses. A moment later a party of men rode through the gatehouse and down the road to the west. Counting the hoofbeats he reckoned there were four of them.

The hoofbeats faded. Absolute silence fell within the castle. Four men; Gonville, Denton and the two men who had held him. Was that all there had been?

The silence was broken by a rat scrabbling around the door outside. Merrivale listened for a moment, his head still clearing, and then sat up straight. Rats were adept at using their claws and teeth. None in his experience had mastered the use of metal tools.

'Who is there?' he demanded.

'It's me, sir,' said Warin of Hexworthy. 'Give me a few minutes and I'll have you out of there.'

The rasping of metal continued. The door lurched, tilted forward and fell into the guardroom with a crash. Warin stood in the doorway, holding up his knife. 'It's an old trick,' he said. 'If you can't open the lock, remove the door. This place is so damp the mortar has gone soft. All I had to do was dig the hinges out of the walls.'

'Is there anyone else still in the castle?'

'No, sir. They went off in quite the hurry.' Warin held out Merrivale's sword and dagger. 'They left these behind in the hall.'

'Where is Master Hull?' Merrivale asked, buckling on his sword belt.

'I don't know, sir. I reckon we should be moving along, lest any of them should come back.'

They hurried away over fields frothing with vapour. The sun was a dim red ball climbing through the fog. A copse of trees loomed up, black dripping silhouettes with two horses tethered beneath their branches. 'Tell me what happened,' Merrivale said as they rode back towards Ravenser.

'They came from the stables behind the tavern and clouted you before I could call a warning.' Warin was silent for a moment. 'This is my fault, sir. You left me on watch.'

'You can't see through walls. This was all carefully planned in advance.'

'Master Hull and I tried to get to you, but there were too many of them. Then another lot came up behind us and knocked me out cold.

When I came around, I was tied over the back of a horse. I managed to slip my bonds and get away across the fens before they noticed I was gone, but I didn't see any sign of Master Hull.'

Perhaps they hadn't taken him, Merrivale thought. According to Wolsthorp, the queen's own household were betraying her.

'How did you find me?'

'I went back to the tavern and followed the tracks of the fellows who had snatched you. When I reached the castle I could see there wasn't a garrison, so I broke in through the postern gate. I made the devil's own noise, but I managed to hide in the kitchen before anyone came out to investigate. I saw them take you to the guardroom and then they rode away.'

'Thank you for following me,' Merrivale said. 'I am grateful to you.'

'What did they want with you, sir?'

'To intimidate me into giving up on the inquisition.'

Warin snorted. 'From what I've seen, sir, frightening you is about as easy as splitting a fart. Were they going to just leave you there?'

'Until I was suitably cold and hungry, and ready to beg for mercy. I don't understand why they attacked you, though. Where were they taking you?'

'Towards the coast, I think. I could hear the sea when I first came to. There's something else, too.'

'What is it?'

'The men who grabbed you were all locals. But the ones who attacked Master Hull and me were foreigners. It was those Piedmontese fellows from London, sir. I'm certain of it.'

'Come on,' said Merrivale, kicking his horse into a canter.

'Where are we going, sir?'

'Back to Ravenser. We need to find Hull.'

Ravenser, June 1339

They found John Hull lying on the wet sand in the morning sun, next to a beached lobster boat. 'He came up with one of the pots,' the boat's master said. 'The rope tying his hands and feet had got wound around the tether. It was the devil of a job lifting him.'

There was no sign of a wound. It would need an expert to tell whether Hull had drowned or had already been dead when he went into the water; nor did it matter. Merrivale knelt on the sand for a moment, looking out over the estuary. In his mind he heard Hull's voice again. *You cannot take pride or honour beyond the grave.*

'Find a priest and arrange for a burial,' he said to the master. 'I will pay for it.'

Crabbe was in the tavern, sitting on the same bench. 'I've heard,' he said.

'Did you see anything of what happened?'

'I heard the fracas outside, two groups of men fighting, but by the time I reached the door they were gone. I'm not as swift on my feet as I used to be.'

'Who were these men?'

'Some of them were local, but there was another smaller group of foreigners. I didn't see Hull at all, or you.'

'How did you come to know Hull? I know your reputation too, Master Crabbe, and you don't strike me as the sort of man to befriend a priest.'

'He wasn't always a priest. Seven years ago he was a man-at-arms in Walter Manny's retinue. I was the admiral of the Scottish fleet, such as it was. Ten ships, all old, none fully manned. When the Disinherited invaded Scotland in '32, they caught my fleet in the Firth of Tay. They had more ships, and their archers shot faster than my crossbowmen. I lost every vessel and every man.'

'Was Hull in the battle?'

'No. I escaped to the shore and made my way south towards Berwick; my home, back then. Hull caught me before I could reach it, and made me his prisoner. The king bought me and paid my ransom in hopes that I would work for him. I refused at first, but the Scots called me a traitor and killed my young son. After that I changed sides and joined England.'

'I'm sorry,' Merrivale said finally. 'Did you hold Hull responsible for your son's death?'

'It was the Scots who slaughtered my innocent boy. Hull was a soldier doing his duty. I respected him.'

'Why did he join the clergy?'

'No idea. Perhaps he just grew tired. We're all sick of war, all of us with any brains or feelings, but we're stuck in the rut and we can't get out. Hull was one of the brave ones who made the change. Who killed him?'

He had been wrong to doubt Hull. The realisation came too late of course; always too late. 'The leader of those foreigners you mentioned,' Merrivale said. 'His name is Aufrej Solaro, a banker from Asti. He is also the agent of Donato de' Peruzzi.'

'Are you going to find him?'

'I will follow him to Ultima Thule, if I must.'

Crabbe finished his ale. 'I've killed plenty of men in fair combat, but I don't hold with murder, especially of clergymen. Hull was a good man. Call on me if you need help.'

'What will you do now?'

'Hull was right, the king has asked me to return to his service. I have been commissioned to raise a fleet to protect the wool ships this summer. I'll be responsible for fending off Doria and his galleys. When do you bury him?'

'Now, I hope.'

Crabbe drained his ale pot and rose to his feet. 'I'll come with you,' he said. 'When the end comes, a man needs his friends around him.'

They buried John Hull in the crypt of Ravener's only remaining church, its windows flooded with the golden light of morning. The grave was half full of seawater and the incoming tide washed against the buttresses outside. In a few years' time, church and grave would no longer exist.

The ferry took Merrivale and Warin back across the estuary to Grimsby and their waiting horses. 'Where now, sir?' Warin asked.

The sun shone brightly on green fields, flecked white with newly shorn sheep. 'London,' Merrivale said. 'I want to speak to an official at the Chancery, a man from these parts named Edmund Grimsby. Then we need to find Stanton and discover whether he has learned anything useful.'

'Have *we* learned anything useful, sir?' Warin asked after a while.

'Gonville and Denton claimed they were acting on the king's orders. But Gonville said something right at the end. "It is not necessary for the king to know everything that is done in his name." I have been in Edward III's service far longer than Gonville, and I know for an absolute certainty that nothing makes him angrier than people acting in his name without telling him.'

'Understandably enough,' Warin said.

'Before the king left England last year, he issued a set of ordinances instructing that *nothing* should be done without his knowledge. Every instruction requires either the great seal or the privy seal, and that means that His Grace must always be notified. But if what Gonville said is true, they are using the privy seal behind his back and issuing orders in his name without informing him.'

Warin considered this for a while. 'You could tell the king what's going on. Then stand back and watch while he bends Gonville over and carves him a new rectum.'

'I have no evidence, and if it comes to my word against Gonville's, the king will believe Gonville. Also, it is possible that Gonville was telling the truth and he really is acting in the king's interests.'

They rode on in silence for a while. 'This is about much more than smuggling,' Merrivale said after a while. 'We have stumbled into the middle of a war for control of the wool trade, with Peruzzi and his myrmidons on one side, and Edmund Gonville and his allies on the other.'

'Which side are we on?' asked Warin.

'Whether Gonville can be trusted remains to be seen. But John Hull was killed on the direct orders of Donato de' Peruzzi. I cannot forgive that.'

13

London, July 1339

London in high summer, the streets teeming with people, market porters and wagon drivers, knife grinders shouting for custom and mendicants ringing bells, hawkers selling everything from eel pies and fresh plums to pots of honey and caged birds. Stone church towers glowed in the hazy sunlight. The city was vibrant with life, a welcome change from the ghostly, drowning harbours of the east coast.

The Court of Chancery lay in New Street on the western edge of the city, next to a small stone chapel. An antechamber led to a plain undecorated hall where clerks worked in rows and dust motes hung suspended in the sunlight coming through the windows. No one spoke; the loudest sound was the scratch of pens on parchment. Yet for all its silence, Merrivale knew, this was a place of power. The Lord Chancellor, who presided over the court, also bore the title of Keeper of the King's Conscience.

As a senior official of the court, Edmund Grimsby had a private office behind the hall, a large room with a window looking onto the apse end of the chapel next door. He was a dry, scholarly man who spoke in precise and legalistic tones. 'I am saddened by the death of John Hull. There was a time at Oxford when I counted him a close friend, and it grieved me when he left to take up the profession of arms. I always felt the church suited him better.'

'So did he, in the end,' Merrivale said. 'Why did he leave Oxford?'

'There was a series of unpleasant incidents between students and townspeople. I assume you have heard of the town–gown riots?'

'I have.' Hull had spoken lightly of the riots, as if he had been a spectator, but it was not hard to imagine a younger version of him being directly involved. Come to that, Grimsby himself was looking a little awkward. Perhaps he had not always been so dry and scholarly.

'Hull was murdered,' Merrivale said. 'I know who killed him, but I want to know why. He deserves better than a nameless grave in a dying town.'

There was a long pause. 'You have requested a search for his killers?'

'Their descriptions have been sent to every sheriff in the east of England, but they will know I am searching for them and I suspect they have already fled the country. I need to ask you some questions about a different matter, if I may.'

Grimsby nodded. 'I will do what I can.'

The door to the room was ajar. Merrivale rose to his feet and closed it. 'Are you aware that untaxed wool is being smuggled out of the kingdom?' he asked, resuming his seat.

'I am. And to save you the trouble of asking, I am also aware that John Wesenham is involved. I was disappointed to learn of this, but not entirely surprised. Will he be punished?'

'Not by me. Edmund Gonville claims to be organising the smuggling in the king's name, to benefit the royal finances. Could he be telling the truth?'

Grimsby pondered for a moment. 'An intriguing concept, but on the whole, it seems unlikely. The wool syndicate is about to collapse and the king is desperately short of money, so much so that he is contemplating the imposition of a new tax.'

'He cannot do that without the consent of Parliament,' Merrivale said.

'And because he needs Parliament's support, it would be most unwise of him to offend the lords and commons by breaking the law. That is why I have doubts about Gonville's claim.'

'Gonville has access to the privy seal. He uses it to give orders, without necessarily informing the king he is doing so. How does he do this?'

'Presumably he has influence over William Kildesby, the keeper of the seal.'

'You mean he is bribing him.'

Grimsby's eyelids flickered. 'That is a serious accusation.'

'And I have no evidence to support it, I know. Why is the king so short of money already? The campaign season has barely begun.'

'But our own army still must be paid and fed, and the German mercenaries the king is hiring are ruinously expensive. And the subsidies he pays our allies on the continent would make your eyes water.'

'Ah, yes,' Merrivale said. 'Brother Willem and Cousin Jan.'

'And his other brother-in-law, the German emperor, and not forgetting the captain general of the League of Three in Flanders, whom the king hopes to entice onto our side. Between them, they are a bottomless pit into which money sinks and is never seen again. But we are facing a crisis. Henry Burghersh, the bishop of Lincoln, is the royal official tasked with paying the subsidies. He reports that he has less than one-quarter of the money he needs to ensure the loyalty of our allies.'

A thought struck Merrivale. 'The money Burghersh receives and remits. I assume this is in the form of bills of exchange, not specie. Who actually handles the money?'

'I believe the bishop has recently turned to one of the Lombard banks, the house of Solaro from Asti, who have a branch in Antwerp. The subsidies are paid through them.'

'Oh, dear God.' Merrivale closed his eyes for a moment. 'One of the partners in the Antwerp branch is a man named Aufrej Solaro. He is also John Hull's killer. Hull was murdered by the king's own banker. But in the name of Christ and all the saints, *why*?'

A bell tolled slowly in the chapel next door, marking nones. 'I have not seen a soul enter or leave the building,' Merrivale said, watching the chapel. 'What order is established there?'

'That is the Domus Conversorum,' Grimsby said. 'It was erected originally for the use of Jewish converts to the Christian faith. But there are very few of them left now, and fewer still want to be seen near the chapel.'

It was almost fifty years since the Jewish population of England had been expelled by the king's grandfather, Edward I. 'Who maintains it?'

'A *proselytus* family provided the funds for its establishment and upkeep. Why do you ask?'

'No reason. Giving myself time while I work out what in God's name is going on. Aufrej Solaro is Donato de' Peruzzi's puppet. What control Peruzzi has over him I do not know, but I believe Solaro and his men killed John Hull, and also attempted to kill myself, on Peruzzi's orders. I imagine he thought we were getting too close to the truth, and decided to put us out of the way.'

'And what is the truth?' Grimsby asked.

'That is what I am trying to work out... Peruzzi wants to take control of the wool trade, perhaps in hopes of raising enough money to restore the fortunes of his bank back in Florence. He has encouraged the smugglers and bribed customs officers to look the other way in hopes of forcing the collapse of the wool syndicate. Even more, I believe he has encouraged some members of the syndicate to smuggle their own wool, presumably on the promise of some greater reward. When the syndicate does collapse, which you say is only a matter of time, Peruzzi will attempt to take control of the wool trade. And the king, desperate for money, will be forced to resort to the new tax.'

He looked at Grimsby. 'Will Parliament agree?'

'On very strict conditions,' Grimsby said.

'Such as?'

'Shall I tell you the Chancery's view? Under His Grace's late father, we saw widespread abuses of power and position, not just by the king himself but by his favourites and courtiers. The result was very nearly a disaster, and even now the problem has not entirely gone away. The present crisis is a golden opportunity to put things right. We intend to increase the power of the institutions of government, including Parliament, in order to create greater stability and ensure such excesses never happen again. Among other things, that means giving government more control over the king's finances.'

Merrivale shook his head. 'The king will never agree.'

'He will have little choice but to do so.'

'No,' Merrivale said suddenly. 'He will go instead to the money markets and borrow from the banks. But he won't be able to raise enough money from English moneylenders to pay our own army and subsidise our greedy allies, so he will have to borrow money from abroad. And Donato de' Peruzzi will be waiting to lend it to him.'

'At ruinous rates of interest,' Grimsby said.

'Even worse. The money Peruzzi lends the king will come from the profits he makes from controlling the wool trade. He will control the kingdom itself in all but name. Which would be bad enough, except that he is also financing our enemies at the same time.'

'If you can prove that, you can bring Peruzzi down.'

'Yes,' Merrivale said bleakly. 'So long as I can do it without bringing down the kingdom at the same time.'

Silence fell. The bell next door had stopped tolling. 'Someone is representing the Peruzzi interests at court,' Merrivale said. 'Do you know who it might be? Bishop Burghersh, for example?'

'I cannot say for certain,' Grimsby said finally. 'But Sir Geoffrey Scrope met with Donato de' Peruzzi during his recent visit to London.'

Merrivale's eyebrows rose. 'Does the Chancery have its own spies?'

For the first time, a little humour crept into Grimsby's voice. 'Did you doubt it?' he asked.

Back at Surnes Tower a letter was waiting, sealed with a familiar seal. Merrivale broke it and read John Stanton's hasty handwriting, and clenched his fist in sudden excitement.

> *I have Aufrej Solaro in custody in Rye. I caught him trying to flee the country. He has promised to tell us about his dealings with Peruzzi, but he insists on speaking to you personally. Come quickly, but be careful. Grimaldi's corsairs raided the Isle of Wight yesterday, and they are moving east.*

Merrivale looked up at the sun. It was nearly midsummer and there were still several hours of daylight left; they could make Sevenoaks by nightfall, take lodging at the hospital there, and reach Rye tomorrow evening. 'We've got Solaro,' he said to Warin. 'Now I'm going to squeeze the truth out of the bastard.'

'Let me alone with him, sir, and he'll soon be singing. Although he might be a countertenor by the time I've done.'

'I don't care what notes he sings,' Merrivale said. 'So long as I can hear the words.'

Rye, July 1339

Smoke filled the sky with haze, turning the westering sun dull orange as Merrivale and Warin rode up to the castle gates. The guards stood watching the smoke, their faces tense. 'What is it?' Merrivale asked.

'Grimaldi burned Hastings this morning. Looks like we're next.' The officer of the guard nodded. 'You'll find Master Stanton inside.'

Stanton came down into the courtyard as Merrivale and Warin dismounted. The serjeant's face was tense. 'How did you find him?' Merrivale asked.

'Word came that a foreign banker was looking to take passage for Antwerp. He wasn't having any luck, because all the big roundships are out at sea hunting the French and the small boats aren't willing to take the risk with Grimaldi bearing down on us. I found him in a tavern down by the harbour, trying to persuade the crew of a crab boat to take him across. I was expecting resistance, but he came along quietly.'

'Expecting, or hoping?' Merrivale asked.

'He'll suffer for Hull's death, but I wanted to give you a chance to talk to him first. I'll take you to him now.'

'Anything else?' Merrivale asked as they climbed up onto the ramparts.

'One of Peruzzi's factors visited Rye several times this spring and paid shipmasters to take untaxed wool across to Flanders. It is generally agreed that he bribed the collector of customs too. No one is prepared to admit it under oath, though.'

Rye resembled the prow of a ship, jutting out into the sea with the castle standing on its highest point. Lurid sunlight glittered off the lapping waves of the harbour, partly enclosed by a long spit of sand. In the distance stones and broken timbers protruded from the sea, the remains of the old town of Winchelsea destroyed by storms fifty years earlier; the new town lay crouched on another hill on the far side of the bay. Clouds drifted low on the southern horizon, glowing white in the sun.

Aufrej Solaro was confined in a room in one of the towers. Two guards stood watch at the door; one produced a key and let them into the cell. Solaro's clothes were ragged and he looked like he had done a great deal of hard travelling, but he rose and bowed ironically as they entered. 'Welcome, Master Merrivale. You arrived more quickly than I expected.'

'Where are the other butchers? Enric and Sgond?'

'Safely back in Antwerp by now, I should think. We travelled by separate routes to avoid drawing attention to ourselves.'

'It would seem you failed. Why did you kill John Hull?'

Solaro's voice was calm, his manner almost arrogant. 'The priest? I had nothing to do with that.'

Merrivale turned to Warin. 'I heard your voice that night at Ravenser,' the groom said. 'You're one of the men who took me.'

Solaro looked at Merrivale. 'You allow your servants to talk for you?'

Warin's fist smashed into Solaro's solar plexus and he doubled over in agony, gasping for breath. Another blow drove him back against the wall and he dropped to his knees. 'My fists do my talking for *me*,' Warin said. 'Tell us what happened to Master Hull.'

'All right,' Solaro said, still gasping. 'We had orders to kill all three of you, but we had not expected Denton's men to arrive at the same time. They took you, Merrivale, before we could get to you.'

'Ordered by whom? Peruzzi?'

'If you think I am going to answer that question, you are even more dim-witted than you look.'

Warin dragged Solaro to his feet and hit him twice more, knocking him against the wall. 'Again, sir?' the groom asked.

'Of course,' Stanton said. 'Don't hold back, either. We want him conscious, but that's all.'

Another blow sent Solaro sprawling on the floor. Warin bent and pulled him upright again, pinning him against the wall. 'For God's sake,' Solaro moaned. 'Enough. Yes, it was Donato de' Peruzzi. We have a partnership with his bank and he… calls on our services from time to time.'

Merrivale stepped forward. 'Peruzzi is trying to destroy the English wool syndicate and seize control of the trade. Am I right?'

'Yes,' Solaro said. 'That is the way of commerce. The strongest dog wins.'

'Your comparison of Peruzzi to a dog is quite apt. And, of course, the lesser curs like yourself will share in the spoils. Who represents the Peruzzi interests at the English court?'

'I have no idea.'

'That is a lie,' Merrivale said. 'Let us continue the conversation we had in London. Your bank is financing the galley fleets of Doria and Grimaldi, while at the same time you are also acting as agents for the English court in Antwerp. The morality of this does not concern you?'

'Of course it doesn't. Money has no loyalty, Merrivale, and it knows no sovereign. One country's money is as good as another's. Our vocation is profit, and we follow wherever it calls us.'

'You have admitted to working with our enemies,' Stanton said. 'When we inform the king, your bank will be finished. Your men will be lucky to escape from Antwerp with their lives.'

Solaro stared at him. 'Go ahead. Tell the king. We will deny everything, of course. Our patron is Bishop Burghersh, the king's friend and confidante, and I think the king will listen to him before he listens to you. Take this tale before His Grace, Merrivale, and you might find yourself deprived of your post. Again.'

Warin hit Solaro in the pit of the stomach and he doubled over, gagging and gasping for air. 'You forget that you are our prisoner,' Merrivale said. 'We will take you to Antwerp and put you to the question before the king. You are a competent assassin, Solaro, but I don't think you are a very brave man. Under torture you will confess everything, rather quickly, I think. And that includes the fact that in financing the galleys, you are merely acting as agent. The money really comes from your partner, Donato de' Peruzzi.'

Solaro straightened, smiling through his pain. 'You think you are very clever, do you not? You will learn soon enough how wrong you are. I have powerful friends, remember. You will not hold me here for long.'

Outside the tower someone was shouting. A bell tolled, sharp urgent notes sounding the alarm. Merrivale ran out onto the rampart, followed by Stanton and Warin. Merrivale shaded his eyes against the red glare of the sun. A big war galley was moving across the mouth of the harbour, oars flashing as they rose and fell. Another followed, emerging from the smoky haze beyond Winchelsea. A pause and then came a third galley and then two more and still more, a dozen ships in all with fighting castles at bow and stern. Smoky sunlight glittered off the helms and armour and weapons of men clustered on their decks. A huge banner flew from the mast of the largest galley, patterned with red and white diamonds; the colours of Carlo Grimaldi, the lord of Monaco.

14

Rye, July 1339

Horns sounded harsh and strident, cutting across the clamour of the bells. Men rushed shouting along the walls, men-at-arms glittering in armour, archers stringing their bows. Merrivale turned to the guards. 'Watch Solaro like hawks. If he escapes, you will pay the penalty.'

The guards saluted. 'Rest assured, sir,' one of them said. 'He'll not get past us.'

Already the lead galley was turning past the end of the sandspit and rowing into the harbour. A few fishing boats lay anchored in its path; the galley rammed one of these and smashed it to splinters, ploughing on through the bobbing wreckage. Pale streaks rushed through the air, crossbow bolts tipped with fire, setting the other boats in flames. The other galleys pushed on through hanging curtains of smoke, drums beating as they turned towards the beach at the foot of the town.

'Grimaldi has timed his attack well,' Stanton said. 'The tide is in. He can beach his galleys just below the walls.'

Merrivale watched the galleys for a moment, listening to the thunder of their drums. 'This is Grimaldi's trade. He is a master of it.'

He turned and ran down the stairs, followed by Stanton and Warin. 'What are you going to do?' Stanton asked.

'Try to stop them.' At the castle gate Merrivale called for the captain of the guard. 'Leave the prisoner securely guarded, but summon every other man you can muster.'

'In whose name do you give orders?' the captain demanded.

'No one's,' Merrivale said. 'But unless you want your town to suffer the fate of Southampton and Hastings, captain, I suggest you listen to me.'

'All right. But I'm in command, do you hear?'

'As you wish,' Merrivale said. He drew his sword and looked down the hill.

Eight galleys had beached now; the other four were cruising offshore, oars rising and falling slowly. Smoke boiled up as the warehouses along the waterfront began to burn. More fire-tipped crossbow bolts arched over the ramparts and landed on the roofs of the lower town. Within a few minutes, these too were burning. 'They'll use the smoke as cover to break down the watergate,' Merrivale said. 'Then they'll come straight up Middle Street and assault the castle. Once that is taken, the town will be in their hands.'

'How do you know this?' demanded the captain.

'Because I know Grimaldi. I saw him take Antibes last year using the same tactics. Get ready.'

A rush of footsteps around them, more archers and men-at-arms arriving on the run. Shouting and screaming broke out down the hill, punctuated by the clash of metal, sword blades and axe heads hammering on armour. Drums thundered, and they heard a ram crash against the gates. More screams, a deep voice shouting '*Anans! Anans! Mòrt al nemico!*'

The gates broke with a sound of splintering wood and rending metal. A roar of triumph filled the air. 'We await your orders, captain,' Merrivale said. He was quivering with anticipation, the familiar rush of wild excitement flooding through him, even as his stomach began to churn.

The captain squared his shoulders and drew his own sword. 'Follow me!' he commanded.

They ran through the streets past Saint Mary's church, the archers drawing arrows from their quivers and nocking. By the time they reached the head of Middle Street the corsairs were halfway up the hill from the harbour, the red and white diamonds blazing on their shields and surcoats.

'Come on!' shouted the captain, and he ran down the street towards the enemy, waving his sword over his head. Black crossbow bolts streaked out and pierced his body in half a dozen places, throwing him headlong onto the cobbles. His sword slid away over the stones, clattering to a halt against the wall of a house.

Stanton was at Merrivale's shoulder, Warin close behind them. 'Kill those crossbowmen!' Merrivale snapped at the archers. 'The rest of you, stay tight together. Run hard, don't stop!'

Arrows hissed through the air and the crossbowmen slumped down, dropping their weapons. The corsairs tried to form a shieldwall but the English men-at-arms hit them before they could close up, and then it was every man for himself in the narrow street, yelling and screaming, swords clashing off armour and biting deep into flesh and bone. Merrivale ducked under one swinging sword and ran his opponent through the body. Withdrawing the blade, he spun around and hacked another man across the neck, sending him reeling back against a wall with the wound spurting blood. Stanton was fighting one of Grimaldi's men-at-arms; the Englishman was unarmoured and there was already blood around his mouth and on his arm. Merrivale swung his sword two-handed, hammering the corsair's vambrace and breaking his sword arm; the man reeled back shouting in pain and Merrivale followed up with a killing blow to the head.

More arrows whirred around him. The enemy were falling back; Grimaldi's men would never run from a fight, but the impetus of the English charge was driving them slowly down the hill. The English archers arrived yelling, shooting at close range before drawing their long knives and piling into the fight.

From the beached ships trumpets began to blow, sounding the recall. Up on the ramparts men were shouting again, pointing out to sea. The four galleys that had remained on watch were pulling swiftly towards the harbour mouth, covering the withdrawal of the others. Stanton staggered up, wiping blood from his lips. 'English ships have been spotted on the horizon. Grimaldi is pulling out.'

He wiped his mouth again, spitting a broken tooth into the palm of his hand and looking at the burning houses down the hill. 'He must reckon he's done enough damage.'

'This is nothing,' Merrivale said grimly. 'You should have seen what he did to Antibes.'

The excitement had gone now, leaving only the sickness swirling in his stomach. He pulled himself together, looking around. Men knelt in the street around them, tending to the English wounded and giving the *coup de grâce* to the injured corsairs. People began to emerge from their houses, some hurrying down to fight the fires along the waterfront. A woman knelt over the body of an English archer, sobbing frantically as she caressed the dead man's face. She had long fair hair, and when Merrivale looked at her he saw Yolande's face. The sickness came back and hit him like a blow and he knelt on the bloody cobbles, trying not to vomit.

Stanton rested a hand on his shoulder. 'Are you all right, Simon?'

'I will be.' Merrivale stood up again, looking at the bruises on the other man's face and the blood drying on his sleeve. 'You need a surgeon. Let's get you back to the castle.'

At the castle, the door to Aufrej Solaro's cell stood open. Solaro himself had vanished. So had the guards who had been on duty outside the door.

'Body of Christ!' Stanton said angrily. 'The guards must have been bought.' He looked up at the sky. 'The bastards can't have got far. We need to start a search.'

Merrivale was still staring at the open door. 'Don't bother. I expect they went down the hill to meet Grimaldi's men. They'll be on the galleys by now, far away.'

He turned to Stanton. 'Who knew you were in Rye, and that I was coming?'

'I reported to the queen that I was here, and that I had sent for you.'

'Then someone in her household must have sent word to the enemy. We shall have to be more careful in future.'

'Mary, Mother of God. Is there *anyone* in this country we can trust?'

'Each other, I hope.' Merrivale clapped him on the back. 'Let us get your wounds patched up and find a flask of wine. I think we need it.'

Merrivale stopped outside the Peruzzi house on Lombard Street. 'I think you should take the lead,' he said to Stanton. 'I want to watch his reactions.'

'It will be a pleasure,' Stanton said. His arm was still in a sling but the bruises on his face were fading.

'Be careful, though. He is a slippery bastard.'

'All reptiles are slippery. I can handle him.'

The same large men in leather jerkins were still on guard outside the house. Stanton approached them. 'I am a royal serjeant. My business is with Donato di Pacino de' Peruzzi. Take me to him at once.'

Scowling, the large men opened the gate. Stanton walked into the courtyard, followed by Merrivale. A servant bowed in greeting. 'The master is in the garden, *signori*. Please follow me.'

Stepping through another gate into the garden was like walking into a different world. The air was quiet, the noise from the street only a faint murmur; the loudest sound was the bubble of a fountain and the humming of bees. Sunlight shone on carefully trimmed grass, rows of fruit trees, parterres of sweet-smelling sage and lavender.

Donato de' Peruzzi sat in the shade of a tree eating jewel-red strawberries from a silver bowl, wiping his lips occasionally on a silk napkin. He did not look up as they approached. 'Master Stanton. I thought you might call. Your visit will be brief, so I shall not offer refreshment.'

'That is ungracious of you, Donato,' said another voice behind them. 'Master Stanton's wounds, sustained during his heroic defence of Rye, must still be paining him. At the very least you could offer him a sustaining draught. Saffron brandy, perhaps?'

They turned to see a man in the brown robe of a Franciscan friar standing with his hands behind his back, smiling. 'Greetings, Simon,' he said. 'You have been busy since we last met.'

'Who is this?' demanded Stanton.

'Allow me to present Raimon Vidal,' said Merrivale. 'Secretary to His Grace Étienne Aubert, the Bishop of Noyon.'

Stanton turned back to Peruzzi. 'I wish to speak with you in private.'

'Allow me to stay,' Vidal said. 'The conversation promises to be an interesting one. Perhaps as a neutral party, I may have something to contribute.'

Stanton looked at Merrivale, who nodded. He could not guess why Vidal was here, but he needed to find out.

'I will come straight to the point,' Stanton said. 'I know you have financed the mercenary shipmasters Ottone Doria and Carlo Grimaldi on behalf of the French crown. You used your profits from the sale of English wool to finance the pirates who prey on our shores. Do you deny this?'

'Of course I deny it. This is pure fantasy.'

'We have the word of Aufrej Solaro. He confessed the entire scheme.'

'Solaro builds castles in Spain. Not a word he says can be believed.'

Vidal intervened. 'Where is Solaro now?'

'We don't know,' Stanton said. 'He escaped during the raid on Rye.'

'There we are,' said Peruzzi. 'No witness, no evidence, no proof.' He picked up another strawberry. 'You may go now.'

Stanton did not move. 'I know about the Solaros,' he said. 'I have made it my business to study them over the past weeks. They are prominent in Italian politics as well as banking, and they are members of a faction known as the Guelphs, who support the papacy and favour France against the empire. In years gone by they have lent money to at least two popes and several kings of France.'

'You too are a Guelph, *signore*,' Merrivale said. 'And Guelphs tend to stick together. At least, they did in Savoy.'

'I advise you to stay away from political intrigue, Merrivale. You are not very good at it, if you recall.'

Stanton walked forward and stood over Peruzzi so that the other man was in his shadow. 'You made several errors,' he said. 'Hiring the Solaros to kill Merrivale was the first. They were clumsy and stupid and they killed the wrong man, a priest named John Hull. He was a friend of mine.'

'I am sorry for your loss,' said Peruzzi, and he ate another strawberry.

'Your second error was to get involved with the wool smugglers. You paid shipmasters and bribed customs officers, and that left a trail we can follow. We have unravelled part of the story already and we will soon uncover the rest. The king will not be pleased when he learns the truth, I think.'

'This is ridiculous,' Peruzzi said. 'I shall of course make a full report of this conversation to your king, telling him how you tried to impugn the reputation of a great and noble house that has served three generations of English kings. When he hears *my* version of events, I do not imagine your employment with him will last much longer. As for Merrivale, when I tell His Grace the full story of his activities in Savoy, he can expect to feel the force of the king's wrath. I only hope he survives it.'

'You might want to think again,' Vidal said.

The silence that followed lasted for several seconds. 'Why?' Peruzzi asked finally.

'Because such actions would not be in your best interests,' the Franciscan said. 'I'm sure you understand what I mean.'

Peruzzi looked as if the strawberries were giving him indigestion. He pushed the bowl away. 'Very well,' he said to Stanton. 'I am certain you have some arrangement in mind.'

'Stop paying Doria and Grimaldi,' Stanton said. 'Tell the Solaros you will no longer be party to the arrangement. In exchange, we will drop the investigation into your smuggling activities.'

'*Alleged* smuggling activities.' Peruzzi thought for a moment, rubbing the bridge of his long nose. 'What do you propose to say to the king?'

'That depends on you,' Stanton said calmly. 'The choice is yours.'

'I admit to none of the ridiculous charges you have levelled at me. However, I will break off my current arrangements with the Solaro bank. Will that do?'

'Admirably,' said Stanton.

Vidal followed them through the house to the front gate. 'Might I have a word with Master Merrivale alone?' he asked.

Stanton nodded and stepped out into the street. 'I congratulate you,' Vidal said. 'You forced Peruzzi to back down, which is not easy.'

'The credit goes to Stanton.'

Vidal smiled. 'As a matter of interest, why let Peruzzi off the hook? You could have compelled him to give up smuggling wool as well.'

'If we had tried, he might have refused the deal outright. This way he salvages a little of his pride, and sending the corsairs home is more important than stopping the smuggling. The damage Doria and Grimaldi have done over the past year is far greater than the export duty on a few sacks of wool.'

'You think they will leave?'

'They are only here because they are being paid. Why did you intervene just now, Raimon?'

'To force a conclusion. Peruzzi would have continued to bluster for some time, but you had him cornered and I saw no reason to prolong the conversation. I know things about Peruzzi that could sink him, and Peruzzi knows I know.'

'I don't suppose you would share these things with me.'

Vidal's eyes were sharp. 'I might. If you come to work for the bishop, as I suggested.'

'You came all the way to England to recruit me into Aubert's service?'

'Of course not. But one takes one's opportunities as one finds them.'

Merrivale stared at him. 'Why really did you intervene?'

'Would you believe me if I told you that I was revolted by the death of your friend the priest? That I believe Peruzzi should pay for his crimes?'

'No.'

'You are suspicious and mistrustful, Simon. It is one of the things I like about you. The house of Peruzzi are, among other things, bankers to the Pope. Undermining them might prove advantageous to my master.'

Merrivale considered this. 'Pope Benedict XII is in fine health, I am told.'

'He is also in his fifties, an age when accidents happen. He prefers engaging in sterile debates about when the souls of the departed are received into paradise to the actual task of governing the church. It is time a man of real stature wore the red shoes.'

'And Bishop Aubert is ready to try them on.'

'His Grace has never lacked ambition. At the moment, he is toying with the idea of playing peacemaker between England and France. If he can broker an end to the war, his own prestige will rise. I came to London in order to test the waters.'

'Why London? Why not the court at Antwerp?'

'Because, increasingly, London is the centre of power and influence in the country,' Vidal said. 'I am sure you understand what I mean. Did you know William de la Pole has returned to London? Ah, I see you did not.'

Merrivale regarded the Franciscan for a moment longer. He wanted to ask Vidal, again, how he had discovered the love affair between Merrivale and Yolande; he wanted to wrap his hands around Vidal's fat throat and squeeze him until the truth came out. But even as the thought came to his mind, something held him back. *How do you want to remember her, Simon? Memories are all you have now.*

He knew Vidal was reading the thoughts in his eyes. 'Stay out of my way, Raimon,' he said.

'I have absolutely no intention of interfering with you. I wish you every success in your endeavours.' Vidal smiled again. 'You and I are alike in many ways, you know.'

'There is no need to insult me,' Merrivale said.

15

London, July 1339

William de la Pole was a tall man, broad-shouldered with red hair and closely trimmed beard; Scandinavian sea rovers had clearly been among his ancestors. 'I hear you have been making trouble for me, Merrivale.'

They stood facing each other in the hall of Pole's London house. The room was brilliant with paint and gilding and cloth hangings with colours like gemstones, a display of wealth as lavish as anything Merrivale had seen. He was reminded what John Hull had said. *God doesn't think he is William de la Pole.*

'I think you have been making trouble for yourself, Master de la Pole.'

'A fighting cock, are you? I don't fear you, you know. Nothing you say or do can touch me.'

'Even the most powerful can fall,' Merrivale said. 'Fortune's wheel brings us all down, in the end.'

Pole planted his hands on his hips. 'Go on, then. Spin the wheel.'

'Thanks to the smugglers, the wool syndicate is about to collapse. Either you and your partner Reginald Conduit know about the smuggling and have done nothing to stop it, or you are actively involved in smuggling yourselves. That in turn raises the question of why you are trying to deliberately undermine the scheme, and with it, the king's finances and his ability to make war against France.' Merrivale paused. 'I shall be very interested to hear your answer.'

'Have you asked Conduit this question?'

'Yes. He attempted to assault me himself, and when that failed he sent his men to attack me.'

'Reginald thinks with his fists. Sometimes I think he consumes too much of his own product. You should have come to me first.'

'I'm still waiting for your answer.'

'It's quite simple, Merrivale. The whole arrangement was badly designed in the first place. There were no adequate checks on how much wool was purchased in, or how it was to be shipped overseas, or whether all the woolsacks that left the country had genuinely been inspected and taxed. Forgery and fraud were rife. If you want to blame someone, blame the royal officials who dreamed up this scheme in the first place.'

Merrivale shook his head. 'That doesn't answer my question. Are you profiting from the smuggling of wool?'

'Of course I am. Many people are, including some much more highly placed than myself. Once the smuggling began, it was impossible to stop. I had a choice, to sit and do nothing while the smugglers undercut my prices and I ended up with unsold wool on my hands, or to move with the market. But if you think Reginald and I set out deliberately to destroy the syndicate, you are wrong.'

Merrivale watched the other man's face. 'Donato de' Peruzzi is attempting to gain control of the wool trade. I wondered if you might be helping him.'

'Peruzzi? I'd rather hang myself than help that vulture. Don't worry, I'm wise to his schemes. He won't succeed, not while I draw breath.'

'I admire your confidence. Peruzzi has powerful allies, and I think some of them have helped to undermine your syndicate. Those royal officials who designed the scheme. Do you think they are taking a share of the profits as well?'

'Of course.'

'Do you know their names?'

'Yes. But I am not going to tell you who they are.'

'Why not?'

Walking across the room, Pole lifted the lid on a gold wine cooler and took out a flask. He poured a small goblet of wine, added water and offered it to Merrivale, who shook his head. Pole drank off the entire goblet and poured another.

'What do you want?' he asked.

'First, the restoration of Queen Isabella's subsidy. Second, the names of those officials who you say created the scheme. Third, I want Aufrej Solaro brought to justice for the killing of John Hull.'

'I will pay the queen mother's subsidy out of my own pocket.' Pole raised a finger. 'That means I'll send the money, but I won't guarantee she will receive the full sum. There are corrupt officials in her household too.'

'Tell me their names, and the names of the king's officials.'

Pole shook his head. 'No. You'll have to find those yourself.'

Silence fell. 'Is money really so important to you?' asked Merrivale. 'So important that you would lie to protect the guilty?'

'The only person I am protecting is myself,' Pole said sharply. 'As for the others, this is not about money, it is about greed. Avarice does strange things to a man, Master Merrivale. Anything of value, no matter how large or small, becomes something to be coveted. The richest man in the kingdom will cheat a widow out of a farthing, just for the satisfaction of doing so.'

'It is always amusing to hear a merchant talk deprecatingly about greed,' Merrivale said. 'Aufrej Solaro fled from Rye with Grimaldi's corsairs. I suspect he is at the bank's branch in Antwerp.'

'Then he is beyond reach of our justice.'

'Not necessarily.'

'Antwerp is in the duchy of Brabant, not England,' Pole said. 'The duke will never agree to arrest the Solaros, and the king will never ask him to.'

'I know that. I'm not talking about arrest and trial.'

'I am a wool merchant, Master Merrivale. I do not deal in assassinations.'

'We both know that isn't true,' Merrivale said. 'Help me, or I will expose your role as a smuggler and lay the proof before the king.'

Pole reached into his pocket and withdrew a small parchment roll. Untying its red ribbon, he handed the parchment to Merrivale. 'Read this.'

I, Edwardus III Rex, hereby pardon Magister William de la Pole for any and all offences he may have committed up to this time, and for any other offences that he may commit in future. Given by my hand on the second day after Michaelmas in the eleventh year of my reign, 1338.

The letter was signed and sealed with the signet, the king's private seal.

Merrivale handed it back. 'The king will ignore this if it pleases him.'

'He will,' Pole acknowledged. 'But I won't do your dirty work for you. And if you are thinking of having me arrested, that will solve nothing. The king is desperate for money, and so long as he remains so, the men around him will always be looking for ways to plunder him.'

Merrivale studied the other man for a long time. 'You spoke confidently about defying Peruzzi,' he said. 'But you're not confident at all, are you? You know Peruzzi has powerful influence at court, and he is starting to press. If he succeeds, he will ruin you; he may even have you killed to get you out of his way. Your back is to the wall, Master de la Pole.'

'I have been in hard places before, Merrivale. I know how to get out of them.'

'And I recognise bluster when I hear it. Will you support the king's new tax?'

'I don't know,' Pole said after a moment. 'I would need to know the details before I decide.'

'And what happens if Parliament refuses to accept the tax?'

'It is already happening. I'm sure the king's advisors will find a way of getting the tax through Parliament, but it will take time, and meanwhile his thirst for silver remains unquenchable. Every banker in Europe knows he will have to go to the money markets. The moneylenders are preparing their *haustblót*.'

'Including you, I assume.'

'Believe it or not, Merrivale, I have the country's interests at heart. I will lend money to the king, yes, and on terms far more favourable than any he will get from the Peruzzis or the Solaros. For a start, I will take his word as his surety. Those bastards will make him pawn his own children.'

'The king is fortunate to have you as his friend,' Merrivale said.

'Very droll. You should take up writing satires, and become the Juvenal of our times.' Pole finished his wine. 'Or come and work for me. You have talent and you have balls. It is a good combination.'

Merrivale bowed. 'Thank you. But I believe the Bishop of Noyon has first call on my services. Do not trouble your servants, Master de la Pole. I shall see myself out.'

Bishop's Lynn, August 1339

'Welcome, Master Merrivale,' said John Wesenham the collector of customs. 'It is good to see you again.'

That statement was almost certainly not true. Wesenham's face was quiet but his eyes showed his nerves. 'May I inquire after your sister?' Merrivale asked. 'Did she cross safely to Flanders?'

'She did, two weeks ago. The Genoese galleys have been far less active since the assault on Rye, and we judged it safe for her to cross.' Wesenham looked worried, for a different reason. 'She seems very unsettled of late. Her mood is difficult to read, but I do not think she is happy.'

'She has a talent that she cannot fulfil,' Merrivale said. 'Think of an artist unable to paint, or a musician prevented from singing.'

'Perhaps.' Wesenham paused for a moment. 'I wondered if perhaps she had formed an affection for you.'

Merrivale smiled. 'And that I might be the cause of her unhappiness? I assure you I am not. Mistress Wesenham's attitude to me seldom exceeds friendly contempt. And my own affections are given elsewhere.'

He thought Wesenham looked a little disappointed. 'Then what brings you back to Lynn?'

'I think you already know,' Merrivale said. 'Who paid you to look the other way to take their wool out of the port?'

'The money came from Robert Denton, the controller. He said to let the wool go. This was the only way to get it across the channel and avoid ruin for everyone in the syndicate.'

That tallied, roughly, with what Pole had said. 'Denton wasn't doing this on his own. Was he following Pole's orders?'

'No. He said the instructions came from someone at court, but he wouldn't say whom.'

Gonville, of course. It has to be. If we can tie Gonville to Peruzzi we can split this whole rotten mess wide open. And I think I might know how.

'Your late shipmaster, James Westacre. I recall you saying he bought out the shares of his partners, including yourself. Was he a smuggler too?'

'Yes. That's how he could afford to buy us out.'

'After he died, what happened to his ship?'

'I don't know. I assume he left it to his family in his will.'

'What was this ship's name?'

'We had christened her the *White Ship*. Not very imaginative, I know.'

White Ship in Flemish was *Witschip*, the ship in which Nicholas le Flemyng had sailed for the Low Countries with a cargo of stolen saffron.

'I assume you intend to denounce me,' Wesenham said. 'I accept this, and I will take my punishment. I ask only that you tell the justices about the threats against me, and remind them that I gave you as much assistance as I could.'

Merrivale looked at him for a long time. 'Denouncing you would serve no purpose,' he said finally. 'It won't bring John Hull back to life, or help me serve justice on his killers.'

Wesenham looked down at his hands. 'I liked Hull,' he said. 'Do you know who killed him?'

'I do.'

'If I can help in any way...'

'Do nothing for the moment. When the time comes, I will call on you to give evidence against the smugglers. In exchange, I will see you are granted a full pardon. Do not fail me.'

'I won't. This is more than I deserve.'

'It is,' Merrivale acknowledged. 'But I don't want to see your sister's reputation dragged through the mud along with your own. Keep your head down, Master Wesenham, and stay safe.'

Castle Rising, August 1339

Queen Isabella received Merrivale and Stanton in her solar, the lead glass windows flooded with sunlight. She wore red silk today, her fair hair pulled back under a cap of gold wire. The light played off the planes of her face, highlighting her clear blue eyes. Merrivale looked for any trace of sorrow over Hull's death, and found none.

Ellerker the treasurer stood behind her, looking pale and rather sick. There was not a cat in sight.

'I have read your report,' the queen said. 'I am pleased to hear that my subsidy will finally be paid.'

'Account for it carefully, Your Grace,' Stanton said. 'Ask for a clear statement of payment from Master de la Pole, and check with your bankers that the amount has been paid in full.'

'My treasurer will see to it. I want justice for the death of my chaplain, gentlemen. I want his death avenged.'

So there was sorrow after all. Merrivale bowed. 'So do we, Your Grace.'

'What do you intend to do?'

'At the moment, our choices are limited. Solaro is in Brabant territory, so recourse to law is out of the question.'

'Yes,' said the queen. 'Cousin Jan guards his sovereignty with great zeal.'

Jan Reginar, Duke of Brabant, was the scion of a family so old they looked down on Charlemagne as an upstart. He had inherited the familial arrogance in full, and tended to treat his cousin King Edward as a junior partner in the alliance. The king, who needed Brabant's seaports and wool markets, gritted his teeth and accepted in silence.

'We also considered more direct action,' Merrivale said. 'I approached a man who I thought could arrange it, but he refused.

On reflection, I believe he was right. Assassinations are difficult, and if it came to light that we had killed Solaro on Brabant soil, the king would be put in a difficult position.'

'I agree that your choices are limited, gentlemen,' the queen said. 'However, doing nothing is not one of those choices.'

'With respect, Your Grace, we never said it was,' said Stanton. 'But as well as seeking justice for Master Hull, there are other matters to consider. Edmund Gonville has been manipulating the wool trade. Gonville claims to be acting on the king's orders, and perhaps he truly believes that he is. But as you yourself said, a threat to the wool trade is a threat to the stability of the kingdom.'

'And it will not end there,' Merrivale said. 'As the king grows short of funds, he is turning to the banks. That means fresh opportunities for men like Donato de' Peruzzi to extend their power.'

The silence that followed was broken by Ellerker, coughing heavily into his hand. The queen glared at him and he held up a hand in apology. Isabella looked back at Merrivale.

'When we last spoke, you warned me that Peruzzi would betray us. I was foolish to borrow money from him in the first place. I will not put myself in his power again.'

'Your Grace is not to be blamed,' Merrivale said. 'The theft of your saffron and the cutting off of the wool subsidy were part of a sophisticated plot intended to make you ever more dependent on Peruzzi for your own finances. In turn, he would have used his hold over you to gain still more influence with the king.'

Ellerker was coughing again. 'Your Grace, I beg your pardon. Have I your permission to withdraw?'

'Please do,' Isabella said irritably. 'Ask the kitchen to give you some honey and water for your rheum.'

The treasurer hurried out. The queen looked at her two remaining officers. 'The king trusts Edmund Gonville, but after this business with the saffron, I do not. Is he working for his own ends? Or is he in league with others at court?'

'The answer is probably the latter,' Merrivale said. 'Having met him, I judge him to be a follower rather than a leader. He is taking orders from someone, I am certain.'

'I will not have my son's trust betrayed in this fashion. If people are conspiring to defraud the king, they must be exposed. I am sending you both to Antwerp with letters to the king. I will tell him what you have told me, and I will urge him to employ you to root out this conspiracy. Tell the king only so much as you think is prudent, but find these men and stop them by whatever means necessary.'

Merrivale bowed. 'With respect, Your Grace, Master Stanton should go alone. I do not think the king would find my presence acceptable.'

Her blue eyes fixed on Merrivale's face, unblinking. 'Leave us, Master Stanton, if you please. I wish to speak to Master Merrivale alone.'

She sat, studying him as Stanton departed. Merrivale was suddenly reminded of Mercuriade of Salerno. *And how appalled both women would be if they knew I was comparing them…*

'I am offering you a chance of redemption,' the queen said. 'Why are you resisting it?'

'Because there is no redemption, Your Grace. The king dismissed me from my post.'

'You failed once. Now you are afraid you might fail again.'

Merrivale's hands clenched. 'I know what it is like,' Isabella said. 'I know how it feels to reach the summit, and fall. I understand what is in your mind.' She paused for a moment. 'This business in Savoy. There was a woman involved, I think. Bohemia's daughter. Did you fall in love with her?'

'That barely begins to describe what happened.'

'It is a mistake to allow one's affections to be engaged. That is another lesson I have learned.'

'Yes,' said Merrivale. 'Me too.'

'What happened in Savoy is only one story, one verse in the poetry of your life. It is done. Move on, and write the next verse. It is in your power.'

Whither we have sunk, whither we hasten, whence we are redeemed. 'Master Hull would probably have told me that I should submit myself to God's will.'

'If John Hull had spouted nonsense like that, I would never have employed him as my chaplain. God ordains that you should go to Antwerp and protect the interests of my son. Or if He has not done so yet, He will once I have put in a word.'

Merrivale smiled a little. 'Yes, Your Grace.'

'I shall tell the king what service you have done for me, and indeed for himself. Do not make the mistakes I made.'

'Forgive me, Your Grace, but I think I have already made them.'

'Then learn from them,' she said. 'Journey safely, Master Merrivale.'

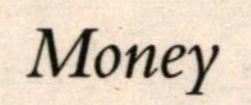

16

Antwerp, September 1339

Tell the king only so much as you think is prudent, Queen Isabella had said, and there was a world of possible meanings in that sentence. There had been plenty of time on the voyage across the German Ocean to decide exactly what she did mean and what story they would tell the king. Edward III was twenty-seven years old, eager, impetuous and devotedly loyal to those he considered his friends. These were strengths that could easily become weaknesses.

Antwerp lay at the mouth of the Scheldt, where the river broadened out into an estuary leading to the sea. Banners, the gold leopards of England on a field of red, and the gold lion of Brabant on black, flew from the towers of the Burcht, the great fortress in the heart of the city. Entering the courtyard through the watergate, Merrivale felt someone tap him on the shoulder and turned to see a tall fair woman with a white silk cowl framing her face, smiling at him.

'The prodigal son returns,' said Alice Bedingfield, lady-in-waiting to Queen Philippa of England, the king's wife. 'Let the slaughter of fatted calves begin.'

Merrivale smiled. 'Alice,' he said. 'It is good to see you again.'

'You too, and you also, John. What news from England?'

Stanton grimaced. 'Little that is good. War and taxes are making the people more unhappy than ever, and Grimaldi and Doria have scorched the coast from East Anglia all the way to the Bristol Channel. I don't suppose there is any chance of a victory over the French, to lift people's spirits?'

'Not much. The king and the army are laying siege to Cambrai, a hundred miles away up the valley of the Scheldt, but it does not seem to be going particularly well. I can give you some good news, though. Grimaldi and Doria have retired from the lists. Word is that their ships are sailing for home.'

Merrivale and Stanton looked at each other. 'How do you know?' Merrivale asked.

'The king's new admiral, Master Crabbe, reported it. He says there is no sign of them on the sea, and the harbours where they normally replenish their ships are empty. They were last reported off the coast of Brittany, sailing south.'

Peruzzi had held up his end of the bargain, which itself was unusual. Merrivale wondered what hold Vidal had over him. But then, he wondered a lot of things about Vidal.

'You are right,' Stanton said, 'that is good news.' He kissed Alice on the cheek. 'I must go. We have letters for the king, and I must make the arrangements for our journey.'

He departed. Alice looked into Merrivale's eyes. 'The king? Has he sent for you?'

'No. I am under his mother's protection, at least for the moment.'

There was a long pause. 'We missed you,' Alice said.

'Likewise.'

'Was she very beautiful? Bohemia's daughter?'

'She was in my eyes. Whether you would have considered her so, I do not know.'

'Do you know what happened to her?'

'No.' Vidal, who almost certainly knew, had said nothing. 'One would hope a father would be merciful to his child, but with Jean of Bohemia anything is possible.'

'I will send word to the queen's sister in Munich. She may be able to tell us something. Have you seen your father? Is he well?'

'He is happy enough and well cared for, but his wits are wandering. There will come a time when he no longer knows who I am.'

Her soft finger caressed his cheek. 'Simon, I am so sorry. You deserved better. We all tried, you know. Geoffrey Scrope spoke to the king, I asked the queen to intervene, but all to no avail. The king's anger was too great.'

'I understand. In his position I would probably have felt the same. No one is to blame but myself, Alice. No one.'

She kissed him. 'Go. We'll talk again when you return from Cambrai.'

Cambrai, September 1339

It was a fine day, full of mellow sunshine, and the sides of the royal pavilion had been raised to let in the air. Standing just inside the door, Merrivale and Stanton could hear the hard thump of trebuchets flinging heavy stones at the walls of Cambrai, and the occasional deeper boom of French cannon replying.

King Edward had just returned from a tour of the siege lines and was still in armour and bright surcoat. A tall man with fair hair and moustache and his mother's brilliant blue eyes, he was not in a happy mood. 'Five days we've been battering them now, and there is barely a scratch on the walls. And cannon. Where the devil did the enemy get those from?'

'I believe the Bishop of Cambrai paid for them himself,' said Geoffrey Scrope.

'Did he, by God. Why don't we have guns of our own? It is intolerable that the French should be better armed than us. I want cannon, Geoffrey.'

'It will take time, Your Grace, and it will cost money.'

'That's what you say to everything. Is there any news of the French army?'

'They are mustering along the Somme, about twenty miles from here. Only about five thousand so far, men-at-arms and ordinary foot soldiers, but more contingents are coming in every day. In a month's time they will have a force superior to ours.'

'Crossbows?'

'None so far. Since Doria and Grimaldi withdrew, the French have struggled to find crossbowmen.'

'So, we have a month to take this damned city.' The king finally looked at Stanton. 'Well? You're here on some business of my mother's, I assume. It had better be important.'

Stanton bowed and handed over Queen Isabella's letter. The king broke the seal and read it. Merrivale saw his eyes flicker and realised the king had reached the passage that concerned himself.

'Her Grace should be more careful about her choice of servants,' the king said.

'Dunham came with the recommendation of Master Gonville, sire,' Stanton reminded him.

The king tossed the letter onto a table. 'Some of the merchants and shipmasters are smuggling wool, and royal officials are colluding with them. So what? Arrest them and arraign them before the courts.'

'It is not that simple, sire. We could easily arrest the customs officers and some of the minor merchants. With others, the situation is more delicate.'

Restless, impatient, the king stirred. His mail coat jingled a little. 'What do you mean, delicate? What are you talking about?'

This was the point where careful diplomacy was required. 'Some of those responsible may be men that Your Grace knows well,' Stanton said. 'They may indeed be here at court.'

King Edward stroked his moustache for a moment. He looked at Scrope. 'Does Moleyns know anything about this?'

John Moleyns was the treasurer of the king's chamber. 'I shall ask him,' Scrope said. 'I will write to London as well.'

'With respect, sire, we have already made inquiries in London,' said Stanton. 'I am sure Sir Geoffrey has weightier matters to attend to.'

'He does,' said the king. 'And frankly, the wool subsidy can go hang. It didn't raise enough money, and I am tired of locking horns with Parliament and my own lord chancellor every time I ask for funds. We need money now, not whenever it pleases the barons to grant it.'

Scrope looked dubious. 'It sets a bad example, sire, if members of your household are pilfering.'

'Yes, yes, all right.' The king gestured to Stanton. 'Carry on, and report to me if you find anything. If some of my clerks *are* stealing from the treasury, I will show them no mercy. Talk to Moleyns and find out what he knows.'

'Where might I find him, sire? And I also wish to speak to Master Gonville.'

'Moleyns is here in the camp,' Scrope said. 'Gonville is back in Antwerp, working with Bishop Burghersh.'

Stanton bowed. 'Thank you, Sir Geoffrey.'

The king waved a hand in dismissal. Stanton bowed again and walked out of the pavilion. 'You too, Geoffrey, if you please,' the king said. He pointed a finger at Merrivale. 'You will stay.'

Merrivale bowed. The king stood, gloved hands on his hips, looking at him. They were the same age, sovereign and subject, and alike in temperament too; perhaps too much so at times. At twenty-seven, Edward III was still feeling his way down the paths of power, still uncertain as to who and how much he should trust. 'I hear a French bishop has offered you a position in his household,' he said.

'It was Bishop Aubert, sire. I have turned him down.'

'Why? He is a rising man. You could have a great future with him.'

'My loyalty is to England, sire.'

'Is it? *Is it?* Did you think of England while you were pricking Jean of Bohemia's daughter?'

'I hoped she might be a useful influence over her father, sire.'

'Oh, really? You were just doing your duty, were you?'

'No, sire,' Merrivale said after a moment. 'I was in love with her.'

'Savoy lost to us, probably for good. Bohemia returned to his French alliance. Doria and Grimaldi in French pay, devastation along our coasts, half a dozen fine towns burned, and all because you were *in love*? Suffering Christ, Merrivale! What in hell's name is wrong with you?'

'I made a mistake, sire,' Merrivale said stonily. 'It happens to all of us.'

'Don't be so god-damned insolent. My lady mother says you have rendered her good service. I accept that, but don't imagine for a moment your blunders in Savoy are forgotten, or forgiven. I want you to look after Stanton.'

That was unexpected. 'Sire?'

'He is a very competent lawyer and he knows how to fight, but he hasn't your talent for work in the shadows. Watch his back and keep him safe while he does his work.'

Merrivale raised his eyebrows. 'May I ask why Your Grace thinks he might be in danger?'

'When my mother's chaplain investigated this business, someone killed him. Do you know who it was?'

'Yes,' Merrivale said, and he rolled the dice. 'Aufrej Solaro from Asti and two of his men murdered John Hull. I believe all three are now in Antwerp.'

'Have you any proof of this?' the king demanded.

'None that would stand up in a court of law.'

'I need the Solaros. I need all the bankers on my side.'

'The Solaros were paying Doria and Grimaldi,' Merrivale said quietly.

Another silence. He wondered whether to mention Peruzzi's role, and decided against it. He did not yet know who Peruzzi's friends were at court. There would come a time when he could expose Peruzzi, but not now.

'How do you know?' the king asked.

'Aufrej Solaro told me himself.'

'I need the Solaros,' the king repeated, although his voice sounded less certain. 'Don't touch them, for the moment.'

Merrivale could see his mind working. 'And later, sire?'

'When I no longer have need of them, they are yours. In the meantime, you have your orders. Look after Stanton, and as I said, watch his back.'

Stanton was waiting a little distance from the pavilion, watching smoke drifting from the ramparts of Cambrai. 'Glad to see you still in one piece,' he said dryly. 'I was expecting you to come carrying your head in your hands like Saint Denis. What did he say?'

'He seems to think you need someone to hold your hand.'

'Really? On balance, I would say it is the other way around.'

'Let's go find Moleyns. I'd like a quiet word with Scrope, too.'

Sir John Moleyns was about thirty, a small man with a sharp, questing face and a shock of wiry hair; he always reminded Merrivale of a terrier. Like Scrope he was a man of many parts, but he had one particular claim to fame; nine years ago, he had been one of the little band of men who followed the young king into Nottingham castle to arrest his mother's lover, Roger Mortimer. For this he had received the barony of Stoke Poges, a vast array of lands in Buckinghamshire and neighbouring counties, and the king's undying friendship. Both Merrivale and Stanton knew him well; he had served in the Scottish wars when Merrivale first became a King's Messenger.

'Yes, I am aware that there are problems with the wool trade,' he said. 'Every year a certain amount of wool goes missing. We call it leakage.'

'Not as much as this year,' Stanton said. 'We think thousands of sacks have been smuggled, perhaps even tens of thousands. That's not leakage, Sir John, that is a flood.'

'What do you want me to do about it? The customs service is the responsibility of the Lord Treasurer in London. I only look after the king's personal finances. Make your complaint to William de la Zouche, not me.'

'But the smuggling means the king is running out of money,' Stanton said. 'And that is your responsibility, Sir John.'

'I don't need you to tell me my duty,' Moleyns said sharply. 'We'll find the money, one way or another. There are plenty of bankers ready to lend to His Grace.'

'Does that include the Peruzzis?' Merrivale asked.

'Yes. Whatever happened in Savoy has been forgiven. For some, anyway.'

Another French cannon boomed, its report echoing in the air. 'Who arranges the king's borrowings?' Stanton asked.

'What has this to do with wool smuggling?' Moleyns demanded.

Stanton chose his words with care. 'We believe some of the king's household may have connived at smuggling. If so, they may be trying to defraud the king in other ways as well. We need to check.'

Moleyns opened his mouth to speak, then closed it again and sat in silence for a moment, thinking. 'Very well,' he said finally. 'I arrange most of the loans, or my clerks do it for me. Other members of the court sometimes introduce prospective lenders, and my staff make the final arrangements. I check the totals and make sure the money is received.'

'Who is he borrowing from?' asked Stanton.

'The Solaros, who have lent him about fifty thousand marks. Several other banks from Florence and Lucca, and some of the smaller banks from Asti. Another Lombard consortium, the Company of the Leopard, wants to get involved but they're rivals of the Solaro, and they have threatened to call in their loans if we deal with the Leopards. There is also a syndicate led by Archbishop Balduin of Trier.' Moleyns grinned unpleasantly at Merrivale. 'You'll know all about him, of course.'

'Jean of Bohemia's uncle,' Merrivale said. 'Who seems to have no qualms about doing business with Jean of Bohemia's enemies.'

'Balduin is a man of God, but he also knows how to turn a profit. His syndicate have promised us three hundred and forty thousand florins.'

'What do the bankers get in return?'

'Repayments of anything up to one and a half times the capital, which would equate to an interest rate of fifty per cent, only we don't call it interest, of course, because everyone knows lending money at interest is a sin. And penalty charges for late repayment, because everyone also knows the king *will* be late, so that is easy money. Balduin's syndicate demanded late payment charges of five thousand florins per month.'

Haustblót, William de la Pole had called it; a blood-feast for the bankers. 'Mother of God,' said Stanton. 'And you agreed to this?'

'Of course. The king doesn't care where the money comes from or what he pays for it. The same goes for the subsidies we send to our allies. He agrees whatever terms they ask, without even attempting to negotiate. For providing just a hundred and fifty men, Prince Rupert of the Rhine asked for five thousand florins plus five florins per man he raises, with payment two months in advance. Good, said the king, sign the indenture and pay him.'

'Everyone profits,' Merrivale said.

'Exactly. What did old Bertran de Born say? To become rich in war, all you need to do is learn to steal well.'

'And you?' Merrivale asked. 'As treasurer of the king's chamber, all this is happening under your authority. Can you not make the king behave more prudently?'

'Have you ever tried pushing water uphill?' Moleyns demanded. 'I have an impossible task, Merrivale. I have to keep the money coming in, because if it stops our army will melt away and the French will hammer us flat. It doesn't matter where the money comes from now. There is no choice. We must carry on.'

Sir Geoffrey Scrope was sitting in his own pavilion, reading a long parchment roll. 'Sit down, both of you,' he said. 'Good to have you back, John. A man of your talents deserves better than to waste away at Castle Rising.'

'It is kind of you to say so, Sir Geoffrey.'

'Not at all. The king needs men he can depend on. How can I help you?'

'We need to ask some questions about the loans the king is taking. We think that the wool smuggling may be part of a wider fraud.'

Scrope's face was serious. 'That has been a concern of mine also,' he said. 'Ask whatever questions you wish.'

'According to the Chancery, you paid a call on Donato de' Peruzzi when you were last in London. Pardon the intrusion, but may I ask why?'

'The Chancery has more eyes than Argus. Yes, I did so at the king's request. I negotiated a loan of forty thousand pounds from the Peruzzi bank.'

'That seems quite a small sum, given the scale of the king's other borrowings,' Stanton said.

'It covered an urgent need. We are in negotiations with the Flemish cities of the League of Three, Ghent, Bruges and Ypres. The captain general asked for forty thousand pounds, which he claimed was necessary to bribe the burgemeesters and aldermen of the cities to join us. We didn't have forty thousand pounds or anything like it, but we were told Peruzzi could raise the money quickly. The king asked me to come to London and make the arrangements.'

'Forgive me, Sir Geoffrey, but was that entirely wise?' Merrivale asked. 'We all know Donato de' Peruzzi's history.'

Scrope frowned a little. 'Yes, he changed sides in Savoy. In fairness, though, he did so because he believed your relationship with King Jean had become compromised. I am not blaming you, Simon, but we all must recognise that your actions had consequences. I cannot say that Peruzzi was entirely at fault.'

Stanton intervened. 'Peruzzi is well known as an adherent of the Guelph faction, and so too are the Solaros. They have a natural affinity with France, our enemy. Should we trust them?'

'Dealing with any bank is risky,' Scrope said. 'At another time we might be more particular about which moneylenders we deal with. At the moment, we have little choice.'

Moleyns had said the same. Merrivale wondered how true this was, or whether the king's advisors were falling into a trap. 'You told us Peruzzi has friends at court,' he said. 'Other people have said the same. Do you know who those friends are, Sir Geoffrey?'

The corners of Scrope's mouth twitched a little. 'I think the question you are really asking is, am I one of them? The answer is no. My loyalty is to the king alone. As for the identity of the others, I have never troubled to speculate.'

'Why not?'

'Because I have other, rather more pressing things to think about. The siege of Cambrai, the French army mustering on the Somme and the Flemish alliance, to name just three. May I offer you a word of advice, Simon? I fully understand your anger, and in your shoes I would feel the same. But do not start a feud with Peruzzi, not now. If you want the king's forgiveness, let the past rest.'

Merrivale smiled a little. 'If only it were that simple,' he said.

Stanton and Merrivale stood on high ground at the edge of the camp, shading their eyes against the sun and looking out towards the embattled walls of Cambrai. The banners of the defenders were specks of bright colours against the blue sky. The cannon boomed again, belching clouds of yellow-white smoke. 'High walls and a wide moat flooded by the river,' Stanton said. 'There is little hope of breaching those walls and absolutely none of undermining them. The only chance is an escalade.'

'And the battlements are well manned,' said Merrivale.

'Yes. I'm glad it won't be me leading the charge. Do you suppose Scrope knows about Peruzzi's double-dealing?'

'He may know, but he doesn't care,' Merrivale said. 'He is carrying out the king's wishes, just like Moleyns. They know there is corruption but they won't stop it. Leakage, Moleyns called it. The price to be paid for getting the king his money.'

'Ask any sheriff,' said Stanton. 'They'll tell you that sometimes you have to ignore petty crimes in order to preserve the greater order.'

'Murder is not a petty crime, John.'

'No.' Stanton looked at him. 'So, what now?'

'Back to Antwerp. It is time we had a quiet word with Edmund Gonville.'

17

Antwerp, October 1339

The late summer warmth had gone, and the west wind smelled of sea mist and cold. Clouds on the horizon held the promise of storms. Dismounting in the courtyard of the Burcht, Merrivale handed over the reins to Warin and followed John Stanton into the hall. Servants brought them warm wine and they slumped down on benches, aching from the long ride.

Alice Bedingfield came and stood in front of them, the corners of her mouth turned down. 'You have returned,' said the queen's lady-in-waiting. 'Are the walls of Cambrai still standing?'

'As strong as ever,' Merrivale said. 'The city is impregnable and the French army is growing in strength. The king hopes the French will advance and he can tempt them into battle while the odds are still in his favour, but that seems unlikely.'

'Of course,' she said. 'The French know we are short of money. All they need do is wait until the cupboard is bare, and we are forced to retreat.'

'You'd have made a fine captain of men, Alice.'

'Better than some.' Alice sat down beside him and helped herself to a glass of wine. 'It is good to see you too, John,' she said to Stanton. 'You must be tired after your long journey, and in need of a rest.'

Stanton smiled. 'I can take a hint.'

He rose and walked out of the hall. Merrivale looked at Alice for a moment. 'How is the queen?'

'She divides her time between quarrelling with her brother and scolding her children. Two of her favourite occupations. I didn't come here to talk about the queen.'

Merrivale said nothing. 'What did the king say?' she asked quietly.

'Actually, he was surprisingly lenient. I escaped with only minor damage to my dignity. Not that I had much of it left in any case.'

She hesitated for a moment. 'I have had a letter from Munich. Yolande is alive.'

He looked at her for a long moment. 'There is more?'

'There is more. She is married.'

He felt as if someone had punched him in the chest. When he could breathe again he said, 'To whom?'

'Guy of Dampierre, the Count of Béthune. One of King Jean's retainers.'

'Someone who will keep me safely away from her. This really is the end. There is no hope now.'

Alice took his hand in hers. 'If there is anything I can do, Simon, you must tell me. Anything at all.'

Harshness and brutality could be endured; it was kindness that eroded the steel wall around his soul. He felt the pain in his chest again. 'There is nothing anyone can do.'

'Weep if you wish to, Simon,' she said gently. 'It is not a sign of weakness.'

He had not realised there were tears in his eyes until then. He brushed them away. 'She filled my soul with light, Alice. I grew up in a time of death and darkness, and my life has been full of long roads. She was all the things I have missed in life, and when I was with her I finally realised why I had been born. And I lost her.'

He sat for a moment, gazing into space. 'No one will ever replace her,' he said.

'No one should,' said Alice. 'At least you had your time together, brief though it was. That is a precious gift, my dear.'

Merrivale looked at her. 'Are you saying that this is the price I must pay for having once been happy?'

'I hope I never say anything that trite. Treasure the memories you have of her, and live a life that is worthy of her.' She paused for a moment. 'Actually, that sounds trite as well. But you know what I mean.'

'Will that make the pain disappear?'

'No,' Alice said. 'We all feel pain, from the moment we lose our innocence.'

'Even you?'

'Yes,' she said. 'Even me.'

Merrivale looked down for a moment. 'I am sorry, Alice. What a stupid and thoughtless thing to say.'

'It is understandable. Outwardly, I know I am the personification of sunshine. That is the face I put on for the world, especially for the queen. But Simon, I have never known the kind of happiness you had with Yolande, never once. And I doubt if I ever will.'

It was said without self-pity, a simple statement of fact. 'You put me to shame,' he said.

'That was never my intention.'

Outside the wind was rising, the storm drawing closer. A vision of his father came to Merrivale's mind, hunched over and staring into the glowing coals of the brazier. *I'm just a burden to you. I'm a burden to everyone…*

He wiped his eyes, crushing the thought. 'Let's change the subject. What can you tell me about Edmund Gonville?'

She looked surprised. 'That odious little squirt? Why do you want to know about him?'

'I have a score to settle with him. He has not been long at court, has he? He arrived after I left for Savoy.'

'Yes. Bishop Burghersh recommended him. The king took to him at once, and he has been a trusted and favoured servant ever since.'

'Why do you call him odious?'

'My dear, he is the most pompous creature God ever created. His father is a merchant who paid for his education at Cambridge, but he acts like he was born to the purple, going about with his nose in the air and treating his servants and underlings like they are so much dirt on his shoes. The rumour is he wants a bishop's mitre.'

'Will he get it?'

'Possibly, if he can persuade some cathedral chapter to elect him. He'll have the king's backing if he does. His Grace thinks the sun shines out of his fundament.'

'He has risen to high office very quickly,' Merrivale said.

'Too quickly, if you ask me. Sometimes I wonder if he is a French spy.'

Merrivale had not considered this. 'His father is French, but he has been settled in England for many years.'

'That means absolutely nothing,' said Alice.

'Why is he in Antwerp? Scrope said something about him assisting Bishop Burghersh.'

'Yes, the bishop asked for his services. Burghersh is handling most of the negotiations with our supposed allies, including handing over the enormous subsidies they demand. He is also leading our negotiations with the Flemings.'

'Will Flanders really join us?'

'The League of Three will, Bruges and Ypres and Ghent. The Count of Flanders and the nobility are still solidly for the French, but they don't have enough power to stand up to the cities.'

'What do the cities want in return?' Merrivale asked.

'Access to markets where they can buy our wool. And money, of course.'

'Forty thousand pounds,' Merrivale said. 'What is Gonville's role in all of this?'

'I don't know,' Alice said. 'Would you like me to find out?'

'It could be dangerous. Men have been killed already.'

'Oh, I shall simply ask the queen. She advises Bishop Burghersh on negotiations with the allies, and she knows everything that is happening.'

Queen Philippa's home county of Hainault was a neighbour of both Brabant and Flanders; the Count of Hainault, Willem of Avesnes, was her brother. There was little she did not know about the politics of her homeland. She was also her husband's most loyal lieutenant, and the 'advice' she gave the bishop was probably something closer to instructions. 'What is this score you want to settle?' Alice asked.

Rain hammered against the windows of the hall, driven hard by the wind. He told Alice about his abduction by Denton's men, and the death of John Hull. 'Aufrej Solaro has returned to Antwerp,' she said when he had finished. 'He lends money to Cousin Jan of Brabant and Brother Willem of Hainault as well as the king, and his house is well protected. If you intend to do what I think you intend to do, be careful.'

'Protected against whom?'

'Their rivals from Asti, a Ghibelline faction known as the Company of the Leopard.'

'Then I want to talk to the Leopards,' Merrivale said.

They could not confront Gonville directly, Stanton agreed; he had both Burghersh and the king as his patrons and his claim to have a writ under the privy seal had probably been true, no matter how that seal might have been obtained. 'How shall we deal with him?' Stanton asked.

'When I saw Gonville at Burstwick, he was full of bluster,' Merrivale said, 'but he was also nervous. He must know we have arrived in Antwerp, but not necessarily why. Let's wait and see how he responds.'

They dined that afternoon with the rest of the queen's household. Bishop Burghersh, a red-faced balding man in black, sat at the head table in earnest conversation with the queen herself. Gonville was on the far side of the hall with some of the queen's clerks, dressed all in black too with a close-fitting cap on his head. He did not look at Merrivale, or acknowledge his presence.

The dinner was good; Queen Philippa liked her food and employed fine cooks. Roast duck with garlic and ginger sauce, beef with a green sauce sharpened with verjuice, stuffed chicken, wafers with jelly and candied quinces were accompanied by a German wine which Stanton pronounced to be pleasant if a little lacking in fire.

After dinner there was music, viols and rebec and shawm warbling their way through Lescurel's '*Douce amour, confortez moi*', and Alice Bedingfield came down to speak to them. 'Gonville handles the transactions between the banks and our gallant allies,' she said. 'He tells the banks how much to disburse and when, and in what currencies.'

Stanton looked puzzled. 'Anyone can do that. Why did Burghersh request Gonville's services in particular?'

'Unless there is something more that we don't know about,' said Merrivale.

Alice looked across the room at Gonville. 'What are you going to do?' she asked, lowering her voice.

'Wait for him to make a mistake,' Merrivale said quietly.

She looked sceptical. 'Waiting for the other side to make the first move? That doesn't sound very much like you, Simon.'

'Circumstances are forcing me to learn patience.'

The same could not be said of Gonville. Now he was watching Merrivale, his pale face quiet, his long fingers twisting around the stem of his wine goblet. Merrivale met his gaze and held it for a few seconds before looking deliberately away. Rising to his feet, he bowed to the queen and walked out of the hall into the antechamber, where he stood looking through the open door at the rain falling in the courtyard. Perhaps a minute passed before Gonville came out to join him.

'What are you doing here?' the clerk demanded.

'I am on the king's business,' Merrivale said.

'The king no longer employs you.'

'Send word to Cambrai if you doubt me.'

Gonville took a step closer. 'I insist on knowing why you are here.'

'Why really did you and Robert Denton abduct me back in June? I'm angry about that, by the way. The rest of my party were attacked and one of them was killed. Thanks to you, I wasn't there to defend them.'

'I am sorry for John Hull's death,' Gonville said. 'But I did what I had to do. As I told you, I was acting in the king's name.'

'Oh, yes, you had a writ. Shall I tell you what I think you were really doing? You claimed the king had authorised wool smuggling, but that was not entirely true. Pole's syndicate had discovered that Peruzzi was trying to move in on the wool trade, and were fighting back. The king sent you with instructions to both sides to stop locking horns and start working together. I suspect the king had forced Pole to agree to this, and you carried Pole's orders to Denton.'

'Who have you been talking to?' Gonville demanded.

'Pole, and Peruzzi. Both were surprisingly forthcoming, and gave us a number of details about their business.'

That could mean anything, of course. He watched Gonville's hands clench and unclench again. 'You are right,' the other man said finally. 'The king desired the trade to be conducted swiftly and without interruption. In exchange, it was agreed that the English merchants would secretly be allowed to export wool free of duty. The king would still receive his share of the profits from the sale of wool.'

'And when I started to sniff around, you saw a risk that this secret arrangement might be exposed. You spun me a story in order to put me off. I still don't see why you had to abduct me.'

'Would you have come willingly?'

'Yes,' Merrivale said. 'I had been wanting to speak to you for quite some time.'

The hands clenched again. 'What about?'

'Ralph Dunham,' Merrivale said. 'You recommended him to the queen mother's household. Why?'

Gonville looked surprised. 'They wanted a reliable clerk. I knew Dunham was a good man, or I thought I did, so I put his name forward.'

'You paid for him to be educated at Cambridge, I believe.'

'Yes. What does this matter? He is dead and the entire unpleasant business with the saffron is closed.'

'Mm,' Merrivale said. 'Yes and no. I think the poison that killed him was procured by one of the crokers, Nicholas le Flemyng. You wouldn't happen to know where he is, would you?'

'Why would I? Westacre brought him into the saffron scheme, I had nothing to do with it.'

'He left Colchester back in the spring, probably bound for Ghent. I wondered if you had heard of him here in Antwerp.'

'No,' Gonville said shortly.

'Very well. Someone in the queen mother's household is still stealing from her. I would like to know who it is.'

Gonville nodded slowly. 'So *that* is why you are here. What makes you think I might know?'

Merrivale looked surprised. 'Did I say you did?'

'Don't play me for a fool, Merrivale. And you are following a false trail. I know all the officials in Queen Isabella's household, and they are utterly reliable. Dunham was a bad apple in the barrel, that's all. If there is theft, as you allege, it must be coming from the minor servants. She doesn't pay very well, so it is not surprising if they pilfer from her.'

Merrivale thought for a moment. 'Very well,' he said. 'I will make further inquiries.'

'How long do you intend to remain at court?'

'A little longer. The king has charged me to work with John Stanton.'

'And what is Stanton's business?'

'The king has sent for his falcons. Apparently, he anticipates having plenty of time to go hunting this winter. Stanton has been ordered to ensure that the falconers and birds arrive in Antwerp without delay. Why this takes two of us, I don't know, but those are the king's orders.' He looked Gonville up and down. 'I am sure we can manage to stay out of each other's way.'

Gonville turned on his heel and left. Merrivale waited for a while, watching the rain. Five minutes later Stanton came out to see him. 'Well?'

'I am not sure which of us told more lies,' Merrivale said. He told Stanton about the falcons. 'It's not much of a story, but it was all I could think of on the spur of the moment.'

'It hardly matters. I doubt he would have believed anything you told him, not even the truth. Did you get anything from him?'

'He let one thing slip. He says he knows all of Queen Isabella's household. If so, that means he knows who the corrupt members are. And of course, they are the ones who have been providing him with information about our movements since the beginning.'

Stanton thought for a moment. 'I have an idea how we might find out,' he said. 'I should have thought of this earlier. Leave this with me.'

'Alice thought Gonville might be a French spy. It was said in whimsy, but I wonder.'

'If so, then whoever gives Gonville his orders is also a French agent. Someone in a position of power in England is also betraying us.' Stanton paused. 'Bishop Burghersh is Gonville's patron.'

'Henry Burghersh, Bishop of Lincoln, former Lord Chancellor, former Lord Treasurer, friend to both Queen Isabella and the king, and about the only man to have served with distinction in the governments of both. Are you saying he is also a French spy?'

'No. Burghersh is loyal to the crown, and besides he already has all the power and riches a man could desire. But he must know Gonville well, and he probably knows who Gonville's associates are. He could at least tell us where to look.'

'We can hardly go and ask him.'

'Not directly, no. But I'll see if I can contrive a meeting with him on some other pretext.' Stanton smiled. 'I'm told he is fond of hawking.'

'See if you can bring him to the lure. I'm going to track down the Company of the Leopard.'

Like the animal for which it was named, the Company of the Leopard proved to be elusive. Three days passed, and it was only a chance conversation with one of the burgemeesters of Antwerp's clerks that finally gave Merrivale a clue. 'I don't know where the Leopards are, or even if they have an office in Antwerp,' the clerk said. 'But Orland Turc will know. You'll find him in Swarte Susters-Straet, last house on the left.'

Swarte Susters-Straet was a narrow cobbled lane with a row of tall houses on one side and a Dominican convent on the other. Merrivale knocked at the gate and waited. After some time, a grille in the gate slid open. 'Who are you?' a voice demanded.

'My name is Simon Merrivale and I am in the service of King Edward of England. I wish to see Orland Turc.'

'Do you have an appointment?'

'No.'

The grille slammed shut. Merrivale knocked again, harder. '*Apri il cancel!*' he commanded. 'Open the gate!'

The gate opened. Two men stood in the archway, one armed with a wooden staff, the other with a short-bladed sword. 'Is this Piedmontese hospitality?' Merrivale demanded. 'Do the men of Asti keep their guests waiting in the streets now?'

'*Pòrs Dé!*' said the swordsman. 'Get out of here, you shit, or I will send you to hell where you belong!'

Merrivale looked at the sword. 'You had better hope you know how to use that.'

'Anton!' said another voice. 'What is going on? Who is at the gate?'

'Someone who claims to be an *Inglèis*,' said the swordsman. 'He asked to see you, Orland.'

A tall man in a red coat and hose walked in from the courtyard. 'Take his weapons,' he said.

Merrivale unbuckled his sword belt and laid his sword on the ground, dropping his dagger after it. 'I did not realise banking was so dangerous,' he said.

'It is in Antwerp,' said the man in red. He turned to Anton, the swordsman. 'Bring him.'

They walked across the courtyard and up the steps into the hall. The man in red walked over to the hearth and spread his hands by the flames, warming them. 'I am Orland Turc de Castel,' he said. 'This is my junior partner, Anton Turc. What is your business with me? And I warn you, it had better be legitimate. We have efficient ways of disposing of our enemies.'

'The Turc family are Ghibellines,' Merrivale said. 'Foes of the popes and France. That means you are also enemies of the Solaros.'

'We are the foes of all Guelphs. What of it?'

'Aufrej Solaro is my enemy also. I think we can help each other.'

There was a short pause. 'What did Aufrej do to deserve your hatred?'

'He murdered a friend of mine.'

Understanding dawned in Orland Turc's face. 'Ah. So it is a blood feud.' He looked at the younger man, Anton, and nodded. A little reluctantly, Anton sheathed his sword.

'I do not know how much help we can give,' Orland said. 'The Solaros are the lords of Asti, and all-powerful. We and the other Ghibelline families have been exiled from the city. We are weak.'

'Not so weak as all that. Tell me about the Company of the Leopard.'

The other two exchanged glances. 'You are looking at it,' Orland said. 'Or part of it, at least. We have banded together with some of the other exiles to form a new banking consortium. As Ghibellines, we of course support the Holy Roman Emperor and his ally, the king of England.'

'And you see an opportunity to do business with England, and recoup some of your family's lost fortunes,' Merrivale said.

'Of course. But the English refuse to see us. They do business with the Solaros instead.'

'The Solaros have a powerful protector, Donato de' Peruzzi. I suspect he is using his influence at court to block you.'

'That is my belief also. I am sorry, but I do not see how you can touch Aufrej Solaro. You cannot arrest him, and assassination and poison will not work.'

'We have tried,' said Anton Turc.

'There is another way,' Merrivale said. 'Donato de' Peruzzi was financing Doria and Grimaldi to attack England. He used Aufrej Solaro and his bank to channel money to the galleys. I put a stop to that, with the result that the galley crews deserted and went home.'

Both of the others stared at him. 'This is interesting,' Orland Turc said slowly. 'Very interesting. I heard the galleys had retired, but I did not know why. When several thousand angry sailors descend on Genoa there will be trouble, not just there but all across Lombardy.'

'I'm not interested in Lombardy's problems,' Merrivale said. 'King Edward does not know that the Solaros were aiding his enemies. If we can find proof that they were doing so, he will cut them off and the Duke of Brabant will close down their bank. The Company of the Leopard can step into the gap and become the king's new Lombard bankers.'

'And without protectors, Aufrej Solaro and his men will be vulnerable,' said the younger man. 'We might settle a few scores of our own.'

'That would be pleasing,' Orland said. 'But finding proof will not be easy. The Solaro records are kept in a secure strongroom, and the last spy we sent into their household was caught and strangled within a day. Taking prisoners will not work either. The Guelphs hate the Ghibellines so much they will tell us nothing, not even under torture.'

'We have tried that too,' said Anton.

Merrivale nodded. 'I can afford to be patient,' he said.

'So can we,' said Orland, and he smiled for the first time. 'The Solaros have held power in Asti for decades; a few more weeks will not matter. My apologies, sir, for our ungracious welcome of you. We are used to being attacked, and we do not always see strangers as our friends.'

Merrivale smiled too. 'Try being a King's Messenger,' he said.

Back at the castle, Merrivale became aware of a commotion in the tower where Bishop Burghersh and his staff had their quarters. He spotted Alice Bedingfield and hurried towards her. 'What has happened?'

'It's Gonville. He is very ill.'

Merrivale hurried up the tower's spiral stairs. A little group of people had gathered outside one of the chambers, peering anxiously through the open door. Pushing his way into the room he found Gonville lying on his side on a bed, his knees drawn up almost to his chin. Jordan of Canterbury, the royal physician, stood over him holding a basin. The sour smell of vomit filled the air. 'What is it?' Merrivale asked.

'Look at his hands,' Canterbury said grimly.

Merrivale looked. Gonville's hands were red and blotchy with small dark lesions on the skin, his fingernails marked with pale white parallel stripes. Edmund Gonville had been poisoned with arsenic.

18

Antwerp, October 1339

Gonville was unconscious and breathing shallowly. 'Who found him?' Merrivale asked.

'His servant,' Canterbury said. 'He came in about an hour ago and discovered his master lying on the floor.'

'Did Gonville call for help before he collapsed?'

'If so, no one heard him. It is possible that the cramps were so painful that he was unable to speak. The servant ran to find me, and we managed to get him onto the bed. I gave him a strong emetic in hopes of expelling the arsenic from his stomach, but I was too late. The poison has already entered his vital organs.'

'Is there an antidote?'

'Not that I know of. All the local guild of apothecaries could suggest was leeches and plasters.'

'How far is it to Ghent?' Merrivale asked.

John Stanton pushed his way through the crowd. 'About thirty miles,' he said.

'Send a messenger as soon as possible. Find Mistress Cassandra Wesenham and bring her here. Tell her Simon Merrivale asks it.'

'I'll carry the message myself.' Stanton turned and hurried down the stairs.

'A woman?' said Canterbury.

'She trained at Salerno and she knows about arsenic.'

They heard Stanton's horse clattering across the courtyard and out through the castle gates. Gonville's breathing was shallow, but at least it was regular. If Cassandra could arrive by tomorrow there might be a chance to save him.

The onlookers began to drift away. Rising, Merrivale looked around the room. It was comfortably furnished with a bed, table, chair and a couple of wooden stools; a charcoal brazier provided heat. Pens, ink and parchment were laid out on the table next to a goblet, a flask of wine and a jug of water. Gonville had been working when he collapsed, but the parchment contained only a partial sentence, *Archiepiscopus Balduinus coronam Vivelin Rus desiderat hoc monet*… Merrivale read this twice, trying to work out what it might mean. Balduinus was presumably Archbishop Balduin of Trier, but what crown might he want, and why? And who or what was Vivelin Rus?

A painted wooden chest stood at one end of the room. Opening it, Merrivale found it was full of Gonville's personal effects including some very well-made clothes of fine wool and silk, a pair of silver cups, and two purses. One was full and bulging with gold florins; the other contained mixed silver coinage, English groats, groschen from Brabant and Holland, and some obols bearing the image of San Sgond, the patron saint of Asti. That might mean something, or it might not… There were no parchment rolls or documents of any kind. Clearly, whatever records Gonville worked on were kept elsewhere.

Jordan of Canterbury touched the sick man's neck, checking his pulse. 'When might he have been poisoned?' Merrivale asked.

'Judging by the symptoms, he had been ingesting arsenic for several days. He must have been feeling unwell, but he said nothing to anyone.'

Merrivale opened the wine flask and sniffed the contents. There was nothing unusual, but of course arsenic was odourless and tasteless. 'Where is his servant now?'

'I sent him away. He was very distressed, and seemed to think he would be blamed for what happened to his master.'

In the kitchen one of the cooks pointed out Gonville's servant, a thin man sitting crouched and shivering on a bench. His clothes were ragged and patched. Gonville, it seemed, did not believe in paying his servants well. It was often thus with the rich; the inability to part with money was one of the things that made them rich in the first place. Merrivale sat down beside him. 'Did you know your master was ill?' he asked quietly.

'He was unwell last evening, sir, sweating and suffering from a headache, but he said it was probably just a rheum. He seemed better this morning, and said he was going to do some work after dinner. He sent me out to buy a bottle of ink. When I returned I found him lying on the floor.' The man hesitated for a moment. 'Is it poison, sir?'

'Yes,' said Merrivale. 'Did you fetch the water and wine?'

'No, sir, that was one of the butler's staff. They always brought it up for him, the same time every day, so he could take a glass while he worked. Will I be punished, sir?'

'No. This is nothing to do with you.'

He went into the buttery and questioned the other servants, who looked helplessly at each other. 'I took his wine up this afternoon, sir,' one of them said. 'But when I knocked at the door he said he had already been served and sent me away.'

'Could someone else have entered the buttery and taken some wine?'

'Yes, sir, I suppose that is possible.'

Butteries were supposed to be kept locked and secure to prevent servants from pilfering wine. Perhaps the staff were trusted here. Or perhaps the pilfering went on anyway, and no one cared. *Leakage*.

'Have you seen any strangers around the castle? In particular, a young man with fair hair and a big nose? He might have been wearing a pilgrim's badge, a scallop shell.'

'I don't recall him, sir. The castle is busy, people come and go all the time.'

That was certainly true. Merrivale returned to the tower and climbed up to Bishop Burghersh's office on the top floor. The bishop was seated behind a heavy oak table, his face redder than ever. 'Will he live?'

'His chances are not good, Your Grace. We have sent for help, but it will take time to arrive.'

'Pity. He's a good fellow. Very useful.'

It was hardly a ringing endorsement of the man whose career Burghersh had fostered and whose services he had especially asked for. 'We should establish an inquisition, Your Grace.'

Burghersh rubbed his chin. 'Any chance it could have been an accident?'

'It is highly unlikely. Arsenic is found in some kinds of paint, but Gonville was not an artist and he did not wear face paint.'

'Let's wait and see if he recovers. If he does, he can tell us what happened. If there is an inquisition, I will handle it.'

Merrivale raised his eyebrows. 'I understand Your Grace is leading the Flemish negotiations. Will you have time?'

'I doubt it will take long. This is clearly the work of French spies. They tried to kill Gonville in order to disrupt our negotiations with the Flemish cities.'

'What about his colleagues here at court? Is there anyone who might have a grudge against him?'

The bishop's eyebrows closed together. 'I said I would handle this, Merrivale.'

'Yes, Your Grace. Gonville kept no papers in his room. May I know what he was working on?'

The red deepened to a shade of purple. 'Of course not! For God's sake, Merrivale, you used to be a King's Messenger! How can you even think of asking such a question? His work was highly confidential and all his papers are locked in a strongbox. Now, if you'll forgive me, I have important matters to attend to.'

Merrivale bowed again and departed. Down in Gonville's room he found Jordan of Canterbury packing up his box of medical instruments. 'At the moment, I can do no more,' the physician said.

'I will stay with him.'

'Call me if his condition worsens. I will send someone to relieve you tonight.'

Merrivale shook his head. 'I will remain here until Mistress Wesenham arrives. Everyone in the castle will know that he is still alive, including the men who tried to kill him. It is quite possible that they will come back to finish what they began.'

He waited all night, listening to the sick man's laboured breathing and the soft sounds of the night in the castle around him. Once or twice he heard footsteps on the stairs, but they passed by the door to the chamber without stopping.

Morning brought wind and rain rattling hard against the shutters. It also brought Stanton and Cassandra Wesenham, sooner than expected. 'I found a boatman willing to take us downriver by night,' Stanton said. 'I won't tell you how much I had to pay him.'

Shedding her wet cloak, Cassandra knelt beside the bed and listened to Gonville's breathing. 'I need hot soup,' she said. 'Beef for preference, but fish will do. And plain pottage mixed with ground-up walnuts or hazelnuts.'

'I'll go to the kitchen,' Stanton said.

Opening her travelling case, Cassandra took out a phial and poured a thick red liquid into a spoon. 'I need to feed him this,' she said to Merrivale. 'Help me open his mouth.'

'What is it?'

'Pomegranate syrup.'

Merrivale held the sick man's head, opening his jaws, and Cassandra poured the liquid slowly down his throat. Gonville coughed once, struggling, but his eyes did not open. 'It will be some time before we see a response,' Cassandra said. 'What treatment has he been given?'

'The physician gave him an emetic.'

She shook her head. 'That only works immediately after the poison is ingested. Once it enters the body the best treatment is to ingest fluids, to try and flush the arsenic through.'

'What about the nuts, and the pomegranate syrup?'

'They are known to be efficacious. I don't know why.'

'You don't?'

She looked at him. 'Sometimes in science we know the effects of things, Master Merrivale, without necessarily understanding their causes.'

'That sounds suspiciously like faith to me,' Merrivale said.

She gave him a level stare, and he bowed his head in contrition. 'Thank you for coming,' he said. 'The royal physician is out of his depth and the local apothecaries are useless. You were the only person I could turn to.'

'I am touched by your faith in me. Master Stanton told me who he is, and why he is important. I will save his life if I can, but I make no promises.'

'I would not ask you to.' Merrivale rubbed his eyes and she touched him on the arm. 'Go and get some sleep,' she said. 'I will send for you if there is any change in his condition.'

Merrivale slept for most of the day, waking only when a hand touched his shoulder. 'Sorry to disturb you, sir,' Warin said. 'The wise woman is asking for you.'

'Don't call her that where she can hear you.' Rising and pulling on his clothes, Merrivale hurried across the courtyard and up to Gonville's room. Cassandra and Jordan of Canterbury stood looking down at the sick man, who was stirring a little. His eyes were still closed and he was only semi-conscious.

'Will he recover?' Merrivale asked.

'Possibly,' she said, her voice cautious. 'What he needs now is nutrition, to force the remainder of the poison out of his organs and help him build up his strength. Continue to give him soup and pottage, as much as he can take.'

'"Certain foods help us to regulate the body,"' Merrivale quoted.

'They do,' said Jordan of Canterbury, 'but I would not have known which ones to use in this case. Mistress Wesenham, you are a miracle worker.'

'Do not thank me yet, sir. He is not out of danger.'

'I understand. Now, you too must rest.'

Merrivale walked her down to the courtyard. 'Why was he poisoned?' she asked as they stepped out into the autumn rain.

'I assume because someone saw him talking to me. They suspected, wrongly, that he had betrayed them and so they ordered his death. We'll probably never know who administered the arsenic, but I'm not interested in them. I want the people who gave the orders.'

'Do you think he will betray them now?' she asked.

'I don't know. I hope so, because if he doesn't, they will try to kill him again. These people don't like leaving witnesses.'

'What about you? They'll try to kill you too, of course.'

'Yes,' he said. 'They will try.'

Cassandra gazed at him. 'Do you really believe you are invincible?'

His expression did not change. 'I have to. Otherwise, nothing makes any sense.'

She was silent for a moment. 'Do you remember the croker, Nicholas le Flemyng?' she asked finally. 'He is in Ghent.'

Merrivale was alert. 'Does he know you are there?'

'I don't think so. I saw him only once, and I don't believe he recognised me. Is he dangerous?'

'I don't know, but take no chances. Stay away from him. How long before I can speak to Gonville?'

'If his health continues to improve, perhaps the day after tomorrow, but not for long. It will be many days before he fully recovers.'

Merrivale met Stanton in the city later that day. 'Have you approached Bishop Burghersh about Gonville's associates?' he asked.

'Yes,' Stanton said, 'and he told me to mind my own business. I'm afraid I lost my temper and demanded whether he knew about the smuggling. He said of course he knew, but what was he meant to do about it? I said there should be a full inquisition led by the Lord Chancellor with authority to take depositions from everyone involved, including the king's own household, and he said that would just be making more work for lawyers like myself. As if I'm somehow going to profit from all this!'

'He wants the whole business to disappear.'

'That's exactly what he said. An inquisition would be a waste of time and money, at a time when we don't have enough of either. We need to get on with concluding the Flemish alliance and winning the war, that's all that matters.'

'And so, the greedy will continue to profit,' Merrivale said. 'They always have done and they always will. We have another problem.'

He told Stanton what Cassandra had said about Nicholas le Flemyng. 'When I saw the signs of arsenic poisoning I thought at once of Dunham. It may be coincidence, or it may be that the same poisoner is at work. Can we find out if Flemyng has been seen in Antwerp?'

'I will make inquiries. What do we do about Gonville?'

'When he wakes, let me talk to him alone. Two of us could make it seem like a formal interview, and put him off. I promise to be gentle.'

Stanton grinned. 'There's a first time for everything,' he said.

Two days later, Cassandra showed Merrivale into Gonville's room. The clerk was sitting up against a bolster, a bowl of fish broth on the table beside him. 'How are you feeling?' Merrivale asked.

'Sick as hell,' Gonville said. 'But still alive, which I suppose is better than the alternative.'

His eyes were dull and the skin of his face was blotchy. 'Not long,' Cassandra warned. 'I will be here in case of need.'

She took a seat on the far side of the chamber, her hands folded in her lap. Merrivale turned back to the sick man. 'I need to ask you some questions, but only if you are strong enough to answer them.'

'Why should I cooperate with you?'

'Because it might save your life. You know they will try again.'

There was a long pause. 'What do you want to know?' Gonville asked finally.

Merrivale held out the document the clerk had been writing when he collapsed. 'What is this about the archbishop wanting a crown? Is this something to do with the loan he has made to the king?'

'Yes,' Gonville said reluctantly. 'Balduin's consortium set very stiff terms. As well as interest and penalty charges, they have asked for custody of the great crown of England, as a pledge to ensure the loan is repaid.'

Merrivale was astonished. 'The king's crown? And you agreed?'

'Moleyns agreed, yes. His is under orders to do whatever it takes to get the money in. The crown was sent under guard to Trier last month.'

There is literally no limit to the king's desperation, Merrivale thought. Small wonder that people are finding it so easy to exploit him. 'You mentioned someone named Vivelin Rus who is advising the archbishop. Who is he?'

'One of Balduin's councillors. I don't know much about him, apart from a few passing references to him in correspondence. *Honorabilis et sapiens Vivelinus Rus*, that sort of thing. He is English, apparently, and his family come from Bishop's Lynn in Norfolk. Is this important to my case?'

'I don't know. Perhaps not.' Merrivale looked at Cassandra. 'Does the name mean anything to you?'

She shook her head. Merrivale watched her for a moment longer and turned back to Gonville. 'I shall come to the point,' he said. 'You were right about one thing when we met at Burstwick, you were indeed carrying out orders to arrange the smuggling of wool. But those orders did not come from the king, and neither did he instruct Pole and Peruzzi to make peace.'

A little more life came into Gonville's face. 'Why did you pretend to believe me?'

'You had the power to make trouble for me, perhaps even get me expelled from court. I thought that if I could throw you off the scent you would lose interest in me. What I did not foresee is that someone would try to kill you. I apologise for that. I should have been more careful.'

'When we last met, did you say *anything* that was actually true?' Gonville asked.

'Yes,' said Merrivale. 'I am bitterly angry about the death of John Hull, and I intend to see justice done. As for you, Master Gonville, if you wish to live you need to start trusting me. Who gave you the orders about the wool?'

Gonville raised his hands to his chest, pressing his fingertips together as if in prayer. 'Moleyns did,' he said.

Oh, Christ, Merrivale thought. 'What did Moleyns stand to gain? Apart from money?'

There was another long silence. 'There are two factions within the court and government,' Gonville said finally. 'One includes Geoffrey Scrope and Bishop Burghersh, and of course the king himself, who are all in favour of prosecuting the war to its fullest extent. They are considering whether the king should formally lay claim to the throne of France, and declare Philip of Valois a usurper.'

'Thus committing us to a very long and bloody war,' Merrivale said.

'You could put it that way, yes. The other faction, including the Archbishop of Canterbury, his brother the Lord Chancellor, Zouche the Lord Treasurer and many in Parliament, are opposed to the war. The collapse of the wool syndicate was to their advantage, because it deprived the king of the money he needed to make war.'

'And you think Moleyns is in league with this faction?'

'I suspect so, yes.'

'You said you had a writ under the privy seal. What about Kildesby, the keeper of the seal? Is Moleyns giving him orders too?'

'Quite possibly.'

'And the plot against the queen mother's saffron was intended to create yet more turmoil,' Merrivale said.

'It was an attempt to gain influence over her, as I am sure you have guessed. The hope was that, in exchange for clearing her debts, she would use her influence on the king to end the war. His claim to the French throne comes through her, after all.'

Gonville was suddenly very tired. Behind Merrivale, Cassandra rose to her feet. 'One more question,' Merrivale said. 'You still have an agent in the queen mother's household. Who is it?'

'I cannot tell you that.'

'Why not?'

Slowly, Gonville turned his head and gazed into Merrivale's face. 'Don't you understand? He is the one who poisoned me.'

The silence that followed lasted for nearly a minute. 'You claim you want to save my life,' Gonville said. 'If I betray this man, I will surely die. My best hope of survival is to get away from him.'

'Give me proof and I will see him hang. Then you will be safe.'

'There is no proof. Only my word against his.'

'You have influence with the king.'

'And he has influence with the queen mother. I cannot take a chance, Merrivale. I need to get away.'

Merrivale thought for a moment. 'Tell the king you are seriously ill and must retire from court for a while. Master Jordan the physician will confirm that you need time to recover. As soon as you are well enough to travel, go to your father in Norfolk and lie low until this is over. I will ensure that you are protected until you depart.'

Merrivale walked downstairs and waited in the courtyard. Cassandra followed him a few minutes later. 'He is asleep. I think it will be some time before he can travel.'

Merrivale nodded. 'What are you not telling me?'

'Vivelin Rus is a Jewish moneylender in Strassburg. His real name is Velvl Roth and he was born in Bishop's Lynn. His family were merchants there before they were expelled.'

Merrivale blinked in surprise. 'The expulsion of the Jews was nearly fifty years ago. He must be an old man.'

'He is in his mid-sixties, yes.'

'Did your family do business with the Roths?'

'More than that.'

'What do you mean?'

She looked around the courtyard. 'For the love of God tell no one about this,' she said. 'I suffer from enough prejudice already. Velvl Roth is my great-uncle.'

'What happened?' Merrivale asked quietly.

'My grandmother converted to the Christian faith in order to marry my grandfather, so she was allowed to remain in England. Her brother Velvl refused to convert and was expelled with the others. As you can imagine, the two families were sundered. I had all but forgotten the connection until I met Mercuriade.'

'I was right,' Merrivale said. 'Everyone involved in this affair knows everyone else. How does Mercuriade fit in?'

'Strassburg is an imperial free city, a place where people who have been expelled from other places wash up on the tide. Mercuriade spent some time there, seeking refuge from persecution against heretics, and she met Velvl. It was she who told him I was studying in Salerno, and he wrote to me. I called on him when I travelled back to England.'

'What sort of man is he?'

'Elderly, of course, but still hale and hearty when I saw him. Very learned and scholarly. He spends much time with his books.'

'Would you write me a letter of introduction?'

'Why?'

'Because his friends have custody of the crown of England,' Merrivale said. 'And I would very much like to know what they intend to do with it.'

She nodded. 'I will do so. Gonville accuses someone from the queen mother's household of poisoning him. Who do you think it might be?'

Merrivale did not answer. It was obvious who Gonville was alluding to, but he could not bring himself to say the name aloud. It was hard to think that someone he trusted might have betrayed him, but a soft voice in a corner of his mind whispered, *why not? It has happened before.*

Antwerp, October 1339

The smell of leather hung heavy in the air in the Vlaeykensgang, a narrow street lined with shoemakers' workshops. A man in a heavy cloak walked up alongside Merrivale and threw back his hood. 'I hear one of your clerks has been poisoned,' said Anton Turc.

'He will recover. Is there news?'

'The Solaros still hold fast to their house, but they are uneasy. Several couriers arrived from the south last week, probably from their branch in Strassburg, and they also had a visitor from Ghent. Since then they have fortified the doors and windows, and their servants have been practising with crossbows.'

The hair stood up on the back of Merrivale's neck. 'Who was the man from Ghent?'

'It took some time to discover his identity, but he is known as Nicolaes Engels. He is a merchant from Colchester in England. Our agent in Ghent says he recently sold a cargo of saffron. Perhaps now he is forming a venture with the house of Solaro. We know they are seeking new partners.'

'Perhaps. When did he leave?'

'Four days ago, I think. Is he important?'

'Yes. Why are the Solaros looking for new partners?'

'There is a rumour in the money markets that their partnership with Peruzzi has ended.' Turc smiled the cheerful smile of a man watching his enemies crumble. 'They are under pressure, I think.'

'Keep watching them. I need another favour, if you will.'

'What is it?'

'I leave tomorrow and will be away for a few weeks. While I am absent, I need you to put a watch on an English serjeant named John Stanton. Record where he goes and whom he meets, every detail you can.'

'Is he working with the Solaros?'

'I don't know,' Merrivale said. 'That is what I need to find out.'

Ghent, October 1339

Walking through the streets, Merrivale heard the rattle of looms and thump of fulling mills overlaid with the rasp of grinding wheels and hammers of forges producing weapons. Armed patrols bearing the badges of different guilds guarded the bridges and public buildings. In Ghent, the largest and most prosperous city of the League of Three, commerce and war went hand in hand, each depending on the other.

The man known in Colchester as Nicholas le Flemyng and in Flanders as Nicolaes Engels had a fine house on the Korenlei. A ship lay moored in the river outside. Merrivale had half expected Flemyng to refuse to see him, but after a long delay he was finally shown into the hall. Two servants stood at the back of the room, both conspicuously armed.

'How did you find me?' Flemyng demanded.

'It was not difficult. You haven't exactly covered your tracks, which in itself is a little surprising. Perhaps you wanted to be found.'

'Of course I haven't covered my tracks! I have nothing to hide.'

'Well, we both know that is a lie. You killed Ralph Dunham and James Westacre, or at least you helped Brigget to do it, and you doubtless intended to kill Brigget as well and steal the remainder of the saffron crop. You stole Westacre's ship and sailed to Flanders, having first asked your paymaster to ensure that Doria's galleys did not molest you.'

'I did not steal the ship! I bought it from Westacre!'

'I don't believe you. You stole Moreno's pilgrim badge, you stole Westacre's ship, you stole the queen mother's saffron; my God, Flemyng, is there anything genuine about you? Is that even your real name, or did you steal that too?'

The two servants took a step forward, but Flemyng held up a hand. 'Be careful, Merrivale,' he said. 'You are on dangerous ground.'

Merrivale watched the other man closely. 'How much is Donato de' Peruzzi paying you for your services?'

A hesitation, a tiny check, and then Flemyng laughed. 'Peruzzi? My God, Merrivale, you really are a fool. You know nothing, absolutely nothing about what is going on. You're flailing around like a blind man.'

'If not Peruzzi, who? Aufrej Solaro? Is *he* your paymaster? We know you called at his house in Antwerp last week.'

'A merchant pays a visit to his banker!' Flemyng said mockingly. 'My God, whoever heard of such a thing? The world is turned upside down. Like I said, Merrivale, you know nothing. I suggest you leave now, before you humiliate yourself any further.'

'You helped to kill two of the queen mother's servants,' Merrivale said. 'Now you have attempted to kill the king's secretary. Flanders is neutral ground for the moment, and so you are safe. But as soon as the alliance with the League of Three is signed, the king will ask the captain general to arrest you. I understand the castle here in Ghent has an impressive array of instruments of torture. By the time we are done, you will be familiar with every one of them.'

Flemyng said nothing. Merrivale bowed, ironically. 'I wish you good day, Master le Flemyng. I am certain we will meet again, very soon.'

19

Strassburg, November 1339

A cold wind swept up the valley of the Rhine. Already there was snow on the mountains to the west of the city. 'The winters are so cold now,' said Velvl Roth. 'The whole world is growing colder, it seems. When I was a boy the sun seemed always to shine, and people made wine even in England. Now I hear the vineyards are all gone, the grapes killed by frost.'

'I am younger than you,' Merrivale said. 'I remember only the rain.'

Roth studied him. He was a sturdy, strongly built man in his mid-sixties with snow-white hair and beard, but his eyes were bright and clear. His robes were dark and he wore no ornamentation apart from a seal ring with a simple device, a spoked wheel. Cassandra Wesenham's letter of introduction lay open on the table before him.

'You are of an age to have endured the famine, I think,' he said. 'It has left its mark on you.'

Cassandra had said that Roth was a friend of Mercuriade, and the experience of meeting him was much the same; Merrivale felt like part of his soul had been exposed. Perhaps wisdom really did come with age, he thought. He wondered if he would live long enough to find out.

Whither we have sunk, whither we hasten, whence we are redeemed. He really would have to find some way of getting those words out of his head.

'You must be weary after your long journey from Antwerp,' Roth said. 'Please be seated. My servants will bring refreshments.'

Merrivale sat, looking around the room. The shelves were full of scrolls and codexes in Latin, German, Greek and Hebrew, and a star map had been painted on one wall. Candles burned in brass candlesticks, clean white spears of flame. Charcoal glowed in ornate cast-iron braziers, making the room pleasantly warm.

Roth followed his gaze. 'Do you read, Master Merrivale?'

'Not so widely as I should like, or in enough languages.'

'That is a pity. In books we find the experience of others mirrored against our own. They remind us of our common humanity.'

'Perhaps that is why some people find them dangerous,' Merrivale said.

The refreshments arrived, hot sweet white wine flavoured with cinnamon and cloves. The wine came from somewhere further down the Rhine; thanks to Stanton, Merrivale had learned how to recognise the various regions where wine was made. Stanton himself had remained behind in Antwerp; among other things, he was still pressing Bishop Burghersh to open a formal inquisition into the attack on Gonville. *He's trying to sweep everything away*, Stanton had said. *He wants to pretend it all never happened. Every time I ask him to do anything, he says the Flemish negotiations must take priority. I know they are important, but a man nearly died.*

True; but Gonville had claimed he already knew the identity of his poisoner, and that it was someone in the queen mother's household. Merrivale was certain in his own mind that Nicholas le Flemyng had a hand in the poisoning, but as on previous occasions, Flemyng might have been working with someone else. Merrivale had thought of confronting Stanton but decided against it. He had asked the Turcs to watch Stanton, and he had left Warin to watch both Stanton and the Turcs; more, he could not do.

He sipped his wine. 'I am extremely grateful to you for seeing me, Master Roth. King Edward has asked my colleague Master Stanton and myself to look into some issues concerning his finances. Would you be willing to answer some questions?'

'Of course. I will tell you what I can, but I am not certain how much help I can give you.'

'In particular, I wanted to ask you about Archbishop Balduin of Trier and the loan he has made to the king. Are you a member of his syndicate?'

Roth nodded. He did not seem perturbed by the question; probably he had been expecting it. 'Actually, I provided the great majority of the loan. Some of the other Strassburg banks have also contributed, and Balduin himself invested ten thousand florins, but the rest came from myself.'

'How was the money transmitted to King Edward?'

'In the form of bills of exchange, made payable to the treasurer of the king's chamber, John Moleyns. Sir John was also paid a commission for helping to arrange the transaction, as also was Bishop Burghersh.'

'Is that common practice?'

'Of course. Money greases the wheels and makes negotiations move more quickly. Moleyns and Burghersh each received a thousand florins for their troubles.'

A thousand florins was a little over two hundred pounds, a considerable sum of money. 'What role did Burghersh play?'

'He made the initial contact with Archbishop Balduin. Moleyns handled the details after that.'

'May I ask who are the other Strassburg bankers?'

'Most are local moneylenders, but there is one outland bank, the house of Solaro. They contributed five thousand florins. I was intrigued by this, as I thought the Solaro branch in Antwerp handled King Edward's business. Sinibald Solaro, the head of the family here, is more involved in lending to King Jean of Bohemia.'

'They saw a chance to make a profit by playing both sides, perhaps.'

'I suspect you are right,' said Roth. 'When it comes to money, the Solaros are even more unscrupulous than Archbishop Balduin, who of course is also playing both sides. Sometimes I think I am fortunate. As an outcast, I have no side to take. I am free to invest where I wish.'

'Do the Solaros and the other banks know that you are a partner in the syndicate?'

Roth shook his head. 'None of them would have touched the venture had they known a Jewish moneylender was also involved. Only Balduin and his secretary know, along with a few people at the English court.'

'Why invest in England? Taking an objective view, the war is not going well for us. Are you certain you have chosen the winning side?'

'Like all bankers, I loan on the basis of risk. England is a wealthy country with a strong government and effective administration. I judge that there is an excellent chance the loan will be repaid.'

Merrivale looked sceptical. 'Kings have refused to repay loans before, especially when they are already short of money.'

Roth smiled a little. 'I have friends at court. They will protect my interests.'

'Do your friends include John Moleyns and Bishop Burghersh?'

Roth sat back in his chair, gazing at the star chart for the moment. 'I am curious,' he said. 'If you wanted information about our syndicate, you could easily have asked your own officials and saved yourself the trouble. Instead, you rode three hundred miles to interview me. That leads me to two possibilities. You suspect there is corruption among your own officials, and are hoping I can provide evidence. Or, you suspect me.'

'There is a third possibility,' Merrivale said. 'Both could be true. Balduin and the Solaros, and indeed yourself, might have ulterior motives in making this loan, and you and they might be working hand in glove with our own corrupt officials. Balduin asked for the great crown of England as security for the loan. What does he plan to do with it?'

'It was I who asked for the crown,' Roth said.

Merrivale watched him for a moment. 'Why? You said you have friends at court who will protect your interests. But perhaps you don't really trust them after all?'

'Moleyns I do not know,' Roth said. 'But I have known Bishop Burghersh for many years. I have lent him money before, when he was Lord Treasurer of England. We have a mutual interest and yes, I do trust him.'

Roth leaned back in his chair. 'But, as you pointed out, kings can be capricious. They are particularly likely to default on loans to Jewish bankers, knowing that no court of law will give us a sympathetic hearing. So, the crown is my security should King Edward fail to repay.'

'You think the crown is worth 340,000 florins?'

'Nothing like so much. Melted down, it would be worth ten thousand perhaps, the gems a few thousand more. Its value is symbolic. It represents the power of the king.'

'That is what concerns me,' Merrivale said. 'I will be frank with you. There is a strong rumour that King Edward intends to formally claim the throne of France. But if his crown should find its way into French hands, he would look ridiculous. No one would take his claim seriously and his allies would melt away. Whatever else happens, the crown must remain safe.'

'Would you like to see it?' Roth asked.

One of the bookshelves had wooden rollers on its feet. Pulled away from the wall, it revealed an oak door banded with iron. Roth took out a set of keys and unlocked the door. 'We will need light,' he said.

Merrivale picked up a candlestick and followed him. A narrow corridor led to another heavy door set into the wall at a right angle. The space was so cramped that it would be impossible to attack the door with a hammer or a ram. Beyond it, a stair led down to a third door, even stronger than the other two and entirely covered with iron plates. It had three locks, each with a separate key.

'I have seen fortresses that were easier to get in to,' Merrivale said.

'That is the general idea,' Roth said dryly.

Beyond the door was a small plain room lined with shelves full of more rolls of parchment. Two large ironbound chests stood against one wall. Kneeling down, Roth unlocked one of these and lifted out a heavy object wrapped in red silk. Placing the object on a table in the centre of the room, he slowly unwrapped the silk and stood back.

Candlelight flickered off polished gemstones and ornate gleaming gold. The crown was conical in shape, not unlike a helmet, braced with four thick gold arches and topped with a cross pattée. Every square inch of the surface was ornamented with gold bezants and cabochon gems; an enormous red spinel was set in the middle of the cross.

'How many people know it is here?' Merrivale asked.

'Only Balduin knows the exact location. King Edward has been told the crown is in Strassburg, but nothing more. The rest of the world believes it is held in the archbishop's palace in Trier.'

Merrivale said nothing. 'As you can see, not even an army could break into this room,' Roth said. 'The crown is safe, and will remain safe so long as it is in my custody. You have my word of honour that it will not be sent to France.'

After a moment Merrivale nodded. 'Thank you,' he said.

Roth wrapped the crown carefully and returned it to its chest and they retraced their steps, locking each door behind them. Back in the library Roth poured more wine. 'You said you had a mutual interest with Bishop Burghersh,' Merrivale said. 'May I ask what it is?'

The door opened and another man entered. A little younger than Roth, he was tall and thin with a receding hairline and black beard streaked with grey. He bowed when he saw Merrivale. 'My apologies, Velvl. I did not realise you had a guest.'

'Join us, please.' Roth leaned forward and poured another glass of wine. 'This is my friend, Rabbi Levi ben Gershon. He knows all the movements of the stars and planets, and he is the finest mathematician since al-Khwarizmi. Levi, this is Master Simon Merrivale, a servant of King Edward of England. Master Merrivale is also a friend of my great-niece.'

Merrivale bowed. 'He wants to know about my connection with Henry Burghersh', Roth said. 'Do you think I should tell him?'

Gershon sat down on a bench. 'What does your niece say of him?'

'That he is an honest man. Mind you, she is still young.'

'Mercuriade of Salerno would also vouch for me,' Merrivale said. 'Unfortunately, she is far away.'

'Mercuriade is wiser than all of us put together,' Gershon said. 'I think you may tell him, Velvl.'

'Very well.' Roth sipped his wine. 'As Cassandra explained, I was expelled from England along with most of the other Jewish residents when I was a boy. Ever since then, like many of my fellow exiles, I have dreamed of returning home. Some years ago, I was able to contact some of our people who had converted to the Christian faith in order to remain in England.'

'The Domus Conversorum,' Merrivale said.

'That is where I found them, yes. I wrote also to my sister who had remained behind in Lynn, but received no reply. Only much later did I learn she had died.' An expression of pain crossed Roth's face. 'I never had a chance to apologise for the harsh words I spoke to her when we parted.'

'She is in Sheol now, where all things are known,' Gershon said gently. 'She is at peace, brother.'

'But I am not. She chose the path of love, believing it to be more important than faith. At the time I thought she was a traitor, and I used words that I am ashamed to repeat. To atone, I have made it my life's work to help our people return to their homes in England. Through the Domus Conversorum, I learned that Henry Burghersh was sympathetic to our cause and I wrote to him asking for assistance. He and I have worked tirelessly to persuade the king's advisors to allow our return. This loan to the king is part of the plan.'

'What do you mean?' Merrivale asked.

'I have agreed to loan the king a considerable part of my fortune. When the loan comes due, Burghersh will ask the king to issue an edict allowing us to return. If he agrees, I will waive repayment of the loan and return the crown, without any charge or fee. The king will keep his money and our people will fulfil their dreams.'

'Will the king agree?'

'Henry Burghersh thinks he will. The king is a practical man and will choose the path of expediency. Of course there will be opposition by some, for the hatred that drove us out of England has not died. But when the people see that we come in peace and act in good faith, I believe they will receive us.'

Levi ben Gershon nodded. 'As the Rambam reminds us, individuals can be wicked but our common humanity is a force for good. Both of our faiths share this belief. It can be a bond that unites Christians and Jewish people, I think.'

'The Rambam?' Merrivale asked.

'I beg your pardon. I refer to the great scholar of our people, Rabbi Moses ben Maimon. Rambam is the abbreviation of his name which he used in his *Guide for the Perplexed*. That is how we all know him.'

Merrivale nodded. 'But the damage done by wicked individuals often outweighs the good of the rest,' he said. 'Earlier, Master Roth, you mentioned corrupt officials in England. You are right, they do exist. What I do not know is whether these men are deliberately trying to harm the king, or are simply acting out of greed.'

'Greed is deliberate also,' Gershon said. 'We sometimes describe greed as a sickness of the soul. But unlike most illnesses, it is a sickness we embrace willingly. Greed is not forced upon us; we choose it and we embrace it.'

'I am a banker,' Roth said. 'Many would say *I* am greedy.'

'You have always seen money as only a means to an end, my friend. You are a righteous man.'

'And what of those who are not?' Roth asked. 'Why does God not punish them?'

'God will do so in time, but He is slow to anger. And God does not always know which way we will turn. He knows what the possibilities are, what choices we can make, but He has no foreknowledge of which road we will choose to travel.'

'And so evil enters the world,' Merrivale said.

'It was already here, my friend. Evil too is a choice we make.'

'Is it?' asked Merrivale. 'My mother and sisters did not choose to starve to death during the great famine. And no hand of man created the famine. That was the work of God alone.'

'Yet God also enabled you to survive,' Gershon said gently. 'Do you ever wonder why?'

'Yes. Nearly every day.'

There was a silence for a moment. 'I am aware that I have not answered your question,' Roth said. 'The point that Levi was trying to make, albeit in a rather circuitous way, is that whether these men seek power or greed is not the issue. Either way, you are facing an organised conspiracy.'

Queen Isabella had made a similar point, though in a different way. Gershon nodded. 'People who steal from kings do not do so lightly. They lay careful plans and cover their tracks so they cannot be caught. You must think of this conspiracy as an equation, a mathematical puzzle that you must solve.'

'A puzzle of unknown size and shape,' Merrivale said.

'I shall again refer you to the words of the Rambam. When we try to describe God, he says, we fail because we do not know what God is. Instead, we should seek to understand what God is not. When we have finally eliminated all the things that God is not, we are left with the pure essence of truth. Then we truly understand God.'

'You are saying that to understand what this conspiracy is, I should first try to define what it is not.'

'That is the logic,' said Gershon. 'You do not look convinced.'

'Do I not? It is better than any advice I have received so far.'

'I do not doubt the existence of this conspiracy,' Roth said, 'but I can tell you nothing about it. As I explained, my involvement in the loan has been kept secret and I have had no contact with anyone except Archbishop Balduin. But there is someone at the Court of Chancery in London who can help you, a man named Edmund Grimsby.'

'I am grateful to you,' Merrivale said. 'I have already spoken to Grimsby and he was helpful, up to a point.'

'Grimsby will help you,' Roth repeated. 'Especially if you tell him I sent you.'

Light suddenly dawned. 'Is Grimsby a convert?'

'No, but his father was once known as Avigdor Roth. He married Matilda of Grimsby, and took her name when he converted. We are cousins in a distant degree.'

Merrivale nodded. 'Master Roth, Rabbi, it has been a pleasure to speak with you. I wish you good fortune with your venture, and hope that you succeed in all your aims.'

'Amen,' said Levi ben Gershon. 'As for you, my son, do not grieve overmuch for the past. The future will bring its own sorrows, and you must be prepared for them. Believe that the God of truth, the God of faithfulness, will watch over you.'

20

Antwerp, December 1339

Warin took the reins as Merrivale dismounted in the courtyard of the Burcht. Overhead the royal standard flapped in the cold wind. 'Anything to report?' Merrivale asked.

'The Turcs are keeping a close watch on the Solaros, and I reckon the Solaros know they are being watched. The Turcs also have a man trailing Master Stanton every time he leaves the castle.'

Merrivale looked around, lowering his voice. 'And Stanton?'

'He spent an hour closeted with Master Gonville before the latter left for England.'

'When did Gonville leave?'

'About a week ago. According to Mistress Wesenham, he's still not in the best of health. Master Stanton also paid several calls on Bishop Burghersh, and since the king's household returned from Cambrai he has also been closeted with Sir John Moleyns.'

Merrivale considered this. 'Anything else?'

'Master Stanton took delivery of a collection of parchment rolls that came in last week. One of the servants told me they were sent from Castle Rising. I don't know if that is important.'

'Has Mistress Wesenham returned to Ghent?'

'Yes, sir. After Master Gonville departed she felt no need to stay.'

'Good. Thank you, Warin. You have done well.'

Stanton was working in his chamber, parchments spread out around him, a goblet at his elbow. He grinned and lifted a wine flask wrapped in woven straw. 'Welcome back, Simon. Have a drop of this to wash the dust away. It's from Cyprus and strong as hell, so take plenty of water.'

The wine was dark, nearly black, and syrupy in consistency. Merrivale added water to his goblet and sipped it. 'Very good,' he said.

'Isn't it? I've not tasted anything like it before. The depth of flavour is remarkable.'

'What is the situation? I see the king has returned from Cambrai.'

'The siege failed, as we knew it would. The army withdrew at the end of October, and the English troops were paid off and sent home until spring. Brother Willem and Cousin Jan have gone home too. There will be no more fighting until next summer, I reckon.'

'What about the Flemish alliance?'

'All but sealed, Burghersh says. The king goes to Ghent next month to meet Jacob van Artevelde, the captain general of the League of Three. There is a rumour that he will make a public claim to the throne of France at the same time.'

Merrivale's eyebrows rose. 'It is decided, then?'

'Artevelde insisted, we are told. He wants to ensure we are fully committed to the alliance. There will be trouble at home, of course. Parliament will be furious that they weren't consulted.'

Merrivale nodded. 'Did Burghersh establish an inquisition into Gonville's poisoning?'

'He says he has proof that Gonville was attacked by French agents trying to disrupt the negotiations with Flanders. Guards have now been posted on the buttery to prevent a repeat occurrence, and the matter is closed.'

'French agents? Do you believe that?'

Stanton snorted. 'Do you?'

'Have you spoken to the king?'

'Only briefly. He has too many other things on his hands, I think. The Flemings, of course, but something is happening back in London, too. I don't know what it is, but he spends much of each day talking with Scrope.'

Merrivale sipped his wine, looking at the parchments. 'May I ask what you are working on?'

Stanton frowned. 'I'm not sure yet. That is to say, I am searching for something in this correspondence but I haven't yet found it. Or perhaps it is staring me in the face but I don't recognise it... What about you? Did you discover anything further about Archbishop Balduin's syndicate?'

'The Solaro branch in Strassburg is involved, but only in a very minor way. Otherwise, all appears to be genuine. Balduin is only interested in the money.'

'And the crown is safe.' It was a statement, not a question.

'The crown is safe,' Merrivale repeated. 'Thank you for the wine, John. I must be on my way.'

One of Bishop Burghersh's servants intercepted Merrivale in the rain-swept courtyard. 'His Grace wishes to see you, sir. He asks you to attend on him at once.'

Red-faced as ever, Burghersh greeted Merrivale as he entered the office. 'Where the devil have you been?'

'Talking to Velvl Roth,' Merrivale said.

'Close the door. How did you find out about Roth?'

'Gonville told me. I am impressed by your broad-mindedness, Your Grace. Not every clergyman would support the return of the Jewish exiles to England.'

'You know about that.' Burghersh closed his eyes for a moment. 'Not a word to anyone, do you understand? I haven't yet discussed it with the king.'

'Why not?'

'Because not all of the money has reached us,' Burghersh said. 'We need Roth to carry out his side of the bargain.'

'He said the money had been sent to John Moleyns.'

'Not all of it. Some of the bills of exchange have gone missing. Moleyns is still trying to trace them. Keep quiet about this, do you hear?'

'Yes, Your Grace,' said Merrivale. 'Why did you wish to see me?'

'I want you to tell that fool Stanton to stop poking around the Gonville affair and leave it alone. The French spies who poisoned Gonville have long since left Antwerp.'

'Do you know who they are?'

'Men employed by your old friend King Jean of Bohemia, I am told. They were spotted in the Botermarkt the day Gonville left for England, but the town watch failed to capture them. There has been no sign of them since. Now, tell Stanton to drop the matter. That's all.'

Anton Turc was waiting for him again in the Vlaeykensgang, where water dripped from the eaves and bubbled in the gutters. '*Salut*,' he said. 'Did you have a pleasant journey?'

'I crossed the Ardennes twice in the pouring rain. What do you think?'

Turc grinned. His initial hostility had quickly vanished, and he appeared to like Merrivale. Perhaps he sensed a kindred spirit, the latter thought.

'Your return is timely,' Turc said. 'The Solaros grow more and more nervous, and Aufrej and his men rarely venture out of doors. There has been trouble back in Italy.'

'What kind of trouble?'

There was excitement in Turc's voice. 'When Ottone Doria's galleys reached Genoa, the crews began a revolution that toppled the aristocracy and brought in a popular government. Now the tides of revolt are spreading all over the country, including Asti. We think the people are preparing to rise up against the Solaros.'

'What will you do?'

'If the Solaros fall, we will seize their property here in Antwerp and claim it in the name of the new regime. We are already making preparations.'

'The Solaros will resist.'

'I hope so,' Turc said. 'I do, with all my heart. Fifty years of oppression and exile demand blood.'

'Be careful. I don't think Cousin Jan would look kindly on a massacre in his streets. You said the Solaros do not go out. Have they received any visitors?'

'Two only. The first Sinibald Solaro, the senior partner in the Strassburg branch, arrived a few days ago. He is still there now.'

Sinibald Solaro was the man who had invested in Balduin and Roth's syndicate. 'What is he doing here?'

'We have not been able to find out, but if I were you, *Inglèis*, I should be worried about this. Yes, the Solaros are lending money to England, but they are Guelph pigs and their hearts will always lie with the papacy and France. If they learn that the crown of England is in Strassburg, they might be tempted to acquire it for themselves.'

Merrivale took a step forward. Water dripped from the brim of his hat. 'Keep your voice down,' he snapped. 'Who told you that?'

'Your *compagn*, Stanton. He told Orland last week. That was careless of him, don't you think? You must hope he did not also tell the Solaros. You recall I said there were two visitors? Stanton called at the Solaro bank a few days after you departed.'

'Could Stanton have visited the Solaro house?' Merrivale asked Warin later that day.

'It's possible, sir. I couldn't watch all the time, not him and the Turcs both.' The groom paused. 'I'm sorry, sir.'

'Yes,' Merrivale said. 'So am I.'

Antwerp, December 1339

Christmas in Antwerp. The great hall of the Burcht was decorated with greenery interwoven with silver and gold ribbons. Every table had an elaborate centrepiece, silver-gilt nefs, gilded boars' heads with gold apples in their mouths, swans carved from paste with silver beaks and jet eyes. The royal musicians wore new uniforms with gold tabards decorated with red leopards. 'I hope you are fond of boar,' Alice

Bedingfield said to Merrivale. 'The hunting has been particularly good.'

At one Christmas on Dartmoor during the famine, the festive meal had consisted of grass and treebark stewed in a pot. Merrivale could still recall the bitter taste. His father and mother had both refused their portions, giving everything to their children. It had still not been enough to save the two girls.

'You would never know the king is nearly bankrupt,' Alice said. 'Where has all the money gone? He has borrowed from practically every bank in Europe. According to rumour, it is nearly impossible to get a loan on the money markets because all the lenders have pledged their credit to England.'

'Rumour exaggerates,' said Merrivale. 'I cannot imagine William de la Pole, for example, lending every penny he possesses.'

'It might depend on what he receives in return. Have you heard? The king has knighted Pole and given him the barony of Holderness. He has also made him a baron of the exchequer, meaning he has the keys to the Treasury. You might as well put a fox in charge of the henhouse.'

Merrivale remembered the great cold hall at Burstwick in Holderness. 'I expect this was all promised a long time ago,' he said.

They stood by the wall, watching the lavishly dressed nobles and knights enter the hall. The king stood near the door, brilliant in scarlet and gold robes, flanked by Sir Geoffrey Scrope and Bishop Burghersh as they welcomed the Duke of Brabant and Count of Hainault. 'Their last feast together,' Alice said. 'We are leaving next month to take up quarters in Ghent, to reassure the captain general that we really are committed to the new alliance. I expect Cousin Jan and Brother Willem will be pleased to see the back of us.'

'The boar certainly will,' Merrivale said.

She cuffed him lightly on the arm. 'You haven't answered my question. Where has all the money gone?'

Voices, laughter and music echoed in the rafters and reverberated back. Under the cover of the din it was possible to have a quiet conversation without being overheard. 'Are things really that serious?'

'Yes, they really are. The royal household is surviving on credit with local merchants. That's another reason for going to Ghent, so we can postpone paying our bills. First the wool money goes missing, now this. What is happening, Simon?'

'I don't know. That is what Stanton and I are trying to discover.'

'Have you discovered yet who poisoned Gonville?'

'A man named Flemyng had a hand in it, but he was acting on someone's orders. I suspect Bishop Burghersh knows something, but he has warned Stanton and I to stay out of the affair.'

A thought ran through his mind. Burghersh had said French agents had attacked Gonville. Nicholas le Flemyng had visited the Solaros, who had a natural political affinity with France. Perhaps there was something there after all; and if so, it made the Solaro involvement in English royal finances even more dangerous. And then there was the killer in the queen mother's household; the household of Isabella of France.

'Perhaps Burghersh put the arsenic in his wine,' Alice suggested.

'This isn't Italy, Alice. Clergymen don't go around poisoning people.'

'My dear, you are so naïve. Poison has been the weapon of priests since the beginning of time. Even Saint Benedict had to leave his monastery after the monks put wolfsbane into his pottage.'

'Burghersh isn't a Benedictine. He maintains it was done by French spies trying to disrupt the talks with Flanders… There is another possibility which is absolutely unthinkable, and yet I cannot get it out of my head.'

'Tell me.'

Merrivale told her. 'I don't know what to do,' he said at the end. 'Do I take this to the king?'

'God alive, Simon. Geoffrey Scrope is Stanton's patron, and you can be absolutely certain he will protect his protégé. If you intend to denounce Stanton, you will need proof so watertight it could sail home to England. Are you sure it is him?'

'I hope I'm wrong. I badly want to be wrong. But the pieces are starting to fit together.'

The queen came down into the hall, blazing with multicoloured jewels, and stood with one hand resting on her belly. Her damsels formed a protective screen behind her. 'I must go,' Alice said. She touched Merrivale's arm. 'What will you do?'

'Wait,' Merrivale said.

Antwerp, January 1340

He waited. The wind blew in bitter gusts from the north, sending snowflakes swirling in clouds around the towers of the Burcht. The royal family and their household prepared to depart; the first heavily guarded boats loaded with baggage had already sailed upriver to Ghent.

A message arrived for Merrivale in the afternoon, delivered by an unassuming man who slipped away without waiting for a reply. *We think the Solaros are preparing to depart. Come quickly, and come armed.*

He had just buckled on his swordbelt when John Stanton came into his chamber, carrying a flask and two goblets. 'Bastard wine from La Rochelle,' he said. 'According to Brother Jofroi of Waterford, it is strong, dry on the palate but with a soft flavour, and very good for both the head and the belly. Have a glass with me.'

'I must go out,' Merrivale said.

'In this weather? Don't be a fool, man. If ever there was a day for staying inside with a glass of wine, this is it.'

'I must go,' Merrivale repeated.

Stanton looked at him. 'You're armed. What is happening?'

'Nothing that need concern you.'

'What do you mean?' Stanton set the flask and goblets down on a table. 'If there is danger, I'm coming with you.'

'No, you are not. Stay here.'

Stanton laughed. 'Stay here, while you go out and fight? Give me a moment while I fetch my sword.'

'No!' Merrivale said. 'I mean it, John. You are not coming with me, and if you try to follow me, I will prevent you.'

'I don't understand.'

Time was short, and he needed to get rid of Stanton. 'You met with the Solaros not long after I left for Strassburg,' Merrivale said. 'Why didn't you tell me?'

'I went to confront Aufrej Solaro and demand to know whether he was still doing business with Peruzzi. I'm convinced the two of them are planning to betray us to France, but I'm not sure how.'

'Did you tell him about the crown?'

'The crown?' Stanton stared at him. 'God above, of course not! I'm not stupid!'

'Aren't you? You told Orland Turc.'

'Turc already knew! God knows how. Simon, what is going on?'

'Soon after you spoke to Aufrej Solaro, the head of the Solaro branch in Strassburg came hurrying north to meet him. That's not a coincidence, is it? The Solaros know the crown is in Strassburg.'

'But I didn't tell them!'

'If not you, then who did?'

'How should I know?' Stanton's hands clenched into fists. 'Body of Christ,' he said. 'You must have had me followed to the Solaro house. How long have you been keeping watch on me?'

'Since I realised I could no longer trust you.'

'Not *trust* me? Holy Mary, Simon, how many miles have we ridden together? I fought beside you at Rye!'

'I'm sure you had to make it look good,' Merrivale said curtly. 'Your employers, whoever they are, would hardly have been pleased if I had cast you off. At least now I know how they were able to track my movements so efficiently. As a matter of interest, how much are they paying you?'

'You utter bastard,' Stanton said.

Merrivale touched the hilt of his sword. 'Be careful. I've had enough of betrayal.'

'As God is my witness, I have betrayed no one.'

'Oaths are cheap.' Merrivale forced himself to relax a little. 'I must go. We will discuss this when I return.'

'We will discuss nothing,' Stanton said, and there was pain as well as anger in his voice. He picked up the flask and goblets and turned towards the door. 'I don't know why you have decided I am a traitor, but it does not matter. We are finished, Simon. Do not ever speak to me again.'

The door slammed behind him. Merrivale stood for a moment, breathing deeply and trying to calm his anger. He had been on the verge of drawing his sword and killing Stanton which, since the other man had no weapon, would have been murder. He told himself to be calm, that Stanton was of more use alive than dead, but the rage did not abate.

He pulled on a heavy cloak to ward off the wind and went downstairs. In the streets outside the castle the snow was blowing harder and thin slush covered the cobbles. The Turc house in Swarte Susters-Straet was dark and shuttered, but the gate opened quickly when he knocked and a servant ushered him inside. In the buildings around the courtyard he heard the rasp of swords being sharpened on grinding wheels.

Orland Turc was in the hall, armed with a sword and dagger and wearing a helmet and a short mail tunic over his coat. Anton and several of his kinsmen were with him. All were grinning broadly. 'The Solaros are about to leave,' Orland said. 'Our watchers have confirmed it.'

'What has happened?'

'Word came through from Asti this morning. The people have risen up and overthrown the Solaros. Their power is broken, and our allies now control the city.'

'Congratulations,' Merrivale said. 'Where is Aufrej Solaro intending to go?'

'We managed to intercept one of their letters. He and Sinibald have orders to close the branch here and fall back to Strassburg. If you want the records of his transactions with Doria and Grimaldi, we need to get into the house quickly before they can take everything away.'

'Where is the house?'

'On the Suikerrei, facing the canal with a street behind it. A barge has come up the canal and docked outside the watergate, so we suspect that is how they are planning to depart. They have put crossbowmen on the roof of the house to protect their escape.'

'Do you have crossbows of your own?'

Anton grinned. 'Even better. We have hired some of your English archers. With our own household and a few others we recruited, we have about forty men in all.'

'What about the town watch?'

'Paid to look the other way,' said Orland. 'They will say they are investigating disturbances in the Grote Markt. We wait until night has fallen. Then we go.'

The English archers were intrigued by Merrivale. 'What brings you here, sir?' one of them asked as they walked through the dark streets.

'The Solaros killed a friend of mine. What about you?'

Snow swirled around them and the archer brushed a few flakes from his beard. 'We were paid off when the army returned from Cambrai. We decided to stay and look for work.'

'We like fighting,' said another man. 'We thought there was more chance of finding it here than back in Chelmsford.'

'Not sure about that,' said a third. 'I've been to Chelmsford.'

The streets were silent and empty. Merrivale wondered if the watch had spread the word, telling people to stay indoors. The Solaro house was brick-built with crenelated gables and a range of narrow windows facing the street. They could see men crouched on the roof, dark shapes dimly glimpsed through the falling snow. Lamps gleamed in the great hall on the first floor and, more dimly, in the floor above.

Merrivale looked at the gate. 'Can we break that down?'

Orland Turc shook his head. 'The planks are four inches thick and banded with iron. It will be an escalade.' He turned to the archers. 'Five of you out on the bridge. If anyone tries to get out through the watergate, shoot them. The rest, cover the grapnel men while they go forward. Once the grapnels are in place, everyone take hold of a rope and start climbing. Remember, our goal is to take the strongroom. We have about an angelus to get down there before they either empty the room or barricade themselves inside. Everyone ready? Let's go.'

'For a banker, your senior partner knows his tactics,' Merrivale murmured.

Anton chuckled. 'Did you really think that banking was all about trade finance and sea loans and pawnbroking for indigent kings? This is our world, my friend.'

The snowfall increased. Someone shouted from the roof of the Solaro house and a crossbow bolt clattered off the cobbles, followed by another. The archers raised their bows and grey-feathered arrows hissed away into the night. The wind was gusty, but the Englishmen were veterans who knew how to allow for windage and two crossbowmen fell from the roof, bodies hitting the street with a heavy thud. Screams sounded from the far side of the house; someone must have tried to get out through the watergate. More crossbowmen appeared in the windows and two of Turc's men went down with bolts through the body, but the English archers shot rapidly and methodically and one after another the Solaro men slumped down dead.

They were under the walls of the house. Men whirled grapnels around their heads and hurled them skyward, listening for the rasp of metal on brick overhead and tugging on the ropes to make sure they were firmly fixed. Merrivale dropped his cloak and laid hold of a rope with both hands, braced his boots against the wall and began to climb. For a few moments he was exposed, unable to draw his sword and helpless if an enemy should appear above him, but the archers had done their work well. He reached the roof and climbed over the gables, stumbling over the body of a crossbowman and smelling the reek of hot blood cooling in the snow.

His mind cleared. He forgot about Stanton and everything else in the world save for the task in front of him. The moment of reckoning had come; Aufrej Solaro, Enric and Sgond were about to die. More men were coming over the battlements and running towards the stair turret. Someone shot at them as they opened the door and then fled back down the stair. Merrivale followed, Anton Turc close behind him. They reached an open passageway lit with oil lamps and ran towards the sound of retreating footsteps. A man jumped out behind them and Anton turned and killed him with a single blow of his sword. Ahead, the footsteps came to a halt.

Merrivale stepped through the door of the chamber at the end of the passageway. The light of another lamp showed a bearded man in a leather jerkin and dark hose, carrying a sword with a long tapering blade. 'I recognise you,' Merrivale said. 'Which one are you, Sgond or Enric?'

'*Maledission.* I am Enric, and you shall die like a pig.'

Merrivale raised his sword and moved straight into the attack. Enric parried the first blow, looking into Merrivale's eyes and seeing his own death. He stepped back, catching the heel of his boot and stumbling. His guard came down, and Merrivale knocked the sword out of his hand and stabbed him through the chest.

'One,' he said aloud.

Down the passageway Orland Turc was yelling at his men to move on and take the next floor. Stepping out of the chamber, Merrivale found another spiral stair leading down, much narrower than the first and probably intended for servants. He took the stair at a run, shoulders brushing the brick walls. At the bottom was another door; he kicked it open and stepped into the great hall. A group of armed men who had been watching the main door turned in surprise to face him. Merrivale walked forward, arm outstretched and bloody sword extended, pointing at one of the men. 'Sgond,' he said. 'Come and fight me.'

Sgond shouted and ran forward, raising his own sword. Merrivale stepped aside, letting the other man's impetus carry him past, whirled around and drove his sword point into Sgond's back. Sgond dropped his sword and fell to his knees, clutching at his wound. His shoulders slumped and he fell onto his face, blood soaking through his tunic.

'Two,' Merrivale said. He turned towards the others, who bolted towards the main door. They had almost reached it when the door opened and Anton Turc raced in, followed by a dozen others. The Solaro men halted, dropping their weapons and raising their hands.

'Leave them,' Merrivale said. 'They're not important.' He ran through the door and downstairs to the ground floor. Anton followed him. Another narrow passage led them to the heavy strongroom door, which was standing ajar. Merrivale pushed the door open and walked into the lamplit room.

Aufrej Solaro stood in the middle of the room, sword in hand. Another man, a little older, dark-haired and bearded, stood behind him. A long dagger was tucked through his belt, and like Turc, he wore a mail shirt over his black tunic. 'Merrivale,' he said calmly. 'I should have killed you that first day in London.'

'And I should have killed you in Rye,' Merrivale said. 'We all make mistakes. Fortunately, we sometimes get a chance to put them right.'

Orland Turc walked into the room. 'This is a vendetta,' he said. 'Our quarrel with this man is far older than yours.'

Merrivale held a hand to stop him. 'If you let me kill him, the Company of the Leopard gets the king's business. If not, the deal is off the table.'

Orland hesitated, torn between passion and profit. 'Very well,' he said finally.

Merrivale walked forward, his eyes never leaving Solaro's face. Solaro waited calmly, sword raised. Merrivale tapped his own blade against it, testing the other man's guard. Whipping the blade away he stabbed low, the point ripping through Solaro's hose and drawing blood from his leg. Solaro cursed, slashing back, but Merrivale ducked under the blow and stabbed again. Solaro parried and for a moment their blades grated together, crossguards clashing and locking. Forcing Solaro's sword aside, Merrivale stepped in close and with his left hand plucked Solaro's dagger from his scabbard and stabbed him in the neck. Stepping back again, he watched Solaro fall to the floor and blood begin to pool around the body.

'Three,' he said softly. 'That is for you, John Hull.'

But killing would not bring Hull back to life. The reaction he always felt after fighting hit him again, stronger this time; his stomach churned and he felt briefly dizzy. The blood on his hands was bright and stinking.

Orland walked forward, looking at the bearded man. 'Sinibald Solaro. How do you wish to die?'

The bearded man spread his hands. 'Not even a Turc would murder an unarmed man. Or would they?'

Anton raised a hand. 'This one is the senior partner in the Strassburg branch, Orland. He will have information that is helpful to us, I think.'

Orland considered this for a moment. Finally he nodded. 'It will be a pleasure squeezing it out of him. Very well, take him away.'

One of the Englishmen ran into the room. 'We've cleared the house, sir. We have some prisoners, but no one got away.'

'Search the prisoners and disarm them,' Orland said. 'If any are members of the Solaro family, bring them to me. The rest can go free.'

'What about the dead, sir?'

Orland nudged Aufrej Solaro's body with his foot. 'Take them down to the watergate and tip them into the canal. The tide is going out. They will be gone by morning.'

Anton fetched an axe, and a series of heavy blows smashed the strong-boxes open. There was no gold or silver, and no bills of exchange. 'They must have sent those away earlier,' Orland said. 'No matter.'

Most of what remained was correspondence with other branches or with clients in the Low Countries. In the second box they found a bundle of tightly bound rolls marked *Correspondentia cum Angliae*, and Orland handed this to Merrivale. 'I hope you find what you are looking for.'

Merrivale was not sure what he hoped. He still felt sick; he had wiped his hands and cleaned his sword, but he could not cleanse his mind. Retrieving his cloak from the street he walked back through the falling snow to the Burcht. It was after curfew, but the guards knew him and admitted him. In the gatehouse he hesitated for a moment.

Whatever Stanton had done, he had done for a reason. Merrivale found it hard to believe that the genial, wine-loving serjeant was as corrupt and venal as Gonville, for example. But something was very wrong, and he needed answers.

He climbed up to Stanton's chamber and knocked at the door. There was no answer. He knocked again, and after a moment, lifted the latch and opened the door. A rush light, guttering down to its end, showed him the open flask of wine and goblet on the table, and the body lying on the floor.

John Stanton had died in agony. His body was rigid, his fingers clenched so hard his nails had bitten into his palms and drawn blood. His mouth was open, his face streaked with strings of saliva. His lifeless eyes stared up at the ceiling, imploring God to make a swift end to his suffering. But God had shown him no mercy.

The future will bring its own sorrows, Levi ben Gershon had said, *and you must be prepared for them*. But nothing could have prepared him for this. Merrivale knelt beside the body and gently closed its eyes, and buried his face in his hands.

21

Antwerp, January 1340

'Hemlock,' said Jordan of Canterbury. 'I'm surprised he didn't taste it.'

'He told me the wine was strong and sweet,' Merrivale said. 'That probably disguised the taste. Whoever poisoned him almost certainly knew this, and may even have supplied the wine.'

The physician squinted into the flask. 'He has drunk most of it. That's unlike Stanton. He enjoyed the taste of wine, but he was also careful. He never drank himself into a stupor, not that I saw.'

'Nor me,' Merrivale said bleakly. 'But on this occasion he was angry and hurt. He drank without thinking.'

Canterbury hesitated. 'There is nothing more I can do. The court leaves for Ghent the day after tomorrow, and I must attend on the king.'

'I will take care of him. He was my friend.'

That was true, Merrivale thought, even if I was too blind to see it. I drove him away. I sent him to his death.

They buried John Stanton the next morning in the vault of the Sint Paulus church, the sound of the memorial mass ringing in the vaults overhead. Several members of the royal household attended, including Alice Bedingfield, standing shivering beside Merrivale, and Sir Geoffrey Scrope in a heavy cloak lined with black fur and matching hat. Scrope insisted, somewhat ostentatiously, on paying the expenses of the funeral and afterwards handed over a heavy purse to pay for more masses for the dead man's soul. He said nothing to Merrivale, but before he departed he rested a hand, briefly, on the latter's shoulder. It was only a small gesture of comfort, but in Merrivale's mind it was still more than he deserved.

After the funeral he walked back to the Burcht with Alice. The weather had cleared and turned colder still; icicles hung from the gables of the houses and frozen snow crunched under their boots. 'I don't think we should go to Ghent tomorrow,' she said. 'This is a dreadful mistake. How many people really believe that Edward can become king of France? Does he himself even believe it?'

'Someone must,' said Merrivale.

'Oh, Scrope believes, and Bishop Burghersh too. France is weak, they keep saying. One more push, one successful campaign, and King Philip's nobles will desert him and he will fall from his throne. But we are two years into the war and there is no sign of Philip's power weakening.'

'A wise man told me recently that England is a wealthy country with a strong government and effective administration. He is betting on us to win.'

'Then he is a fool of a gambler. Where is our wealth? We have mortgaged everything we have to pay for the war. Where is the strong government, when the king's own ministers are plotting against him?'

'What do you mean?' Merrivale asked.

'Come, Simon, you must have heard the rumours. Archbishop Stratford is opposed to the war, and firmly against any notion of claiming the throne of France. Many high officials in London agree with him.'

'Everyone knows that. Disagreeing with the king is not the same as plotting against him.' Merrivale paused. 'What are you saying, Alice?'

She stopped, looking around. 'The queen told me about the great crown,' she said quietly. 'She wanted to make sure a few trusted people knew the truth, so the crown could be protected if need be. She didn't want to hand over the crown in the first place, and said she would sooner serve as a hostage herself. If the crown should fall into the hands of the French… Well. I don't need to spell it out.'

'I have seen the crown,' Merrivale said. 'It is safe.'

'Nothing is ever safe, not when betrayal and greed are rotting us from within.' She bit her lip. 'Why did John Stanton die? Burghersh is raving about French spies again, but I don't believe it.'

'John also knew about the crown. Did you tell him?'

'No, the queen did, for the same reason she told me. She trusted him.'

'Which is more than I did,' Merrivale said bitterly. 'The person who killed him was also trying to kill me. We were meant to share that flask of wine.'

'Why didn't you?'

'Because I thought he was working with them. I had convinced myself that he was the enemy.'

'Oh, Simon,' she said quietly, laying a hand on his arm. 'I am so sorry, my dear, so very sorry.'

They walked on. 'Consider this,' Alice said. 'If you had died too, who would be there to avenge you and John? No one would ever know why you had died. At least now there is a chance for justice.'

'So, of the two of us, why did John have to die? Why not me?'

'You sound like a soldier, mourning his dead comrades and wondering why he has been spared. Never mind why. There are people in this world who still need you, Simon. Think of your father. Who could care for him, if you were gone?'

'The monks would look after him. They have a duty of charity.'

'Very well, think of the king. *He* needs you, now more than ever. He has so few people around him whom he can truly trust.'

The queen mother had said something very similar. 'I want to see him,' Merrivale said. 'But I don't know if he will see me, not now. He told me to watch over Stanton, and I failed him. Again.'

'What will you do?'

'John had sent for some parchments from Castle Rising. I don't know why they were important, but there might be a clue as to who killed him and why. I also need to go through the correspondence we took from the Solaro house.'

Alice raised her eyebrows. 'What were you doing at the Solaro house?'

'Cleaning it. Please don't mention that I was there.'

'Of course not. What were you hoping to find?'

'Proof that the Solaros and Donato de' Peruzzi are working with the French. I know they are, Alice, I can smell it in the wind. I just need to find proof.'

'When you find it, come to me,' Alice said. 'I will see that you get your audience.'

Back at the castle, his mood as bleak as the winter wind, Merrivale climbed up to Stanton's room. Stanton's strongbox was locked, but the keys were in his purse on the table. Opening the box, Merrivale found a little money, silver pennies and groats and a few Brabant groschen. The rest of the box was full of parchments, tightly rolled and bound. He unrolled them one after another and began to read.

All of the documents were letters. Some were from Stanton himself to Peter Ellerker, the queen mother's treasurer; others were from Ellerker to Edmund Gonville. Most of these dealt with mundane matters, but Merrivale rerolled two of them and put them into the pocket of his cloak. The final letter, unsigned and unsealed, sent a quiver of shock down his spine. Stanton might not have known who this letter was from, but Merrivale had seen Donato de' Peruzzi's handwriting before and recognised it at once.

'Oh, my friend,' he said softly. 'If only you had told me.'

'Told you what?' said a voice.

Merrivale looked up. Geoffrey Scrope stood in the doorway, still in his fur-lined cloak and hat. The jewelled clasp of the cloak sparkled in the sunlight.

Merrivale bowed. 'Your pardon, Sir Geoffrey, I did not realise I had spoken aloud. I wish John had told me where his family lived, so I could send his effects to them.'

'That was a kind thought,' Scrope said. 'As it happens, I know his family well. I will see to it.' He paused for a moment, eyes searching Merrivale's face. 'You were fond of him.'

'Everyone who knew him was fond of him. Everyone, that is, except for the men who killed him.'

'Burghersh thinks it was French agents.'

Merrivale shook his head. 'Do you believe that, Sir Geoffrey?'

'Henry Burghersh believes French spies live under his bed,' Scrope said dryly. 'What is your view, Simon?'

'Stanton was a minor official. If the French have penetrated our court so thoroughly, why did they not attack someone more senior? Yourself, for example?'

Scrope paused for a moment. 'Good point. I hadn't thought of that.'

'Does the king know what happened to Stanton?'

'I told him yesterday. He was full of sorrow and anger, much as we all are, and he has charged me with conducting an inquisition. Will you assist me?'

'I will do what I can,' Merrivale said.

'Good. Stay here in Antwerp, see if you can find out who got into the Burcht and how the poison was administered. I must go with the king and queen to Ghent tomorrow. Report to me there when you have news.'

Merrivale bowed. Scrope paused for a moment. 'There are rumours of some sort of affray in the city yesterday evening. Do you know anything about it?'

'I have heard nothing,' Merrivale said.

'If you do, be sure to let me know. If there really are French agents in Antwerp, we must all be on our guard.'

'Of course, Sir Geoffrey.'

'I shall send a servant to pack up John's effects,' Scrope said. He shook his head. 'What a waste, what a terrible waste. He was a good man.'

Merrivale waited until the sound of Scrope's footsteps had faded, and put the letter from Peruzzi into his pocket with the other two. He wondered who had found these letters at Castle Rising and sent them to Stanton. It certainly would not have been Ellerker himself, and that left only one other, rather unlikely choice. Locking the strongbox, he took a final look around the room and stepped outside, closing the door firmly behind him.

Whence we are redeemed... There would be no redemption, no rest, until the men who murdered John Stanton were dead. They were powerful men and protected and it would take time to build a case against them, but he could wait. His moment would come.

Back in his own chamber Merrivale sat down with another bundle of parchments, the ones from the Solaro strongroom, and began to read. Most of the documents were accounts, transfers of money from *domus Per* to *domus Sol*, the house of Peruzzi to the house of Solaro, dated 1338 and 1339. These, it was fairly easy to guess, were the payments destined for Grimaldi and Doria; records of the onward payments to the two captains would probably have been destroyed, if they ever existed at all. Other, more formal records detailed Solaro's loans to the English crown along with commissions paid to John Moleyns, the treasurer. There were also receipts for the loans, each bearing the treasurer's seal. Taken together, the loans amounted to about seventy thousand marks, more than Merrivale had expected.

Two of the other accounts made him sit up straight. One was a payment of five hundred marks to *magister Reg de Conduit vintner Lond*. Why had the Solaro bank been sending money to Reginald Conduit, the hot-tempered London wine merchant and presumed wool smuggler? The second document recorded a payment of one thousand marks to *Nicolaus Flandrensis mercator Gand pro domino Donato de' Peruzzi*. The document was dated after Nicholas le Flemyng had moved to Ghent. Clearly, Peruzzi had instructed Solaro to make this payment, but why? Was it for a service Flemyng had performed at the time, or earlier while he was still in England?

It might be enough, he thought. I was looking for a link between Peruzzi and Gonville; I haven't found it, but the connection with the saffron plot more generally is beginning to emerge. Whatever the case, he was certain that Gonville had more to tell.

The last parchment was a letter addressed to Aufrej Solaro and dated to the previous summer, and it made the hair stand up on Merrivale's neck.

> *To the worthy and esteemed magister Alfredo Solaro, greeting. It is known that you, along with Donato de' Peruzzi of Florence, Niccolosio Bartolomei of Lucca, Alessandro de Bardi, William de la Pole, Reginald Conduit, John Pulteney and sundry others, have been lending money to the king without the consent of the lords and commons of England. Know that these loans do not have the sanction of the lords and commons of England, and that they are contrary to the ancient rights and customs of the kingdom. All transactions must be conducted through the Exchequer, not the king's personal treasurer. If you fail to comply with this demand, certain matters concerning your bank and its transactions may become public knowledge, in particular your conspiracy with sundry other parties to evade lawful duties and taxes on wool exports, and the aid and comfort you and your associates gave to Carlo Grimaldi, Ottone Doria and others in the service of the king of France during their piratical attacks on English towns and ships. Take heed of this warning, or bear the consequences.*

There was no signature, but the letter was sealed with the privy seal of England.

Merrivale sat staring at the letter for a long time. The passage about ancient rights and customs was nonsense; kings had been borrowing money privately for decades in order to get around the restrictions the great institutions of state – Parliament, the council, the Exchequer, the Chancery – attempted to place on them. Now, as Grimsby had said, those institutions were exerting their power and attempting to clip the king's wings.

Those same officials had known all along about the wool smuggling and the house of Solaro's collusion with the enemy. They knew and they said nothing, preferring to use their knowledge as a weapon in the struggle with the king. By blackmailing his bankers into refusing to lend to him, they hoped to undermine the king himself. Meanwhile, in Southampton and Harwich and Rye and all along the southern and eastern coast of England, people had died.

Merrivale called the following day at Swarte Susters-Straet and found the Turcs in a state of high excitement. 'We failed to seize any of their assets,' Orland Turc said. 'We found no specie or bills of exchange, nor is there any sign of the loan book. But Sinibald Solaro has given us detailed information about the network of Solaro clients across the Low Countries. We can now take over that network and make it our own.'

'After fifty years in the shadows, profit and power are now within our grasp,' said Anton, whose approach to the world was a simple one.

'What did you do with Sinibald?' Merrivale asked.

'After we had wrung him dry, we let him go,' Anton said. 'It would have seemed ungrateful to do otherwise. We'll finish him eventually, of course. We're going to set up a branch of our own bank in Strassburg and drive him out of business.'

'And remember our bargain,' Orland said to Merrivale. 'The Company of the Leopard stands ready to serve His Grace. Remind him that we are Ghibellines and supporters of his brother-in-law the emperor. He can trust us.'

'I shall pass on your message. Have you heard any rumours about French spies in Antwerp?'

Orland shook his head. 'We understand that another of your men has been poisoned. Do you suspect the French?'

'Possibly. It would help if I could find out who had put poison into a flask of La Rochelle wine.'

Orland looked sharply at Anton. 'We found a barrel of La Rochelle in the buttery of the Solaro house,' the latter said.

'And hemlock?'

'None, but they could easily have acquired it from an apothecary.'

Merrivale walked through the snowy streets of Antwerp, knocking on the doors of every apothecary's shop. The story from each was the same; yes, we have hemlock in stock, we use it in small amounts for potions to treat coughs and chest complaints, but we have not sold any raw hemlock. Finally, at a small shop near the river, a woman who reminded him of an older version of Cassandra ran a hand through her white hair and stared at him. 'Is this about the dead Englishman?'

'Yes. Tell me whatever you know. No harm will come to you.'

She looked disbelieving. Merrivale laid several coins on the counter. 'Tell me what you know,' he repeated.

'A man came into my shop last week. He wanted some arsenic to kill rats, but I said I didn't have any so he asked for hemlock instead. I sold him a quarter of a pound of hemlock root.'

'You cannot kill rats with hemlock,' Merrivale said.

'I know. So did he.'

'Can you describe him?'

Her reply left no room for doubt. The man who had purchased the hemlock was Nicholas le Flemyng.

Ghent, January 1340

A barge brought Merrivale upriver from Antwerp, passing fields white with snow and cottages with smoke coiling blue from chimneys. Watching the spires of Ghent lift over the horizon, Merrivale felt his stomach tighten with a mixture of anticipation and anger.

But he was too late. The house on the Korenlei was empty, and neighbours confirmed that Nicolaes the English merchant had departed in his ship the previous day. Some of the crew had said they were bound for London.

Cassandra Wesenham's shop was in a narrow lane just off the Vrijdagmarkt. Business seemed to be brisk; she had two assistants, and a steady stream of people came and went through the door. She smiled at the sight of Merrivale. 'I thought you would turn up sooner or later. How are you?'

'May we talk in private?'

She led the way into the back room, the air thick with the smells of aromatic herbs; he recognised the tang of saffron among them. 'What is it?' she asked.

He told her about Stanton's death. Her eyes grew wide. 'You were fortunate,' she said.

'I don't feel very fortunate. Is there anything more you can tell me about Nicholas le Flemyng, anything at all?'

She shook her head, still shocked. 'Not really. I have already told you about the visits to my shop. Apart from that I barely spoke to him.'

'Did James Westacre say anything about him?'

She thought for a long time. 'I recall him saying once that Flemyng is ambitious,' she said finally. 'He wants to be the biggest fish in the pond, was how Westacre put it.'

'After he came to Ghent, Aufrej Solaro paid him a thousand marks on behalf of Donato de' Peruzzi. I think Peruzzi had procured his services and used the Solaro bank to pay him at arm's length, just as he did with the corsairs. Flemyng was in Antwerp when Gonville was poisoned, and he was there again and made a purchase of hemlock not long before John died. We can draw our own conclusions, I think.'

Her eyes widened a little. 'Where is Flemyng now?'

'On a ship, bound perhaps for London. He knows the alliance with the League of Three is about to be signed, and decided to get out of Ghent before we ask the authorities to arrest him. I need to find him and force a confession out of him.'

'But why would he sail to London?'

The same thought had bothered Merrivale. 'He must know someone there who can hide him.'

'And equally, there must be someone here in Ghent who can tell us more about him,' she said. 'I will ask some questions.'

'Please do, but keep yourself safe, Mistress Wesenham. The dangerous times are just beginning.'

Do not think about what the plot is, but what it is not. When we eliminate everything that is impossible, the Rambam had said, we arrive at the truth. It made sense; inasmuch as anything made sense.

The English court had settled into the Gravensteen, the gloomy grey castle overlooking the river that had once been home to the exiled

Count of Flanders. The courtyard was busy with servants, huntsmen carrying bunches of wild duck tied with string around their necks, fishermen with baskets of fish and eels, carts full of firewood and coal. 'We are preparing for another feast,' said Alice Bedingfield. She looked unusually gloomy. 'It is settled. His Grace will claim the throne of France tomorrow at midday. He will make a pubic proclamation in the Vrijdagmarkt.'

'You said you could get me an audience. Can it be in private, with no clerks or advisors present?'

'It shall be done.'

He waited in the castle hall, feeling time slip slowly by, trying not to think about the past. Grey winter light washed softly through the high windows. Distant bells rang nones and fell back into silence. He thought about Hull, and Stanton, and Yolande, and wondered if the guilt would ever fade.

We speak of many kinds of gnosis*: who we were, what we have become, where we were, whither we have sunk.*

A whisper of motion; he looked up, startled, to see one of the red-coated royal pages standing in front of him. 'Master Merrivale? The king will see you now.'

The king's chamber was hung with thick wool hangings to seal in the warmth. King Edward stood in front of the fire, hands behind his back. His wife Queen Philippa reclined on a padded seat beside him. She wore a red velvet robe that did nothing to conceal the fact that she was seven months pregnant, and a jewelled coif covering most of her black hair. Alice Bedingfield stood behind her.

'I told you to look after Stanton,' the king said.

'And I failed, sire,' Merrivale said. 'Again.'

King and subject stared at each other for a few moments. 'Very well,' Edward said. 'Make it brief.'

'You might wish to read this, sire.' Bowing, Merrivale handed over the letter to Aufrej Solaro. The king read it slowly, nodding a little as he reached the end.

'Sealed with the privy seal, by God,' he said, and his voice was reflective rather than angry. 'Where did you get this?'

'From the strongroom of the Solaro bank in Antwerp.'

'So, you were behind that business. I thought I told you to leave the Solaros alone until I no longer need them.'

'You no longer need them, sire. The Ghibellines have taken control of Asti and driven the Solaros out. It is only a matter of time before the entire bank fails. The Company of the Leopard is taking over their business.'

The queen's brown face was impatient. 'I told you. You should have dealt with the Leopards in the first place.'

'Yes, I remember,' King Edward said sourly. 'Are these allegations true? The Solaros were involved in smuggling and in supplying money to the French?'

'Yes, sire. Throughout this time they were acting as clients of Donato de' Peruzzi, who is one of the associates mentioned in the letter. I am certain that whoever wrote this letter knows this also.'

'Have you proof of Peruzzi's involvement?'

'Not directly, sire, but there is another thing. Edmund Gonville and John Stanton were both poisoned by a man named Nicholas le Flemyng, an adventurer who may also have had a hand in two murders in England. Aufrej Solaro paid Flemyng for his services, but again, he did so on behalf of Peruzzi.'

He handed over the parchment confirming the transaction. The king's brow furrowed as he read it. 'Have you told Geoffrey Scrope about this?'

'Not yet, sire. I will inform him, of course, but I wanted you to see this first. I'm afraid there is more. We already knew the Solaros were making payments to Doria and Grimaldi, and we found documents in their strongroom that indicate Peruzzi had a hand as well. I am afraid there is little doubt that both were acting secretly in the French interest.'

The king stood silent for a moment, the parchments still in his hand. 'Solaro and Peruzzi conspired to attack my servants,' he said slowly. 'They betrayed England to our enemies. And someone in high office in England, with access to the privy seal, knew about this and did nothing to stop it.'

The queen looked at her husband. 'This fits with what we are hearing from London,' she said.

'Yes… This could not have come at a worse time, of course. Tomorrow I shall publicly claim the throne of France. There will be no turning back after that.'

'The timing of Stanton's murder was no coincidence,' the queen said. 'The archbishop and his friends cannot stop you from claiming the throne, but they can and will undermine you in other ways.'

The king nodded. 'It is time I returned home and dealt with Archbishop Stratford and his coven,' he said. 'I shall begin by reminding them who is the true king of England. *And* of France, by God.'

'Do nothing rash,' the queen warned. 'Return by all means, but don't confront Stratford. Negotiate with him.'

'I'd rather hang him,' the king said, 'but you are right. I still need his support, at least for the moment. I shall depart for England directly after the ceremony. Geoffrey Scrope and Henry Burghersh will come with me. Merrivale, you will accompany me too. I shall need a King's Messenger.'

'Sire?'

'You heard me. I am reappointing you to your post. Find Scrope and tell him to have a ship prepared for our departure. Make it so.'

22

Westminster, February 1340

The whole world is growing colder, Velvl Roth had said, and there were times when Merrivale wondered if he was right. London was in the grip of a bitter frost, the sun shining red through clouds of smoke from thousands of chimneys. The Thames had frozen solid, trapping moored ships and barges in the ice. From the gardens of the palace of Westminster they could see the spires of the city cold and hazy in the distance.

'I owe you my thanks,' said Geoffrey Scrope. He was dressed all in dark fur again, Russian sable with fur-lined gloves as well. Condensation from his breath had frozen into tiny icicles in his beard.

'For what, Sir Geoffrey?' asked Merrivale.

'For saving me from myself. I told you Donato de' Peruzzi had friends at court. You have probably guessed by now that one of those friends was myself.'

Merrivale waited. 'I was convinced,' Scrope continued. 'No, to be honest, I *allowed* myself to become convinced that Donato de' Peruzzi was willing to work with us again, despite Savoy. As I told you, I can see his point of view there.'

'I understand,' Merrivale said.

'When His Grace informed me that Peruzzi had been colluding with the French, especially those butchers Doria and Grimaldi, I refused to believe it at first. My pride would not allow me to admit that I had been gulled.'

'Peruzzi is a snake,' Merrivale said. 'You are not the first to be deceived by him, nor will you be the last.'

'Well, his hour of reckoning is fast approaching. I have advised the king to absolve himself of repayment for all the loans he received from both Peruzzi and the Solaros.'

Merrivale considered this. 'Is that entirely wise? Reneging on loans tends to make the other bankers suspicious. They will wonder if they can trust us in future.'

'There is that risk. But Peruzzi must be punished. There is a point of principle at stake.'

Not to mention your pride, Merrivale thought. 'Without its English revenues, the Peruzzi bank may collapse completely,' he said.

'I shall shed no tears if it does. Will you continue searching for Nicholas le Flemyng?'

'In Ghent people said he was on his way to London. It may be a false trail, but it is all we have.'

Scrope nodded. 'Good hunting,' he said.

The atmosphere in the palace of Westminster was tense and febrile, and reminded Merrivale of the final days in Savoy. Once again, he tried to stop thinking about Yolande, and once again he failed.

He could not deny, though, that his mood was a little lighter. Being reinstated as a King's Messenger had something to do with that; he had restored his pride, and he could afford once again to pay for his father's care at Frithelstock. He thought about the old man, searching for fond memories, but all he could see was Yolande's face and then the bodies; Stanton lying dead on the floor, Hull tangled in rope surrounded by a pool of seawater, the white-shrouded corpses being lowered into their graves on Dartmoor.

The officials arrived on a cold and bitter morning, when the wind sent snow scudding in long streams across the ice of the Thames. Merrivale stood outside the hall, watching as they entered the court-yard. John Stratford, Archbishop of Canterbury and president of the council, tall, white-haired, imposing, a man who had served at the very highest levels of government for more than a decade and had once been the king's closest and most trusted advisor. His brother Robert

Stratford, the Lord Chancellor, greying, a little hunch-shouldered, his face watchful. William de la Zouche, the Lord High Treasurer, his clasped fingers twisting in front of him. William Kildesby, the Keeper of the Privy Seal, small with a sharp, angular face.

Sir John Pulteney was there too. He had entered with William de la Pole, but he left the others and walked across the courtyard to join Merrivale. 'I hear you have been reinstated,' he said. 'Congratulations.'

'Thank you. What is happening, Sir John?'

'The king has summoned us to discuss the imposition of a new tax. He wants us to push it through Parliament.'

'A new tax? I thought the king was relying on the money markets.'

'I think even he is beginning to realise that he has borrowed more than is prudent. So, he has presented us with demands for a new tax of one-ninth. The proceeds of one in nine sheaves of corn, one in nine sacks of wool and one in nine of the new season's lambs. Townsmen and those without lands will be taxed at one-fifteenth of their moveable goods.'

Merrivale was silent for a moment. 'Will Parliament accept?'

'They will demand very heavy concessions in return. And the king will have no choice but to agree to their demands. He is overwhelmed with debt, and he knows there is no other way out.'

'I wonder if the king will see it that way… Sir John, I have a question about William Kildesby, the Keeper of the Privy Seal. We have reason to believe that Kildesby may no longer be loyal to the king. Is it possible that he has turned against His Grace?'

Pulteney frowned. 'It depends on what you mean by loyal. There are many men like Archbishop Stratford, and indeed myself, who are loyal to the king but disagree with him on matters of policy. I judge Kildesby to be one of those.' He looked sharply at Merrivale. 'Are you saying there is more to it than that?'

Merrivale did not answer directly. 'Is Kildesby associating himself with Stratford and his party?'

'Very much so. He wants a bishop's throne, and I suspect Archbishop Stratford has promised him one.'

'Indeed. If you were the king, how would you go about winning Kildesby's loyalty back.'

Pulteney looked briefly amused. 'Is Kildesby so important? Ah, control of the privy seal, of course. You could go one better than Stratford. The Archbishop of York is gravely ill, I am told. If he should die, the see of York will be vacant. Do you see what I mean?'

'I do,' Merrivale said. 'Thank you, Sir John.'

Inside the hall a trumpet sounded. 'I must go,' Pulteney said. He walked away across the snowy courtyard, joining the others processing into the hall. Merrivale watched him go, a few more pieces of the puzzle slowing fitting themselves together in his mind.

An hour later the officials departed, most of them grim-faced. Merrivale waited until Kildesby came out and followed the Keeper of the Privy Seal through the gates and out into the icy road that led back towards London. The wind plucked at him, making his ears tingle. 'A moment, Master Kildesby, if you please,' he said.

Kildesby turned, his face framed with a fox fur hood that make him look a little like a fox himself. 'The errand boy, restored to favour. I didn't miss you while you were away.'

'In a moment, you may wish I had never returned. I should like your explanation of this.'

He handed over the letter addressed to Aufrej Solaro. Kildesby read it quickly, eyes darting across the parchment and down to the wax seal. 'What of it?'

'How does this come to have the privy seal?'

'That is none of your business, messenger. As keeper of the seal, I am accountable only to the king.'

'And it is the king who is holding you to account now,' Merrivale said. 'The king must know everything that goes out under this seal, he made that clear before he departed for the Low Countries. Why was he not informed of this document?'

'How should I know? I have an office full of clerks, Merrivale. I cannot be everywhere, watching everything they do. One of them must have made a mistake.' Kildesby paused. 'How did you come by this document?'

'I seized it from its former owner, and you are lying to me. You knew about the wool smuggling and you knew about Peruzzi.'

'I am serving the king's best interests. And you, Merrivale, are meddling in matters far above your station.'

'So people keep telling me. You haven't answered my question.'

'And I won't answer it. I am not responsible to you, errand boy.'

'No, you are not. But I shall watch you, Kildesby. If I find you are betraying the king, not even the privy seal will protect you.'

London, February 1340

Merrivale met Edmund Grimsby three days later in the cloister of the Domus Conversorum, the little chapel for Christian converts next to the chancery. The building was empty and silent in the late morning. Snowflakes curled down through the air, shrouding the black limbs of trees in the garden.

'A great deal has happened since we last met,' Grimsby said dryly.

Merrivale looked around. 'Was it your father's family who built this place?'

'They did, although I am not sure how much good was achieved. In these tormented times, faith is a refuge for the weak and a luxury for the strong. Those of us in the middle do not reap much benefit.'

'Did Velvl Roth write to you?'

'Yes. Do you intend to expose me?'

'Expose you? As what?'

'Prejudice runs deep. If it became known that I was the son of a Jewish convert, at the very least I would be deprived of my post. If people learned that I supported the return of our Jewish compatriots from exile, it would probably be far worse.'

Merrivale reached inside his cloak and pulled out the letter to Aufrej Solaro. He waited until Grimsby had read it. 'Did you know about this?' he asked.

'I did not.'

'But someone did know, and now another good man is dead.'

Grimsby paused. 'You are implying that there is some connection between resistance to the king's policies, and the machinations of Peruzzi and Solaro.'

'I don't know if there is or not. That is what I am trying to find out.'

'Archbishop Stratford is a determined man, but he would not kill to achieve his ends. I would not follow him if it were otherwise.'

Merrivale handed over two more parchments, the ones recording payments to Reginal Conduit and Nicholas le Flemyng. 'I would appreciate your views on these.'

Grimsby read the documents through, brow furrowed. 'I don't know of Nicholas le Flemyng, but a thousand marks is a sizeable sum.'

'According to the last report, Flemyng was sailing from Ghent to London on his roundship, the *Witschip*. The Chancery has its own spies, you said. Can they find him?'

'If he is in London, yes. I am puzzled by this payment to Conduit.'

'Was he borrowing from the Solaros?'

'Conduit lends money, he doesn't borrow it. This must be payment for a service.'

Merrivale nodded. 'That was my thought also. A commission, perhaps? A fee for arranging another transaction, or making an introduction to someone?'

There was a long silence. 'Possibly the latter,' Grimsby said finally.

'An introduction to whom? I cannot force you to tell me, but I need to know.'

'Conduit is close with my own superior, the Lord Chancellor, Robert Stratford. He owes Conduit a great deal of money.'

Silence fell once more. Snow continued to fall, soft and white.

'Blood of Christ,' Merrivale said finally. 'Peruzzi is manipulating all of you, through the Solaros and Conduit and whoever else is working for them in London. He is trying to influence policy in his favour. If you force a confrontation with the king, he will find a way to profit from it. He will already have laid his plans.'

'But surely that threat no longer exists,' Grimsby said. 'The Solaro bank is collapsing, and the king has refused to repay Donato de' Peruzzi and exiled him from the kingdom.'

'That won't stop Peruzzi. He is like the kraken, able to strike from the deep, and his tentacles are everywhere. Who else does Conduit know? He has lent money to the king in the past, and he was a leader of the wool syndicate. Who is his contact at court? John Moleyns?'

'No,' Grimsby said. 'It was Edmund Gonville.'

Merrivale closed his eyes for a moment. He had been looking for a link between Peruzzi and Gonville; now, indirectly, he might have found one. 'That makes sense,' he said finally. 'And Moleyns himself. Can you tell me anything about him?'

'He is jealous of William de la Zouche, the Lord Treasurer. He would love nothing better than to see Zouche disgraced and out of office, preferably with himself installed in Zouche's place.'

'Why? He already has wealth and power.'

'Yes,' Grimsby said. 'But power is like strong wine. The more men have of it, the more they crave.'

Merrivale nodded. 'I hope you achieve your goal,' he said. 'You and Roth. If you will permit me, Bishop Burghersh seems an odd choice for an advocate.'

'On this matter, at least, I believe Burghersh to be sincere. He believes genuinely that the decision to exile the Jewish people was wrong.'

'Can it really be done?' Merrivale asked. 'Even if the law is relaxed and Roth and his people are allowed to come home, will the rest of England accept them?'

'I don't know,' Grimsby said finally. 'I hope so, but ignorance and superstition are a deep seam running through our country. At the very least the Jewish people would require royal protection. At a time when war and taxation are already making the king unpopular, would he risk still further damage to his reputation?'

The answer to the question hung unspoken in the air between them. 'Does Roth realise this?' Merrivale asked.

'I have tried to explain, but it is not easy. This is Velvl's great purpose in life, and it is not a cause he will abandon easily. He hopes that we can find a way.' He looked at Merrivale. 'And you? What will you do now?'

'Seek justice,' Merrivale said. 'John Hull's killers paid the price for their crimes, and Stanton's will do the same.'

'It may take a long time.'

'I can wait,' Merrivale said.

Castle Rising, March 1340

'Thank you for receiving me, Your Grace,' Merrivale said. 'I shall endeavour not to take up too much of your time.'

'Take as much as you wish,' said Queen Isabella. 'Time is one commodity that I have in plenty.'

They were in the great hall rather than her usual painted chamber, probably because the hall was warmer; the wind, scooping up moisture from the North Sea, was keen as a knife. A tabby cat lay stretched out before the hearth, sound asleep.

'Shortly before he died, John Stanton received a quantity of correspondence from the office of your treasurer, Master Ellerker,' Merrivale said. 'Can you tell me who acquired those documents for him?'

'I did,' the queen said. 'Master Stanton wrote to me asking for help. I sent Ellerker on an errand to Bishop's Lynn, and while he was gone I entered his private office and took away the requested documents.'

'Have you dismissed Ellerker, Your Grace?'

'No. Master Stanton recommended that we keep this matter quiet until he could return and present a proper case against him.'

Merrivale drew out two of the letters he had taken from Stanton's room. 'These are copies of letters Ellerker sent to Gonville. The first shows that both were aware that Ralph Dunham intended to defraud you of the saffron crop, and were party to the fraud. In the second letter, Ellerker informed Gonville that John Stanton had gone to Rye and that I intended to join him there.'

The queen's blue eyes were cold. 'I read the letters before I sent them to Antwerp. I know their contents.'

'Ellerker was also in direct contact with Donato de' Peruzzi,' Merrivale said. 'It was Peruzzi who passed the word to Carlo Grimaldi.'

He laid the third letter on the table. 'This was written by Peruzzi,' he said.

Isabella looked at the letter. 'I did not know who wrote that letter, nor did I understand its import. It says that Ellerker should take steps to improve security in my household and keep me safe. He should ensure that I am surrounded by loyal men. After the treachery of Dunham and Brigget, I thought this was a wise move.'

'Loyal to whom?' Merrivale asked. 'There is an old Florentine saying, *sicuro, com' un uccello in gabbio*. Safe, like a bird in a cage. Peruzzi had always planned to use you in order to influence the king. When the saffron plot failed, he decided to infiltrate your household using Ellerker as his instrument. He has used this tactic before; it is how he intended to manipulate the Count of Savoy, before he decided he could make more money working for the other side.'

'This letter. Is it why Stanton was killed?'

'I thought so at first, but I realised that I was meant to die along with Stanton. Possibly Peruzzi thought Stanton had shown the letter to me and decided to eliminate us both, but my instinct tells me that is unlikely. Peruzzi is responsible for Stanton's killing, but someone else gave the orders that sent him to his death.'

'Have we enough evidence to hang Ellerker?' the queen demanded.

Merrivale shook his head. 'There is nothing to connect him directly to a capital crime. But, there is nothing to prevent Your Grace punishing a treacherous servant.'

Isabella turned to her lady-in-waiting. 'Summon him.'

Ellerker had not changed; still the same close-set eyes and nervous tics, his hands twisting in front of him. Merrivale took his arm and drew him to the table, pointing down at the parchments. 'You recognise these,' he said.

'Yes,' said Ellerker, his voice little above a whisper.

Merrivale turned to the queen. 'What is your command, Your Grace?'

'That groom of yours. Is he as strong as he looks?'

'Yes, Your Grace.'

'Take this vermin down to the stables, and order your man to give him thirty strokes with a horsewhip. After that, take him to the gate and throw him out. If I ever see him again, I will cut his throat myself.'

Ellerker opened his mouth to speak, and Merrivale hit him a back-handed blow across the mouth that started blood pouring from a split lip. 'Come with me,' he said grimly.

After it was all over and he had washed the blood from his hands, the queen received him once more. 'I like you and you are useful,' she said. 'I am looking for a steward to manage my household. Are you interested?'

Merrivale bowed. 'If Your Grace should ever need my services again, you have only to command. But until then, I would prefer to stay with the king.'

'I thought you would say as much. My son, for all his faults, has an ability to inspire loyalty in others. When he learns to use that ability well, he will become a fine leader of men. At the moment, he is too trusting. It is a fault in our family,' she added.

'It is a fault in most families,' Merrivale said. 'Thank you again, Your Grace. I owe you a debt.'

Isabella smiled, a little wryly. 'It is good to be on the credit side of the account for a change,' she said. 'Keep yourself safe, Master Merrivale.'

23

Larling, March 1340

Edmund Gonville had still not fully recovered. His skin was pale and dry and his lank hair fell down over his shoulders. His hands trembled a little. 'What do you want?' he asked, his voice dull with resignation.

They were in the hall of Gonville's father's manor in Norfolk. There was no sign of Gonville senior; hiding among his books, probably, while sending his weak, ill son out to face trouble alone. *Whereas I left my weak, ill father to face an uncertain future alone. It has been over a year since I saw him last. Will he still know me?*

'The truth,' Merrivale said.

'The truth,' Gonville repeated. 'What is truth? Who among us is able to recognise it?'

'We can try.'

'Suppose I tell you what you want to know. What will you do to me?'

'That depends. However, if you do *not* cooperate, you will go to prison. The oubliette in Norwich castle is an unpleasant place. I don't think a man in your condition will last long there.'

Gonville said nothing. 'Think of your rectories,' Merrivale said. 'Think of the benefices you have been given, the offices you hold, the bribes you have taken. You are a wealthy man now. Do you wish to turn your back on all of that?'

The silence continued. 'We have Ellerker's correspondence,' Merrivale said. 'We have proof that you were involved in the saffron plot. Peruzzi used you and Ellerker in an attempt to control the queen mother, first by putting her in his debt and later by manipulating her servants. After you were poisoned, you tried to protect Ellerker by suggesting that John Stanton was behind the attempt on your life.'

'Yes,' Gonville said eventually.

'But Stanton didn't try to kill you. Who did?'

Gonville sighed. 'It was one of the saffron crokers. The one from Colchester, Nicholas le Flemyng.'

'Go on.'

'He called on me a few days earlier. He claimed to have a sum of money he was willing to invest in a loan to the king. Knowing the man, I very much doubted this and I told him to stop wasting my time and sent him away. But I wanted to know his real purpose in coming to Antwerp, so I instructed one of the servants to follow him and report back to me. After leaving the castle, Flemyng went straight to the Solaro house.'

'The wine that poisoned you. Did it come from La Rochelle?'

Gonville looked surprised. 'Yes, it was. Very good quality, too. I was pleased when a servant told me they had acquired a cask.'

'Did you recognise this servant?'

'Why would I? One menial looks very like another.'

'The wine came from Aufrej Solaro,' Merrivale said. 'He also made a payment to Flemyng, on behalf of Donato de' Peruzzi.'

The surprise deepened. 'Why would Peruzzi want to kill me?'

'I said he paid Flemyng, I didn't say he gave the order. Flemyng was Peruzzi's agent, but I think he was loaned out for the occasion. Have you thought any more about why anyone would want you dead? Had you made enemies at court?'

'Apart from you? None that I know of. There were the usual grumbles, of course. I had risen to a high post very quickly, and people were jealous.'

'You owe your place to the favour of Bishop Burghersh.'

'He recommended me to the king, yes, but others found me useful as well. I have considerable skill with numbers.'

'What does that mean?'

'I know how to manipulate accounts,' Gonville said. 'Specifically, I know how to create accounts that give a false picture of a financial position. I can make money appear where it is not, and hide it where it is present.'

Light began to dawn on Merrivale. 'Was this the special work that Burghersh wanted from you in Antwerp?'

Gonville hesitated for a long time before answering. 'To secure the Flemish alliance, we had to promise a subsidy of forty thousand pounds,' he said finally. 'The captain general demanded proof that we could pay, but we didn't have enough money. So, I diverted the funds from the king's chamber to Bishop Burghersh and created two sets of accounts, one showing the real position, the other indicating that the forty thousand was still lodged in the treasury of the king's chamber.'

'What do you mean, you didn't have the money? Sir Geoffrey Scrope arranged a loan for forty thousand pounds from Peruzzi. Where did that money go?'

'I made it disappear,' Gonville said bleakly.

'Were you paid for this service?'

'I received a commission of a thousand pounds.'

'Was the forty thousand pounds ever paid to the Flemings?'

'I assume it was. I was attacked before the transaction could be completed.'

'John Moleyns would have seen those account rolls. Did he not suspect anything was wrong?'

'He knew all about it,' Gonville said. 'I expect he was also paid a commission.'

'For God's sake! Did *no one* see what was happening?'

'Why would they? This is not real money, Merrivale. It is not gold or silver, or even bills of exchange. This money is invisible, passing from ledger to ledger and account book to account book. A clever man can make those books say anything he wants, so long as all the accounts appear to balance in the end.'

'What were you doing before you were summoned to Antwerp?'

'I worked with Moleyns on the loans coming from foreign banks. Balduin's syndicate, and also the Solaro and Peruzzi loans.'

'Very well,' Merrivale said. 'Moleyns says the Solaros had made loans to the king totalling fifty thousand marks. I took documents from their strongroom indicating they had lent over seventy thousand. What happened to the other twenty thousand?'

Gonville looked at him with red-rimmed eyes. 'Need I spell it out for you?'

'No. Did you take a commission on these transactions too?'

'For hiding the money in the accounts, yes. Some other court officials also received a share. The bulk of the money was remitted to England.'

'Who received it?'

This time the silence was longer even than before. 'Reginald Conduit, the London wine merchant,' Gonville said finally.

'Ah, yes, of course. You are Conduit's connection at court. You look out for his interests. Aufrej Solaro paid Conduit five hundred marks last year. Do you know why?'

'How do you know this?'

'Answer the question.'

'Conduit needed to make payments to members of Parliament, especially in the commons. We didn't have the money, but somehow Peruzzi found out about it and stepped in. He instructed Solaro to make the payment.'

'Those payments Conduit made were not simple largesse to his fellow members of Parliament, were they? They were bribes, to encourage them to resist the will of the king.'

'I will not answer that question.'

'You don't have to. Where can I find evidence of this?'

'Nowhere. We covered our tracks completely.'

Gonville looked exhausted. He would not be able to continue the conversation for much longer. 'One more thing,' Merrivale said. 'You told me in Antwerp that you thought Moleyns might be in league with the Stratfords and their party. Was that true?'

'It was. But as I told you, I cannot prove it.'

Merrivale rose to his feet, looking down at the sick man. 'You asked what the consequences will be. You will not return to court. The king will be informed that you have decided to retire from public life and devote yourself to good works. Take your stolen wealth and spend it where it will do good for other people. Do that, and I might consider that justice has been done.'

'I shall do so,' Gonville said quietly. 'This is my penance. I am facing the end of my life, and now I must seek redemption.' He looked up at Merrivale. 'Who redeems *you*, King's Messenger?'

'I will tell you at the end of the road,' Merrivale said.

Southwark, March 1340

The snow had melted now and the ice was breaking up in the Thames. Walking across the bridge from London, Merrivale looked out through the gaps between houses and saw great translucent slabs grinding together as they drifted down towards the sea. Rain pattered on the roofs of thatched houses and ran in steady streams from the eaves.

Edmund Grimsby met him at St Mary's dock outside the priory of St Mary Overie. Water dripped from the brim of his hood. 'We must be careful,' he said. 'The Lord Chancellor has set men to spy on me. I don't know whether he questions my loyalty, or he has some suspicion about my family. The first I can deal with, but not the second.'

Merrivale nodded towards Warin, standing at the head of the dock. 'If anyone tries to interfere, he will deal with them.'

Grimsby pointed to a ship moored next to the dock, a roundship of perhaps fifty tons burden, with a single mast and furled sail. 'That is Nicholas le Flemyng's vessel, the *Witschip*. He himself is not aboard, but is currently living at the Tabard. He stays inside most days and rarely goes out. He seems to be waiting for something, or someone.'

'Thank you,' Merrivale said. He hesitated. 'If I were to provide you with a set of accounts, could you spot whether someone had falsified them in order to commit fraud?'

'I am a trained auditor, so yes, I should be able to do so. Will I know what I am looking for?'

'I can give you a few clues. First, I need to get my hands on the accounts without the man who owns them realising they are missing. That may not be easy.'

'Who owns them?'

Merrivale gazed at the ship. *I cannot do this alone*, he thought. *Sooner or later I will have to trust someone.*

Another voice in his mind said, *you trusted too many people in Savoy, and you paid the price.*

I know. But Grimsby has played fair so far.

'John Moleyns,' he said.

'You *are* playing with fire,' Grimsby said. His voice had lost its usual dry tone.

'I know. The men who went to Nottingham ten years ago are the king's sacred band, his praetorians. He will stand by them to the end, and it will take incontrovertible evidence to break his trust. But Moleyns is betraying the king.'

'Is there some connection between him and Flemyng? And Peruzzi?'

'That is what I need to find out,' Merrivale said.

Grimsby nodded. 'If you can acquire these accounts, bring them to me. I will do what I can.'

The inn known as the Tabard stood just off the high street. The courtyard was full of people watching a cockfight, shouting and shaking their fists in the air while the birds circled each other, scratching at the ground and bobbing their heads. Neither looked much like it wanted to fight, Merrivale thought. Perhaps it was the rain.

He nodded to Warin, who melted into the crowd. Pushing through a group of pilgrims in grey cloaks, Merrivale entered the common room. The air smelled of stale ale, woodsmoke and sweat. Two women in bright gowns and painted faces looked at him hopefully. He tapped a servant on the shoulder. 'Where is Nicholas le Flemyng?'

The servant held out a hand. Merrivale put a halfpenny into his palm. The servant looked at it for a moment, then closed his hand. 'First floor gallery, third door.'

Merrivale climbed the stairs to the gallery overlooking the courtyard and lifted the latch on the door, moving swiftly inside with his hand on the hilt of his dagger. He need not have bothered. The room was empty apart from a bed and a charcoal brazier, which was stone cold. 'Body of Christ,' he said.

'Blasphemy,' said a voice behind him. 'But, in this case, understandable.'

Merrivale turned to see a brown-robed Franciscan friar smiling back at him. 'Welcome, Simon,' said Raimon Vidal, folding his arms across his chest. 'It is good to see you again.'

'What are you doing here?'

'As always, serving my master's interests. Bishop Aubert continues to cherish hopes of negotiating peace between France and England.'

'Does your master believe in unicorns? Two months ago, King Edward laid claim to the throne of France and denounced Philip of Valois as a usurper. There is no chance of peace now.'

A roar went up from the courtyard below. Vidal grimaced. 'Cockfighting is such a vulgar sport, don't you think? I agree, the auspices are not good, but the bishop is a tenacious man. Once his heart is set on a goal, he is not easily dissuaded.'

Merrivale studied him. 'Where is Nicholas le Flemyng?'

'Somewhere safe.'

'What do you want with him?'

'Nothing. I find him boorish and not a little objectionable. But the bishop has decided to recruit him into his service.'

'Oh? In which commodity is Bishop Aubert planning to invest? Saffron, or poison?'

Vidal chuckled. 'You would have to ask the bishop. I was ordered to find Flemyng, and of course, keep him safe from you.'

Merrivale nodded. 'A word to the wise. If he offers you a goblet of wine, don't drink it.'

'I have already taken that into account.'

The two prostitutes had come upstairs and were walking along the gallery, knocking on doors and calling out for custom. 'I understand they are known locally as Winchester geese,' Vidal said. 'The Bishop of Winchester owns most of the brothels in Southwark, so that makes sense. But I fail to understand the allusion to geese.'

'Perhaps they sound the alarm when a stranger approaches.'

'Indeed? When I approached them, I found them to be most welcoming. But then, I have always said the English are a hospitable people. Perhaps if you tell me your interest in Flemyng I could broker a deal.'

'Surely you already know. He murdered one man, attempted to murder another and was involved in at least two other cases of poisoning.'

Vidal raised his eyebrows. 'Really, Simon, is that all? In these days such trivial offences are hardly worth bothering about. What you really want, of course, is to know the name of his paymaster. Do you suspect Donato de' Peruzzi?'

'Yes.'

'Think again. Peruzzi has indeed employed Flemyng's services and found him useful. But Peruzzi needed desperately to stay in the English king's good books so he could continue to make profitable loans. Why would he poison two of the king's most trusted servants?'

Merrivale considered this for a moment. Disappointed, the two women had drifted away. 'Who, then?'

'I have no idea. It doesn't really interest me. But if I were you, given the rifts that are opening up in your court and government, I should start looking much closer to home.'

'I will find Flemyng,' Merrivale said. 'And neither you nor the bishop will deny me.'

'There is another way, Simon. Accept the bishop's offer to join his service, and he will give you access to Flemyng.'

'I have already returned to the king's household.'

'Then let us hope that is a choice you do not regret.' Vidal studied him for a moment. 'You puzzle me,' he said. 'Most people have a weak spot, and when I find it I can bend them to my will. What is your Achilles heel, I wonder? It certainly isn't women. You appear to have forgotten Yolande quite thoroughly. Does her fate not trouble you at all?'

'Shut up, Raimon.'

'A dazzling woman. Quite the fairest ornament of Bohemia's court. I've heard her compared to Helen of Troy. How did Dares Phrygius put it?

'*The face that overthrew all Asia and took pride*
That she set lords on fire, and tore the world in war,
And won an ugly fame for beauty without shame.

'But of course, she is married now and so she is unobtainable. Do you suppose she still remembers you fondly, or is all her affection given to her new husband?'

'You have no idea how close I am to killing you,' Merrivale said. 'You and I have nothing more to say to each other, Raimon. Go in peace.'

He had said he would wait, but he could only wait for so long. Events were threatening to spin out of control. At Westminster the preparations for the next session of Parliament were under way, and the air hummed with tension. Merrivale sought out Geoffrey Scrope.

'I have a delicate question for you, Sir Geoffrey. Have you ever had cause to suspect the loyalty of Sir John Moleyns?'

Scrope's eyebrows rose. 'Why do you ask?'

'Edmund Gonville suspects him of intriguing with the archbishop's party,' Merrivale said.

'Does he now? Let me answer your question this way. If my right hand suspected John Moleyns of anything, I would order my left hand to cut it off. In the king's eyes, Moleyns is untouchable. You have been restored to favour once, Simon. Be grateful for that, and keep your peace.'

24

Westminster, April 1340

King Edward gestured towards the rain-splattered windows of the painted hall. 'Can no one shut them up?' he asked.

Even though it was raining, a group of several hundred people had gathered in the road outside the palace. The sound of singing came clearly into the hall where the king stood with his officials, Scrope and Burghersh with Merrivale waiting quietly behind them, facing Archbishop Stratford and his brother the Lord Chancellor.

Our prince of England
By the counsel of his gentlemen,
At Westminster after Easter
He made a great Parliament.
The charters agreed were written on wax;
They were held too near the fire
And now all are melted away.
Hundred, chapter, court and shire
All go the devil's way.

'We have dispersed them several times, sire,' the archbishop said. 'Each time they return. We are reluctant to use force for fear of provoking a confrontation.'

The king shook his head in disgust. 'With respect, sire, we have more urgent problems,' said the Lord Chancellor. 'Parliament is demanding concessions before it will consent to the new tax.'

'What does it want?'

'The power of scrutiny over the collection of the tax, and a voice in future decisions concerning expenditure, not just of this tax but all royal revenues.'

Sir Geoffrey Scrope shook his head. 'I do not advise this, sire. The lords and commons are welcome to scrutinise the tax collectors, but how the money is spent is none of their business. Once the money has been collected and handed over to the king's chamber, it belongs to you. It is yours to do with as you please.'

Outside in the spring rain the singing went on.

Might is right
Light is night
And fight is flight
Because might is right, the land is lawless
Because night is light, the land is faithless
Because fight is flight, the land is shameless

Archbishop Stratford shook his head. 'We must be careful, sire. There will be resistance to the tax collectors, we may be sure of that, and with the people in their present mood it would not take much to turn that resistance into open revolt.'

'Damn the people!' Bishop Burghersh thundered. 'Shall they be allowed to thwart the king's will? *You*, my lord Archbishop and *you*, my Lord Chancellor, are responsible for seeing that his orders are carried out!'

Stratford stared at him. 'I am your superior, my lord *bishop*. You will respect my office.'

Burghersh's face went redder than ever, and his fists clenched. 'You are my superior in matters spiritual, my lord. In the temporal realm, I obey only the king.'

'Peace!' Geoffrey Scrope said sharply. 'We need to remember who the real enemy is, my lords. The galleys may have withdrawn from our coasts, but France has still managed to raise a fleet of more than two hundred ships. They are calling this the Great Army of the Sea. We need to raise a fleet to match theirs, and an army capable of defending our new allies in Flanders and carrying the war to the enemy. We need ships and crews, men-at-arms and archers, bows and arrows and cannon and stone shot, and we need them now.'

He looked at the archbishop and the chancellor. 'You are servants of the king. Your task is to see that his wishes are carried out.'

There was a moment of silence. The archbishop stirred a little. 'May I inquire as to Your Grace's intentions?'

'I am returning to Flanders as soon as possible,' the king said curtly. 'I have already wasted far too much time here. Give the commons whatever they demand, but bring me the money from the Ninth, my lords. That is my command.'

Silently, the Stratfords left the room. The king sighed. 'Will this work?' he asked.

'It will if they follow orders,' Scrope said. 'The yield from this tax should be considerable, far higher than the wool revenues.'

'You should have been more severe with them, sire,' said Burghersh. 'We must make clear the penalties if they fail.'

'God damn it, Henry, I can't execute bishops for failing to collect taxes. What will the Pope say? Is he using Bishop Aubert to spy on us?'

The last question was directed at Merrivale. 'The bishop is playing some game of his own,' the latter said. 'One of his agents is in London. I am having him followed.'

'I don't trust Aubert. I don't trust any of those bastards in Avignon. The sooner we break the French hold over the papacy, the better.' The king made an impatient gesture. 'And I certainly don't trust the Stratfords. I still suspect they had a hand in the failure of the wool syndicate. Could they have done so?'

Burghersh glanced at Merrivale. 'It is certainly possible, sire. We need to keep a close watch on them, and the Lord Treasurer too.'

Scrope stroked his beard. 'May I make a suggestion, sire? When we sail for Flanders, leave Sir John Moleyns behind. Instruct the Lord Treasurer that Sir John will examine all of his accounts. Sir John knows every sharp practice there is, and if anyone tries to defraud us he will be sure to spot it.'

'Sound advice,' the king said approvingly. 'I will speak to Moleyns myself.'

Whoever rows against the flood
Of sorrow shall he drink
Now one is two
Weal is woe
And friend is foe
Because one is two, the land is without strength
Because weal is woe, the land is without pity
Because friend is foe, the land is without love

Scrope laid a hand on Merrivale's shoulder as they walked out of the hall. 'I have reflected since we last spoke,' he said. 'No one can be above suspicion, none save the king himself.'

'You are testing Moleyns,' Merrivale said.

'Exactly. Have a private word with Zouche and instruct him to keep a careful watch on Moleyns, too. If either is cheating us, the other will spot it.'

'Unless they both are. Sir Geoffrey, may I repeat His Grace's words? Will this work?'

'It will work. One victory, Merrivale. One victory will be enough to shake Philip of France from his throne. But first, we need that money.'

Heed the words of the Rambam. Do not ask what the plot is, but instead ask what it is not.

Neither the archbishop or the chancellor had spoken out against the war, they had only warned of the risks. Similarly, the people chanting in the rain outside the palace were not protesting against the war; they were angry about injustice and corruption. If unrest broke out, as Stratford had suggested it might, that would be the reason.

Back at Merrivale's lodgings, Warin was waiting. 'I followed the Franciscan as you ordered, sir. He went to a big house up by the Temple and let himself in through the postern. I asked around, and folk say the house is owned by the Keeper of the Privy Seal.'

'Let us go,' Merrivale said.

The house was outside the western walls of the city, on rising ground overlooking the rain-splattered waters of the Fleet. The gates were shut and the house appeared dark. 'The postern is around the back,' Warin said.

The door was locked. Merrivale unhooked the pin from his cloak and inserted it into the lock, waggling it until the door clicked open. 'That's an interesting skill, sir,' Warin murmured.

'I'll teach it to you.' They stepped quietly into the empty kitchen, climbed the stone stair beyond and walked into the screens passage. The door to the hall was closed but they could hear a murmur of voices, easily identifiable as Vidal and William Kildesby. Merrivale stepped closer to the door and listened.

'Is your king not disturbed by the size of the French fleet?' Vidal asked. 'I doubt if he can raise enough ships to counter them.'

'So do I,' Kildesby said. 'But Edward is desperate for a battle. He seems to think victory will solve all his problems.'

'Will it?'

'Of course not. You must have seen the mood in the streets.'

'I heard the songs, yes. I thought they were directed more towards the king's officials than the king himself. Edward is popular, and he is clever enough to know how to milk that popularity. If you are trying to curb his ambitions, Kildesby, I don't give much for your chances.'

'Wait until the new tax fails,' Kildesby says. 'When the country is bled white and the king still doesn't have enough money to win the war, things will change.'

'Will the tax fail?'

'There are men determined to see that it does.'

'Will you tell me their names? If you do, I will double the payment you are currently receiving.'

Merrivale pushed the door open. 'And I will double whatever Vidal pays,' he said. 'Go on, Master Kildesby. Name them.'

Kildesby's sharp nose seemed to grow even more pointed. 'Merrivale! How did you get in?'

'Through the postern,' Merrivale said. 'You might want to install a stronger lock. Do you really know who these people are, or are you just boasting to attract Vidal's attention?'

Kildesby said nothing. 'I'm afraid you have been gulled, Raimon,' Merrivale said. 'He may be Keeper of the Privy Seal, but he knows nothing of importance. Neither side really trusts him, you see. The Stratfords believe he is still secretly loyal to the king, and the king's party hate him for publicly adhering to the Stratfords.'

'You don't know what you are talking about,' Kildesby said sullenly.

'Raimon, I need to speak to our friend alone. If you step into the screens passage, my man Warin will escort you outside. Treat Warin with respect. He is very good at hurting people.'

'Like master, like man,' Vidal said in a rare flash of temper. He stood up and strode out of the hall, brown robes flapping around his ankles. Merrivale turned back to Kildesby. 'What is he paying you for? Information?'

Kildesby was silent again. 'You do realise this is treason,' Merrivale said.

'Treason? His master is a bishop, a prince of the Church. He is not our enemy.'

'Étienne Aubert is also a Frenchman. Body of Christ, Kildesby, how could you have been so stupid?'

'He paid well,' Kildesby said finally.

'I'm sure he did, but there is more to it than that. I lied to Vidal just now because I needed to get him away from you before you did something even more stupid, like naming the men who are conspiring against the king. Why did you side with Stratford? What did he and his friends promise you?'

'A bishop's mitre.' Kildesby looked suddenly defiant. 'Don't try to threaten me again, Merrivale. I have powerful protectors now.'

Merrivale feigned surprise. 'Threaten you? That is the last thing on my mind. I have come here to buy you.'

'What can you possibly offer me?'

'The Archbishop of York passed into the kingdom of heaven last week, and the see is vacant. The chapter will be looking for a new candidate. The king has already nominated you and will give you his full support.'

The foxy face looked stunned. '*York!* Are you serious?'

'Very. You would be the second most powerful prelate in the land.'

'I haven't even been ordained as a priest.'

'We will arrange the ceremony,' Merrivale said. 'It doesn't take long.'

'Holy Mary... What does the king want in exchange?'

'First, end this arrangement with Vidal. Second, surrender the privy seal. Third, cease your association with the Stratfords.'

Cunning crept into Kildesby's face. 'When I am ordained archbishop, then you shall have the privy seal. Not before.'

'Very well. But if you use the seal on any document that affects the tax of the Ninth, or in any other way that furthers Parliament's power at the expense of the king, his support will be revoked and I will inform him of your dealings with Vidal. Is that clear?'

'Quite clear,' said Kildesby. He paused for a moment. 'Why are you doing this? What do *you* want?'

'Isn't it obvious? I want you, and the privy seal, removed from the game.'

'You won't win,' Kildesby said. His eyes glinted a little. 'But then you're used to losing, aren't you, Merrivale? You had plenty of practice in Savoy.'

Merrivale hit him a back-handed blow across the face, rocking him back in his chair. 'Never speak of Savoy to me again. Is John Moleyns working with the Stratfords?'

'How would I know?' Kildesby said sullenly, rubbing his cheek. 'It is as you said. I cannot be trusted.'

'Nevertheless, I am sure the dean and chapter of York will make you very welcome,' Merrivale said. 'Keep your word, Kildesby, and we shall keep ours.'

Outside the rain had trailed off. Merrivale, Vidal and Warin walked down to the wooden bridge over the Fleet and stopped, looking down into the turgid stream. 'Is this where you intend to dispose of my corpse?' Vidal asked. His face was composed again, the earlier anger smoothed away.

'Another time,' Merrivale said.

'What, then? I thought we had nothing more to say to each other.'

'You were wrong. What is your master's relationship with Donato de' Peruzzi?'

'You've finally worked that out, have you? It is quite simple. Bishop Aubert desires to be pope one day. Peruzzi thinks he has the right qualities, and is backing him financially.'

'Which explains why you stepped in to whisk Nicholas le Flemyng away from me. You did it as a favour to Peruzzi. But what if the Peruzzi bank collapses?'

'The bishop will find another patron. I don't imagine he will need to look very far.'

'The money the bishop instructs you to pay Kildesby, and doubtless others too. Does it come from Peruzzi?'

'I am only a humble Franciscan, Simon. Such matters are far above me.'

'I will take that as an affirmative. I need something from you, Raimon.'

'I see. Depending on what it is, I might comply. It will be interesting to have you beholden to me.'

'That's not quite how it works,' Merrivale said. 'I need you to procure some accounts from the strongbox of Sir John Moleyns, the treasurer of the king's chamber.'

'Forgive me, Simon, I must be growing hard of hearing. I thought I heard you say that you wanted me to steal private papers from one of the king's closest advisors. Surely that cannot be the case.'

Merrivale said nothing. Behind him, Warin shifted from one foot to the other.

'What makes you think I have the ability to do this?' Vidal asked.

'I have known you for many years, Raimon. I would not have asked you if I didn't know of the wide scope of your talents.'

'For the sake of argument, what happens if I refuse?'

'You will be arrested as a spy.'

'And Bishop Aubert will intervene, and I will be released.'

'I thought that too, before I listened to your conversation with Kildesby. However, the bishop seeks influence in England. If it became public knowledge that his own secretary had been acting as a spy at court, it seems entirely plausible that he would throw you to the wolves in order to save his own reputation. What do you think? You know him better than I do.'

'I think you have read his character with great accuracy. If I perform this service for you, how do I know you will keep your word?'

'You don't. You have a simple choice. Do as I ask, or you will be arrested and sent to the Tower.'

'How refreshing it must be to see the world in such binary terms. You're a shit, Simon. But so am I, so I suppose we deserve each other. What documents do you want?'

'I will give you a list,' Merrivale said.

London, May 1340

'I will come straight to the point,' Merrivale said. 'Sir John Moleyns has been assigned to work with you to ensure the tax of the Ninth is collected fairly and in full, and to see the money is remitted to the king. We need you to keep watch on him and check his accounts.'

William de la Zouche, the Lord Treasurer, stared hard at Merrivale. He was a stocky man in his early forties, already with a few flecks of grey in his hair. He looked like he had not been sleeping well. 'Why?' he demanded.

'The king does not need to give reasons,' said Merrivale.

'Is Moleyns no longer trusted?'

Merrivale said nothing. Zouche leaned back in his carved oak chair. 'The chancellor has already told me that Moleyns will be working in my office, checking *my* accounts. Now you want me to check on him as well. We are supposed to spy on each other?'

'There is no question of spying, my lord. The king is merely concerned to see that the accounts are rendered accurately and the full sum of the tax raised is remitted to him.'

'The king doesn't know a damned thing about this, does he? No, don't bother to reply. I already know the answer.'

'Do we have your cooperation?' Merrivale asked.

'No, you don't. Blood of Christ, I am already in an impossible position. The ultimate responsibility for collecting this tax and remitting it to the king rests with me as Lord Treasurer. If anything goes wrong, it is my head on a spike. I will not get caught in the middle of whatever game the Stratfords and Scrope and Burghersh are playing.'

'I am surprised to hear it. I thought you were a loyal adherent to the Stratfords and their party.'

'Not any more. I've had enough, Merrivale. I'm tired of the scheming and the intrigue. I heard a new chant in the streets this morning, do you know this one?

'*Half of what is raised in the kingdom does not come to the king.*
Since he has not got the whole that he was promised,
The people are obliged to give more, and thus they go hungry,
For the taxes which are raised are not all given to the king.

'People are angry about the corruption, Merrivale, and by God I don't blame them.'

'So what will you do? Go out into the streets and join them?'

'I might have been tempted, but I have had a better offer. The dean and chapter of York have offered me the post of archbishop. I have already informed the Lord Chancellor that I am resigning as treasurer.'

'The king will not be pleased,' Merrivale said after a moment. 'He has recommended Kildesby for the archbishopric.'

'Yes. The chapter's response was, *anyone but Kildesby*.'

Merrivale thought for a moment. 'With respect, why did the dean and chapter at York choose you? There must have been other candidates.'

Zouche looked momentarily uncomfortable. 'Yes, I confess I was surprised. But the dean made it clear that I was the first choice. Bishop Burghersh had written to them, strongly recommending me. His word counts for something.'

'More than the king's?'

'So it would seem,' said Zouche.

'We have been duped,' Merrivale said to Sir Geoffrey Scrope later that day.

Scrope shook his head in annoyance. 'Stratford guessed we were going to put Moleyns under scrutiny. Or perhaps he just doubted Zouche's loyalty. Either way, York was the bribe to remove Zouche.'

'And we have also lost our hold over Kildesby. Do you think this is Stratford's doing? Zouche told me it was Henry Burghersh who wrote to the chapter and put his name forward. Or is Burghersh also playing us false? Has he too gone over to Stratford's faction?'

Scrope looked suddenly tired. 'God knows,' he said quietly. 'Until last month I would have said Henry was as loyal to the king as I am myself. Now, I am starting to doubt everyone.'

'If Parliament approves the tax of the Ninth, Stratford's faction will try to interfere with the collection of the tax, or attempt to delay remittance of money to the king. Or both.'

'How do you know this?' Scrope asked.

'I don't, for certain. But I would bet good money on it.'

'Then we shall have to be doubly vigilant,' Scrope said bleakly.

London, May 1340

The commissions of array went out, instructing men and ships to assemble and prepare for service overseas. Word came from Kent; the Great Army of the Sea was passing through the straits between Calais and the North Foreland, their hulls and sails so numerous that they obscured the sea itself. Bells rang the alarm and archers and men-at-arms hurried to defend the coasts, but instead of attacking England, the huge fleet moved on to Flanders and dropped anchor in the estuary of the Zwin, blocking access to the Flemish seaports. Word came from the queen in Ghent, speaking of panic in the streets.

Time passed. The days grew longer and warmer. In the fields of Essex the army began to assemble; columns of men-at-arms in armour and jingling harness, bright surcoats and banners blazing in the sun; troops of archers, lean muscular men in russet and green with longbows resting on their shoulders; wagons full of flour and salt pork, siege equipment, bundles of arrows, portable forges and grinding wheels, coal and firewood. In the ravaged harbours of the east coast, ships began to assemble and carpenters went aboard to build fighting castles. Cannons were carried out of their foundry in the Tower of London and tested on the green outside, rattling windows with their noise and filling the air with clouds of yellow smoke.

Raimon Vidal called at Merrivale's lodgings, carrying a sack bulging with parchment rolls. 'You realise I have read all of these and know their contents.'

'And probably made copies,' Merrivale said. 'I know you hate getting your hands dirty, so I presume you hired someone else to undertake the actual theft. Are the loose ends tied up?'

'I am offended that you should even ask. I said I have read these accounts, but I do not understand them.'

'That is because these documents were created by a very skilled man. Fortunately, I know another man who can interpret them.'

'I am curious, Simon. I do not like secrets, especially ones I don't already know.'

'Then you are doomed to disappointment. Instead, I offer you a piece of advice. Tell Bishop Aubert to stay out of English politics for the time being. The next six months could be dangerous, and he wouldn't want to end up on the wrong side.'

'I told you that you were playing with fire,' Edmund Grimsby said.

'It is a hazard of my profession,' said Merrivale. 'What have you found?'

'Very large sums of money are being received by the king's chamber, but never rest there for long. Sometimes the money moves to other household accounts. Sometimes it disappears entirely.'

'That should not be surprising. We know the king is spending money like water.'

Grimsby shook his head. 'I can see the expenditures, but there is much more to it than that. Someone has been moving money around very quickly, almost like sleight of hand, in order to deceive the auditors. I admire the skill of whoever did this. They are an artist.'

'I know who did it,' Merrivale said. 'What I need to know is why.'

'All of this trickery was designed to cover up a series of immense frauds. The loans from the Solaro bank, for example, totalled about seventy thousand marks. I calculate that only about thirty thousand actually reached the king's hands. The rest was stolen.'

Merrivale closed his eyes for a moment. 'And the other loans? The same?'

'I fear so. Most of them have been plundered. Of the vast loan made by the Bartolomei bank from Lucca, only about a third reached the king's treasury. And I can only find about forty thousand florins of the money lent by Archbishop Balduin's syndicate.'

'Mary, Mother of God! That is three hundred thousand florins missing!'

'Yes. A Tartar horde would not have been more thorough in their pillaging.'

And the king had been forced to leave his pregnant wife defenceless in Ghent, unable even to pay the archers of her bodyguard. Merrivale felt a sudden surge of anger. 'Are there any clues as to who took the money, or where it is now?'

'No,' said Grimsby. 'Which means there is little chance of recovering it. And Balduin's syndicate have the great crown in their possession.'

'Which they could break up and melt down, or sell to the French. Either of which would humiliate the king.'

'Is that the aim of the conspiracy?'

Heed the words of the Rambam. 'That is the obvious conclusion, isn't it? But nothing about this entire case is obvious. Is there anything we can use to prosecute Moleyns?'

Grimsby shook his head. 'There is nothing indicating he is responsible. There was one reference to a payment of twenty thousand marks from Moleyns to the London merchant Reginald Conduit back in January, but that appears to be a repayment of an earlier loan. We could make a case that Moleyns should have spotted the thefts, but that only amounts to incompetence, not corruption.'

'Yes,' Merrivale said slowly. 'And Moleyns himself will know by now that the documents are missing. He will have prepared a convincing story, or perhaps even created new documents that tell a different story. And he is the one the king will listen to, at least for the moment. Where are the accounts now?'

'Hidden in the Chancery archives. Don't worry, they are perfectly safe. Do you know how many thousands of rolls of parchment we have? A man could search for a year and never find them, unless he knew where to look.'

Merrivale nodded. 'Thank you, Master Grimsby. I am in your debt.'

'What will you do now?'

'The king travels to Harwich tomorrow,' Merrivale said. 'I am bidden to attend on him there. We sail for France as soon as the winds favour us.'

'I shall pray that God watches over you,' Grimsby said.

Westminster, May 1340

The palace was full of activity, servants packing boxes and chests in preparation for the move to Harwich. Merrivale sought out Geoffrey Scrope.

'Moleyns paid Conduit twenty thousand marks earlier this year,' he said. 'It could be the repayment of a loan, but this payment was made at a time when the king's chamber was all but bankrupt. Where did the money come from? We already know that Conduit received money from Aufrej Solaro to bribe his fellow members of Parliament to oppose the king.'

Scrope's face was grim. 'Leave this with me, Merrivale. Not a word to anyone, do you hear?'

'Yes, Sir Geoffrey.' Merrivale watched Scrope's back as the latter walked away. *That is the problem*, he thought bleakly. *We all have too many secrets.*

25

Harwich, June 1340

Fifteen months had passed since Ottone Doria's raiders had reduced Harwich to smoking ruins. Since then much of the town had been rebuilt, although the rasp of saws and thump of hammers still echoed in the streets. The inn known as The Bear was all raw masonry and pale new-cut timbers, but Merrivale felt he could still smell smoke lingering in the air.

'According to the latest reports, sire, the French fleet is still anchored in the Zwin,' Sir Geoffrey Scrope said. 'They may have two hundred and fifty ships by now, and many of their vessels are larger than ours.'

The English fleet lay at anchor nearby in the estuary of the Stour. The forest of masts and yards looked impressive, but some of the ships were only around thirty tons burden.

'What are the Flemings doing?' King Edward asked.

'There is not much they can do, sire,' said Bishop Burghersh. 'They have no ships of their own, and they are facing a French army mustering on their southern border. If the French fleet lands troops in the north, they will be caught in the jaws of a vice. The captain general begs us to send aid quickly.'

'The best way to aid the Flemings is to defeat the French,' the king said. 'What is the last thing the French admirals will expect us to do?'

The bishop rubbed his chin. 'Their fleet is far more powerful than ours and is anchored in a secure position. They must imagine they are safe from direct attack.'

'Then they are in for a rude awakening,' the king said. He looked around at his captains. 'I said I wanted a battle, and by God we're going to have one. Tell the shipmasters to start their preparations. Organise the ships into groups of three, two full of archers and the third with men-at-arms. I want every ship fully armed and provisioned for a long fight. You have your orders, gentlemen. Make it so.'

The captains filed out of the room, Scrope and Burghersh following them. The king turned to Merrivale. 'You will return to Ghent immediately with messages for the queen and the captain general. John Crabbe will give you passage.'

'Yes, sire,' said Merrivale, bowing.

The king watched him for a moment. 'I need to trust the people around me,' he said. 'I need to know that I can rely on them.'

'Yes, sire.'

'So, tell me the truth. John Moleyns thinks Scrope may be intriguing against him. Do you know anything about this?'

Merrivale chose his words with great care. 'We have discovered a financial transaction between Sir John and Reginald Conduit. It is probably nothing more than a repayment of a loan, but when I informed Sir Geoffrey he felt this connection required further investigation.'

'Of course there is a connection. Conduit lent us money last year, and Moleyns handled the transaction.'

'Was it wise to take money from Conduit, sire?' Merrivale asked after a moment.

'One day, Merrivale, I will have a conversation with you where you don't question my authority. Are you suggesting Conduit cannot be trusted?'

'He had a relationship with the house of Solaro, and by implication, with Donato de' Peruzzi. Similarly, Sir John also had a connection with Aufrej Solaro. We found records of several commissions being paid to Sir John in exchange for help in arranging loans.'

'For Christ's sake, what are you saying? That *Moleyns* cannot be trusted?'

'I am quite certain that all of Sir John's transactions are legitimate, sire. But Sir Geoffrey felt it would be prudent to investigate.'

'Why was I not informed of this earlier?'

'Sir Geoffrey said he would inquire into the matter personally. There is no need to concern the king, he said.'

'But I *am* concerned! If I can't trust John Moleyns, who can I trust? He has been at my side for ten years, for Christ's sake!'

'Sire, there is no evidence that Sir John is untrustworthy.' That was almost true; certainly there was no evidence that would hold up in a court of law. 'As I said, Sir Geoffrey is merely being prudent.'

'Prudent,' the king said, as if the word has a bad taste. 'Very well, I will let this rest for now. We have too many other things to do to.' He jabbed a finger at Merrivale. 'But next time you learn something that might affect one of my household, don't go running to Scrope. Come straight to me. I don't care who is involved or how serious the issue might be, I want to know. Is that clear?'

'Yes, sire.'

The German Ocean, June 1340

John Crabbe's ship was called the *Dobeler*, a big weather-beaten round-ship with a stone-throwing engine mounted just in front of the mast, and a comforting number of archers and crossbowmen on board. The wind was fair from the west, and Harwich soon disappeared into the sea mist behind them. 'I can't take you to Antwerp or Ghent,' Crabbe said. 'The French have sea patrols all around the Zwin and the mouth of the Scheldt. I'll put you ashore at Testerep instead, and you can make your way overland from there.'

'Thank you.'

'Did you ever find the men who killed John Hull?'

'Yes.'

Crabbe did not ask what happened. 'And did you put a stop to the smuggling?'

'It turns out that wool smuggling was only the surface of the problem,' Merrivale said. 'There is a power struggle within government as well.'

The shipmaster nodded. 'I said as much. It's dog eat dog in London. Everyone wants to build their own empire. Sometimes piracy seems like a clean and honest living by comparison.'

Merrivale remembered what Hull said, just before he died. *Money buys you power, and power gives you access to money. It was ever thus.*

He gazed out over the rolling grey sea. The mast creaked, and the ship's rigging hummed a little in the stiff wind. Water rushed past the hull. *Heed the words of the Rambam*, he thought. Power was involved, yes, but was this really a political struggle? What if the quarrel between the king and the Stratfords was being whipped up by men – on both sides – who stood to profit from it?

And behind everything, of course, was the sinister figure of Donato de' Peruzzi. Bishop Aubert and Vidal had made Theophilus's bargain, a pact with the devil in which they sold their allegiance in exchange for Peruzzi's money. So had Nicholas le Flemyng. How many others had done the same? Gonville, certainly. Kildesby? Moleyns, the king's close friend? And where did Bishop Henry Burghersh fit into all of this?

At Peruzzi's direction, the queen mother's saffron had been stolen, the wool trade had been plundered and a great portion of the money the king had borrowed had been siphoned off. There was every chance that the tax of the Ninth would be plucked bare as well; Gonville was no longer available, but other creative masters of the account rolls would doubtless be found. And of course, John Hull and John Stanton had been murdered, along with Westacre and Dunham, while Nicholas le Flemyng was still free to roam the face of the earth.

What else might Peruzzi be seeking? Where might he turn his attention next? A memory turned over in the back of his mind, of the cellar in Strassburg, candlelight gleaming off gold and gemstones, and Velvl Roth's voice saying, *the crown is safe*.

Merrivale turned to Crabbe. 'You used to be a pirate. I need you to think like one now. What would you do if you knew where the great crown of England is?'

'Is it held securely?'

'Yes.'

'Then I would wait until it comes time to move it. Goods are always at their most vulnerable when being transported from one place to the other. I would study the ground, lay my plans, recruit the men I needed, and wait.'

'It might take a long time.'

Crabbe smiled. 'A good thief always knows how to wait,' he said.

Yes. So does a King's Messenger.

Closer to the Flemish coast a light mist descended once more, cutting visibility to about a mile. Crabbe ordered his crew to shorten sail and the *Dobeler* crawled forward over the oily dark waves, the lookouts peering ahead and trying to spot the lighthouse at Oostend on the island of Testerep. A distant murmur could be heard over the noises of the ship, the sound of waves rolling up on the beaches.

Someone shouted. Merrivale turned to see two long narrow wolf-like shapes emerging from the mist, high-prowed galleys with white sails decorated with enormous red crosses. 'That's the cross of Saint George!' someone said.

'There are no galleys in our fleet,' Merrivale said sharply. 'That is the device of Genoa. For Christ's sake, don't tell me Doria is back.'

'No,' said Crabbe, staring at the ships. 'This is a rogue Genoese captain, a man named Barbavera. I know him, I've crossed swords with him before.' He studied the two galleys. '*Dobeler* is a fast ship and we have the wind in our favour. We'll get you to Flanders, Master Merrivale, never fear.'

'And while I am landing, the galleys will cut you off from England. You'll have to fight to get past them.'

Crabbe smiled. 'I can deal with Barbavera. You need to worry about how he knew where to find us.'

'The king gave me his instructions in person. No one else was present. What about you?'

'A messenger brought the order, but it wasn't one of the royal pages. He wore the livery of Henry Burghersh, the bishop of Lincoln.'

Testerep could be seen now, a white line of glimmering surf washing up on its beaches. The galleys were falling behind; as predicted, they were turning now to cut off *Dobeler*'s escape route back to England. 'Who else knows this?' asked Merrivale.

'I said nothing to anyone, mostly because I thought nothing of it. I assumed Burghersh was carrying out the king's wishes.'

'Keep this to yourself,' Merrivale said.

'Oh, don't worry. I've learned three lessons during the course of my life. Never accept false money, never get pinned against a lee shore and never pick a fight with a bishop. I'll stay well away from Burghersh.'

Ghent, June 1340

The canals stank in the summer heat. Even behind the high walls of the Gravensteen the smell of sludge hung heavy in the air. Inside the castle the atmosphere was tense; outside, armed gangs fought each other in the streets. 'The factions who favour the French are growing bolder,' Alice Bedingfield said. She looked tired and drawn, thinner than when Merrivale had last seen her. The winter had been long and full of strain.

'The French fleet is holding fast in the Zwin,' she said, 'and their army is marching towards the southern borders of Flanders. The captain general has only a handful of militia at his disposal. Everyone's nerves are at full stretch.'

'The captain general was supposed to raise thirty thousand men!'

'Indeed, but Bruges and Ypres won't send troops. They say they need to defend their own cities first. Everything is unravelling, Simon.'

'Is the queen safe?'

'So far. Come, I will take you to her now.'

Queen Philippa looked tired too. She had given birth to a son three months earlier, and had not yet fully recovered. 'What word from my husband?' she asked directly as soon as Merrivale entered the room.

'He is on his way, Your Grace. The fleet was preparing to sail from Harwich when I departed. He sends you this letter.'

He bowed, handing over the parchment. The queen broke the seal and read it quickly. 'He intends to challenge the French fleet? With half as many ships?'

'He is certain of victory, Your Grace.'

'Send word to the chapel, Bedingfield. Tell the priests I want them down on their knees praying for victory from lauds until matins, every day from now until we hear word from the fleet. Yes, I know what you are about to say. I'll find some way of paying them.'

She looked back at Merrivale. 'Have you seen the captain general?'

'Not yet, Your Grace. I have a letter for him also. The king asks that he send the Flemish army north, to ward off a possible landing from the ships in the Zwin.'

'He can't do it. The French are already mustering in the south at Saint-Omer and Arras, and they have reinforced their position at Tournai. If they choose to strike downriver they could be here in two days, and the captain general's men are in no condition to oppose them. They are short of weapons, short of money and short of numbers, and I am sitting helpless here in Ghent wondering how in the name of Christ we got into this mess.'

'Bruges is not far from the Zwin,' Merrivale said. 'Perhaps the militia of Bruges, at least, could be sent to defend the shore.'

'Suggest it to the captain general when you see him. What about this new tax? How much money has it raised?'

'So far as I know, nothing yet. The new lambs are still being gathered in, shearing season has only just begun, and the corn will not be harvested for another two months. The officials are trying to organise advance payments based on the presumed value of the harvest, but this is taking time.'

'Unless he brings money, the king can expect a cold welcome in Flanders,' Philippa said bluntly. 'The treaty we signed with the League of Three promised a subsidy, but not a penny has yet been paid. The captain general is starting to ask questions.'

Merrivale's eyebrows rose. 'According to Gonville, the subsidy should have been handed over. There was some delay while the money was found, but that was resolved. I can ask Sir John Moleyns to confirm this.'

The queen's brown face darkened. 'Moleyns will tell you whatever he wants you to hear.'

'Does Your Grace distrust him?'

'I dislike him intensely. Him and Rowton and all the others who forced their way into Nottingham castle ten years ago and surprised my mother-in-law in bed with her lover. Hardly an act of gallantry, was it? There were other ways of arresting Mortimer that would have been less humiliating to the queen. But the king insists on treating them like heroes.' She sighed. 'Perhaps I am letting my feelings cloud my judgement. But I am not certain that Moleyns deserves the trust my husband reposes in him.'

'May I ask why Your Grace thinks this?'

'He is in charge of our finances, and our coffers are empty. Where has the money gone?'

Their eyes met for a moment. She knows, Merrivale thought. Or at least, she suspects.

'I suspect it has been hidden very skilfully, Your Grace,' he said quietly. 'It is possible that we may never recover it.'

'You are talking about embezzlement. By whom? The men who killed John Stanton?'

'Yes, Your Grace.'

The queen continued to stare at him. 'Do you know who they are?'

'I know who one of them is. I cannot yet say for certain about the others.'

'Have you told the king?'

'Not yet.' *I don't care who is involved or how serious the issue might be*, the king had said, *I want to know.* But there were some truths for which he was not yet ready.

The queen read his thoughts without difficulty. 'I understand,' she said. 'You need more proof before he will listen to you. But be careful, Master Merrivale. They missed you when they came for Stanton. They may not miss again.'

Cassandra Wesenham looked up in surprise as Merrivale walked into her shop. 'Welcome back. I did not realise the king had returned.'

They stepped into the quiet back room, out of earshot of her apprentices. 'The king is on his way to attack the French fleet,'

Merrivale said. 'God help us all if he fails. Are you safe here, Mistress Wesenham?'

Her eyes widened a little. 'So far the factions have been preoccupied with killing each other. There have been no reports of attacks on foreigners.'

'That may change if we are defeated. If ever you feel you are in danger, go to the Gravensteen and ask for Alice Bedingfield, the queen's lady-in-waiting. She will help you.'

'Thank you,' Cassandra said.

'I tracked down Nicholas le Flemyng in London, but he fled before I could speak to him. I wondered if he had returned to Ghent, but his house is empty.'

'The house is no longer his. It was seized by his creditors a few months ago, in exchange for outstanding debts.'

Merrivale was surprised. 'Debts? He received a payment of a thousand marks late last year. What has he done with it?'

'According to the gossip, his family are notorious spendthrifts. His father fled originally from Ghent to England because he could not pay his debts. There were also rumours that both father and son were colluding with the pro-French factions here in Flanders.'

'And now the son is in the service of a French bishop. If you hear any further rumours about Flemyng, please send word to me. You can leave a message with Mistress Bedingfield if I am absent. She, at least, I can trust.'

Ever since the voyage from England Merrivale could not stop thinking about the crown. Vidal had claimed he did not like secrets, but in fact he was extraordinarily good at ferreting them out. If Vidal and the bishop knew about the crown, then almost certainly so did Peruzzi, which meant the situation was even more dangerous than he had first thought. They would stop at nothing to get their hands on it and use it as a weapon of influence in either France or England. Or, possibly, they would simply sell it to the highest bidder, at a price a bankrupt England could not afford.

He reached the fish market, passing barrels of eels, fresh cod as long as a man's arm, lobsters in spiny black armour, and turned towards the bridge leading to the Gravensteen. A man stepped out of the crowd and grinned at him. '*Bondì*, Simò,' said Anton Turc. 'It is good to see you again. I hope your time in England was profitable?'

'In a manner of speaking,' said Merrivale. 'What are you doing here?'

'Looking for you. Orland received word that you would be coming.'

The market was busy but they were speaking in Piedmontese; no one around them could understand a word. Merrivale looked at him sharply. 'Word from whom?'

'Sir John Moleyns, the king's treasurer.' Turc grinned again. 'Do not be so suspicious, Simò. Orland is a senior partner in the Company of the Leopard and responsible for the loans the company is now making to England. Thanks to you, of course. Moleyns told us you were returning, and suggested that if we have any concerns about the loans we should contact you.'

'Do you have concerns, Anton?'

'Of course. If you were in our place, so would you.'

'The king will not renege on your loans,' Merrivale said. 'He refused to pay Solaro and Peruzzi because they betrayed him. Show yourselves to be trustworthy, and you have nothing to fear.'

'That is not what keeps us awake at night. We paid an additional commission to Moleyns in return for his guarantee that the contracts would be honoured. We are more concerned about what happens if the French defeat you. Your position is precarious, Simò. The French army is large and well-armed, and their fleet is so vast that you can walk across the Zwin by stepping from one deck to another, never getting your feet wet.'

'Don't believe every rumour you hear,' Merrivale said.

'It is not a rumour, I have seen them with my own eyes. Everyone says the French will destroy your own fleet with ease. Without ships, you will be cut off from your allies in Flanders, and the French can resume attacking your harbours and coasts. If that happens, what hope is there that the king can repay his loans?'

'The queen has ordered her chaplains to pray for victory. Perhaps you should do the same.'

Anton looked sceptical. 'God will favour the side with the most ships. You have other problems too. The Solaro exiles are gathering in Strassburg under the leadership of Sinibald Solaro, and have called on King Jean of Bohemia for aid. He has taken them under his protection. King Jean also believes that his uncle, Archbishop Balduin, has custody of the great crown, and has demanded that the archbishop hand it over to him. Balduin has refused. But sooner or later, the king will learn the truth.'

Vidal. Something cold crept down Merrivale's spine. 'Do *you* know the truth?' he demanded.

'Stanton told us only that the crown is in Strassburg. Presumably one of the other banks there has custody of it.'

'Are there many banks in Strassburg?'

'Oh, yes. All the banking houses from Florence and Lucca have branches there. The Company of the Leopard will soon open a branch there too. I shall be the senior partner.'

'Congratulations,' Merrivale said.

The bells of Sint-Jacobskerk next to the Vrijdagmarkt began to ring, clamorous and urgent. Within moments bells from the Sint-Nicolaus and Sint-Jan churches had joined in, tolling out over the rooftops and canals. People stopped and stared around them, wondering what this portended. Merrivale saw fright in many faces.

'An alarm, perhaps?' Anton Turc said speculatively. 'Or a tocsin of victory? And if so, whose victory?'

Back at the castle, Merrivale found Alice Bedingfield hurrying through the hall, her face streaming with tears. He caught her arm. 'What is it? What has happened?'

'The French fleet is destroyed, but the king is gravely wounded,' she said with a sob in her voice. 'Master Jordan the physician sent word. The queen is leaving within the hour to be by his side.'

'I will go with you.'

'Yes, you are summoned as well. Master Jordan asks you to bring the apothecary Mistress Wesenham to the king. Find her quickly, Simon. We have not a moment to lose.'

26

Sluis, June 1340

Anton Turc had not exaggerated; the long sea inlet known as the Zwin was covered with ships. Some were blackened with fire; others showed dark streaks on their hulls where blood had run from the scuppers, and arrows protruded from their timber sides like porcupine quills. The tide was out and the masts and timbers of other ships protruded from the mud. This was all that remained of the Great Army of the Sea.

Sluis was a huddle of brick houses looking out over the inlet. A boat was drawn up on the foreshore, John Crabbe waiting beside it. 'How is the king?' demanded Queen Philippa.

'He was shot in the leg with a crossbow bolt, Your Grace. Master Jordan extracted the bolt, but he is concerned that the wound may be festering. That's why he sent for the apothecary.' There was sympathy in Crabbe's weathered face. 'Your Grace must not fear unduly,' he said. 'I have seen men recover from worse wounds.'

'Take me to him,' the queen said.

They stepped into the boat, the crew bowing their heads in salute and taking up positions at the oars. The boat made its way across the rippling waters towards the royal flagship, the *Thomas*. Alice Bedingfield looked around. 'What is that?' she asked, pointing to a long mound of fresh earth on the far bank of the Zwin.

'That's where we buried the French,' Crabbe said. 'The ones we could recover, that is. Most are at the bottom of the sea. There were so many, the fishermen claim the lobsters have begun to speak French.'

The boat bumped alongside the clinker hull of the *Thomas* and Merrivale and Crabbe climbed aboard, reaching down to help the women up. The queen, Alice and Cassandra were ushered below. Merrivale turned to Crabbe. 'Will he live?'

'You can never tell with infections.'

No one mentioned what would happen if the king died. His eldest son and heir, Edward of Woodstock, had celebrated his tenth birthday just a few days ago. Another regency would leave England weak and vulnerable.

Merrivale looked around at the battle-scarred ships. 'So, you beat the odds. How?'

'The French admirals were fools,' Crabbe said. 'Rather than sailing out into open water where they could manoeuvre and encircle us, they chose to remain at anchor here in the Zwin. We formed up just as we would on land, a ship full of archers on each flank and another with men-at-arms in the centre. The archers cleared the decks of each French vessel, the men-at-arms boarded and finished off anyone remaining, re-embarked, moved on to the next enemy ship and did it again. It was more of a slaughter than a battle.'

'Did any of them escape?'

'Barbavera and his galleys waited until dark and made a run for it. A few others followed, a dozen in all.'

'Perhaps now our coasts will be safe from attack.'

'Don't bet on it,' Crabbe said. 'France still has plenty of ships, and there is talk of hiring more from Castille. But at least we now have enough ships of our own to mount a stronger defence. Some of the prizes we took were vessels the French had seized from us earlier in the war.'

'I thought I recognised some of them.' Merrivale pointed. 'That's the *Christopher*, isn't it? And that cog next to her looks familiar as well.'

'The *Witschip*. She was crewed by Flemish sailors loyal to France.'

Merrivale knew now where he had seen the ship. Three months ago it had been moored at St Mary's dock in London. 'Did any of her crew survive?'

Crabbe shook his head. 'Some jumped overboard and swam ashore, but their compatriots waiting on the bank killed them all as soon as they landed. The rest died on the deck. What is your interest in her?'

'I am trying to trace her owner. He is a man named Nicholas le Flemyng, from Colchester among other places.'

'If he was on board, he is now dead. But he might have employed a shipmaster rather than sailing himself.'

'I don't think Flemyng was a nautical man.'

'What do you want with him?'

'He killed a friend of mine.'

Crabbe pursed his lips. 'Being a friend of yours must be a hazardous occupation.'

Merrivale ignored this. 'What will you do now?'

'*Dobeler* returns to England in a few days to help transport supplies across to Flanders, but I am bidden to join the army when it lands. I am an engineer as well as a shipmaster, and the king wants my services.'

Crabbe departed for his own ship. Merrivale leaned on the rail in the sunlight, watching water bubble past the hull as the tide came in. Half an hour later Geoffrey Scrope came on deck, one hand swathed in a bandage. He looked tired, his brow furrowed with worry.

'How is the king?' Merrivale asked quietly.

'His fever is down and he is resting comfortably. Your friend the wise woman is skilful, it seems.'

'She is an apothecary,' Merrivale said. 'She studied at Salerno.'

Scrope seemed uninterested. 'His Grace is also much better for seeing the queen. The bond between them is very close, and he has been worried for her safety.'

'Understandably.'

Scrope looked at him. 'Were you waiting to see me, Simon?'

'Yes. I think Nicholas le Flemyng has returned to Flanders. Would it be possible to ask the captain general to make a search for him?'

Scrope frowned. 'I will make the request, but I am not hopeful. The captain general has many other things to occupy his attention. As have we all.'

'The inquisition into John Stanton's death has not concluded. And surely, catching a French spy would be a priority.'

Scrope was suddenly alert. 'Do you think Flemyng is a spy?'

'He is employed by Bishop Aubert, who is French. That should be enough to convince the captain general.'

'Very well,' Scrope said after a moment. 'I will speak to Artevelde when we reach Ghent. No promises, but I will see what I can do.'

Much later Cassandra Wesenham came on deck, wiping her hands on a cloth. She looked tired, but she smiled when she saw Merrivale. 'The wound was indeed infected,' she said. 'But we have cleaned it thoroughly and Master Jordan and I are satisfied there is no longer any poison in the wound. Now he needs rest and food to regain his strength.'

'He will live?'

'It will be a couple of weeks before he can walk unaided, but he will live.'

'Thank God,' Merrivale said quietly.

'Bishop Burghersh is doing exactly that. He has ordered a mass to celebrate the king's recovery. The queen was kind enough to say they should be thanking me rather than God. They offered me a reward but I refused it.'

'Why?'

'Because I was simply doing my duty as a subject of my king. And also, they need the money more than I do.'

'The last is certainly true…' Merrivale looked around, but there was no one close enough to hear them. 'Do you ever think about your family, Mistress Wesenham?' he asked. 'The ones the old king drove from their homes and sent into exile?'

'My Jewish family? Yes, I do sometimes. My brother does not, he rejects that part of his heritage entirely. But then, he has a family of his own and his position to think of. Because I am a woman alone, and because of my profession, I sometimes feel like I too am an exile. I am glad I met my great-uncle and heard his story.' She glanced at him. 'Why do you ask?'

'Something you said reminded me of Velvl Roth. I would advise you not to make public your connection with him, especially not to Bishop Burghersh.'

She looked surprised. 'I don't make a habit of talking about Jewish relations, and Bishop Burghersh is too busy bothering God and fawning over the king to have time for a lowly apothecary. But I shall heed your advice.'

Ghent, July 1340

The bells rang out in the streets and marketplaces once more, in thanksgiving this time for the safe return of King Edward of England to his faithful allies in the League of Three. The king, still limping heavily and leaning on a stick, greeted the captain general in the Vrijdagmarkt before a cheering crowd. The captain general welcomed the king and made a speech praising his great victory. No one said anything about money.

The streets of Ghent became calm once more. The pro-French factions, disheartened by the disaster on the Zwin, melted away. Within days the first companies of English men-at-arms and archers arrived, followed by long trains of wagons laden with supplies and weapons, including of course the king's pride and joy, his new cannon fresh from the armouries at the Tower of London. Wincing a little, the king mounted his horse and, followed by Geoffrey Scrope, Merrivale and the archers of his bodyguard, rode out of the city to inspect them.

John Crabbe greeted them in the meadow beside the Scheldt where the cannon had been set up. There were four of them, long tubes bound with black iron hoops resting on wooden frames with heavy braces to support them. The king slapped his thigh, forgetting his injury for a moment. 'Well done, Crabbe. Are they ready for action?'

'All four were tested in London, sire. We have two wagon loads of shot and an ample supply of powder.'

'Excellent,' the king said briskly. 'What do you say, Geoffrey? These will knock a few holes in the walls of Tournai, don't you think?' He and Scrope walked around the guns, the king still talking quickly about how best to site the guns and how long it might take them to breach the walls. Crabbe watched for a few moments and turned to Merrivale.

'I have discovered where Nicholas le Flemyng is. Or at least where he was.'

'Oh?'

'He found another crew from somewhere, and together they stole the *Witschip*. Three days ago they cut her out from her moorings at night and sailed out of the Zwin before anyone could stop them.'

'Where did they go?' Merrivale asked, though he had already guessed the answer.

'The ship was spotted a few days ago at Nijmegen on the river Waal. They appear to be travelling up the Rhine.'

Strassburg was on the Rhine. 'One of the crew appears to be a Franciscan friar,' Crabbe continued. 'Some sort of renegade, perhaps, or one of those Spiritual Franciscans that have been excommunicated. Emperor Ludwig is giving them shelter in Munich, so perhaps that is where they are bound.'

'Perhaps,' Merrivale said. 'Thank you. I am grateful for the information.'

'I don't know how much good it will do you. If they go to Munich, they are out of your reach.'

'No,' Merrivale said. 'I know how to find them.'

Back at the castle, on the orders of his physician, the king retired to rest. Merrivale sought out Geoffrey Scrope and told him what Crabbe had said. 'I think Flemyng and Vidal are trying to steal the great crown.'

'They won't succeed,' Scrope said. 'Archbishop Balduin has it safely in custody.'

Either Scrope did not know the real truth, or he was concealing it well. 'Balduin's nephew, Jean of Bohemia, is demanding that the crown be handed over to him,' Merrivale said. 'If King Jean is working with Bishop Aubert and Donato de' Peruzzi, there is a real danger of the crown falling into enemy hands.'

'And if Balduin does hand over the crown, we will refuse to repay the loan,' Scrope said. 'He wants the money, Merrivale. Trust me, the crown is safe.'

Merrivale said nothing. 'I know you want to see Flemyng hang,' Scrope said. 'So do I. Letters will be sent to our ambassador in Munich, instructing him to speak to the emperor and request that Flemyng be arrested. Justice will be done, never fear.'

'I am glad to hear it, Sir Geoffrey. Do I understand that we are intending to march against the French at Tournai?'

'As soon as our allies finish mustering their troops, yes. The Hainaulters and Brabanters are joining us before Tournai, while the Flemings attack the French garrison at Saint-Omer, further west.'

'And this time we have enough money to pay the army, and our allies?'

'Funds from the taxation of the Ninth are starting to come in.'

That was not exactly a full answer. 'Sir Geoffrey, have you thought further about our conversation in London? About Moleyns and Conduit and Burghersh?'

Their eyes met. 'I have thought of very little else,' Scrope said.

Ghent, July 1340

A letter arrived, addressed to *Magister Simon Merrivale, nuncius regus*. The red wax seal bore the device of a spoked wheel.

> *To the esteemed Magister Merrivale, greeting. When we met, I judged you to be an honest man who would always be true to his word. Therefore I pray you now to be honest with me again and tell me truly what I may expect. The repayments on the loan our syndicate made to King Edward are several months overdue. Archbishop Balduin has written to Sir John Moleyns and Bishop Burghersh, reminding them of the penalties for late payment, but has received no response. We begin to fear the loan will not be repaid, that His Grace the king will absolve himself of the debt as he did with the Solaros and the Peruzzis.*

The archbishop and our other partners are growing restive. Balduin, may God esteem his soul, speaks of breaking up the great crown and melting down the gold, or perhaps selling it to his nephew King Jean of Bohemia, who is most desirous of gaining possession. Because of the respect I have for the king and for Bishop Burghersh, I wish to prevent this from happening. Can you tell me truly whether we may expect repayment in the near future?

I am your humble servant, Velvl Roth.

As he had done in Antwerp, the bishop had chosen to locate his office in a tower at the top of a long stair. Merrivale wondered if this was so he could see his enemies coming.

Burghersh's face had darkened in the summer heat until it was almost the colour of beetroot. 'What is it?' he demanded.

Merrivale laid the letter in front of him. 'I thought you should see this, Your Grace.'

The bishop read the letter quickly, his eyes glaring. 'This is none of your business,' he said.

'Will the loan be repaid?' Merrivale asked bluntly.

'Are you hard of hearing, Merrivale?'

Merrivale kicked the door shut with his heel. 'Two things bother me,' he said. 'First, you promised Roth that you would advance the cause of the return of the Jewish exiles and their families to England. Yet so far as I can see, you have sat on your arse and done absolutely nothing to help them.'

'You insolent bastard! I could have you whipped for this!'

'You could try. Second, Roth and Balduin and their partners agreed to lend three hundred and forty thousand florins to the king, but only about forty thousand ever reached the royal coffers. If I was a suspicious man, I would say that someone made a promise to Roth in exchange for his money without ever intending to repay the loan. Instead, this man kept most of the money for himself. Would that man by any chance be you, Your Grace?'

Some of the choler went out of the bishop's face and voice. 'Very well,' he said. 'Yes, I planned all along to fleece Roth. I told him that if his wretched people were ever to return to England he would have to prove his good faith first by making a loan to the king. It worked; he agreed to hand over the money. And no, I never intended to repay him.'

'His syndicate holds the great crown as a pledge.'

'Set your mind at rest. The crown will be safe no matter what happens. I have Archbishop Balduin's word on this.'

Merrivale considered this. 'You lied when you said you would speak to the king. You had no intention of helping the Jewish people return from exile.'

'Of course not! Old King Edward had every right to drive them out. The Jews were the king's property, his to dispose of as he wished. Why should I undo his good work?'

'Lying is a sin,' Merrivale reminded him.

'Not to a Jew. God's law does not apply to them. But if you accuse me of stealing that money, Merrivale, I will break you. The king was angry with you after Savoy, but by God, that was nothing compared to the wrath that will descend on your head now.'

Merrivale rested his hands on the bishop's desk, leaning forward until their faces were only a foot apart. 'Well, someone certainly stole it,' he said. 'It had to be either you or Moleyns. Is that why you intervened in the York election? To get Zouche out of the Treasury so Moleyns could do his work without interference?'

Just for once Burghersh's face lost some of his arrogance. 'What do you know?' he demanded.

'Enough.'

'What do you intend to do?'

'That depends on you. If you keep your promise to Roth, I might say nothing. If you don't, the devil will be lighting a special fire in hell just for you.'

Oudenaarde, July 1340

Halfway between Ghent and Tournai, Oudenaarde was a prosperous banking and cloth-making town which until now had remained aloof from the conflict. Seeing the approach of the allied army, the burgemeester and councillors had hastily professed friendship with the League of Three, but clearly not all of the townspeople agreed. Most had locked themselves in their homes, shuttering their windows and barring the doors. The town square was silent and empty, rippling with heat waves.

The king's lodgings were in the aldermen's hall on the north side of the square. A page ushered Merrivale into a chamber where the king stood leaning on a stick, brooding over a map spread out on a table. The map, Merrivale saw, showed the defences of Tournai, formidable walls and towers on both sides of the Scheldt connected by fortified bridges.

They were alone in the room. Merrivale bowed. 'I trust Your Grace's injury is healing well?'

The king rubbed his leg. 'Well enough. I gather we have you to thank for procuring the services of Mistress Wesenham. Master Jordan is keeping her with us until the wound is fully mended.'

'I am glad to hear it,' Merrivale said. 'How may I serve Your Grace?'

'Everything is falling apart in London. That bastard archbishop is up to his tricks again. Money is being collected from the taxation of the Ninth, but nothing is coming through to us. Already we are short of funds, and the campaign has barely started. Merrivale, I want you to find out what is happening and put a stop to it. You have my full authority.'

Merrivale drew a silent breath. 'Sire, you said in London that if I learned anything, I should come straight to you.'

The king looked up. 'What is it?'

'John Stanton and I were investigating the theft of money from the royal treasury. It has taken time to assemble the evidence, but this was no casual pilfering by clerks. Tens of thousands, perhaps even hundreds of thousands of pounds are missing. Edmund Gonville was one of those involved.'

The king's hand tightened on his stick. 'You have proof of this?'

'Gonville confessed it himself. I promised that if he gave evidence he would not be prosecuted.'

'Did you now? You took a great deal on your own shoulders, Merrivale.'

'I did what had to be done, sire. Gonville is only a minor player in this particular game. We can afford to let him go.'

'God damn it, I trusted him! I favoured him, gave him lands, benefices, rewards. Why did he repay me like this?'

'If it is any consolation, sire, I think he regrets it bitterly. His actions nearly cost him his life. My point is that Gonville was acting on instructions. Someone is defrauding you on a huge scale. They plundered the wool trade, they stole much of the loans you received and now they are taking funds from the Ninth.'

'I know that! Did you not hear what I just said?' the king demanded. 'Stratford and his friends are the ones responsible. Put a stop to them!'

'Sire, with respect, there is no direct evidence that the archbishop is involved in any way. In my view—'

The king interrupted him again. 'I don't care what your view is. Find some evidence against the archbishop.'

Merrivale tried again. 'Sire, it was Donato de' Peruzzi who turned Gonville against you. He has turned William Kildesby, too, and Reginald Conduit, and I believe he has also turned Sir John Moleyns. How many others, I cannot say. But I believe he has made an approach to the Bishop of Lincoln.'

'Henry Burghersh! Have you taken leave of your senses? There is no more loyal or honourable man alive.'

Unless you are Jewish, Merrivale thought. 'I did not say the bishop had responded favourably, sire. I merely said an approach had been made.'

The king walked restlessly across the chamber to the window, stick tapping on the red tiles. 'So, the plot is not confined to London. These bastards are corrupting members of my own household. By God, I will not have it.'

He turned back to Merrivale. 'Peruzzi may or may not be involved, but I know who my real enemies are. Go to London and bring me the evidence I need so I can arrest these treacherous shits and hang the lot of them. Make it so.'

There was a knock at the door and the page entered, bowing. 'Sir Geoffrey Scrope and the Bishop of Lincoln to see you, sire.'

'Send them in.' The king looked at Merrivale. 'That will be all.'

Merrivale bowed as the two men entered; Scrope nodded in response but Burghersh ignored him. As he closed the door he heard Burghersh say, 'I don't know what you see in that fellow, sire. His insolence is beyond measure.'

'He is also a loyal servant,' the king said. 'Yes, he made a bad mistake in Savoy, but otherwise he is competent and useful. I'm sending him back to London to keep watch on Stratford and his friends.'

'An excellent idea, sire,' Scrope said. 'And unlike my friend Henry, I have a high opinion of him. He is trustworthy, which is more than can be said for many.' He paused. 'I am afraid there is bad news, sire. The Flemings have suffered a heavy defeat at Saint-Omer. The French sallied out and slaughtered them in the open field. What remains of their army is retreating.'

'Christ,' the king said. 'What do we do?'

'We must carry on, sire. We still have the men of Hainault and Brabant. With their aid, we are strong enough to take Tournai.'

'Very well, we march tomorrow. We'll make camp at Avelgem and move on to Tournai the following day.'

Silently, Merrivale walked downstairs and out into the sweltering afternoon. His own lodgings were across the street in a fine big house belonging to a local merchant. Climbing up to his chamber he stood for a while by the window, looking out over the square. The king's orders troubled him. He was more convinced than ever that Stratford was a distraction, and that the quarrel between the archbishop and king was being manipulated to distract the king and his servants from the real threat.

I don't need to be in London, he thought. *I need to be in Strassburg*.

Someone knocked at the door. He opened it to find Alice Bedingfield standing outside, holding a sealed roll of parchment. 'Is it true you are going back to London?' she asked.

'Yes. How did you know?'

'The queen has just spoken to the king.' Alice handed over the parchment. 'She asks you to deliver a letter for her, to her children.

She was going to send it by the usual courier, but decided it would be safer with you.'

'I am honoured by Her Grace's trust.' Like the king, Philippa was both tough and sentimental; her older children, son Edward and daughters Isabella and Joan, were at Windsor and she missed their company.

'When do you depart?'

'Now. If I hurry I can catch a boat downriver to Antwerp, and take a ship from there.'

'I'll find you some food while you pack.' Alice disappeared downstairs and Merrivale opened his travelling bag and packed a few clothes and necessities. It did not take long; King's Messengers travelled light. Down in the hall he found bread and ham on the table and Alice bringing a jug of dark brown liquid from the buttery. Merrivale peered at it. 'What is this?'

'Beer,' she said. 'One of the local monasteries brews it, using hops rather than gruits. I suppose that explains its colour.'

'Why hops?'

'Because gruits are taxed and hops are not. Like everything else in life, it comes down to money.'

Merrivale poured a tankard and drank it down. It tasted bitter and lacked the aromatic flavours of gruits, but it was not unpleasant. He cut a slice of ham. 'Where are the servants?'

'Hiding from us, I suspect. There is a common belief in these parts that Englishmen have tails.'

'Good God. Really?'

'The French have been spreading lies in hopes of persuading people not to cooperate with us. The more gullible have begun to believe them. Shall I send a message to the landing and order a boat?'

'No, I will go directly. Thank you, Alice.'

She smiled a little. 'Someone needs to look after you from time to time. Are you still thinking about her?'

'Every day. But you were right, Alice. I would rather have had the time we had, than nothing at all.'

'Then you are ready to start living again,' she said.

Whither we hasten, whence we are redeemed…

His vision had become blurry. He blinked, trying to clear his eyes, and opened his mouth to speak but his tongue had gone numb. The room began to spin, and a sudden tremor made his body go rigid. His last memory was of his knees giving way as he fell towards the floor.

Blood

27

Tournai, August 1340

The world spun through darkness and splinters of light. He was aware sometimes of lying on a cot, but the cot itself was whirling through a vortex, trembling like a ship in a storm. People appeared as if out of a mist, bending over his cot while coloured lights flickered around them.

His father, gaunt and haggard, his face full of concern, his lips moving, his voice echoing down a long tunnel, *what are you doing lying there, boy, get up, there is work to be done, the fire needs tending, the cows must be milked, all the servants are dead and someone needs to bury them, get up, get up!*

John Stanton, holding up hands with pale stripes on his fingernails, *you of all people to fall for that trick, drinking poison, what were you doing? This wine is very good, red and sweet, full of fire to make the blood strong, but it won't do* you *any good, my friend, you need saffron brandy, not wine.*

Alice Bedingfield, holding out a cloth to mop his brow. The cloth was cold; he attempted to pull her arm away, but had no strength. 'Hush, Simon,' she said softly. 'Lie still.' He realised he was not dreaming and tried to hold onto the moment, but something sucked him back into the void.

His mother and sisters, silent, holding out their hands and begging for food. He looked around wildly, trying to find anything he could give them, but there was only emptiness, the rain falling on the moor. When he looked back they were already fading away, disappearing into the mist.

Yolande, walking towards him in a shimmering gown of green, her hair unbound, smiling and holding out her hands. *Simon! Oh, Simon,*

I love you, love you, love you, love you, echoing on the wind but as she drew closer her face contorted with fury and she drew a knife, screaming at him, *you bastard, you left me to die!* before stabbing him in the chest. He felt no pain, but when he looked down, blood gushed like a fountain from the wound.

Darkness fell once more.

Far above his head a tiny dot of grey light appeared in the blackness. It was impossibly far away, but he reached for it nonetheless and felt himself beginning to rise, like a swimmer surfacing after diving into a deep pool. It was thus that he had learned to swim, jumping into ponds high on Dartmoor.

The grey dot grew brighter and larger. Suddenly he was surrounded by blinding light that stabbed at his eyes. He was lying on his side on a cot, but this time the cot was not moving, or at least not much. Something outside went *thump*, sending a little tremor through the ground. A hand touched his neck, feeling for a pulse, and he realised that his heartbeat was fast and irregular.

Something about the hand seemed familiar. Despite the brilliant light he opened his eyes and looked up. His vision was still blurry but he could just make out Cassandra Wesenham's face framed by a white wimple. He tried to speak but the effort was too much and he closed his eyes again. He felt her hands lift his head and something trickled between his lips and down his throat. He had just time to realise it was saffron brandy before his stomach revolted. He vomited, body convulsing from head to foot with spasms, and the blackness returned.

More hallucinations, some full of horror, interspersed with intervals of wakefulness. Gradually the intervals grew longer and, he supposed, closer together. Whenever he woke Cassandra gave him cordials and broth, eventually graduating to pottage. He learned to keep it down, or at least most of it.

Eventually he found a voice, wavering and rasping in his ravaged throat. 'What happened?'

'There was poison in the beer,' she said quietly. 'A mixture of wolfsbane and a very strong syrup of poppies. The flavour of the beer hid the taste.'

'You saved my life.'

'I know the antidotes for each poison, but not for both mixed together. Your own strength has saved you, so far. But you are still very weak.'

Another *thump* in the distance. 'Where are we?'

'In the camp outside Tournai. That sound is our cannon battering at the walls.'

'Aren't you supposed to be tending to the king?'

'It is by the king's express order that I am here.'

He was still thinking about this when darkness fell again.

Gradually he began to sleep more normally, though the hallucinations continued at intervals; worryingly, sometimes while he was still awake. Alice Bedingfield came to visit, sitting down beside his cot, her lovely eyes full of pain. 'Simon, I am so sorry.'

'Why?'

'I saw a jug of beer in the buttery and assumed one of the servants had left it out. I had no idea. I wish I had drunk it myself.'

'I don't.'

He closed his eyes. When he opened them again she was still sitting in her blue gown, but now she had a tabby cat's head and a jewelled collar. He forced himself to ignore this. 'Has anyone spoken to the servants?' he asked.

The cat mewed. 'Sir Geoffrey did. They were in their own quarters all afternoon, keeping away from the English devils. The owner and his family had gone away to Ghent so were not even in the house. Simon, dear, don't die. We need you.'

'I have no intention of dying,' he said, and closed his eyes.

Later Cassandra came to feed him pottage, meat broth with peas and pepper. The warmth spread through his body and for the first time he could feel a little strength in his limbs. 'Have you known Mistress Bedingfield for long?' she asked.

He had to think about this. 'Since I joined the king's service.'

'Are you and she lovers?'

He started to laugh, but the effort hurt. 'Why do you ask?'

'Because it might give her a motive for trying to kill you.'

A long moment passed. 'Alice did not try to kill me,' he said. 'We are friends, but not lovers. Her interests are directed elsewhere.'

'Then who put the poison in your beer?'

'Someone who wanted, very badly, to stop me from going to England,' he said, and closed his eyes again.

He puzzled on this, slowly pulling the broken, dreamlike fragments of his mind together. Stratford might have wanted to stop him, or Moleyns, or Conduit, but they could not possibly have known he was coming. The king had only given his orders shortly before the attack.

Burghersh knew that he had seen Moleyns's secret accounts. *My dear, you are so naïve. Poison has been the weapon of priests since the beginning of time.*

Tournai, September 1340

Days passed, turning into weeks. His strength returned slowly, but the hallucinations continued, alarmingly unpredictable. The poison had attacked his nerves as well as his mind, Cassandra said, and the full extent of that damage came to light when he tried to walk for the first time; his legs refused to answer the command of his mind, and he overbalanced and fell flat on his face. It happened again the next time, and the next.

Slowly and patiently Cassandra and Alice taught him how to walk again, taking his weight on their shoulders and holding him upright, manipulating his legs until he could take slow, shuffling steps. When

Alice was on duty with the queen, Warin came in and took over. 'Where have you been?' Merrivale asked the first time he appeared.

'Keeping watch outside, sir. I've recruited a couple of lads I know from Devon to stand with me. I wanted to taste your food, too, but Mistress Wesenham is doing that herself. She knows what to look for, she says.'

By the end of another week he could walk unaided, albeit with slow shuffling steps. There came an afternoon when he found himself alone; Alice was with the queen, Cassandra had gone out to gather herbs and Warin was asleep. He dressed with infinite slowness and pulled on his boots, an effort that caused spirals of light to glow behind his eyes. Rising, he walked slowly outside and stood for a moment, feeling the sun on his face for the first time in a month.

The two men Warin had recruited were on watch, leaning on their bows. Both were short, stocky men with dark hair. They touched their foreheads in salute. 'It's good to see you up and about, sir,' one said.

'Thank you. What is your name?'

'I'm Robin Pinn, sir, from Sidmouth. This here is Jack Giffard from Torrington.'

'Torrington? Do you know Frithelstock Priory?'

'Of course, sir,' Giffard said. 'Warin says the old gentleman in the infirmary is your father, is that right?'

Flames were shooting out of the sun, streaking across the sky. Merrivale concentrated with an effort. 'Yes. Is he well, do you know?'

'Yes, sir. I see him out for walks sometimes, with some of the young ladies. I think they're looking after him fine, sir.'

He knew logically that this was good news, but he felt nothing. 'I am going for a walk myself. Tell Mistress Wesenham when she returns.'

'Yes, sir.'

A cannon boomed. He turned and walked slowly towards the noise. Giffard and Pinn looked at each other; Pinn nodded, and Giffard moved silently to follow Merrivale. A flock of rooks flew up from some nearby trees, cawing raucously. Gradually his eyes took in the scene around him, the huddled tents of the besiegers' camp bright with banners flying in the wind, the grey walls of Tournai and the towers of its cathedral on the hill beyond, the gushing yellow smoke of the cannon drifting slowly on the wind. A ship lay moored in the Scheldt not far away, and as he stared at it the ship seemed to rise into the air; either that or the world was falling away below it. He felt dizzy and reached out an arm to steady himself. I should turn back, he thought, and he tried to do so but once again his legs refused to obey.

He saw, or thought he saw, two men in the middle distance, talking. One wore armour and a surcoat of blue with a yellow bend; those were Geoffrey Scrope's arms, but the figure inside the armour was hunched and stooped with a face like a goblin. The other man was goblin-like too, except his face resembled that of Nicholas le Flemyng, the man who had killed John Stanton and was now far away on the Rhine attempting to steal the great crown of England. Sudden mist clouded his eyes, and when it cleared both figures had vanished. Another cannon fired, shaking the air; the smell of brimstone drifted on the wind.

Someone appeared alongside him; the real Geoffrey Scrope this time, only not in armour and wearing a plain blue coat and hose rather than a surcoat. 'It is good to see you up and around, Simon. We thought we had lost you.'

'You nearly did,' said Merrivale, fighting down the urge to vomit. 'I must return to my quarters.'

'I'll help you, sir,' Giffard said quietly behind him.

Scrope laid a gentle hand on his shoulder. 'I shall call on you as soon as I can. Now that you are feeling better, we have matters to discuss.'

Scrope came to his pavilion two evenings later, just as Merrivale was finishing a meal of pottage flavoured with beef broth and herbs. He was growing tired of pottage, but Cassandra had warned that he still needed to be careful about what he ate. He had lost weight, and his coat hung loosely on his arms and shoulders.

Scrope turned to Cassandra. 'Mistress Wesenham, I would like to speak to Master Merrivale in private, if I may.'

Cassandra bowed her head and withdrew. Scrope pulled up a wooden bench and sat down opposite Merrivale. His face looked tired in the lamplight. 'At the king's orders, I have conducted an inquisition,' he said. 'I don't know who administered the actual poison, and we may never know. None of the apothecaries in Oudenaarde was willing to admit selling either wolfsbane or poppy syrup in quantities needed to kill a man. But as you said about Stanton, what really matters is who gave the order.'

Merrivale waited. 'Everything points to someone from Stratford's faction,' Scrope said. 'Someone knew you were being sent to London and wanted to stop you. However, as I'm sure you have worked out, the instructions could not have come from London as the attack happened almost immediately. That means the man who gave the order to kill you may still be here, with the army.'

'You know what I am about to say, Sir Geoffrey.'

'Yes, I know.' Scrope closed his eyes for a moment. 'Back in Ghent I said that money from the taxation of the Ninth was starting to come in, but I spoke too soon. It is clear that Stratford and his brother, the Lord Chancellor, are holding back money. They will stop at nothing, it seems, to ensure that this campaign fails and the king is discredited.'

'Is the campaign failing?' Merrivale asked.

'We attacked Tournai twice while you were ill. During the first assault we lost five hundred men. The second attack against the fortified bridges cost us another two thousand. Our allies are quarrelling with each other and our cannon are unable to breach the walls. And the French army sits at Bouvines ten miles away and mocks us, knowing we are running out of money and time.'

'Now that Zouche has resigned as treasurer, who is responsible for the income from the Ninth?'

'A new Lord Treasurer has been appointed, but he has not yet taken up his post. John Moleyns has sole responsibility now. And to answer your next question, yes. Our reports from London make it clear that he is taking orders from Stratford.'

'But as you said, Moleyns is in London,' Merrivale said. 'We cannot avoid this point any longer, Sir Geoffrey. Did your inquisition consider Henry Burghersh, the Bishop of Lincoln, as a potential suspect?'

'It did,' Scrope said after a moment. 'And I found no evidence that could link Burghersh to the attack on you. However, his motives for some of his other actions require explanation. I must think carefully about how to lay this before the king.'

'Be careful, Sir Geoffrey. You could be putting yourself in danger.'

'It is too late to turn back, Simon. We must follow this road wherever it leads us.'

Whither we hasten, whence we are redeemed. Mercuriade's words had haunted him over and over in his hallucinations and nightmares; once he had seen them written in blood on a wall. Even in his dream that had seemed in poor taste.

The dreams had told him the bitter truth; that even if by chance he could make his way back to Yolande, there was no certainty that she would welcome him. Love could turn to hate, all too easily. He had lost her, and for this there could be no redemption.

Tournai, September 1340

With both of her patients on the road to recovery, Cassandra Wesenham returned to Ghent. Merrivale continued to walk through the camp each day, slowly regaining his strength, listening to the booming of the cannons. Sulphur swirled through the air, mingled with the stale smell of defeat. A week later a party of Hainault men-at-arms in the service of Brother Willem rode into a French ambush near Bouvines and were decimated. The survivors claimed that the Duke of Brabant's men had failed to support them, with the result that Cousin Jan and his troops threatened to leave the army and go home. The captain general's men, already demoralised by the losses they had suffered, prepared to follow them.

'It's over, sir,' Warin said.

'Yes,' said Merrivale. 'Though whether our captains realise it is another matter.'

A thick fog hung over the valley of the Scheldt. The towers of Tournai were ghostly shapes in the mist. An archer, an Essex man in tattered russet coat and hose, came though the camp to Merrivale's pavilion. Merrivale looked at him. 'I recognise you from Antwerp,' he said.

'That's right, sir, I'm one of the fellows who came with you to the Solaro house. Someone is out on the front lines asking for you.'

'Who?'

'A Franciscan friar, sir, or at least he wears a friar's robes. We caught two of them trying to slip through the lines. We were going to kill them, but this one said he knows you.'

'Did he give a name?'

'Yes, sir. He calls himself Aimeric de Gensac.'

Raimon Vidal and his companion stood waiting in the fog. 'Ah, Simon,' the former said cheerfully. 'We do meet in the oddest places. I was sorry to hear you were unwell. Was it something you drank?'

'What are you doing here?'

'As always, straight to the heart of the matter. I once said that I admire this, but on reflection I think you would do well to develop a line in small talk. It might help you cultivate some of the Aristotelian virtues, like friendliness and patience.'

'I don't need a lecture on virtue from Raimon Vidal.' Merrivale nodded towards the other Franciscan. 'Who is your friend?'

'It doesn't matter. I have a message from Bishop Aubert for your king. The bishop has persuaded King Philippe of France to negotiate a truce. His envoys are waiting at the hamlet of Espléchin. You will find the terms are generous.'

'Why would the French want to make peace?'

'Because King Philippe is a devout man who desires to avoid the shedding of any more Christian blood. Also, his tax-farmers are even less efficient than your own and he too is growing short of money. He needs peace so he can pay off his army.'

'And King Edward's claim to the French crown? Will he enter into negotiations over that?'

'That was not mentioned. In any case, I understand Philippe is hopeful of establishing his own claim to the crown of England.'

Merrivale looked him in the eye. 'Do you know where it is?'

'Did *you* really believe I would answer that question?'

'So you don't know, and this is all a bluff. Where is Nicholas le Flemyng?'

Vidal looked vague. 'Do you know, I am really not certain. I hope the bishop has not mislaid him.'

Merrivale looked at the archers. 'Hold them here while I report to the king. If I do not return by nones you have my permission to kill them both.'

The king's pavilion was dark in the fog, banners hanging limp from their masts. Geoffrey Scrope greeted him in the lamplit interior. 'Simon? What is it?'

Merrivale told him and Scrope nodded. 'I'll take you to His Grace at once. Burghersh is already with him.'

All three men listened while Merrivale repeated what Vidal had said. 'Is this man reliable?' the king asked at the end.

'No. But I think the offer is genuine.'

Burghersh nodded. For once he looked shaken, his usual aggression quite gone. He had nearly been killed a few days earlier when a party of French men-at-arms sortied from Tournai and attacked the camp. Perhaps he is contemplating his own mortality, Merrivale thought.

'We have reports from other sources that our adversary is short of money,' the bishop said. 'Sire, I think we must accept the truce. Our own position is growing untenable, and we must fall back on Ghent before our allies desert us entirely.'

There was silence for a moment. 'By God, it sticks in my throat,' King Edward said finally. 'But there is no help for it. Geoffrey, Henry, you will handle this personally. Ride to Espléchin and meet their envoys, and get the best terms you can.'

He looked down at his hands. 'I will order the marshals to make preparations for breaking camp. Tomorrow, we return to Ghent.'

28

Ghent, November 1340

Summer had flown by and another winter was setting in; already in the morning the fields around Ghent were white with frost. Merrivale found it hard to believe that it was nearly two years since the disaster in Savoy. Two years since he had last seen Yolande, whom he would never see again. In his calmer moments he knew this was for the best, but those moments never lasted long. All too soon the pain returned; mingled, more and more often now, with dark explosive anger.

Back at Ghent the allied army fell apart. The German princes denounced their commanders for incompetence and departed for home, taking their expensive retinues with them. The Hainaulters followed them; most of the men of Brabant had already melted away. The Flemings, still smarting from their losses at Saint-Omer and Tournai, fell into their old habits of fighting among themselves. In the Gravensteen, the king sat down with the captain general, Brother Willem and Cousin Jan to discuss how to keep the alliance together. Accusations of betrayal and bad faith were hurled on all sides, and the king's allies accused him of planning to abandon them. Finally, in order to hold the alliance together, King Edward swore an oath that he would remain in Ghent and not return to England. Muttering darkly, Cousin Jan and Brother Willem agreed to accept this.

Merrivale called on Cassandra in her shop. 'I have so much to thank you for.'

She smiled, and for a moment her face lightened. 'My work is my vocation. No thanks are needed.'

Merrivale shook his head. 'Throughout this entire affair you have been a voice of reason and common sense. I will never forget your friendship.'

'You speak as though the end is coming.'

'It is, very soon. One way or the other.'

He met Anton Turc at a tavern on the Korenmarkt, and after buying a flask of wine they walked up to the gallery above the common room where they could talk without being overheard. 'I have news for you,' the young banker said. 'Nicholas le Flemyng and the *Witschip* are at Koblenz. It is where the Moselle river meets the Rhine.'

'I know where it is. What is he doing there?'

'My guess is that he is waiting for orders. The Solaros know the great crown of England is in Strassburg, and will be moving heaven and earth to find it. But if they fail, it may be necessary to extract the information from Archbishop Balduin. He is at his home in Trier, on the Moselle river.'

'I suspect Balduin is more than capable of defending himself.'

'Against poison?' asked Turc. 'And your enemies have also made another move. Prepare yourself for some bad news, Simò. There is a rumour that the king is secretly in negotiations with Donato de' Peruzzi.'

Merrivale buried his face in his hands. 'Suffering Christ,' he said.

'Indeed. Peruzzi's original loan will be reinstated, and he has agreed to guarantee future payments to the allied princes, Brabant and Hainault, and the captain general of Flanders. But the crown of thorns will seem a light burden next to the price Peruzzi has demanded for his services.'

'Oh? What is the price?'

'Custody of the great crown,' Turc said.

There was a moment of silence. 'Peruzzi's allies intend to put pressure on Balduin to hand over the crown,' Merrivale said. 'But Balduin is stubborn as an ox. The only thing that will persuade him is repayment of the loan in full.'

'Perhaps that is what they are planning to do,' Turc said. 'The question in my mind is, why is the king prepared to trust Peruzzi once more?'

'He isn't. I doubt very much if the king knows anything about this. Are you still going to become senior partner in Strassburg?'

'I am. I depart next week.'

'Anton, I may need your help again. Will you give it? I cannot promise anything in return.'

Turc smiled. 'We are bankers,' he said, 'but we are also men of Asti and we remember our friends. Send word to me, and I will come.'

Ghent, November 1340

The great hall of the Gravensteen was cold, so cold Merrivale could see his own breath steam. The king's household controller had ordered the fires to be kept low in order to save money. The strongboxes were empty of silver and the tradesmen of Ghent, like those of Antwerp, were now refusing credit to the king's servants.

A Flemish steward appeared, rubbing his hands. 'There's a man at the gates asking to see the king, sir. His name is Kildesby, and he says he comes from England.'

English soldiers would probably have recognised Kildesby, but the gates were guarded by Flemish troops; not to protect the king, but to ensure that he remained inside. The king had sworn a solemn oath, but clearly Cousin Jan and Brother Willem and the captain general did not trust him to keep his word. The king and his household were effectively the prisoners of their own allies.

'Admit him,' Merrivale said.

Kildesby walked briskly into the hall a few minutes later, wrapped in a long cloak. His hood was trimmed with fox fur, accentuating his sharp features. He stopped suddenly when he saw Merrivale.

'Surprised to see me?' the latter asked.

'Take me to the king,' Kildesby snapped.

'Why do you want to see him?'

'My message is for His Grace, not the errand boy. Take me to him.'

The king was in his solar, wrapped in a thick wool robe. Scrope and Burghersh were with him, as were the queen and Alice Bedingfield, both the latter with woollen mittens on their hands. A single candle burned on a side table, adding a little luminance to the grey light coming through the windows. Merrivale bowed. 'Master Kildesby to see you, sire.'

The king looked up in surprise. 'What is your business here, Kildesby?'

'I have information of great importance to lay before Your Grace.' Kildesby paused for a moment. 'But I require something in return.'

Everyone stared at him. 'You dare to bargain with the king?' demanded Burghersh, his red face glowing with anger.

'I was promised the see of York, but the chapter chose William de la Zouche instead. You, my lord bishop, advised them to do so. I want you to withdraw your support for Zouche, and I want the king to recommend my appointment to the Pope in Avignon.'

'By God,' the king said in wonder. 'You *are* attempting to bargain.'

Kildesby bowed. 'With the greatest of respect, sire, I am asking for what is rightfully mine.'

Burghersh looked like he was about to erupt. Geoffrey Scrope held up a hand. 'You are right,' he said to Kildesby. 'You were made a promise, and that promise will be kept. We will do everything we can to smooth your path. I will draft the letter to the Pope myself, and it will go out under the king's signet.'

He glanced at Burghersh, who hesitated for a moment and then nodded. 'Will that do?' he asked Kildesby.

'It will,' Kildesby said.

'Then speak,' said Scrope.

Kildesby drew a deep breath. 'Archbishop Stratford and his brother the chancellor are plotting to make themselves masters of England. Already they are disregarding the king's wishes and instructions, giving orders in the king's name but in reality serving their own ends. They have withheld money raised by the taxation of the Ninth, depositing it in the treasury rather than sending it to Your Grace.'

The king's fists clenched. 'Have they, by God!'

'Now they are preparing to strengthen their grip on power,' Kildesby went on. 'They have won over most of the officials in the Chancery and Treasury, as well as the Lord Mayor and aldermen of London. Many of the rich merchants are willing to support them too. Reginald Conduit and William de la Pole are the leaders of these, along with Sir John Pulteney.'

'Are they planning to seize the throne?' demanded Scrope.

'They have denied this, but there are many rumours. One suggests that they will seize the young Prince of Wales and bring him to London. The king will be deposed on account of his absence from the kingdom, and Archbishop Stratford will rule as regent on behalf of Prince Edward.'

Queen Philippa spoke for the first time. 'So why are you here, Master Kildesby?' she asked. 'The triumph of the Stratfords seems assured, given how many powerful men they have behind them. Don't you want to be on the winning side?'

'I am a loyal subject of His Grace,' Kildesby said self-righteously. 'I would never plot against him.'

'Christ give me strength,' the queen snapped. 'You are here, Kildesby, because you see an advantage for yourself. Since the day you were spawned, you have never done a single thing that does not benefit you. I ask again. Why are you here?'

Kildesby looked taken aback. 'I don't understand, Your Grace.'

'I see I shall have to answer my own question,' the queen said. 'You hope to goad us into retaliating against the plotters, attacking them before they attack us. When they have been dismissed and disgraced, we will reward our servant Kildesby by promoting him. Is that right?'

'He still isn't answering, Your Grace,' said Alice Bedingfield.

'He doesn't need to.' The queen looked at her husband. 'Send this creature away. We need to talk.'

'I will escort Master Kildesby downstairs, sire,' said Merrivale.

King Edward shook his head. 'Stay where you are. We may need you.'

Two royal pages were summoned to take Kildesby back down to the great hall. King Edward waited until the door closed behind them and looked at Scrope. 'Do not write that letter,' he said.

'Sire, I never intended to.'

The king turned to his wife. 'What is on your mind?'

'Kildesby has exaggerated the situation for his own benefit,' she said, 'but there may be some truth to what he is saying. It is unlikely that even he would tell so egregious a lie. If there is a plot stirring in London, we need to kill it now before it takes root.'

'I agree,' the king said grimly. 'Especially if those bastards are withholding funds from the Ninth.'

'That would explain why so little money is coming through,' said Burghersh. 'Unfortunately, so long as we remain trapped here in Ghent, there is very little we can do.'

There was a long pause. 'Then I must return to London,' the king said. 'There is no other choice.'

Burghersh looked appalled. 'Sire, you swore an oath not to leave Ghent.'

'Really?' said the queen. 'You're a bishop, for God's sake. Absolve the king of his oath, and we're done.'

Burghersh bowed. 'My apologies, Your Grace. I meant to say that relations with our allies are difficult enough already. If the king leaves Ghent it will be taken as a sign of bad faith. We should appoint an inquisitor to look into this plot by the Stratfords, while we remain here in Ghent and prepare to raise a new army in the spring.'

Edward turned on him. 'Raise a new army, Henry? With what?'

The bishop said nothing. 'No more prevarication,' the king said. 'This time, we take action. Henry, Geoffrey, you will remain here with the queen. I shall depart for London as soon as possible.'

'It could be dangerous,' Scrope said. He saw the expression on the king's face and raised a hand. 'I was thinking of Her Grace, sire, not myself.'

'Cousin Jan and my brother and the captain general will be furious,' the queen said, 'but they will not dare harm me. I am one of them.' She looked at the king. 'Go. Do what you must.'

Burghersh was still uneasy. 'The Gravensteen is watched, sire. How do you propose to escape?'

The king looked at Merrivale. 'That is where you come in,' he said.

The cold had deepened and the boat, a long black barge with a covered canopy over its mid-section, crackled through thin panes of ice as it nosed up to the watergate. Merrivale took hold of the painter and drew it inside, tying the rope around the mooring post. 'Did they see you?' he asked.

Robin Pinn, Devon fisherman turned archer, took off his cap and grinned. 'We made sure they noticed,' he said, pointing at the ramparts overhead. 'I reckon they'll be on their way down now.'

The other two boatmen, Warin and Jack Gifford, made the boat fast. Released from their indentures at the end of the campaign, the two archers had chosen to join Merrivale's service instead. He had welcomed them; Pinn was lively and humorous, a man who could find a bright spot in everything, while Giffard was quieter and more calculating, but both were tough, reliable and deadly shots with a longbow.

Merrivale turned towards the stair turret and waited. A few moments later a young Flemish militia captain in a close-fitting metal cap and dented breastplate came hurrying down the stairs. 'What is that boat doing here?' he asked, pointing.

'The king sent for it,' Merrivale said.

'Why does he want a boat?'

Merrivale shrugged. 'How should I know? When he gives orders we obey them, without asking stupid questions.'

'I shall report this to the captain general.'

'Do whatever you like.'

By nightfall there were more guards on the ramparts and two boats anchored in the river opposite the watergate. 'They don't really trust us, do they, sir?' asked Warin.

'No,' said Merrivale. 'And they are quite right not to.'

The following morning a party of horsemen rode up to the main gate of the Gravensteen, halting on the bridge over the moat. Their leader wore a magnificent silk cloak lined with black fur and a matching fur hat with a jewel pinned to its front. 'I am Heer Christoffel van Zandhoven, magistrate of Antwerp,' he announced. 'I demand to see King Edward of England.'

'What is your business with the king, *meneer*?' demanded the officer of the guard.

Heer van Zandhoven looked down his nose. 'Some members of the king's household incurred debts during their stay in our city last year. I am here to see that those debts are paid, or to seek redress through the courts. Here is my letter of authority.'

He handed over a parchment sealed with several impressive seals, including the familiar lion of the duchy of Brabant. The officer read it quickly. 'Good luck getting money out of the English,' he said sourly. 'You chose cold weather for riding, *meneer*. Why not come by water?'

'There is ice in the lower Scheldt already and I have no mind to be frozen in for the winter. Will you open the gates, or not?'

Antwerp was an important trading partner of Ghent, not to be offended. The officer gave the order and the gates swung open, and the magistrate rode into the courtyard. His men followed him, nine in all, cloaked and hooded against the cold. Quite an entourage for a magistrate, the officer thought; but Antwerp men always did have an inflated sense of their own importance.

Two hours later the gates opened and the magistrate and his party rode back out again. 'Did you get what you came for?' the officer asked.

'All is arranged to my satisfaction,' said Zandhoven. He paused for a moment, as if debating with himself. 'Have you put a close watch on the watergate?' he asked.

'Yes. The entire castle is secure.'

'I hope you are correct, *meneer*. I saw men inside the watergate, preparing a barge and making ready to sail. They were loading supplies as if for a long journey.'

The officer stiffened. 'You said there was ice in the river. They cannot get away by water.'

'Downriver, I said. There is nothing to stop them going upriver to Kortrijk and making their way overland to the sea.' The magistrate paused again to let this sink in. 'Guard them closely, *meneer*. If the king escapes your custody, the Duke of Brabant will be most displeased.'

The officer touched the brim of his hat. 'Thank you for the warning, *meneer*. Journey safely.'

The magistrate touched spurs to his horse and trotted across the gate, followed by his entourage. Turning left, they followed a narrow street parallel to the river until they came to the Graupoort, the gate guarding the Antwerp road. The captain of the guard at the gate remembered Heer van Zandhoven and waved his party through. The magistrate was clearly in a hurry, spurring his horse again, and the whole party cantered away up the road through the suburbs. Not until they were out in open country did they rein in and halt.

One of the party threw back his hood. Watery sunlight shone on his fair hair and moustache. 'Thank you, Master Turc,' said King Edward of England. 'You played your part with great skill.'

Anton Turc, resplendent in magistrate's robes, bowed in the saddle. Other hoods were thrown back to reveal Merrivale, Warin, the two archers and several of the king's own servants. One of these was Kildesby, whom the king had insisted must accompany him to England to bear witness against the plotters. Merrivale thought that Kildesby did not look very happy about this.

'What about your men?' Kildesby asked. 'Can they be trusted?'

Turc's original entourage had changed clothes with the king and his party before sitting down to hot drinks and food in the great hall of the castle. 'They will say nothing,' Turc said. 'They will make their way out of the castle one at a time. No one will suspect them.'

'Nonetheless, when the barge does not sail as expected, the Flemings will realise the trick we have played on them,' Merrivale said. 'We must make haste, sire.'

Kildesby looked shocked. 'They would not dare pursue the king.'

'They would,' the king said grimly. 'And once they learn the news, Brother Willem and Cousin Jan will join the chase.'

He looked at Turc. 'You have done well. You will be rewarded for this.'

'I beg Your Grace to remember the Company of the Leopard,' Turc said, bowing again. 'That is all the reward I seek. I wish Your Grace well, and God speed you on your journey.'

Damme, November 1340

It was a little over thirty miles to the port of Sluis on the Zwin, where John Crabbe would be waiting with the *Dobeler*. The direct route lay through Maldeghem, but the Duke of Brabant had a garrison there; to avoid this, the king's party veered away westward, coming in late afternoon to the town of Damme.

The streets were quiet, brick houses shuttered against the cold. Roofs and gable ends bore traces of snow. They stopped outside a tavern and dismounted to rest their horses, and Giffard and Pinn were sent inside to fetch hot wine and ale. 'How much further?' asked the king.

'About eight miles,' Merrivale said. 'There is a straight road from here to Sluis. We should be there before nightfall.'

Edward nodded. 'We must hope the Zwin has not yet frozen. If it has, Crabbe's ship will be trapped in the ice.'

'What do we do if it has?' Kildesby asked.

'We will think of something else,' said Merrivale.

Kildesby muttered under his breath. His pointed nose was white with cold and he looked more unhappy than ever. Something murmured in the air and died away. Merrivale listened, and heard it again.

'Horsemen,' he said. 'Coming this way. Someone must have alerted the garrison at Maldeghem.'

The king nodded. 'Fetch those men out of the tavern. All of you, to horse.'

Warin bolted into the inn and ran out a moment later followed by Giffard and Pinn, all three throwing themselves into the saddle. The king was already moving, followed by Merrivale and Kildesby. 'How did they discover us so quickly?' the latter gasped. 'Who betrayed us?'

'Perhaps they worked it out for themselves,' Merrivale said. 'Stop asking questions and ride.'

'It's good to hear you being insolent to someone else for a change, Merrivale,' the king said, looking around. 'They're coming fast. Use your spurs.'

The horses leaped forward, racing up the road towards Sluis. A broad canal, its banks fringed with ice, ran beside them. Looking back, Merrivale saw a column of light horse emerging from the huddled houses of Damme, their lances like porcupine quills against the darkening sky.

'Thirty at least,' he said, 'and their horses are fresher. They are gaining on us, sire.'

'We can hold them off, sire,' said Robin Pinn. He touched the longbow slung across his back. 'Take a few of them with us, at least.'

'No,' the king said sharply. 'If blood is shed, the alliance will be ruined forever. Put your heads down and ride as if the devil himself is pursuing us.'

They used their spurs again and the horses responded, but the Brabanters were still closing in behind them. Ahead, the houses and spires of Sluis drew closer, lamps gleaming in the falling dusk and reflecting out across the waters of the Zwin where the wreckage of the French fleet protruded from the mud. More lamps shone from the deck and mast of a big roundship anchored just offshore. They galloped through the town to the foreshore and stopped, jumping down from the saddle. A boat pulled away from the roundship, rowing steadily towards them, but it was too late. The pursuing horsemen rode up slowly, reining in a few yards away.

Their leader raised a hand to his hat in salute. 'Greetings, Your Grace. By order of my master the Duke of Brabant, I must ask you to accompany me back to Ghent.'

'Tell your master my business takes me to England,' the king said. 'I shall return when that business is concluded. He has my word on that.'

The leader shook his head. 'I doubt if the duke will consider that to be sufficient, sire.'

'Then take this instead.' Reaching inside his cloak, the king pulled out a purse and threw it to the horseman. The clink of money could be distinctly heard. 'There are twenty marks of silver for you and your men to share,' Edward said. 'Return to your master and say you were too late.'

The man thought for a moment, weighing the purse in his hand. Then he touched his cap again and turned and rode back through the town, followed by his men. The king let out his breath. 'Thank Christ for that,' he said. 'If he had asked for more, we were doomed. That was all the silver I have in the world.'

The boat grounded on the soft mud behind them. The king stepped in, followed by Kildesby and the others. Merrivale boarded last of all, sitting down by the thwarts and watching the retreating Brabanters, his mind still racing.

He had counted on the ruse giving them a day or two's grace, more than enough to allow them to escape to England. Instead, someone had realised the king was missing almost at once, in time for a message to be sent to Maldeghem ordering the garrison to arrest them.

Kildesby had asked who betrayed them. Someone inside the Gravensteen had realised the king was departing and informed their allies; and that someone could well have been Kildesby himself.

29

London, November 1340

Midnight, the torches over the watergate of the Tower of London glinting off the oily dark water of the Thames. The sentinels on the walls leaned on their spears, half asleep in the cold wind.

Something stirred in the darkness, a giant wing sweeping over the water. One of the watchmen cried out in alarm. 'Jesus! What is that?'

'It's a ship!' another man said. 'Christ, whose is she?' French raiders had not yet sailed up the Thames, but there was a first time for everything. The ship drew closer, gliding over the water. 'Who goes there?' the first man yelled.

A voice roared back at them from the deck of the roundship. 'It is your king!' shouted John Crabbe. 'Open the gate, *now*!'

There was a moment of stunned silence before the Tower burst into activity. By the time *Dobeler* had furled her sail and moored at the landing place, the watergate was open. More torches blossomed in the courtyard beyond, illuminating the enormous bulk of the White Tower. A gangway was lowered and the king strode down it, cloak billowing behind him. Merrivale and the others followed. The guards knelt, bowing their heads. 'Where is the constable?' the king demanded.

'He is not here, sire.'

'What do you mean, *not here*?'

'He is… He is not in the castle, sire.'

'For Christ's sake! Where is the deputy constable?'

'In-in-in bed, sire,' stammered another.

'Drag him out of it. Mary, Mother of God, this is the premier fortress of England! The mint is here, the armoury, the treasury! And I arrive to find the constable is off in some whorehouse, his deputy is sound asleep, and the whole place so badly guarded that a couple of old women with brooms could sweep the garrison away! By Christ, someone will pay for this!'

The guards still knelt, one of them shivering a little. The king bellowed at them. 'Well? What are you waiting for? Turn out the rest of the garrison! I want every last mother's son formed up outside the great hall in five minutes. *Go!*'

They went. The deputy constable emerged, wearing a cloak over what was fairly obviously his nightshirt. 'Your Grace, we did not expect—'

'Be quiet. Here is a list of names. Arrest every man on that list and bring them before me in the great hall.'

The deputy constable squawked with horror. 'All of them, sire? Now?'

The king took a step forward. 'Your one hope of keeping your post, Sir Robert, is to carry out my orders to the letter. And yes, God damn it, *now*!'

Within moments the streets of London were full of the sounds of running feet, fists pounding on doors, splintering wood. One by one the men on the list were brought to the Tower and taken into the painted hall where the king sat before the high table, Merrivale and Kildesby standing behind him. Robert Stratford, the Lord Chancellor. The master of the rolls, and every other senior judge and secretary in the Chancery; only Edmund Grimsby was missing. Sir John Moleyns, arguing furiously with the men who had arrested him. Andrew Aubrey, the mayor of London. Reginald Conduit, wearing only a cloak and a pair of drawers, a bruise swelling on the side of his face. William de la Pole, smiling faintly. Sir John Pulteney, glancing at Merrivale and nodding a little as he looked around at the others.

When the last prisoner had been brought in, the king rose to his feet. 'Well, well,' he said, his voice full of contempt. 'I am reminded of the words of my ancestor, Henry II. What miserable vipers and traitors have I nurtured and promoted, who will let their king be treated with such shameful contempt. Where is Archbishop Stratford?'

'We searched his residence, sire,' said the deputy constable. 'He fled before we arrived. We have detained all the others on the list, as you can see.'

Edward ran his eye over the prisoners, coming to rest on Robert Stratford. 'Lord Chancellor, you are an ordained priest and I cannot try you in a civil court. But you are dismissed from your post with immediate effect. By God's grace you may depart.'

Stratford turned on his heel and stalked out of the room, his face set like stone. The king spoke again. 'The rest of you will be taken to cells while I decide your fate.'

Moleyns knelt, looking up at the king. 'Sire, there has been some mistake! I am your loyal servant!'

'No, John,' the king said quietly. 'There has been no mistake. You have betrayed my trust and my friendship. Now you must pay the price.'

Two guards gripped Moleyns by the arms and dragged him still shouting out of the hall. The king turned to Merrivale. 'There is one more arrest, I think.'

'Yes, sire.' Merrivale clamped a hand on Kildesby's shoulder and motioned to the guards. Kildesby cried out with alarm. 'Me? What have I done?'

'You know damned well what you have done,' Merrivale said. 'You spun us a fable in hopes that you could profit from it. The queen saw through you, of course. Which post do you have your eye on? Lord Treasurer or Lord Chancellor? Or even Canterbury? Denied one archbishopric, you hoped Stratford would fall and you could set your sights on another.'

Silent with shock, Kildesby was marched out of the hall. A long silence followed. 'They are all thoroughly frightened, sire,' Merrivale said finally. 'I think you have achieved your objective.'

'Yes.' The king's voice was quiet once more, almost reflective. 'Tonight was necessary, I think. I have reasserted my authority, and my officials know now that I am not to be trifled with. They wanted to curb my power, and I have shown them that I will not accept this.'

'What will you do with them, sire?'

Another sovereign might have resorted to summary executions, but King Edward was learning wisdom. 'I am not a tyrant,' he said. 'They will be arraigned before the King's Bench and the law will take its course. For those involved in corruption, fines and confiscations of property will be a salutary lesson. For those who tried to thwart my will, like the Stratfords, depriving them of their offices will be punishment enough.'

'William de la Pole will claim that he has your pardon. And I do not believe Sir John Pulteney has committed any real offence.'

'Then he has nothing to fear from the courts. Pole is more complicated. I must decide whether the harm he has done outweighs the good services he has rendered.'

Merrivale hesitated. 'Your lenience does you great credit, sire. However, in order to find the men who killed John Stanton and defrauded your treasury, I may need to threaten a few people.'

'You have my full authority. Do whatever you must.'

'Welcome,' Edmund Grimsby said dryly. 'You find us a little quiet today.'

The Court of Chancery was silent as a tomb. Nearly all of the offices were empty, their occupants currently behind lock and key in the Tower; only a few frightened-looking clerks were at work in the hall. They glanced at Merrivale and lowered their heads.

'I take it I have you to thank for my liberty,' Grimsby said.

'I explained to His Grace that you are assisting the inquisition.'

'I have Moleyns's records here. There is something I had overlooked when we last spoke. I think you need to see this.'

The document was a simple parchment roll, addressed to Aufrej Solaro and authorising the payment of a thousand marks to Nicholas le Flemyng. There was no name, but the parchment was sealed with red wax bearing the image of a pear. 'Peruzzi,' Merrivale said slowly. 'This matches a document I found in the Solaro strongroom. We now have a direct link between Peruzzi and Moleyns. Thank you, Master Grimsby. This is very useful.'

'What happens next?'

'Warrants have gone out for the arrest of most of the collectors and controllers of customs on the east coast. Conduit is already in hand, of course. Most will be dismissed, and some will go on trial for corruption. We already have a fair amount of evidence against them, from John Wesenham in Bishop's Lynn and from some of the customs officials in Rye.'

'There is a rumour that these men have been arrested because they are part of a conspiracy against the crown,' Grimsby said. 'I must tell you that I do not believe such a conspiracy exists.'

'Neither do we. Kildesby arrived in Ghent spinning that story in hopes of provoking the king into action. His aim, of course, was to distract us away from the real plot. The king agreed to play along with Kildesby in order to discover the real conspiracy and its true objectives. I think I already know what that is, but I need more evidence.'

'Are you able to tell me what the real plot is?'

Merrivale shook his head. 'I could, but it would expose you to danger. You have run enough risks for us already.'

He looked out of the window towards the Domus Conversorum next door, icicles hanging from its eaves. 'There is something else,' he said. 'Bishop Burghersh never intended to support the return of the Jewish exiles. He deceived Roth, and you, in order to get his hands on Roth's money.'

Grimsby was silent for a long time. 'One knows, of course, that prelates can be just as venal and dishonourable as the next man,' he said finally. 'All the same, I find this shocking. This will hit Roth very hard. He has spent much of his life working towards this end. Have you told him yet?'

'No,' Merrivale said. 'But I will. As soon as my business in London is finished, I shall return to Strassburg. He deserves to hear the news in person.'

'Good afternoon, Master Kildesby,' Merrivale said, looking around the bare little room in the White Tower. 'I trust your cell is comfortable? Have you seen any sign of rats?'

'Not so far,' Kildesby said.

'Perhaps we can bring you some. We wouldn't want you to be lonely.' Merrivale gestured to a writing table and bench by the window. 'There is parchment, pen and ink, and I shall light a candle. Be seated, and I shall dictate the terms of your confession.'

'My what?'

'Please write as follows. I, Magister William Kildesby, do solemnly affirm the following. Item, that I deceived my sovereign lord the king by pretending that I had discovered a conspiracy to overthrow him. Item, that I deceived my sovereign lord the king by suggesting that certain of his officials were disloyal and working against his interests. Item, that I deceived my sovereign lord the king by using the privy seal, of which I was keeper, to issue instructions to the banker Aufrej Solaro that were against the king's interests. Item, that I deceived my sovereign lord the king by concealing evidence of numerous frauds and thefts from the royal treasury, particularly those committed by Sir John Moleyns. All of these things I swear to be true, and I beg for the king's mercy and hope that he will see fit to grant me clemency.'

Kildesby sat open-mouthed, staring at him. 'Why in God's name would I write that?'

'Because if you don't, by nightfall your head will be on a spike over London Bridge, with the ravens fighting each other for a chance to peck out your eyes.'

'You can't do that! I am entitled to a trial! I demand the chance to defend myself!'

Merrivale raised his eyebrows. 'This is not a time for quibbling, Master Kildesby. Confess to me, or to the ravens. It is up to you.'

Kildesby was shaking now. 'You arrogant shit. You came from nowhere, Merrivale, and nowhere is where you will go. The king will discard you when he no longer needs you, just like he does all of us.'

'I am sure you will enjoy watching that,' Merrivale said. 'So, make sure you are still alive to see it happen. Let us start again. I, Magister William Kildesby, do solemnly affirm...'

Because he was of higher status than the others and had once been the king's friend, John Moleyns had been given a better room, part of the constable's old quarters high up in the White Tower. A fire burned in a hearth at one end of the room and the walls had been plastered and painted white with red floral designs.

Moleyns was sitting by the fire reading a small codex when Merrivale walked in. '*Antiocheis*, by Joseph of Exeter,' he said, holding up the book. 'I am rediscovering the pleasures of literature. I so rarely have time for reading.'

'You may have much more time in the near future,' Merrivale said.

The door opened again and Sir John Pulteney entered, looking grave in a dark robe trimmed with fur. 'I have asked Sir John to join us,' Merrivale continued. 'It is important that we have a reliable witness.'

Moleyns rose to his feet. 'Witness to what?'

'Please don't waste our time and yours by pretending ignorance. I have your missing account rolls. I have already shown these to Sir John Pulteney, who concurs with the opinion of the Chancery auditor I engaged earlier this year. You are guilty of numerous thefts from the king's chamber, including money from the wool revenues and loans that you and Bishop Burghersh helped to negotiate. Some of the money was passed on to other people, but a considerable amount was diverted for your own benefit. Sir John, can you please confirm that this is correct?'

'I can,' Pulteney said. 'The thefts were cleverly concealed, but once I knew what the auditor had found I was able to follow the trail myself. I am prepared to give evidence at a trial.'

'There will be no trial,' Moleyns said. 'I'm the king's friend.'

'So am I,' said Pulteney dryly. 'Yet here I am.'

'There *will* be a trial,' Merrivale said, 'and you have reason to fear its verdict. William Kildesby has already confessed that he knows of your involvement in these crimes.'

Moleyns scoffed. 'Everyone knows Kildesby will say anything to protect himself. Lying under oath means nothing to him.'

Merrivale nodded. 'As well as your own records, we also found references in documents taken from the strongroom of the Solaro bank in Antwerp.' He laid a document on the table before Moleyns. 'Read this.'

'Solaro paid a thousand marks to Nicholas le Flemyng,' Moleyns said. 'Again, so what? This incriminates Peruzzi, not me.'

Merrivale laid the second document, the one Grimsby had found, on the table beside the first. 'Flemyng was paid for killing John Stanton, and probably for attempting to kill Edmund Gonville,' he said. 'Because we found this in your own records, the court will infer that you knew of this, and perhaps that you were working with Peruzzi.'

'Again, so what? Of course I was in correspondence with Peruzzi. He was making loans to the king.'

'And when it comes to light that Peruzzi financed the killing of Stanton? And that you had begun negotiating with him again? And that you had promised Peruzzi custody of the great crown? I think you will have much to fear then. Aiding and abetting the murder of a royal official is a capital crime. It could even be considered treason.'

Moleyns said nothing. Sir John Pulteney cleared his throat. 'Why would Peruzzi involve himself in the killing of Stanton?'

'Who can really say what Peruzzi's motives are, apart from profit?' Merrivale asked. 'In this case, though, it seems fairly clear. Peruzzi has powerful allies at court, men very close to the king. They realised that Stanton and I were close to discovering their identity. They asked Peruzzi to supply the services of Nicholas le Flemyng, his tame poisoner.'

Moleyns said nothing. 'The rope, the knife and the fire await you,' Merrivale said. 'Time to bargain.'

'What do you want?'

'A sworn statement from you, with Sir John as witness. You will name the men who have been working with Donato de' Peruzzi to defraud the king, and who gave the instruction to kill John Stanton.'

Moleyns stood for a long time, staring out of the window over the courtyard. 'It was bound to come to an end sometime,' he said finally. 'It may as well be now.'

Moving to his writing table, he cut a small piece of parchment, dipped a wooden pen into an inkwell and wrote briefly. As soon as the ink was dry he handed the parchment to Merrivale. There were just two names. The first, as expected, was that of Henry Burghersh, Bishop of Lincoln.

The second was the king's friend, advisor and mentor, Sir Geoffrey Scrope.

'One more thing,' Merrivale said. 'Do these men know where the great crown of England is?'

'Yes,' said Moleyns. 'And they are making ready to capture it even as we speak.'

He debated a long time over what to do. He knew how strongly the king felt the ties of loyalty and friendship. Giving the order to arrest Moleyns had been one of the hardest things King Edward had ever done, and he was still feeling the pain of betrayal and loss. If asked to indict Scrope and Burghersh, no matter what the evidence against them, he might well dig in his heels and refuse.

Merrivale wrote a letter, laying out what he knew. The letter ended with a plea.

> *I believe that Your Grace is the only person who can persuade the king to do what must be done. I know that this is a great imposition, but I beg you to consider making the journey to London.*
>
> *Your humble and obedient servant, Simon Merrivale, nuncius regus*

Four days later he stood on the top of Saint Thomas's tower, the White Tower behind him and the roofs and spires of London spread away to his right, while a ship with the queen mother's banner at the masthead moored at the watergate. He watched Queen Isabella come ashore, waited for some time, and then walked downstairs and across to the Lanthorn Tower where the king had his lodgings. A page bowed. 'The king is expecting you, sir. Please follow me.'

Isabella sat in a high-backed chair, her skirts arranged in her lap. The king stood by the window, his face set. 'Tell me,' he said.

Merrivale told him. 'Sir John Moleyns will give further evidence, I am certain. He fears for his life.'

'Rightly so. I should hang the conniving bastard here and now.'

'No,' Isabella said. 'You need his evidence.'

'Very well. He can have his life but not his liberty. He will rot here in the Tower until I say otherwise.'

'And Bishop Burghersh and Sir Geoffrey Scrope?' Merrivale asked. 'What is your will concerning them, sire?'

The king bit his fingernails. 'Are you quite certain, Merrivale?'

'The evidence against the bishop is already very strong. He and Moleyns worked closely together, and I suspect an inquisition will find that he has helped himself to tens of thousands of pounds from your treasury. He also tried to cover up any inquisition into the poisoning of Edmund Gonville, his own protégé. I strongly believe that he ordered the attempt on Gonville's life.'

'What about Stanton?'

'I thought that was Burghersh also, but I believe now it may have been Sir Geoffrey. He came to Stanton's chamber the day after he died and gave orders for the taking away of all of Stanton's personal effects, ostensibly to return to Stanton's family, but probably to hide evidence that may have incriminated him. He later learned you were intending to send me back to London, and tried to kill me again in Oudenaarde. While recovering from the poison, I had a hallucination in which I overheard him talking to Nicholas le Flemyng. I now realise it wasn't a dream at all; it really did happen. And of course, Flemyng is the man who murdered Stanton and tried to kill me.'

The queen mother sniffed. 'Three poisonings, and only one was fatal? Not very competent.'

Her tone of voice implied she would have made a better job. 'We had a good apothecary,' Merrivale said.

'Who is this Flemyng?' the king asked.

'An adventurer,' said Merrivale. 'He is currently in the service of Étienne Aubert, the Bishop of Noyon, but he still answers to Peruzzi's call. He was last seen travelling up the Rhine and according to Moleyns, his masters have ordered him to steal the great crown.'

A long silence passed. 'Must we do this?' the king asked.

The queen mother raised her head. 'You are fair and just to your friends, and that is wise,' she said. 'To your enemies, you must show the opposite face, and that too is wisdom. You gave no mercy to Roger Mortimer. You must give none now.'

'The crown is to be returned safely,' the king said. 'That is your first priority, Merrivale. Find the crown and bring it back.'

'Yes, sire.'

'After that, I want this done quietly. There must be no public scandal, is that clear? England's reputation among our allies has already taken a battering. I want nothing that will give rise to more gossip.'

Merrivale bowed. 'It shall be done, sire,' he said.

30

The Rhine, December 1340

'You once told me that goods are at their most vulnerable when being transported from one place to another,' Merrivale said. 'How would you protect them?'

'Are you asking me to think like a pirate again?' asked John Crabbe.

'No. Like a man who is trying to stop the pirates.'

The forested hills on either side of the river were dusted with snow. The lower slopes were covered with vineyards, which reminded Merrivale of John Stanton; Rhenish wines had been among his favourites.

The river's dark waters bubbled past the *Dobeler*'s hull. They had paid their toll at the Pfalz and were passing the village and castle of Bacharach to starboard; more castles could be seen on the hills ahead, towers looming out of the mist. The valley of the Rhine was rich, and where there was wealth, violence usually followed.

'The best way is to throw them off the scent,' Crabbe said. 'Give them a false lead to chase, while you take the cargo out safely by another route.'

'That is sound thinking. The question is, which is the safest route?'

'I am wondering something else,' Crabbe said. 'Why are we going to Strassburg?'

Back in London, presented with the king's authority and asked to give passage to Merrivale, his groom and two archers, Crabbe had asked no questions. Thereafter he had concentrated on working his ship, crossing the German Ocean through a winter storm and navigating the difficult river currents of the Waal and the Rhine. But their destination was fast approaching now, and it was time the shipmaster knew the truth.

'Last year, the king entered into a financial arrangement with the Archbishop of Trier and several bankers,' Merrivale said. 'A pledge was given to the archbishop as security. I am here to see that the pledge is returned.'

'By pledge, you mean the crown.'

'For God's sake. Is there anyone in the world who *doesn't* know?'

Crabbe smiled. 'You expect opposition. From whom?'

'We have a choice,' Merrivale said. 'The Solaro family still have a banking house here, and Jean of Bohemia has taken them under his protection. Bishop Aubert also has agents in the game, including Nicholas le Flemyng who has a ship and crew of his own. They sailed up the Rhine some time back. All of them, of course, are dancing to a tune called by Donato de' Peruzzi.'

'So the bishop's men and Bohemia's are working together?'

'I suspect so. It would not be the first time.'

He was not certain of this, of course. Aubert was subtle and clever, and might well be working with Peruzzi out of expediency as he wove some plot of his own. Peruzzi's attitude to Vidal had been curious, to say the least.

Pale sunlight washed over the river, reflecting off the snowy banks. Crabbe studied the currents in the water. 'If the wind holds fair from the north, we'll be in Strassburg in another day. What happens when we arrive?'

'The enemy do not know the exact location of the crown. As you said, they are waiting until someone tries to move it. Then they will strike.'

Crabbe nodded. 'And when we arrive, they will know the moment is at hand. You in particular will be watched. What do you propose to do?'

'Get in quickly, retrieve the crown and get out again before they can move against me.'

'They will pursue you, of course. How will you shake them off?'

'I shall improvise.'

Crabbe smiled a little. 'Now you do need to think like a pirate.'

'What do you mean?'

'See that tower up ahead, the one at the water's edge? It is called the Mouse Tower. Legend has it that a cruel overlord who lived in the tower refused to feed his people during a famine. When they protested, he killed them. To avenge the people, an army of mice attacked the tower. Trapped inside, he was unable to escape and the mice ate him alive.'

Merrivale studied the approaching tower for a moment. 'Yes,' he said. 'I see what you mean. Now all we need is a tower in the right place.'

Strassburg, December 1340

The guard boats intercepted them in the river half a mile from the city's northern walls. '*Guata Tàg, m'n Härr. Wàss isch äira s'Gschaft do?*'

Crabbe answered in the same Elsàss dialect. 'I am a merchant of *Angland* and I desire an audience with the bergermaischter. I have letters of introduction from my king.'

'You are the second English trader to come here in recent weeks,' the captain of the guard commented. 'Why is Strassburg so important to England now?'

'We are hoping to expand the wool trade,' Crabbe said. 'We are looking for new markets, away from the war in the west. This Englishman. Is he the owner of the *Witschip*?'

'Do you know him?'

'He is an old friend. Where may I find him?'

'Perhaps her crew can tell you. You will find the *Witschip* moored next to the covered bridges. *Ä ammel*, you may pass.'

Mist drifted in fine tendrils across the Rhine, half obscuring the painted houses of the city. On the right lay the Grand-Île, cathedral towers blurry silhouettes in the fog; to the left were the faubourgs. Ships and barges were moored on both sides of the river, and men unloading cargo turned to watch them pass. Most of *Dobeler*'s crew were concealed inside the fighting castles. The few men on deck stood silent, watching the city drift past them.

The channel grew narrower, bending around to the west. They saw the covered bridges, fortified and turreted, barring entrance to the city proper. Several more ships were moored here including an English roundship, her clinker hull scarred and weather-beaten. Merrivale pointed. 'There she is.'

Crabbe turned to his crew. 'Ready the sweeps. Board her as soon as we're alongside. And remember, no killing.'

The sail came down. Sweeps were extended through ports in the hull and the men on deck bent their backs, propelling *Dobeler* forward. Almost silent save for the oars rising and falling, the ship crept towards the bridges. Men on the *Witschip*'s deck watched them, curious but not yet alarmed.

'Now,' Crabbe said.

The steersman threw himself against the tiller. *Dobeler* changed course, aiming straight for the other ship. Men rushed out of the fighting castles, some joining the crew on the sweeps, others raising weapons. Too late, the *Witschip*'s crew realised what was happening. A crossbow thwacked and a black bolt buried itself in one of the castles, just before *Dobeler* rammed into the other vessel with a crunch of splintering wood. Merrivale jumped down onto the *Witschip*'s deck, reversing his sword and smashing the hilt into the face of a man who tried to bar his way. Warin and the two archers followed him as *Dobeler*'s men swarmed over the deck, clubbing down anyone who opposed them.

In half a minute the fight was over. The *Witschip*'s crew, those that were still conscious and upright, dropped their weapons and raised their hands. 'Where is Nicholas le Flemyng?' Merrivale demanded.

'In the city,' one of the men said in Flemish.

Crabbe turned to his crew. 'Disarm them all and send them ashore. Post a strong guard. If they try to come back, stop them.'

Sullenly, clutching at broken arms and bleeding heads, the *Witschip*'s men filed down the gangway to the dock and disappeared into the misty streets beyond the bridges. 'I reckon you have about an hour before they return,' Crabbe said.

'I know.' Tense, his nerves twitching with the prospect of more violence, Merrivale turned to Warin, Pinn and Giffard. 'You know what to do.'

'Yes, sir,' said Warin.

Cloaked and hooded against the cold, Merrivale walked down the gangway and into the streets of Strassburg. Beyond the covered bridges he found a fair, squares and streets full of stalls selling root vegetables, meat, live chickens, spices, sweetmeats and candied nuts, buttons, gloves, pins and needles. A mason sat on his bench chiselling a stone figure for a tomb, leaving a blank indentation on the head where a face could be inserted later. Bolts of velvet and Italian brocade were bright splashes of colour in the mist. Voices sounded all around him, most talking in Elsàss, others in dialects of High German or the harsh tones of North French. Once a voice called out in Piedmontese and Merrivale turned sharply, but it was only an elderly man in long robes beckoning to his dog.

On the far side of the Grand-Île the streets were quieter. He waited a while, making certain no one was watching, and knocked at the gate of Velvl Roth's house.

A moment passed before a grille in the door slid open. 'I am Simon Merrivale, messenger from the king of England,' Merrivale said quietly. 'I am here to see Master Roth.'

'You are welcome, *m'n Härr.* The master has been expecting you.' The door opened long enough to admit Merrivale and then closed again, quickly.

Velvl Roth received him once again in the library with the star chart on one wall. He looked much the same, white hair and beard reflecting the candlelight, but there were more lines on his face. With him was a woman, clad all in white with long white hair, her face enigmatic in the light; Mercuriade of Salerno.

'I received your letter a few days ago,' Roth said. 'I found it puzzling. You said that you feared an attempt might be made to steal the crown, and that I should be vigilant. I have followed your advice, but all has remained quiet. Indeed, there has never been a time when we Jews in Strassburg have been more at peace. Your people are too busy fighting each other, it seems, to have time for persecuting us.'

'That may not last,' Merrivale said. 'You have done well to protect the secret so far, but time is running out. Master Roth, I have no choice. I must humbly beg you to hand over the crown to me so I may return it to England.'

Roth surveyed him for a long moment, his eyes bright. 'Humbly beg,' he said. 'Words you have chosen with care, I think. You do not intend to take the crown by force?'

Merrivale shook his head. 'Not even if I could.'

'I see. Do you bring me news about the repayment of the loan?'

'That is one of the reasons I am here.' Merrivale paused for a moment. 'Master Roth, I am deeply sorry. Bishop Burghersh has played you false. He has not spoken to the king about the return of your people to England, nor does he intend to do so. He only promised in order to entice you into loaning money to the king.'

The silence that followed lasted for nearly a minute. Mercuriade sat, watching them both. 'Does the king know of my offer?' Roth asked. 'To waive repayment in exchange for allowing our people to return home?'

'I do not think so, no.'

'And my money? What has happened to it?'

'Burghersh stole most of it. The rest was distributed to his friends and accomplices. If it is any consolation, you are not the only one they defrauded.'

'The money does not matter. It was only ever a means to an end. I have spent the last fifty years working to help my people come home again. All of my hopes and dreams rest on this venture.'

Merrivale said nothing. After another long silence Mercuriade stirred and spoke. 'We are not always granted our wishes, Velvl. The father who knows all sometimes sees fit to deny us. You know that.'

'But why?' Roth asked, his voice soft with sorrow. 'Why, when my intentions are good?'

'Because it was not destined to be, my friend. The father has other plans for you. Listen to His will.'

'I have not your humility, Mercuriade. I believed in a great cause, and it became part of me. Its failure is like a dagger through my heart. I have no reason now to go on living.'

To his own surprise, Merrivale heard his own voice speaking. 'There are always reasons to live, Master Roth. Sometimes they are hard to find, but they are always there.'

Mercuriade looked at him. 'You have learned since we last met,' she said quietly. 'It is written in our own scriptures. *I went forth from Him who is eternal, and I come again into my own place when I return*. During the journey to and from the eternal, we must find reasons to carry on, even when the road is hard and full of sorrow. You will find a new purpose, Velvl. I am certain of it.'

Roth looked at Merrivale. 'Answer me truthfully,' he said. 'Is there any chance, any chance at all, that the king will allow our people to return?'

'There might be, but that is not the problem. Unfortunately, the ignorance and superstition that led to your persecution in the first place have not dimmed. If your people attempted to return now, there is every chance that they would be slaughtered as soon as they landed.'

'Even if they had royal protection?'

Merrivale shook his head. 'High taxes and a failing war mean the king's star has dimmed. He cannot afford to make himself still more unpopular.'

Roth gazed at him, unblinking. 'Then I have been betrayed.'

'Yes,' Merrivale said. 'You have.'

'I shall require repayment of the loan.'

'Again, I am sorry. But the king does not have the money to repay you, not now. And I must warn you that perhaps he never will.'

'In that case, he will not see his crown again.'

Merrivale nodded. 'I understand. You could break up the crown, sell the gems, melt down the gold and realise a small portion of what you are owed. Much more money could be realised by selling the whole crown. Many are eager to buy it, not least King Jean of Bohemia and Bishop Aubert. They in turn would make even more profit by selling it on to King Philip of France, who would dearly love to lay hands on it.'

'It would be a fitting revenge on those who betrayed me,' Roth said.

'It would. On the other hand, master, you gave me your word that the crown would be safe.'

'So I did. But your people also promised that the loan would be repaid.'

'Those who made false promises will be punished. Please do not blame the king, or England, for their falsehoods.'

Roth gazed at the star map on the wall. He seemed to have grown older during the course of the conversation.

'So this is the end,' Roth said finally.

'For the moment, yes,' said Mercuriade. 'But not forever. Times change.'

'They will not change in my lifetime.'

'But our lifetimes are only a moment in eternity. Wait, Velvl. The time will come.'

His eyes cloudy with sorrow, Roth shook his head. 'It is my own fault, of course. I heard what I wanted to believe, and ignored the evidence to the contrary. But I wanted Burghersh to be an honest man, I *needed* him to be honest, and so I behaved as if he was.'

'I am truly sorry,' Merrivale said. 'I wish it was otherwise.'

'Yes, I believe you do.' Roth looked at Mercuriade. 'You are wise, wiser even than Rabbi ben Gershon. What would you do if you were me?'

'I would follow my heart,' Mercuriade said.

Roth nodded slowly. 'Despite this betrayal, I do not blame the king,' he said. 'Nor do I wish to see England humiliated. It is the country of my birth and I still cherish a love for it, as one might remember the flowers that bloomed in one's youth. Long ago, before the world became colder.'

Roth rose to his feet, opening his desk and taking out his keys. 'You shall have the crown, Master Merrivale. I shall keep the loan contract, but I will not press for payment. But ask the king to think kindly of me, and our people.'

The crown was delivered in a plain wooden box banded with iron. Merrivale tucked the key into his pocket and put the box under his arm, pulling his cloak around him as he stepped out into the street. The fog had lifted a little and a weak sunlight sparkled off wet cobbles. The fair was a distant murmur in the air. He walked quickly towards the sound. If he could lose himself in the crowds he would be safe, and from the fair it was a short distance to the covered bridges and the ships lying beyond them.

On the heels of the thought, a voice spoke behind him. 'Greetings, Simon. Destiny has a habit of throwing us together.'

Merrivale turned to see Raimon Vidal standing in the middle of the street, a cloak over his brown robe. 'Very clever,' the Franciscan said. 'Hiding the crown of England with the old man. Who would ever have guessed?'

'Don't tell me you didn't know,' Merrivale said.

'Much though it pains me to admit it, on this occasion you outfoxed me. I knew the crown was in Strassburg, but assumed it was with one of the Italian banks. The idea of Archbishop Balduin joining forces with a Jewish moneylender does rather make my head spin.'

'It appears that Balduin is broad-minded as well as avaricious.'

'Yes. His nephew King Jean wanted to arrest him and apply hot irons to his feet until he told us where the crown was. Perhaps in hindsight we should have done so. But never mind. All has turned out well in the end.'

'Is this the end?'

'Very nearly. Although I can help you settle your score with Nicholas le Flemyng, if you wish. I assure you, I had nothing to do with his attempt to kill you. Someone else instructed him to do that.'

'I know.'

'Bishop Aubert thought he could use Flemyng, but rather disappointingly for a murderer, he turned out to have no loyalty whatsoever. He accepted work from whoever paid him.'

Merrivale made an impatient gesture with his free hand. 'You have many talents, Raimon, but you talk too much.'

'On the contrary, I have talked for exactly the right length of time. Enough to allow my friends to move into position and bar your escape. Turn around, slowly.'

Merrivale turned. Sinibald Solaro stood in the middle of the street, hand resting on the hilt of his sword. He wore a metal breastplate; the five men behind him had knives and staves and heavy leather jerkins.

Holding onto the box under his cloak, Merrivale bowed. 'I presume you have come for the crown,' he said.

'Not quite,' Solaro said. 'We have also come to kill you. You killed my cousin in Antwerp. Blood demands blood.'

Merrivale turned back to Vidal. 'It's not just you,' he said. '*All* of you talk too much. You could have killed me, stolen the crown and been away by now. But no, you had to indulge your love of rhetoric. And now, it's too late.'

Another man ran into the street, waving his arms. '*Pressa!*' he called. '*Vit, vit!* They are coming!'

'Who is coming?' snapped Vidal.

'The pirates! They have archers and crossbowmen! Run!'

Vidal was away in a moment, lifting the skirts of his robe and haring down the street. Solaro lingered for a moment, still gripping his sword. 'I do not care about the crown,' he said. 'I want blood.'

'So you said.'

Solaro spat on the cobbles and ran after the others. Warin appeared at the end of the street, knife in hand, flanked by Pinn and Giffard with bows strung and arrows at the nock. Half a dozen of Crabbe's men followed, crossbows level in their hands. Merrivale walked towards them, still holding the box.

'Have they gone, sir?' Warin asked.

'They ran like rabbits. Quickly, back to the ships.'

Flemyng had two choices; he could try to retake his ship by force, or he could appeal to the authorities. Wisely, knowing who he was up against, he chose the latter. A quarter of an hour after Merrivale and the others returned to the *Witschip*, a phalanx of heavily armoured spearmen marched out of the gate beside the covered bridges and spread out along the waterfront. A party of men-at-arms rode after them, followed by two men wrapped in furs and wearing gold chains around their necks. Banners floated above them, the red bend on a white field of the city of Strassburg and the black eagle on gold of the Holy Roman Empire.

The taller of the two, who had a long face with hollow cheeks and lantern jaw, reined in his horse and hailed the *Witschip*. '*Ehren uff s'Däck! Wär isch äijerer Maischter vu Scheff?*'

Crabbe stepped across from the *Dobeler*, still moored alongside. 'I am John Crabbe, master and admiral in the fleet of King Edward of England. Who might you be?'

'I am the imperial viscount of the free city of Strassburg.' The tall man waved a gloved hand at his companion. 'This is the bergermaischter of the city. In the name of Emperor Ludwig, we demand that you give up this ship and restore it to its rightful owner.'

Crabbe glanced at Merrivale. 'That is exactly what we are doing. The *Witschip* was part of the French fleet in the battle on the Zwin, and was taken there as a legitimate prize of war. She belongs rightfully to King Edward of England.'

Merrivale held aloft a parchment. 'I hold here the king's authorisation to seize the *Witschip* and return her to England. The king also demands the arrest of Nicholas le Flemyng, an English subject who is wanted on charges of piracy and murder. This document is sealed with the king's privy seal.'

At a nod from the viscount, one of the men-at-arms approached the gangway and Merrivale handed him the letter. There was a pause while the viceroy read it. The seal was genuine; Kildesby, a broken man, had sealed the document in London without demur.

'Very well,' the viscount said. 'A court will be convened to determine the true ownership of this vessel. Until the court reaches a verdict, I shall take the ship into custody on behalf of the emperor.'

Crabbe shook his head. 'No, *m'n Härr*, I cannot allow that. My orders are to surrender this ship to no one, not even the emperor himself.'

'*Gott s'Blüat, Maischter!* You are not in England now! This is the empire and the emperor's rule is law!'

'*You* are in the empire,' Merrivale corrected. 'According to the law of the sea, this ship is sovereign territory. You cannot arrest us or touch us.'

The bergermaischter, who looked cold and like he wanted to be somewhere else, spoke up. 'Be reasonable. The ship will be perfectly safe until the court determines its ownership.'

'But its cargo will not,' Merrivale said. 'I am a King's Messenger, and I have custody of the great crown of England. It will remain on this ship, as will I and my men, until we can return the crown to London.'

A stunned silence fell along the waterfront. 'The English crown?' asked the bergermaischter, his face a picture of incredulity. '*Müatter Gott*, what is it doing here?'

'It is a long story,' Merrivale said.

The spearmen were still staring at the ship. The viscount and the bergermaischter conferred behind their hands. Finally, the viceroy nodded reluctantly.

'In order to ensure the safety of the crown you may remain aboard, but you will not be allowed to depart until the court has reached its decision. You will also allow my men to board your ship and ensure you do not try to escape.'

'How long will the court take?'

'The evidence must be examined and discussed. A day, perhaps two.'

Crabbe looked at Merrivale, who nodded. 'We agree,' Crabbe said.

Orders were given, and five imperial men-at-arms dismounted and boarded the *Witschip*, looking around wide-eyed as if they expected to see the crown lying on the deck. The crew ignored them. Merrivale turned to Crabbe. 'Did you send the message?'

'One of my best men departed just after you left. Will your friends be waiting?'

'They will. They are reliable.'

Crabbe looked doubtful. 'I've never yet met a banker I could trust.'

'I said they were reliable,' Merrivale corrected. 'I never said we could trust them.'

31

Strassburg, December 1340

The day passed without incident. Dusk fell early, thick with freezing fog. Crabbe moved back and forth between the two ships, speaking quietly to the men on watch. Torches were lit, their flames surrounded by haloes in the mist. Warin and the two archers went below in search of a place to sleep. The imperial men-at-arms kept watch in turns while their comrades slept too. Merrivale stood near the forward castle, wrapped in his cloak and staring into the fog. From the city, invisible bells tolled the hours, vespers, compline, matins.

In the small hours a wind stirred, lifting the fog. The eastern horizon was a rim of grey light. The bells rang again, sounding lauds. Standing on the deck of the *Dobeler*, Crabbe raised his fingers to his mouth and whistled. The crews of both ships sprang into action, manning sails and sweeps. The imperial men-at-arms, roused by the noise, reached for their weapons but a dozen men converged on them, knocking them down and ripping their swords away before binding them hand and foot. Merrivale bowed to them. 'My apologies, gentlemen, but I fear we cannot wait for your court's deliberation. We are departing now.'

'This is an outrage!' their leader said, struggling against his bonds. 'The emperor himself will hear of this!'

'Yes,' Merrivale said. 'But by then it will be too late.'

The light was growing. *Dobeler* slipped her moorings and turned on the current, heading downriver. *Witschip* followed, sail billowing as the breeze filled it. Someone shouted from the ramparts, and a trumpet sounded the alarm. 'Do they have cannon in Strassburg?' asked Jack Giffard.

Merrivale pointed to the towers. 'No, but they do have stone-throwers.'

Pinn looked down at the water, gauging the speed of the current. 'They'll have to be damned quick to hit us.'

Up on one tower the arm of a catapult was already being wound back. A moment later the arm sprang to the vertical, hitting the crossbar with an audible thwack, and a thirty-pound stone shot splashed into the river behind *Witschip*'s stern, throwing up a fountain of water. More catapults were in action, but Pinn was right, the ships were moving fast and the artillerists could not turn their weapons quickly enough to follow them. Then they were out of range, Strassburg sliding away astern.

Up ahead the guard boats were pulling hard out into the river, men bending their backs at the oars; one of them was already dead ahead of *Dobeler*, an officer standing up and shouting orders to heave-to. Too late, he realised that *Dobeler* had no intention of stopping. The crew threw themselves at the oars again, but the boat was still gathering way when *Dobeler* ground over the top of it, smashing the hull to pieces and throwing the men into the water. *Witschip* followed, ploughing through a swirling mass of broken planks and oars, and both ships surged away downriver.

'I'd say Master Crabbe has done that before,' Robin Pinn said.

The sun rose, golden light pouring over the floodplains along the Rhine. Away to the west the mountains of the Vosges were brilliant white with snow. Merrivale stood in the bow of the *Witschip*, shading his eyes in the light and looking for the tower he had spotted on the way upriver the day before. He found it, a stone spike standing up from the frozen pools and marshes that fringed the river's left bank.

'Crabbe! There is the tower!'

Dobeler's sail came around a little and she lost way, allowing *Witschip* to run up alongside her. 'Are you certain you can do this alone?' Crabbe asked. 'Some of my men can stay with you.'

'You've risked enough already. God speed you on your journey home.'

Crabbe's men climbed aboard their own ship, leaving Merrivale, Warin and the two archers along with the bound and trussed men-at-arms. Crabbe raised a hand in salute, and *Dobeler* pulled away downriver. Robin Pinn took the helm of the *Witschip*. 'What are your orders, sir?' he asked.

'Run her aground,' Merrivale said. 'As close to the tower as you can.'

Silence fell, broken only by the ripple of water around the hull. The winter sun was low, a glittering brass ball not far above the horizon. The river bank grew nearer. Merrivale pointed to a patch of sand. 'There.'

A minute later *Witschip* slid gently onto the sand and came to a halt. Pinn drew his knife and slashed the halyards, and the sail fell to the deck. Merrivale stooped over the imperial men-at-arms and cut their bonds, waiting while they rubbed their limbs and struggled to their feet. 'You may go,' he said. 'Strassburg is only about ten miles away.'

'We will not forget this,' the leader said sullenly.

'I don't care,' Merrivale said. 'Go.'

Stiffly, the men climbed over the side and dropped onto the frozen sand. Merrivale watched them start to make their way back upriver. Pinn and Giffard were already busy spreading pitch over the deck and sail. Merrivale lit a torch and set fire to the pitch, watching as flames and smoke began to rise from the deck. When the ship was well and truly alight, he dropped the torch and picked up the wooden box.

'Time to go,' he said.

The four of them dropped over the side and walked across the marshes towards the tower, slipping and sliding a little on the ice. Behind them the smoke of the burning ship rose and caught the wind, spreading out like a stain across the sky. 'Nobody could possibly miss that,' Pinn commented.

'Let's hope not,' Merrivale said.

The tower stood where the marshes began to give way to fields and hedgerows. Once it had been a watchtower, built during the time when the towns of the Decapolis along the upper Rhine were at war with each other; before the Empire established peace. Now it was abandoned, the curtain wall largely collapsed, its stone plundered for building work elsewhere. A stable stood behind, its roof fallen in. Looking down, Merrivale saw the faint indentation of hoofprints in the frozen ground; a party of horsemen had been here, probably not long before.

He looked around, scanning the fields, but saw no sign of movement. The roofs of a town could be seen in the distance to the north. Closer at hand to the west, a dense belt of forest stretched away towards the mountains. He closed his eyes for a moment, feeling his stomach beginning to churn, his limbs tingling despite the cold.

At the foot of the tower a stone stair led up to an empty doorway. Inside was a chamber full of bird droppings and rotting straw. Kneeling down, Merrivale laid the box on the floor and heaped straw over it. He heard Warin's voice, calling sharply. 'They're coming!'

Horsemen were riding fast over the fields from the south. Merrivale ran back down the stair and followed Warin and the archers, who were already running towards the forest. 'We'll be safe when we get to those trees,' Giffard said.

'Yes,' said Merrivale. 'Unless there are bears.'

The archer looked alarmed. '*Bears?*'

'On Dartmoor we have wolves,' Warin said. 'If it's not one thing it's another.'

'I'd sooner face bears than horsemen in the open,' said Pinn. 'Begging your pardon, sir, but I think we need to run faster.'

Merrivale looked around. The horsemen were gaining rapidly. Some of them came sweeping around to the west, cutting them off from the forest. There was no chance of escape. He held up a hand. 'Stop.'

They stopped. 'Make ready,' Merrivale said, 'but shoot only on my command.'

Pinn and Giffard strung their bows and drew arrows from their quivers, nocking them. Merrivale counted the horsemen; eleven in all, four with crossbows. The only one not obviously armed wore a plain brown cloak. Merrivale watched him, wondering a little. Had Vidal come to claim the crown for his master, and make sure it stayed out of Jean of Bohemia's hands? Or were they all working together?

Not that it matters. The result will be the same.

The horsemen slowed, circling around them. Sinibald Solaro spoke, his voice clear in the cold air. 'Hold your positions. I shall kill Merrivale, and then we shall take the crown and go.'

'How do you intend to do that?' asked Vidal.

'I shall challenge him to single combat. I do not think he will refuse me.'

'What about me?' demanded another man. His hood fell back and Merrivale recognised Nicholas le Flemyng. 'That ship was all I had left in the world, and now this bastard has burned it! I owe him a death.'

Smoke from the ship could still be seen in the distance. 'You won't fight me, Flemyng,' Merrivale said, his voice full of contempt. 'You wouldn't dare face me. Your trade is poisoning people from the shadows, like a coward.'

'Do not listen to him,' Solaro said sharply.

'Go to hell, Solaro. This dog has escaped me twice before, but he'll not get away this time.'

He urged his horse forward, but Solaro seized him by the arm. 'Let him go,' said Vidal.

Puzzled, Solaro lowered his hand. Flemyng trotted forward, sword in hand. 'Go on,' he said to Merrivale. 'Draw your blade.'

'I don't need it,' Merrivale said.

Flemyng kicked his horse into a gallop. Raising his sword, he aimed a hard stroke at Merrivale's head. Merrivale ducked under the blow, grabbed Flemyng's arm with a grip of iron, dragged him out of the saddle, slammed him onto his back on the frozen ground, ripped the sword out of his hand and stabbed him through the heart, all in a single fluid motion. Flemyng gave a convulsive shiver, and died.

Nausea exploded in the pit of Merrivale's stomach. He doubled over, retching, and then raised his head and looked at Sinibald Solaro. 'Come on!' he screamed. 'What are you waiting for?'

Solaro hesitated, and Vidal raised a hand. 'No more fighting,' the Franciscan said. 'We came for the crown, not to indulge in childish vendettas. Hand it over, please, Simon, or with the greatest of regret, I shall order our men to shoot you.'

Merrivale stood still, panting for breath. He felt light-headed, and for a moment the hallucinations came back; it was Yolande, not Flemyng, who lay before him in a pool of blood. 'I don't have the crown,' he said. 'I gave it to John Crabbe, with orders to take it directly to England.'

'You are lying!' snapped Solaro.

'Of course he is,' said Vidal. 'Simon Merrivale regards his duty as a sacred trust. He was sent to retrieve the crown, and he will carry out that mission or die in the attempt. He would certainly never entrust an object so precious as the great crown of England to a man of Crabbe's reputation.'

Merrivale shouted at him. 'So where is the crown, you damned fools? Do you see it anywhere? Am I wearing it? I'm telling you, I sent the crown with Crabbe!'

Vidal rubbed his gloved hands together. 'You feared pursuit, of course. Faced with being caught in the open, you decided to hide the crown, talk your way out of trouble in your usual inimitable style, and come back for it when the danger had passed. But it won't work, Simon. Not this time.'

'Where did he hide it?' demanded Solaro. 'He can't have buried it, the ground is too hard. Where else could it be?'

Vidal sighed. 'I have always assumed that bankers were men of high intelligence, but perhaps things have changed. If you look towards the smoke coming from the late Master Flemyng's ship, you will see a ruined tower. Search there, and I suspect you will find the crown.'

Merrivale glared at Vidal. 'You utter bastard.'

'Don't take it to heart, Simon. I know how your mind works, remember? Solaro, what are you waiting for? Search the tower!'

Solaro pointed to his four crossbowmen. 'Guard Merrivale and his men. If they move, kill them. The rest of you, follow me.'

The other four wheeled their horses and followed Solaro, cantering back towards the tower. Merrivale watched them dismount, tether their horses and go one by one up the stair and inside. Looking around, he saw Pinn and Giffard had lowered their bows but still had arrows at the nock. He wondered how long to wait.

He saw a flicker of movement around the ruined stable, a man leading a black horse quietly away. After a moment he mounted and rode towards them. Vidal's eyes narrowed. 'Who might this be?'

'His name is Anton Turc,' Merrivale said. 'He is senior partner in the Company of the Leopard's bank in Strassburg. If you turn, you will see more of his men coming up behind us.'

A compact company of horsemen rode out of the shelter of the forest, spreading out into an extended line as they crossed the frozen fields. Vidal opened his mouth to speak again, just as the tower exploded in a cloud of smoke. Stones arched through the air leaving more trails of smoke behind them, bouncing and skidding on the hard ground. Roof timbers hovered for a moment before falling back to earth. When the smoke cleared, the tower was gone; only a heap of smouldering rubble marked the spot where Sinibald Solaro and his men had died.

The crossbowmen were still staring at the tower when Merrivale nodded to his archers. Two arrows hissed in the air and two of the crossbowmen fell dead from their saddles. An expert longbowman could draw an arrow, nock and release in under five seconds, and Pinn and Giffard were experts. One of the surviving crossbowmen realised what was happening and lifted his weapon, but before he could squeeze the trigger Giffard's second arrow struck him in the chest. Pinn shot the fourth man a fraction of a second later, his body hitting the ground with a hard thud.

Merrivale turned towards Vidal, sitting motionless on the back of his horse. 'Answer one question for me, and answer it honestly, if you are capable of such a thing. How did you discover the truth about Yolande and myself?'

Vidal stared back at him, the reins clutched in his hands. 'You really do not know? Can you not guess?'

'I want to hear it from you.'

'She told me herself,' Vidal said. 'She wanted to end the affair, and knew she had to do something extraordinary to drive you away.'

The shock was not so great as he expected; perhaps because he was waiting for it. 'If you are lying, Raimon, I will gut you like a fish.'

'You could do that anyway. I am unarmed and you could kill me in a moment. But you stand there, holding your ground, because you know I am telling the truth. Why would I invent this?'

'You would summon the devil himself to your defence, if you could.' Merrivale swallowed the bile in his throat. 'You are free to go.'

Vidal bowed in the saddle. His own voice was bitter with defeat. 'That is very gracious of you.'

'Don't take it to heart, Raimon,' Merrivale said. 'I know how your mind works, remember?'

Vidal turned his horse and rode away towards Strassburg. Anton Turc and his men arrived a couple of minutes later, the former grinning and carrying the crown's wooden box resting on the pommel of his saddle. 'I thought you were going to barricade them inside the tower and set it on fire,' Merrivale said.

Turc's grin broadened. 'I think you will agree this was simpler and more effective. There was less risk to myself, too. I put the gunpowder on the second floor and laid a trail down the back stairs into the stable. All I had to do was hide there, light the train and ride away.'

'They might have searched the stable as well as the tower.'

'There was little risk of that. They were Solaros, and like all Solaros they could only think about one thing at a time.'

'Where did you get the gunpowder?'

'From your people. When your army retreated from Tournai in the autumn the captains were so desperate for money that they sold everything they no longer needed, including surplus gunpowder. We bought it for a good price.'

Turc lifted the box. 'I brought the crown back, too. I found where you had hidden it, and guessed you wouldn't want to be digging it out of the rubble, not in this weather. It weighs a bit, doesn't it?'

'Gold is heavy. You of all people should know that. Are you going to hand it over?'

Turc looked at his men. 'I'm not sure. Now that I have it, it might be nice to get the credit for returning it to King Edward myself. There might be a reward on offer. Or I could do what Solaro and Vidal were planning to do, and sell it at auction. There will be plenty of bidders, I think. I envisage a large profit.'

'You could do that,' Merrivale acknowledged. 'You might change your mind, though, once you have seen it.' He reached into his pocket and pulled out a black iron key, tossing it to Turc. 'Take a look.'

Turc unlocked the box and opened it. He stared for a moment, and then upended the box. A shower of small stones fell out, bouncing and rattling on the ground.

After a moment Turc smiled again. 'It is probably for the best,' he said. 'God knows how much trouble I would have got into. And, I would have been sorry to lose our friendship. As a matter of interest, where is the crown?'

'Far away downriver by now, and making its way home to England,' Merrivale said. 'Ironically, it turned out that the only one I could really trust was the pirate.'

Ghent, December 1340

'I will make this brief,' Merrivale said. 'The king wants this matter dealt with privately. There must be no public disgrace. Both of you will die here in this room, and the queen will announce with great regret that you have perished of illness. Your bodies will be given a decent burial and masses will be said for your souls. Those will not save you, of course, but they might make the fires of hell seem a little less warm.'

Scrope said nothing. Burghersh's face was more choleric than ever. 'By God! You dare to threaten us?'

'I am not threatening you, I am telling you what will happen. Here is the king's writ. Read it.'

Merrivale laid a parchment on the table. Burghersh picked it up and began to read. 'May we know what we are accused of?' Sir Geoffrey Scrope asked calmly.

'Theft and fraud. Procuring the murder of John Stanton and the attacks on Edmund Gonville and myself. Indirectly, you are also responsible for the death of John Hull. And finally, you attempted to steal the crown of England, which is treason.'

'This is absurd!' Burghersh said angrily. 'These charges have absolutely no foundation whatsoever! At the very least we demand a proper trial. We shall appeal to the queen.'

'I have just come from the queen. She knows her husband's mind and agrees with him. It is by her order that you will die, here and now.'

Burghersh sat still, his mouth open as reality began to sink in. Scrope picked up the document and read it too, laying it down with a sigh. 'I don't suppose there is any chance the king will change his mind?' he asked.

Merrivale shook his head.

'There are two of us and only one of you,' Scrope said.

'There are. But in the highly unlikely event that you could overpower me and escape from the castle, your crimes will be made public, your lands and fortunes will be confiscated and you will be declared outlaws. You have been offered an honourable death. I advise you to accept it.'

Burghersh was still silent. 'Yes,' Scrope said finally. 'That would seem to be the wisest course. We knew the risks, of course, from the beginning.' He looked up at Merrivale. 'You must admit we were nothing if not audacious.'

'You were,' Merrivale said. 'But you went too far. Whipping up the idea of a conspiracy against the king in London was a mistake. The more I heard about it, the less sense it made. So, I listened to the words of the Rambam. I came to understand your plot, not by learning what it was, but by uncovering what it was not. Politics had nothing to do with the case. Right from the beginning, your only motivation was greed.'

'Not only,' Scrope said. 'There was also the thrill of the chase. I wanted to see how far we could go. You are too young to remember, but there was a famous case during the reign of the king's grandfather when someone broke into Westminster Abbey and stole the royal treasure. I always wanted to do something like that. When Peruzzi offered to help us, it was too good an opportunity to let pass.'

'You had power and wealth greater than most people can imagine,' Merrivale said. 'But still you wanted more.'

'Of course,' Scrope said quietly. 'There is always more.'

Merrivale lifted a heavy pottery jug and put it on the table, along with two cups. 'This is a cordial of hemlock, sweetened with honey and a little saffron to make it more palatable. It was supplied by an apothecary well versed in the art of poisons. There is more than enough here to kill you both.'

Cassandra had refused to have anything to do with an execution, until he told her about Burghersh's betrayal of Velvl Roth. After that, she had mixed the preparation herself.

Both men stared at the jug. Burghersh's mouth opened a little. Scrope's calm vanished. 'Let us go,' he said sharply. 'We will make restitution, return the money we have stolen.'

'There is no need,' Merrivale said. 'We already know where it is. Recovering it will present certain difficulties, but I think we can manage it.'

'Name your price, Simon. Whatever you ask, we will pay it.'

'How long have we known each other, Sir Geoffrey?' Merrivale said quietly. 'And how is it that you still do not understand me?'

Scrope said nothing. 'Are we allowed any final requests?' Burghersh asked.

'No,' Merrivale said. 'What you have is already much more than you deserve.'

He walked out of the chamber, closing the door behind him and locking it. The guards in the antechamber watched him. 'No one goes in or out until I return, on pain of death,' Merrivale said. 'Is that understood?'

One of the guards lifted his chin a little. 'Who you are to give us orders, *meneer*?'

'I am a King's Messenger,' said Merrivale, and he turned and walked away down the stairs.

Acknowledgements

We would like to start by thanking Bruce Campbell, professor emeritus at The Queen's University of Belfast, good friend and also Marilyn's PhD supervisor. Large portions of the research for this book were drawn from her PhD work on the *Nonae* (the taxation of Ninths) and Bruce was the person who brought this source to her attention and encouraged her to use it for her PhD.

Thanks also to Victoria Goldman and Heather Adams for reading the manuscript prior to submission; we are grateful to both for their advice. We should also single out a few particularly valuable sources used for this book. Matt Raven's article 'Wool Smuggling from England's Eastern Seaboard, *c.*1337–45', published in *Economic History Review* in 2022, is a detailed look at wool smuggling during the period and a mine of information. T. H. Lloyd, *The Medieval English Wool Trade* and J. H. Munro's article 'Wool-Price Schedules and the Qualities of English Wool in the Later Middle Ages', published in *Textile History*, gave us valuable background information. We read widely on the growing, sale and use of saffron, but the work we always came back to for a definitive account was Sam Bilton's excellent *Fool's Gold: A History of British Saffron*. And for anyone wanting to know about tabby cats in the Middle Ages, Kathleen Walker-Meikle's *Medieval Pets* is the place to go looking.

Thanks as ever to Jon Wood, our agent at RCW, and to Kit Nevile and all the team at Canelo. Owing to personal circumstances we made a lot more work for them than usual. This is particularly true of Kit, and we are grateful for his patience and forbearance, as well as his belief in these books and support for Simon Merrivale. Thanks to Chere Tricot for a diligent copy-edit, and to Andrew Davis for an excellent cover that sets the tone for the book and, we hope, the rest of the series. Thanks also to Gary Beaumont for drawing the maps at the last minute.

And finally, thanks must go to the oncology teams at North Devon Hospital and the Royal Devon and Exeter Hospital, especially to the nurses and other staff of the Cherrybrook Unit and the Yarty Ward at RD&E. Their kindness and care have helped us to get through a time of darkness, and without them this book would not have been written. Thanks also to the ELF volunteers who supplied tea and biscuits during chemotherapy treatment; they were a great help during the editing process, much of which took place on Cherrybrook.